"For you see, Your Grace, the longer you sit there, the greater the likelihood that I will accept your offer…

"You are not moving, Your Grace."

He reclined and shuffled to cross one leg over the other.

"Your Grace," Abigail persisted, "I would not be a good duchess. People would always remember me from my come-out. Your family will not be pleased at all…I am not beautiful. I have no connections. I have nothing to offer you. I am going to count to three, very slowly. You must take your leave while you have the chance, Your Grace, for if you are still here by the time I have finished counting, I warn you that I shall accept your proposal and you will leave here an engaged man. I only have so much self-discipline, you see, and part of me sees you as quite the answer to all of my problems.

"I am warning you…

"One…

"Two…

"Two and a half…" Oh, lord, he still had not moved.

Abigail dropped her hands. "Three," she said.

He was watching her with something that looked like it might be amusement. He lifted one ducal eyebrow. Before either of them could say anything, Betty entered, carrying a tray with both tea and a plate of sandwiches upon it. She set it down carefully on the table beside Abigail.

"Thank you, Betty," Abigail somehow managed. Both she and the duke sat quietly until Betty once again had disappeared. "How do you take your tea Your Grace? Sugar? Milk?"

Lady Saves the Duke

by

Annabelle Anders

Lord Love a Lady, Book 3

Lady Saves the Duke

COPYRIGHT © 2019 by Annabelle Anders

Cover Art by *Debbie Taylor*

The Wild Rose Press, Inc.
PO Box 708
Adams Basin, NY 14410-0708
Visit us at www.thewildrosepress.com

Publishing History
First Tea Rose Edition, 2019
Print ISBN 978-1-5092-2427-2
Digital ISBN 978-1-5092-2428-9

Lord Love a Lady, Book 3
Published in the United States of America

Dedication

To Mary Balogh.
For inspiring me to create new worlds.

~

And to my mom,
for buying me my first Mary Balogh book.

~

A special shout out as well
to all the members of my Facebook Group,
A Regency House Party!
Thanks for letting me rant, asking your opinions,
and just keeping me motivated.
You Ladies Absolutely ROCK!

Chapter 1

Miss Abigail Wright had not planned to attend a house party this summer. She'd not planned on attending any parties ever again. She was fine, thank you, dwelling at her father's modest home, Raebourne, for as long as she was able.

But plans—her plans anyway—often materialized entirely differently from her intended scenario.

Which might explain why Abigail now sat, frustrated, on the delicate chair at her mother's bedside. The furniture in her mother's room was fashioned in the Queen Anne style, including the large canopied bed, desk, and side tables. Her mother liked all things around her to be delicate and feminine.

"But, Mother," Abigail implored, "I do not *want* to go to a house party! I have been looking forward to spending the summer with my cousin *here*, at Raebourne."

Her mother's eyes remained closed as she reclined against several carefully arranged pillows. Her left foot was elevated as well—not exactly doctor's orders; he'd said it was only a bruise and could bear weight any time—but Abigail's mother insisted she must rest it for several days. And now she was insisting the "girls" needed a more capable chaperone than she herself could provide with her injury—such as it was. Thus, her reasoning for sending them to Raven's Park.

Which was ridiculous. Both Abigail and her cousin, Penelope, had long since passed the age where they required any chaperone other than each other.

"The arrangements have been made. Your Aunt Emily assured me the Spencers are more than happy for you and Penelope to join the house party." She sighed heavily. "Please do not be difficult about this, Abigail. After all your father and I have done! All the scandal we've put up with. We do not expect arguments at every turn."

Abigail looked down at her hands and resisted the urge to clench them tightly. At the age of seven-and-twenty, she was quite dependent upon her parents, and they often used the situation to treat her as a child. One mistake! One mistake and her future turned from one of hope and optimism to one of dependency and insecurity. Except she was determined to find some happiness, some joy, despite her circumstances.

"But we were not invited, Mother!" Abigail whispered on an exhale. She knew she was a burden to both of her parents. Their ever-present worry hung over her like a thick, black cloud.

Mr. Bernard Wright, although not a man of great fortune, was a man of property. When the estate was initially established, a life estate was to always be in place for the widow. This ensured security and comfort for Mrs. Wright as long as she lived but left Abigail to fend for herself upon the unfortunate event of her father *and mother's* deaths. Both of her parents constantly reminded her that she must set herself up either as a wife to some country gentleman or a companion to an aging relative. Otherwise, she faced abject poverty eventually.

She would *not* be destitute. She had a few ideas. And, as a last resort, she *could* find a position as an elderly person's companion. She could not contemplate marriage. She'd lost that prospect upon her epic failure in society.

She pushed these worries aside. She would enjoy her life for now, for she may not always be so fortunate. Her father, although more dependent upon spirits than she would like, was still very healthy and vigorous. As was her mother.

Except for when her mother did not wish to be, which was the case today.

"Your uncle and aunt have assured me you will be welcome," her mother repeated. She opened her eyes and looked sidelong at her daughter. Studying Abigail's gray day dress and frayed white pelisse, she added, "And do wear some of your prettier dresses, dear. You look almost fetching when you put forth an effort." She touched her index finger to her cheek. "Give me your kiss goodbye now. I have told Coachman John you and Penelope must leave at sunup tomorrow. I shall still be abed. I don't want you to miss any more of the house party than you already have."

All spring, Abigail had anticipated Penelope's visit. The simple pleasures she'd looked forward to enjoying with her cousin, such as attending choir practice, visiting friends, and taking long walks around the village, were to be scrapped for a blasted summer house party. Abigail's mother refused to accept defeat where her only daughter's matrimonial prospects were concerned.

When Penelope had arrived two days ago and

informed Abigail's mother that her parents, the Baron and Baroness of Riverton, were attending a house party at Raven's Park, a cunning gleam appeared in Mrs. Wright's eyes. The Ravensdale family consisted of three very single, very eligible sons who were likely to be in attendance, one a viscount and the other two mere misters. But sons of an earl, nonetheless.

Abigail leaned forward, dutifully kissed her mother's powdered cheek and gave her a gentle hug. Her mother was bound for disappointment. Abigail knew better than anybody that her mother's hopes were, in truth, unrealistic. At Abigail's advanced age, she was all too aware of her own lack of appeal to any man seeking a wife. Aside from being on the shelf, she was certain that, although not an antidote, she could boast no real claim to beauty. Her mother called her plump. Penelope was kind enough to refer to her as voluptuous.

Abigail had long resigned herself to the unfortunate truth that her breasts were more prominent than those of most ladies and her hips more rounded as well. She did not feel overly large, as a person, for she was short in stature and somewhat petite. And ever since…well, she could no longer summon the enthusiasm required to maintain a slim, fashionable figure. It would serve no purpose at this point. And for this reason, she had no intention of forgoing cakes and biscuits with her tea. A girl needed some indulgence in her life, after all. Especially when one could only look forward to a very long future as a spinster.

Closing the door behind her, Abigail forced herself to smile. She would simply have to adjust her attitude and enjoy this unexpected journey. She mustn't fear it. All would be well. Contentment was a state of mind, after all.

And so early the next morning, feeling light of heart, Abigail climbed into her parents' ancient traveling carriage, along with her cousin, en route to a party to which she had not been invited. She refused to dwell upon her mother's unreasonable expectations. The day was too beautiful to be ignored. In addition to the fresh air and blue skies, she was embarking on this adventure with her dearest friend in the world.

"What a glorious summer this is turning out to be! So much sunshine. Everything is blooming, and the meadows are overflowing. It was kind of Lady Ravensdale to allow us to join your parents. Do you not think so, Penelope?" She'd embrace her usual optimism with a bright and determined smile.

Penelope snorted. "Oh, good one, Abby. Surely, your mother must give up on us at some point. Has she never seen the sons of Lord Ravensdale? Does she not realize they are handsome, charming, and wealthy? Does she not realize that when they choose to take wives, they will be able to select from the most beautiful and youngest ladies in London?" She ended her rhetorical questions with a roll of her eyes and then looked back out of the carriage window to watch the rolling scenery.

Abigail absorbed Penelope's words. She herself had never laid eyes on any of Lord Ravensdale's sons. She had heard about them, of course. Such a prominent family as the Spencers often received mention in the newspapers and gossip sheets. Their only daughter, in fact, had made quite a splash a few weeks ago by calling an end to her engagement with the Duke of Cortland.

The girl must be either very brave or very foolish. Abigail could never imagine exercising such assertiveness on her own behalf. Abigail looked forward to meeting Lady Natalie Spencer, however, a girl who could take matters into her own hands with such bravado. Abigail sighed and closed her eyes.

After a few hours, the carriage crested a hill and turned into a gated driveway. This must be Raven's Park. Ah, yes, it was. The name of the estate had been elegantly scripted into the decorative iron entrance. As the carriage made a slight turn, a large Georgian manor situated in a protected valley came into sight. The patchwork of neatly tended holdings they had been traveling through gave way to a cleverly landscaped park, the perfect setting for the stately mansion. The façade of the great home was liberally covered with ivy and closely surrounded by copses of trees, lawns, and haphazard wooded areas. The exterior, a whitewashed limestone, contrasted with the greenery surrounding it. In spite of its size, Abigail found it pretty and homey.

The carriage halted, and the steps were pulled down. Both of Penelope's parents, as well as a few others, had stepped outside to greet them.

The men sported tailored suits with well-pressed cravats and shining boots while the women, not to be outdone, wore dresses made of fine materials accessorized with expensive pendants and draping pearls. These people represented some of the highest sticklers of the ton. They lived a different life from the rest of humanity.

A uniformed footman opened the door and reached inside the carriage to assist Penelope and Abigail outside as though they had travelled from Buckingham

Palace rather than the tiny village she'd grown up in.

"You girls certainly made it here quickly. I should have known your mother would have jumped at such an opportunity." The scent of Penelope's mother's perfume engulfed Abigail as she allowed her aunt to embrace her properly. The baroness, although outwardly welcoming, betrayed her discomfort in her pinched lips and disapproving appraisal of Abigail's dress.

Abigail smoothed her skirts, which had certainly wrinkled over the course of the journey. She didn't wish to embarrass her aunt any more than their arrival obviously did.

And then the Earl and Countess of Ravensdale stepped forward as the baroness presented her. Although considerably older than herself and Penelope, they were a handsome couple indeed.

"Welcome to Raven's Park. I'm *so* delighted the two of you could join us." The countess's words made it sound as though they'd been invited along with all of their other guests. If Lady Ravensdale was put out by their arrival, she certainly did not show it. Even the earl, who ought to be haughty and aloof, acknowledged their arrival with a pleasant nod.

Abigail wanted to believe such a welcome to be genuine but could not ignore her feelings of doubt. Even the servants appeared to be turned out better than she. Such elegance all around her!

"My daughter, Natalie," the countess declared, "will show you ladies to your chamber." She ushered them inside to where the young beauty awaited them. "And I'm so sorry the only available accommodations are on the upper floor." The countess winced.

The servant's quarters. Abigail plastered on a smile, wanting to apologize for their arrival for the hundredth time already. Deep breath. Smile.

With a faraway look in her eyes, Lady Natalie stood off to the side while her mother said all the right things.

Abigail envied her poise, her calm. Seeing her now, Abigail understood how the girl had been bold enough to jilt a duke. Although beautiful, the girl exuded goodness. Dressed in the latest fashions, Lady Natalie did not act with any disdain toward her mother's uninvited guests.

Painfully aware of the circumstances surrounding their arrival, however, Abigail could not help but feel contrite for their presence. "I hope our arrival is not an inconvenience, my lady, even though Aunt Emily said your mother had assured her it was not. My mother was quite out of sorts with herself for her inability to chaperone us adequately. We both assured her it was not necessary, but confined to her suite, she expressed that we would be subject to all manner of indiscretions. She does have an extensive imagination."

Lady Natalie and Penelope had a prior acquaintance, and so there was no ice, so to speak, to break there. And of course, her cousin would not bend to normal pleasantries. "A bunch of tripe, Abigail. Aunt Edna saw the opportunity to expose us to some bachelors yet again and came up with the most transparent of excuses."

Lady Natalie did not seem offended, but she did look a bit confused. She turned toward Penelope questioningly. "But there are no bachelors here, really." And then she caught on. "My brothers?"

At this point, Abigail spoke up so as to smooth over yet another of Penelope's bouts of brutal honesty. "You have no need to worry, my lady. There is no danger to your siblings—as I am sure you can gather on your own." She added the last with a gesture at herself, in her wrinkled traveling dress.

Lady Natalie did not look at her apparel, however. She stared directly into Abigail's eyes as though she could read more about her there. And then, as though having made her decision, she nodded brusquely. "Nonetheless, I am glad of your company." She continued leading them up the stairs. "As much as I enjoy my mother's friends, it will be a pleasure to have the companionship of ladies closer to my age. Mother has planned a garden party for this afternoon, inviting everyone who lives within a day's drive, mind you, but not one of them below the age of forty. I think the boys will have set up some games. If not, we'll find some other entertainment." Lady Natalie grimaced. "But you shall have a few hours to rest before the festivities begin."

They reached the landing and followed her down the long corridor. Upon opening the door to their chamber, Lady Natalie then took her leave, as though she had other things to tend to. What did the daughter of an earl need to tend to, Abigail wondered.

The room consisted of two small beds, two desks, and two dressers. Although the furnishings were somewhat austere, the view from the window made up for them in spades. It overlooked the entire front of the park, which included the lake and part of the wilderness walks. Abigail sighed. Perhaps one day she would live in a home such as this, as a companion or governess.

But she did not wish to think about that now. Turning to Penelope, she smiled enthusiastically. A garden party would be lovely! Despite feeling gauche and somewhat frumpy, Abigail determined to enjoy herself. Planned or not, she would have a pleasant summer with her cousin.

****

Alex Cross, the Duke of Monfort, had not expected to attend any house parties this summer. In fact, he *never* attended house parties. As a rule, he'd normally consider them to be a complete waste of time, filled with insipid conversation and banal entertainments. He'd only accepted the invitation when the Earl of Ravensdale promised a tour of his estate, which boasted one of the most modern irrigation and canal systems in Great Britain. Impulsively, the duke had made an exception.

And the inspection of the canals, which was completed the previous day, had been enlightening. He was inclined to consider some of the innovations for his own estates—there were nine, to be exact. The Monfort ducal seat, Brooke's Abbey, had been modernized most recently. It would not require any renovations. Looking out the window of the Ravensdales' elaborate library, Alex contemplated when he could express his regrets and abandon the party earlier than planned. For it was becoming apparent that the Earl of Ravensdale had other motives behind his invitation. In a thoroughly undignified manner, the earl had pushed his daughter into the duke's presence at every opportunity. He'd obviously not abandoned his ambitions for her to become a duchess.

And while Alex considered her a pretty little thing,

he was not inclined to take another wife any time soon. He had done so once, with tragic consequences, and would delay the inevitable for as long as he possibly could. He would eventually need to beget another heir. The son his now-deceased wife had produced for him had been killed in a freak accident at the tender age of three. And although any reasonable person could surmise it was unlikely to happen again, Alex was reluctant to put it to the test.

He snapped his attention back to the present in time to glance out the window at the sounds of an approaching carriage, rather ancient by the inordinate amount of clattering it made. Late guests, Alex thought in an abstract manner, not the least bit curious as to whom they might be. He would leave tomorrow.

But he was not committed to it. Contrarily, the thought of returning to any of his properties was not as satisfying as it ought to be.

While in London this past spring, he made the decision to release the mistress he had kept for nearly two years. He'd been forced to do this because as the latest season had progressed, the beautiful Mrs. Elise Gormley had increasingly become somewhat possessive and, even more worrisome, emotionally attached. The widow's disturbing and passionate displays had not only irritated and embarrassed Alex, but they'd led to a premature end to what ought to have been a long and satisfying physical relationship. Whereas in the beginning, their time together had been filled with giving and receiving sensual pleasures, tears and reprimands took over during the latter stages. A man did not engage a mistress so she could treat him like a recalcitrant husband. And although Elise had been an exceptional beauty and had known how to please him in bed, Alex had not been willing to allow their arrangement to evolve from that of mistress and client to anything else. In releasing her, he gifted her with a rather expensive set of ruby earbobs, bracelet, and necklace, and informed her of his decision in no uncertain terms.

He was right to end it, he'd decided, when she'd protested with sobbing and pleas, which quickly evolved into various curses and a pair of her slippers being flung at his head.

Not inclined to avail himself of whores, he'd also been unwilling to complicate his life with any of the more willing ladies of his own ilk.

He'd remained celibate since that occasion, nearly six months ago.

Even so, Lady Natalie, the earl's daughter, tempted him not in the least. She was very young and a lady of quality. Not at all the type of situation he wished to contemplate. What he ought to do was return to London and seek out a new mistress. Perhaps he would do just that in the fall, during the Little Season. He would curtail his urges for now.

His attention was caught again, outside, as he realized the new guests were not elderly at all. In fact, the women appeared younger than he had assumed—although not young enough to appeal.

Ah, delightful, a pair of spinsters. One of them was tall, thin, and gangly—somewhat familiar, in fact. Oh, yes, Riverton's daughter. She was known to be a bluestocking and something of a liberal. Her auburn hair was pulled back into a tight knot behind her head, and her dress fell colorless and wrinkled.

The other woman appeared, perhaps, to be even more of an antidote. Much shorter, she wore a wrinkled gown over an unfashionably plump figure. She had mousy brown hair, but her eyes stood out large and expressive. The two women were quite a study in contrasts. Whereas Miss Crone was tightlipped and looked bored, the shorter woman's heart-shaped face sparkled with enjoyment. What she found so enjoyable about life, Alex could not imagine. He dismissed them from his mind and turned away from the window.

He paced a few times and then stepped outside of the large library doors. The excitement of the new arrivals carried indoors. He had no wish to become a part of it. Turning on his heels, he stalked in the opposite direction and made his way to the billiards room. Dignified quiet settled around him once again.

He then proceeded to rack the balls and play a rousing game of billiards against himself.

****

Oh, how could she? How could she? Abigail wanted to wail as she began unpacking the slightly familiar dresses from her trunk. These were not the dresses she had packed herself. No, they were the dresses she had worn years earlier, while having her season in London. Although less worn than what she had initially intended to bring, they were not at all modern. Worse than that, they were not quite the proper size. She could kill her mother! She did not wail, but she did moan, drawing Penelope's attention to the dresses.

"Oh, Lord, Abby!" Penelope declared, holding up one of the pale-colored day dresses. "Why on earth would you pack these old things?"

Abigail merely looked at the dresses forlornly. "I did not. This is the work of my mother. She must have ordered Betty to do it." Lifting the dress all the way out, she pressed it to her face and moaned again. It reeked of mildew. "Oh, Penelope, this is horrible! These were made up ages ago! I'd be surprised if any of them even fit me. Most likely, now, they are all too small."

Penelope pondered the dresses and then began sorting through them. "Surely not. We will merely cinch up your stays a little tighter than normal." Raising the dress to her own face, she sniffed suspiciously. "Wipe them with a lavender-soaked cloth and allow them to air." She gave Abigail a rueful smile. "Unfortunately, my dresses would not work, or you know I would gladly share them with you—not that they are any more fashionable than these." And then she allowed a giggle to escape. "Can you imagine you wearing one of *my* dresses?"

In spite of her present predicament, Abigail could not help but to laugh at such a notion. The mere thought of cramming her much rounder curves into a dress made for Penelope's tall, slim form brought back a little of her good humor.

With grim determination, Abigail searched for a dress that might be the most forgiving, opened the window to allow in some fresh air, and then went in search of a housemaid. She would not allow this most recent calamity to ruin her visit.

****

It required a considerable amount of tugging and pulling, but Penelope miraculously managed to tighten Abigail's stays just enough so she could fit into a pale green muslin day dress that had been one of her favorites the year of her come-out. The restricting garment, however, pushed Abigail's bosoms up prominently, causing them to bountifully spill over the top of her stays. Unable to remedy the situation, both of the girls agreed the bodice was stretched too inappropriately taut to be seen in public. Abigail would have to keep herself covered with a wrap. If the garden party were scheduled just a bit later, Abigail could have let out a few seams and resewn the garment for a better fit, but it was not. She hadn't enough time to complete such a task. Abigail would keep her shawl snugged up closely about her at all times. If only the heat could have held off a few more days. Drat, but this would not be a comfortable afternoon.

Feeling not just a little self-conscious, Abigail, with Penelope, found her way outside where the two girls claimed iron chairs conveniently placed in the shade near the lake. A nearby jetty anchored a few rowing boats that had been cleaned and set out for guests to use. It would be lovely to go out for a ride, but Abigail had no expectations of doing any such thing. Her sigh was overheard by her cousin.

Penelope caught Abigail's gaze and gestured with her fan farther along the shore.

In rolled-up shirtsleeves and tightly fitted breeches, three men, nearly identical in coloring and mannerisms shuffled about in a leisurely fashion. Ah, they must be the unobtainable Ravensdale brothers.

"The nearest one is Peter Spencer." Penelope pointed out. "And then there is Stone and of course Darlington."

Although similar in looks, each gentleman exhibited subtle differences. Peter wasn't as brawny as his older brothers, and the oldest, the viscount, stood slightly taller than his siblings. They joked and jostled with one another in a familiar, easy manner.

A fourth gentleman, however, one who had not removed his jacket, kept himself apart from the younger men. He held a cane and wore a top hat. With feet planted firmly on the ground, shoulder's width apart, he gazed out at the lake.

"Who is that?" Abigail asked Penelope. Penelope travelled to London each year to participate in the season, even though she wasn't actively seeking a husband, and so she knew almost every notable person.

Penelope turned her head to identify who Abigail referred to. "Oh, Abby, he is the Duke of Ice, quite a tragic figure." At Abigail's questioning glance, she continued, "Well, he is not really the Duke of Ice, he is the Duke of Monfort, but it is the moniker he has been given by much of the ton. He is not friendly or sociable but, from what I understand, has due cause."

"What happened?" Abigail tried not to inhale too deeply, her bodice becoming more uncomfortable the longer she sat.

"I believe it occurred three years ago," Penelope began earnestly, lowering her voice. "The duke and his wife had returned to his ducal seat just before Christmas, a bit north of Bristol. I believe it is called Brooke's Abbey. Anyhow, the duchess took the children out onto the lake to skate, and the ice broke through. From what I understand, the duke saw it happen but could not reach them in time." With a pointed glance toward the man in question, she finished her story by adding, "His son was three and his daughter five. Before the bodies could be recovered, the temperature dropped and the lake froze over. So sad and ironic, really. Had they waited even a few hours, the ice would not have broken through."

A lump formed in Abigail's throat. Nobody, she thought, *nobody* ought ever to have to endure the loss of a child. It was surely the most horrible thing to befall a person. "If he is so unsociable, why do you think he is here?"

Penelope shrugged. "It is not that he is never seen out in society. It is rather his manner, his address. He seems to lack any warmth whatsoever."

Abby looked back at the lone man. "Hmmm..." was all she could say. Dreadful. Truly dreadful. And then the man, as though he sensed their attention, turned and looked over where they were seated. He raised a quizzing glass to one eye and regarded them for just a moment. A moment in which he quickly perceived the two ladies to be of no interest to him whatsoever. He dropped the glass and turned back to regard the lake.

Well.

It would have been common courtesy to at least acknowledge them in some way. A nod, even, would have done the trick. It was not as though the lawn was teaming with guests yet. Abigail pulled her shawl more tightly about her and a droplet of sweat trickled between her breasts. This situation with her wardrobe really was beyond the pale. Her mother deserved to be strangled. Abigail dismissed such thoughts, however, and forced another smile as Lady Natalie crossed the lawn toward them from the house.

Penelope laughed softly, and Abigail raised her brows. In a missish dress made up of pink muslin and an abundance of lace, the earl's daughter wore her hair in tight golden ringlets. For some reason she'd shed the elegance of earlier in favor of less sophistication. How was it that she still carried herself with such dignity and confidence?

"It's a lovely afternoon, is it not?" Her blue eyes sparkled, and her smile was sincere.

But Penelope could not be contained. "Oh, my lady, what on earth are you doing dressed in…pink, of all colors?"

More guests were drifting onto the well-kept lawn. Abigail looked about anxiously, hoping Lady Natalie did not take offense. Abigail loved her cousin, *absolutely adored her*, but in moments like this, she wished Penelope didn't have to behave so very contrary to proper decorum.

Luckily, Lady Natalie remained unfazed. "My maid is having one over on me." She did not even pretend not to know what Penelope meant by her uncomplimentary question. "But what of you, couldn't you spare even the barest nod toward fashion in your attire? You are not a matron after all, and," she said with a glimmer of audacity in her eyes, "not all of the men here are married and over fifty."

In unison, three feminine gazes turned in the direction of the dashing Ravensdale men as they casually set the posts for a game of horseshoes. Penelope sighed again, this time with theatrical appreciation. "They do present an abundance of manhood, at that."

Abigail stifled a giggle. Penelope did not often admit herself smitten by any man whatsoever. Indicating her fan, which was ironically clutched in the same hand in which she was holding her shawl about her tightly, Abigail imitated Penelope's tone of voice. "Dear cousin. Fan yourself, my dear, lest you faint from palpitations."

All three allowed their laughter to bubble over at the hilarity, but Abigail quickly reined hers in with an inward wince. Drat. Double drat and fiddlesticks! Her bodice had loosened slightly when a couple of stiches gave way with a barely perceptible *rrrip.*

Best not to test those that remained. She was going to kill her mother!

****

The duke stood staring out at the water. This wasn't the first time he'd caught persons whispering as they gawked at him. It happened all the time. Before the accident, he had been gazed upon with a sense of wonder and awe. As a peer of very high rank, men often had looked upon him with respect and envy, women with romantic sighs and sometimes an all too obvious hunger.

Now they all regarded him with a somewhat morbid fascination. He knew society referred to him as the Duke of Ice. He was not an idiot, after all. But life was too short to suffer fools gladly. And many of those who mingled in the ton could aptly be referred to as fools. Why should he make an effort to make them feel more important than they already were?

Giving in to the pull of curious stares, the duke turned to his left and looked across the lawn. The shorter of the two spinsters quite unabashedly inspected his person. With a not very kind need to make her uncomfortable for doing so, he fingered his quizzing glass and slowly raised it to his left eye. Oh, heavens, but she was plain, even if her eyes were rather large and expressive. Alex allowed his glass to drop and turned away.

He really must take his leave of this party soon. Except…except he had promised his hostess he would remain for the entire two weeks, and as a gentleman he was not comfortable breaking his word—without a sufficient reason, that is.

A quartet of strings tuned their instruments in the distance, and servants scurried to and from the house. A banquet of savory and sweet delicacies had been set out along with lemonade, tea, and champagne. The Earl and Countess of Ravensdale did not throw a garden party in half measures—even if local gentry made up most of the guests. He was quite certain he would find himself surreptitiously spied upon by many who would never have the courage to meet him face to face.

He would instruct his valet to prepare for an early morning departure. Surely there must be some urgent need for which he must return to Brooke's Abbey immediately. He would sort through the mail he had received to see if he could find a matter requiring his attention. He had no desire to fabricate a completely untrue excuse.

Just as he made his decision, a heavy hand fell upon his shoulder. "Monfort, what are you doing over here when there is a bevy of young ladies unattended in such a pretty setting?" The earl's voice rang hearty and cheerful. Where business matters were concerned, Ravensdale had proved to be a serious and sober man. It was unusual for the earl to dabble in such a feminine pursuit as matchmaking.

He would not be rude to his host, the duke decided.

Even if it meant he must give a scant amount of attention to the daughter. "What indeed?" he responded, allowing the earl to lead him toward the tree where the spinsters were now seated with Lady Natalie and another gentleman. Just as he might have guessed, three rowboats bobbed along the nearby jetty. And yes, Ravensdale intended Alex to row his daughter about the lake. He did not mind rowing.

In fact, he did not mind lakes. Although many people assumed that he did—since the accident.

It was just that Lady Natalie was looking very feminine and very *young*, elaborately dressed in pink lace with an abundance of ringlets dancing on her head. Far too young. When he did eventually remarry, he would find a sophisticated widow, perhaps, one who would present him with an heir and possibly a spare, and then be content with living her own life. He would be crystal clear from the beginning as to what type of an arrangement he would expect.

The duke had no inclination toward seeking great affection within marriage. He had attempted to do so once and found it to be a messy situation indeed. It would be nice if he could find satisfaction in bed within his marriage, however. For he did believe in fidelity. He did not wish to make any vows before God and mankind that he did not intend to keep.

Marriage could wait for now.

The earl presented the spinsters along with another gentleman for what he declared to be the most romantic of opportunities. Alex vaguely took note of the names: Lord Hawthorne, Miss Crone, and Miss Wright.

Ignoring the spinsters, he bowed and offered his arm to his host's decorative daughter. He did not need to invite her onto the lake with him. Her father had already done that.

"Er...Thank you, Your Grace." Was she as reluctant as himself?

Alex supposed he ought to make an attempt at conversation, but what did one say to a child, practically fresh from the nursery? He could make some trivial comment about the weather, but refused to default to such banality.

"This summer promises to be a warm one," she commented beside him.

But that he could complete this little jaunt as quickly as possible.

Stepping into the recently cleaned craft, Alex steadied it and reached out his hand to assist his passenger aboard.

"I need my parasol!" She gasped in protest and pulled out of his grip. Perhaps she was as unwilling as he to be managed by her father.

Without notice, she shoved the spinster with the large eyes toward him and dashed off in the opposite direction.

The plump one. The—God help him—smiling one.

Miss Wright.

It seemed he was to partner a different lady altogether than he had originally thought. Wonderful.

Except that in order to prevent the woman from falling into the water, his arms reached out to grasp her about the waist leading him to inadvertently spread one hand over the surprisingly sweet fullness of her derriere. Unable to stop her momentum, she had fallen forward and pressed herself up against the front of him. His own traitorous body took that moment to take notice of the softness of her womanly curves and the clean floral scent of her soap.

Chapter 2

Completely of its own volition, his left hand gave a discreet and oh-so-subtle squeeze. His right hand, much better behaved, grasped her shoulder and steadied the lady so she could pull herself away and stand on her own. Her large eyes opened even wider for just a moment before a rush of words let loose from her mouth. Quite a full mouth at that; her lips looked soft and plump just as…

"Oh, my lord! I am so sorry. I nearly knocked you into the lake!" And then she laughed. "More likely, I nearly fell in myself! I most definitely have your quick reflexes to thank that I am not this moment taking an afternoon swim!" She smiled as she found her seat and settled herself into the boat. He grudgingly admitted to himself that her smile transformed her plain features. Hopefully she wasn't a giggler. He did not wish to spend the next thirty minutes or so having to suffer girlish tittering.

But she wasn't quite a girl. She was, he guessed, closer to thirty than twenty.

"Thank you, my lord, er…Your Grace? Oh, I know I ought to know better, but would you prefer me to call you my lord or Your Grace? I am not really a servant, you know, but I am also barely considered gentry."

Oh, good God! Was she truly as rustic as this?

"You may call me Duke, or Monfort. It is of no matter." At her confused expression, he clarified, "Your Grace is fine."

"It's just that it has been quite some time since I spent any time in polite society," she jabbered along, sounding unrefined and more than a little sheepish. Why was that, he wondered? He would not ask.

"It has been nearly nine years since my come-out..." She trailed off.

He took hold of the oars and expertly steered them away from the shoreline. The lake wrapped around a small island. He would make one circle and then deposit this chit back on the lawn. He would more than have done his duty for the afternoon and then might feel better justified for leaving the house party a week early.

She looked up at him, seemingly surprised by her utter lack of discretion. "I was eighteen at the time. I am now nearly twenty-eight. It is startling to imagine that I have not been to London since then. And in the village where my parents live, well, there is not really any nobility in the area. A few vacant estates—well, not vacant, and not abandoned, really, but the owners do not ever visit their homes. It always seems like such a waste to me. These grand manors, cared for by servants with nobody enjoying them."

The girl was a chatterer. He was not surprised. She relaxed as they floated along and allowed one hand to drift into the water. She had removed one of her gloves and was now clutching it in the same hand that held tightly to her shawl. Why was she wearing a shawl? It was damnably hot today.

"Not that I am one to judge, mind you." She must have come to the conclusion that perhaps he himself had an estate or two that went unlived in. "I believe, however, with so many people in want, the owners ought to at least make something of an effort to be a part of the community they preside over." And then she jumped slightly and pulled her hand out of the water quickly. "A fish!" She leaned over and peered into the water. "A fish swam right by my hand!" She had absentmindedly let go of her shawl and was holding both hands up in the air to illustrate the size of the fish. "It was this long! It nearly touched me! I have never before seen such a large fish, alive, so very close! And what gorgeous colors, silvery blues and greens! Oh, I knew a boat ride would be lovely today. I looked out at this lake and thought to myself what a lovely treat it would be to ride out on top of the lake in a boat."

She continued speaking about nature and whatnot, but Alex's attention had been completely lost when she dropped her shawl. For there before him, and he did not think he was exaggerating, were the most glorious breasts he had ever been afforded the privilege to gaze upon. They were creamy white, round, and plump, and he could just make out dusky rose tips pushed up by her stays.

Her dress was apparently experiencing some sort of a malfunction.

She was also quite oblivious to her present circumstances as she continued reaching into the water and swirling her fingertips in its refreshing coolness. Leaning forward, she thrust herself into an even more provocative pose, causing the duke to clutch the oars tightly to stop himself from reaching out to touch her. And, as though he were a raunchy schoolboy, he unbelievably found himself growing hard. It was not as though he had not seen numerous sets of breasts, but there was something incredibly arousing about seeing them in such an inappropriate setting being displayed by such an unlikely woman. And they were, in truth, really quite exceptional.

He cleared his throat and pulled at his cravat. Unfortunately, he could not make his eyes look away from her. "Er…madam."

"It really has been a delightful summer, thus far, would you not agree?" she continued conversing cheerfully. And then, finally realizing that she had been chattering quite unrelentingly, she paused. With a bit of a perplexed look, she tilted her head slightly. "Is there something the matter, Your Grace?"

The duke finally dragged his eyes down to look at the oars where his hands gripped them. "Madam, you must…Er…Please forgive me but…ah…" Oh, good lord, he hadn't been at a loss for words since before he'd gone off to school. "Your dress, madam."

He met her gaze again just before she glanced down at herself. And in that instant, all of the light and joy which had been bubbling out of her just moments before were completely extinguished as her face crumpled in upon itself. She looked around frantically for her shawl, he presumed, but could not locate it. Especially while attempting to cover herself with distraught hands. The shawl had fallen to the bottom of the boat beneath her seat and was somewhat hidden.

The duke locked the oars in place and reached forward to retrieve it for her. As he did so, however, she squealed and jumped back, falling off her seat and landing in an inelegant heap on the bottom of the boat. Alex slowed his movements and picked up the shawl.

Meeting her frightened eyes, he gently tossed it to her.

She wrapped herself quickly and turned her face away from him. Pulling her knees up in front of herself, she continued to lie on the floor of the boat in a curled up ball. She was quite motionless but chanted to herself in a hoarse whisper, "Oh my God, oh my God," over and over again.

For the thousandth time, Abigail wished she had never come. And for the *ten*-thousandth time, she wished her mother to perdition.

She did not know how she could ever face the very handsome, if cold and distant, duke again. And if she could not ever face him again, how would she be able to get out of the boat and go back into the house? Surely she could not complete the trip around the island curled up on the floor like this? Oh, it would have been better had she fallen into the lake initially, when Lady Natalie had pushed her into the boat.

Even better still, she ought to have cried off the garden party altogether so she could alter the dresses. It had been utterly, completely, moronically stupid of her to wear a gown that was so obviously not capable of modestly restraining her...her...well, the bane of her existence.

Oh, and she had been enjoying herself so completely, too. The wonder of having a fish swim right alongside her hand, with the sun shining down through the trees and sparkling on the deep green of the water. Why did it all have to be ruined? What was she to do now? *Oh God, oh God, oh God...*

"You shall not see any more fish that way, Miss Wright." A bored-sounding masculine voice interrupted her extreme bout of self-pity. And then the voice sounded closer. His hand touched her shoulder. "Come now, let me help you back up so you may enjoy the rest of your boat ride." His hand squeezed her shoulder slightly, as though he could impart some courage to her so she might sit up and turn around once again.

Could she do this? Could she pretend that nothing, absolutely nothing had happened? How much had he seen? Oh, she knew, he had seen everything. The seam must have given way when she'd stumbled onto the boat. She must have dropped her shawl when the fish touched her hand. Oh, he'd seen everything.

"Come, now, give me your hand, Miss Wright."

Abigail took a deep breath and tried to turn her body without allowing either of her hands to lose grasp of her shawl. It was quite awkward. The duke had one foot planted on the bottom of the boat and the other on the seat she had vacated. He must be very confident in his own balance, she thought abstractly.

And apparently realizing that she was not going to give him a hand so he could assist her, he reached down, grabbed her under the arms, and pulled her onto the seat.

With barely any effort at all, he had her once again firmly planted upon the wooden bench where she'd been a few moments earlier. This time, however, she faced away from him. The boat rocked as he found his own seat again as well. "You are not injured, are you, Miss Wright? From falling?"

She forced herself to shake her head. "I am not," she spoke in a trembling voice coming out barely more than a wisp of air. "Thank you." At an utter loss as to what to do next, Abigail closed her eyes and attempted to breathe evenly.

So now, was she to keep her back to him for the next twenty or so minutes as they traveled about the island? Was she that much of a coward? The longer she hid her face from him, the more impossible it would be to ever face the man again.

She hated the thought of herself as a coward.

Not giving in to the desire to bury her head in her hands, yet still clutching the shawl tightly about her, Abigail took a deep breath, lifted her knees, and spun about to face him.

Well, she did not actually face him. She kept her head bent forward and watched his hands and legs as he smoothly pulled on the old wooden oars. His tan breeches were tight, and his muscles contracted as he pulled and lifted in an unhurried rhythm. How long since she'd last been alone with an unmarried man?

Abigail dragged her gaze away from his breeches and settled it somewhere more appropriate.

Hands. Oars. Whereas his thighs appeared almost brutish, he gripped the handles of the oars easily with elegant, long-fingered hands.

His hands did not look like those of a typical nobleman. Although manicured, they looked capable and strong. He wore one ring on each hand, and they sparkled intermittently as the sun caught either one or the other. Since he had not removed his jacket as the other gentlemen had, she could not see past his wrists.

"My late wife made her come-out nine years ago as well," he said out of nowhere, as if their conversation had never been interrupted. "She was Lady Hyacinth Glenmore as a girl," he mused, almost as though he were alone. "It does not really seem so long ago, and yet, it is like another life."

His words pulled her gaze back up to his face. He stroked the water with the oars steadily, occasionally looking over his shoulder to be certain of his direction. Abigail took the moment to view him as more the person he was and less the legend. His dark hair was not as perfect as it had been earlier. The wind had lifted a few dark strands so that one dangled roguishly across his forehead. His lips were tight and his nose a bit hawkish. He looked more relaxed than he had earlier, though. Hysterical laughter threatened to overcome her when she determined that all it had required for the Duke of Ice to melt was for her to expose her bosoms to him.

She could not dwell on that right now. If she did, she'd possibly burst into tears.

So instead, she considered his words.

Lady Hyacinth Glenmore. Yes, she remembered the lady. Abigail had never spoken with her, but no one who had been present that year would have missed knowing who Lady Hyacinth was. The war had just ended. The season was crowded with newly returned officers and decorated soldiers. One lady stood out among the hundreds of debutantes.

She was a true beauty. Tall and slim, with an aristocratic bearing, she outshone the rest of them without even trying. She portrayed a cool and remote image. And, Abigail remembered, the girl had quite quickly become engaged to a duke.

This duke, apparently.

And now, she was no longer of this earth. Even though she had not really ever met the lady, Abigail's throat tightened to now perceive that the beautiful girl she had watched from afar had died—in such tragic circumstances, no less.

Abigail licked her lips and somehow brought herself to speak. "I knew of her. I did not know her, of course. She was, well..." Her voice trailed off. And then, after a pause, she asked, "That is when you met her?"

The duke swung his eyes back toward hers. When truly focused on her, they were a bit disconcerting. They were a light gray—no—silver, the color of the moon. Abigail shivered slightly, in spite of the warmth of the day and her shawl.

"Yes." He did not expound on his answer. He stared away from her once again.

Suddenly, Abigail imagined him with a wife and two children. She imagined the terror he must have suffered when he had not been able to save any of them. She barely knew him. She had not known Lady Hyacinth.

But she had an incredibly soft spot in her heart for the children. She would not need to have known them to feel grief upon their passing. "I am so sorry for your loss, Your Grace. Nothing anybody says, I know, can ease the pain of losing them, but I cannot keep myself from telling you how sorry I am that they are no longer with you." She looked down at her hands and tied and retied the loose ends of her shawl nervously. He truly was not an easy man to converse with. He had such a coldness about him.

She was grateful for his change of subject, although she wondered at it, as he had not since been forthcoming in any way.

She wished she could reach into the water again and watch for a daring fish to swim by. That simple pleasure was over, however. No longer did the air feel inviting and the water, magical. Now she only felt the discomfort of her stays, the stifling heat of her shawl, and a stinging embarrassment from earlier.

The duke was unusually uncomfortable. They had journeyed only halfway around the island, and he could not abandon her on shore for another fifteen minutes at least.

He pulled harder on the oars in an attempt to move things along more quickly.

He did not know why he had brought up the subject of Hyacinth. Perhaps it had been Miss Wright's mention of her come-out being nine years ago. This summer would have been his ninth wedding anniversary. Elijah would have been six and Marigold, eight.

And yes, Miss Wright had remembered his wife as a debutante. Likely, no one would *not* have remembered her. She had garnered attention wherever she went, a diamond of the first water. Arrogant and overly confident, Alex had decided he must have her for his own. And he had.

"You only had the one season, then?" he asked her. Not that he wished to know anything more about this rural-minded spinster, but he wished to move the subject away from himself. He did not speak of the accident. With anybody.

Ever.

She looked up from her hands with those large eyes of hers. "Oh…yes." She seemed as uninclined to speak of that time as he was.

"You did not care for London? You wished to return to the country, to your parents?"

"I…" She sighed heavily. "Not all of us have such choices. I did not find a husband that year as my father had hoped. He could not afford a second season." She went to emphasize her words with her hands, but stopped, thinking better of it, and then continued. "I am content. I must be. When choices are removed, shouldn't one make the most of one's situation?" It was her turn to look away. She bit down on her bottom lip as though she would stop herself from saying more.

"There are no marriageable gentlemen in your village? Surely you have a beau waiting for you in this place of rural comfort?" A part of him, a small part, did not wish to think of this bundle of femininity shriveling up as an old maid. It would be something of an abomination, he thought, that there never be a husband to appreciate those breasts.

At that, he pulled himself up short. He did not need to conjure up such images again. It had been difficult enough to cool his ardor earlier, and he did not wish to have to do so again. She clutched at that shawl for dear life now. He made note of that fact with a twinge of regret.

She shook her head. "I am quite happy to remain unmarried." But he sensed more behind her words. Her voice trembled as she asserted her contentment.

She had a nice complexion, he thought absently. Even skin that looked soft to the touch. Her hair had loosened from the chignon tied at her neck. Tendrils had escaped to curl softly about her nape.

Not the antidote he had originally decided her to be.

But still quite rural and quite unrefined. Socially, she was not even as elevated as Elise. He pulled hard on the oars again. She was far beneath him. He had not even known of her existence the season he married Hyacinth. She would have been a wallflower, most likely.

Her voice interrupted his thoughts. "Did your children resemble you or Lady Hyacinth more?"

He was not certain he would answer her question. Damned impertinent of her to attempt to discuss his deceased family so openly with him. He had not invited any person of his acquaintance to discuss them since he'd laid them to rest three years ago. His sister, Margaret, had made attempts, but he emphatically gave her every indication that her efforts would be in vain. She'd eventually capitulated and did not mention their names anymore. Had he, inadvertently, invited Miss Wright to discuss them when he'd mentioned Hyacinth? Damn his eyes, he supposed he had.

"Elijah had his mother's eyes," he found himself remembering. "But Marigold's were gray, like mine." Marigold's eyes had been a relief. He'd never been quite certain where Elijah had been concerned. Nonetheless, the boy had been his. He'd made it so.

"I'm sure they were both beautiful." Her eyes misted wistfully, as though she could picture the children herself.

"They had a beautiful mother," he said.

Miss Wright shrugged slightly. "And a beautiful father." Then, seeming surprised at her own words, one hand let go of her shawl and flew upward to cover her mouth. Her eyes were wide.

The duke found himself chuckling. "If you say so, Miss Wright." He'd never been called beautiful before. He regarded the woman in front of him. Had anybody ever called her beautiful? He thought, most probably, not. There was something innately attractive about her, however. Unbidden, his hand recalled the feel of her bottom when she'd nearly fallen into the boat. That had not been well done on his part at all. He was supposed to be a gentleman. He really must find a replacement for Elise.

"You say you do not plan to marry," he reminded her. "And yet you sound as though you would welcome motherhood." How had no one in her village recognized her...considerable assets?

She turned her head away and looked into the water. Just when he began to think she would not answer, she spoke quietly, "No."

"You do not wish to have any little boys to chase after? No little girls' hair to braid?"

Again she spoke softly. "No."

Hmm...apparently not a subject on which she wished to converse.

"So you will live with your parents for the rest of their lives? And when they die? Is your father's property unentailed? Will you be a woman of property then?" He was not sure what prodded him to torture her like this. She just seemed so...*resigned* to her life, and this irritated him for some reason. He must be bored.

"No." Again she spoke softly.

She was keeping her head in the sand then, preferring to ignore the uncertainty of her future. What a dreadful life! What a stroke of bad luck it must be to be born a female. He would not probe any further. Obviously, she did not wish to discuss the topic.

"So you will become a governess? Or a companion? Are you trained for anything at all?"

This time she stared back at him and lifted her chin slightly. Glaring into his eyes, she spoke firmly this time. "Perhaps." Regaining her composure, she made an attempt to turn the tables on him. "And you, Your Grace? Do you plan on begetting an heir anytime soon? I imagine you will have to marry again in order to accomplish such a feat. Will you be shopping on the marriage mart next spring? Or will you wait until you are a doddering old fool, take a wife a quarter of your age, and impose an old man's body on her?"

Well, then. She was a feisty little thing. He studied her intently. "Touché."

They sat in silence for several moments after that, the only sound the swishing of the water as he moved the oars back and forth. Miss Wright sat straight-backed and stiff on the bench seat. She was no longer enjoying the water and watching for fish. It was a shame such a small delight was now to elude her.

"A seamstress." She broke into the quiet. "Hopefully. I am not trained for any other sort of employment, really." And then, "I try not to think about it."

She was a fool. A man would never leave his destiny up to the fates to decide. To a man who controlled nearly everything around him, this attitude toward the future appalled him. She deserved whatever fate awaited her.

Ah, at last. They were moving closer to the jetty now. He steered the boat expertly and then tied it off on a post. She stood tentatively. He could tell she would have liked to climb out without assistance but could not do so while clutching tightly at her shawl.

The duke took matters into his own hands.

Standing firmly himself, with feet widespread, he took hold of her waist and turned her toward the dock. Giving himself only a moment to rest his hands along her hips, he lifted her effortlessly up and out. Once on deck, she turned back to face him, blushing profusely.

"Thank you, Your Grace." She looked as though she wanted to turn and flee but could not quite bring herself to do so. Lowering her voice, she bent toward him with tremendous uncertainty. "You will not tell anyone? About my..." She was even more flushed now than she had been before.

"Attempt at seduction?" He simply could not help himself.

She straightened abruptly with outrage on her face. "It was not! You know it was not!"

He laughed for a minute before forcing himself to answer her soberly. "I am sorry, Miss Wright. You are absolutely correct." He sobered. "And no. No one will ever know. I give you my word."

Apparently reassured, she simply nodded and then turned.

But it did improve upon my day.

Chapter 3

After handing off the boat to other waiting guests, the duke stepped onto the grass and strode toward the vacated iron chairs now sitting empty in the shade. He lowered himself and then pondered the guests around him. Despite his repugnance at her countrified and obviously impoverished life, the events of the last forty minutes had proven to be somewhat diverting. He did regret, however, bringing up the subject of Hyacinth. Speaking of her was like pulling a scab off a wound that had never properly healed. And he had done it himself. Did she pity him? He glanced around to observe her once again, but Miss Wright had disappeared. Likely she'd gone to repair her dress.

He almost chuckled to himself as he considered the reaction she would have when she looked into a glass and realized how much of herself she'd displayed to him.

Any other young lady, upon suffering such a complete indignity as Miss Wright had, would have not had the courage to turn around and face him for the duration of their excursion. Another lady, he was certain, would have sat with her back to him and made no effort at further conversation.

And that would have been a wise course of action.

But Miss Wright had surprised him and truth be

told, impressed him slightly by turning herself around and facing him, even if she had not been able to meet his eyes right away. Ah, it was this surprise that had caused him to make the comment referring to his marriage. After all, what did one say to a woman of gentle birth who had quite unintentionally exposed her bosoms to him for all of two entire minutes?

She'd been enjoying herself immensely before he'd pointed out the catastrophe that had unknowingly befallen her. And in her smiles, she *was* somewhat pretty.

And then he remembered the fear on her face when he had leaned over to retrieve her shawl. The look in her eyes, the startled demeanor of terror that had overcome her, revealed that she had thought for a fraction of a second that he was going to pounce upon her in some way. Had she really thought he would take advantage of the situation? If he'd been that sort of man, she ought to have realized he would not have brought the matter to her attention at all.

Foolish chit.

"Monfort..." A jovial voice interrupted his thoughts. "I have been hoping I would get a chance to converse with you sometime this week."

Ah, the solitude he craved would elude him after all.

The uninvited interloper was Hector Crone, the Baron Riverton. He was in his fifties, portly, and his hair was diminished to just a smattering of gray tufts combed across the width of his scalp in hopes of hiding the shine of his head.

"Riverton." Alex barely acknowledged the baron. Resting his elbows on his knees, he studied the shine of his boots. They were well worn but also well cared for. Alex reached down and brushed some stray grass off one of them.

The baron was not to be deterred. Instead he began congratulating Monfort for the awards and achievements he had accumulated with the horses bred and trained at Brooke's Abbey. Alex allowed himself to become somewhat engaged in that his horses were as close to him as any person had been over the past few years. He accepted the baron's praise stoically. As the conversation ensued, it became apparent the baron was fishing for an invitation to tour the duke's horse arena and facility. The stables at Brooke's Abbey were renowned.

Alex owned more than one sizeable estate and thus allowed his housekeepers to grant tours to genteel visitors. He was not so willing, however, to give strangers access to Brooke's Abbey, where he normally chose to reside. He would not invite the baron to tour his equestrian facilities.

When the baron realized an invitation was not going to be forthcoming, he redirected the conversation in a direction for which Alex had even less enthusiasm. "Saw you took my niece for a nice trip around the lake, Your Grace," he said, taking Alex slightly by surprise.

"Your niece?"

"My wife's brother's gel." The baron grimaced. "She doesn't get out much since her scandalous behavior in London. Years ago, mind you, but some slights can never be erased, you know? Heh heh…Hope she behaves herself. Family associations aren't always the thing."

"Indeed" was all the duke said. He had no idea

what the man was rambling on about.

"I'd presume she cannot set so much as a toe in London ever again." The man was flushed with the heat of the day as he feigned sympathy for the young lady's plight.

Based upon the forty minutes Alex had spent with the young lady, he'd be willing to wager that any scandal Miss Wright stepped in had been through ignorance rather than intent. Did her foolish relation not realize the worst possible thing he could do for his niece was revive it?

But the baron continued, "Nearly ruined the entire family. Unfortunate for her…utterly dependent upon her parents now with no marital prospects whatsoever. No man wants to tie himself to damaged goods. My poor brother and sister-in-law. Never would have taken her for one of those types, though, if you get my meaning."

"Not at all." The image of Miss Wright's bosoms flashed through Alex's mind. Was it possible that the exhibition in the rowboat had been contrived? Had it been an invitation of sorts?

"My daughter, Penelope, is quite attached to her cousin, unfortunately. It is not a connection I have ever encouraged. But Penny's quite independent. Never thought my own daughter would turn out to be such a bluestocking. Anyhow, embarrassing that my sister-in-law thought it fitting to send her to Raven's Park. Luckily, the Spencers aren't high in the instep. Otherwise, I'd have put my foot down. Bad enough to be related to the little doxie; I shouldn't have to put up with her in polite company," the baron rambled on. "Well, no harm in a little country party, eh? She didn't bore you too much, did she? I imagine she would have been mute with fear, in awe of yourself, Duke."

"She was quite charming." Alex found himself defending her. Had he really said that? Charming?

The baron gave the duke a rather worldly look and leered. "Oh, I imagine she can be. But she is a lady, nonetheless, heh, heh." And then he had the temerity to wink!

Alex had had enough. He stood up abruptly and straightened his jacket. He did not wish to encourage a connection with Baron Riverton. Nodding haughtily, he turned on his heel and left. Damned unfortunate relation for the lady to have. Damned unfortunate indeed.

****

Abigail did not wait for Penelope and the viscount's boat to return. She left a message with one of the servants for her instead and hastily returned to the small chamber they shared on the third floor. Once inside, she removed her shawl and faced the only mirror in the room.

Oh, God. He most certainly had gotten an eyeful. Abigail could hardly bear looking at herself. The dress had torn so thoroughly, she appeared to have no bodice at all. And those dreadful stays did nothing to preserve her modesty. In fact, they'd merely pushed her breasts up and out as though they would burst forth from her person. Abigail covered herself with her hands and groaned. She could only hope he would keep his promise and not tell another soul about it. He was a man, though, and they had a tendency to joke about this sort of thing. Hopefully the duke would be different. Hopefully he was not so cruel.

Turning away, she struggled to remove the dress

but could not untie her stays herself. Frustrated, humiliated, and tired, she wrapped herself in her dressing gown and lay down on the bed. Face down, she closed her eyes tightly.

You do not wish to have any little boys to chase after? No little girls' hair to braid? He could not know how those words would torment her. She decided she would give herself a moment, just a moment, to yield a few tears. It had been a few months since the last time. In spite of the self-control she could usually impose on her emotions, she was coming to realize the pain was not ever going to go away. She would carry it forever.

After releasing some of her pent-up tears, she dabbed cold water on her face and then sought the attention of one of the maids walking in the corridor outside of her room. The housemaid obliged happily and untied the stays so Abigail could change back into the dress she had traveled in earlier that day. She then spent the rest of the afternoon altering a few of the dresses. Sewing was something she was both good at and enjoyed. Not only did she open up some seams, but she removed a few flounces and embellishments which had gone out of fashion. When she focused hard enough on her task, she could almost convince herself that nothing out of the ordinary had happened earlier in the day.

Almost.

Penelope returned much later.

"You missed all of the excitement, Abby!" Penelope's eyes sparkled, and her cheeks glowed an unusual pink. "This tiny dog jumped into the lake, and Natalie jumped off her boat after it and sank like a stone. Thank heavens for Lord Hawthorne. An honest to goodness hero. Saved Natalie and her little dog. Both are wet but none the worse for their dunking."

"She maneuvered the earl into being her partner." Abigail hadn't thought much of it at the time, she'd been too concerned with being thrown into the duke's boat. She'd thought she'd heard something about Lord Hawthorne and a kidnapping but refused to judge people based upon such gossip. "Do you suppose she has a tendre for him?"

Penelope had been examining some of Abigail's handiwork but set the dress down to consider the notion. "I can't imagine Ravensdale would allow such a match. Hawthorne's considered something of a pariah in London."

"And yet he is welcome in their home," Abigail pointed out.

Penelope shrugged and then went back to examining Abigail's perfect stitchwork. "Darlington cheats at horseshoes."

"I'm to assume he beat you, then?" Abigail laughed. Penelope and her blasted competitiveness. "Don't tell me you accused the viscount outright?"

"Of course I did!" Her cheeks flushed again. Abigail knew her cousin well. Although Penelope would never admit to it, her cousin had been head over heels in love with Ravensdale's heir for nearly a decade.

And the viscount treated her like an annoying sister.

This, Abigail suspected, was why Penelope eschewed marriage to such a degree.

"What was it like being alone with the duke?" Penelope changed the subject. "That was not well done of Natalie."

Abigail focused all of her attention on threading her needle. "Fine. He was quite pleasant."

If she concentrated on the thread and the needle, rather than the events which had taken place on the boat, she might be able to keep Penelope from suspecting anything untoward had occurred.

Penelope flopped onto one of the single beds and stared at the ceiling. "Darlington has the most annoying perspective on how Parliament ought to be run. He thinks the House of Lords…"

Abigail tuned out her cousin's monologue but thanked heaven for her distraction. She could not tell even her closest confidante about the humiliation she had suffered. It was far too painful and embarrassing to think about, let alone share. Penelope eventually took a short nap, but Abigail worked diligently on the gown she would wear this evening. She would not risk a repeat of this afternoon's catastrophe.

By the time the dinner gong echoed throughout the large manor, Abigail was quite pleased with her efforts. Her dress for the evening, a light yellow muslin, had short puffed sleeves and splashes of embroidery at the hem and below the bodice. She had let out the seams on the bodice to make it comfortable and modest. Overall, she deemed herself presentable enough. She did recheck her seams one last time, however. She would never allow *that* to happen again.

She only wished she did not have to see *him* this evening. If she never came face to face with the Duke of Monfort again, she could almost pretend *it* had never happened. For all intents and purposes, he did not seem like a nice man.

And yet, he had promised he would not tell anybody about her dress. She knew for a fact not all gentleman would have done the same. She hoped, oh, she hoped he would not speak of it, as he had promised.

In all honesty, she was also forced to admit to herself that he had been kind to her when she had been lying on the bottom of the boat. He had not done anything to further embarrass her at a time when she had been most mortified. Again, something she would not expect from all gentlemen.

When she had looked down and seen her bared breasts, she had wished that she would die, then and there. She was not being dramatic about this either. And then, when she thought he might be reaching out to touch her, *to touch them*, she had been terrified. It had been the most frightening moment of her life.

No. It had not. But it had been close.

No. Not really.

And then she had flinched when he'd only been reaching down to retrieve her shawl from the floor of the boat. How foolish of her! He had, in fact, been rather kind.

Except when he hadn't been.

Abigail determined, as she and Penelope descended the staircase, not to dwell on *the incident*. It was forgotten, and she was going to enjoy the evening. She even felt almost pretty. There were many people here, and she hoped to be friendly and learn about their interesting lives. She set out to enjoy herself. She was quite unwavering.

She and Penelope entered the richly furnished drawing room, unnoticed of course, and made their way to a loveseat that was pleasantly situated beside the large fireplace. No fire burned tonight. It was far too warm for that. The servants had utilized the hearth instead to showcase a beautiful flower arrangement. The fragrance delighted as did the effect.

Shortly after the two single ladies sat down, Lady Natalie joined them dressed in far more sophisticated apparel than she'd worn earlier that afternoon. No pink. No flounces. Rather a fashionably cut gown that set off her figure and coloring to perfection.

And an unrepentant grin.

Nonetheless, Abigail knew her manners, and the girl had nearly drowned earlier that day.

"My lady, I do hope you are feeling well after your frightening experience this afternoon? And the little pup, has he recovered too?" Lady Natalie and the dog both might have died if not for the quick actions of Lord Hawthorne. In light of the younger girl's experience on the lake, Abigail needed to rethink her own perspective on what had happened with the duke.

"Please, call me Natalie. And Baby Bear and I are both unscathed by this afternoon's events." Natalie smiled.

Abigail loved the dog's name! "Baby Bear is his name, oh, how adorable! I have always wanted a pet, but my mother is allergic and could never tolerate an animal in the house."

"Your mother barely tolerates other humans about—"

Abigail sent Penelope a warning look. The woman was her *mother*, after all.

"Do let's sit. I cannot believe how warm it has been these past few days." The blonde beauty fanned herself and then impishly turned toward Penelope. "Did my brother charm you as you took your turn about the lake? Please tell me he was not a dreadful bore conversing on agricultural outputs and trading prices."

"He was quite charming, but yes, in fact, that is exactly what we discussed. Why would such a topic be considered boring?"

Abigail knew Penelope too well. "I'm sure it was at Penelope's instigation." She wished Penelope could move on from the unattainable viscount. "Penelope avoids anything resembling flirtation or romance when a gentleman dares attempt such with her. She is determined to remain unmarried. As am I."

"And what of yourself?"

Apparently Abigail was not to be spared.

"Did you avoid flirtation as well? Was it necessary to do so with the duke this afternoon?"

Aha! Lady Natalie was not unaware of her unfair antics! "Naughty of you to pair me with Monfort. A duke, no less! What was I to do when plunked down in a boat with a *duke* of all things, for nearly forty minutes? What does a grown woman, one for all intents and purposes on the shelf, speak of with a duke? Very naughty indeed, Lady Natalie." Abigail could hardly believe her audacity at chastising the daughter of a earl. But it had not been a kind act on the young lady's part!

"And what *does* a woman who is practically on the shelf discuss with a duke for forty minutes? Pray tell us, Miss Wright."

The image of her bosoms exposed came instantly to mind, and Abigail couldn't stop the heat from climbing her neck. Fear struck her, again, that the duke would not keep her secret. She swallowed hard, but when she went to speak nothing came out.

A commotion at the entrance drew her gaze to the door, and all thoughts of the duke vanished. First her heart stopped, and then it raced at the sight of the familiar but unwelcome person who'd just entered the drawing room.

In her mind, she remembered another time, another place—a dark place with nothing but his hard beady eyes and his clammy bold hands. She had hoped never to lay eyes on him again. She should have known. The ton was interconnected. He would not have disappeared from the face of the earth merely because she wished it so. All of the air swooshed out of the room. She wondered that those around her could not hear her heart pounding.

The somewhat dusty and disheveled man was accompanied by two other similar creatures, but they went unnoticed by her as Abigail fought the spinning darkness threatening to overtake her.

She barely noticed when Penelope's hand reached over to squeeze hers reassuringly.

****

Standing alone in the drawing room, Alex absentmindedly noticed that Miss Abigail Wright wore a gown that was not going to allow any further glimpses of her attributes today. Such was his first thought as he watched her enter the drawing room. Surprisingly, the woman he had earlier considered an antidote had somehow caught his imagination. Perhaps this was because he had gone more than a few months now without any sex. But as he allowed his eyes to remain on her person, he recognized…something.

Although she lacked any level of presence, she managed to be alluring. She smiled too much, with full lush lips, and she dropped her gaze to her hands often, as though ashamed of herself. But when she did that, when she tipped her chin downward, attention was drawn to the delicate arch of her neck—the fragility of her shoulders and back.

A fitted bodice and lacy fichu covered the modest glimpse of cleavage allowed by her dress. The dress fit her snugly and emphasized the contrast between her breasts and waist.

She had her hands primly folded in her lap, lifting them when she spoke to punctuate her words.

All in all, she possessed an unexpected appeal.

And he was tempted.

He would not avail himself of whores, but he wouldn't mind a discreet affair. Now that could certainly make this house party more interesting. She was different from any other woman he had ever contemplated bedding. Perhaps that was her pull. Lifting his glass, he took another sip of the rich wine Ravensdale had made available to his guests and reconsidered his options.

Alex deliberately made his demeanor as uninviting as possible. This way, he could avoid situations involving tedious small talk. He repulsed most people easily with a tightening of his jaw and slight narrowing of his eyes. Most persons found those two subtle movements enough to steer into another direction completely. A rather useful technique which left him free to observe.

Miss Wright, although subdued, had recovered herself enough to join what most likely would be daunting company. In her own words, she had described herself as barely gentry. How must she feel to be mingling with individuals who nearly all held some form of title? And yet she sat tall and proud. She glanced around the room with a cheerful smile and a sparkle in those expressive brown eyes of hers.

She was chatting gaily with her cousin and Lady Natalie for a few moments before the duke noticed the very life flow completely out of her.

Her eyes became vacant, and all color left her face. She froze, staring at the doorway. What on earth?

The duke's gaze swiveled toward the door just in time to see four late visitors being escorted away by Stone Ravensdale, the second son to the earl. He had gone to school with one of the "gentlemen" who were dressed in traveling clothes and could not have appeared more out of place. Hugh, yes, the Viscount Danbury. But the others were rabble rousers, from what he could remember.

Odd.

The Spencers were known as a wholesome type of family, and it would be unusual for one of the sons to entertain the likes of Damien Farley. Yes, that was the bulkier man's name. The duke could not recall the names of the other two. He did remember, though, that Farley had a tenuous claim to nobility. Rather more valuable, likely, was his talent for attaching himself to naïve lordlings with more fortune than brains.

And the men's appearance had been enough to cause Miss Wright to look as though she had seen a ghost. Her cousin, Penelope, had reached over and covered Miss Wright's hand protectively. Monfort watched as color gradually returned to Miss Wright's complexion. What the devil was all of that about? Even more vexing, why the hell did it matter to him?

****

In spite of the long day, a large supper, and a few sips of sherry, sleep eluded Abigail. She tossed and turned for hours but could not find any position in which she could relax for long. When she closed her eyes, she could not chase away the image of Damian Farley. Age had done nothing to improve his appearance. His eyes were a bit more bloodshot, his hair a bit thinner, and his skin somewhat sallower. Why was he here? Had he remembered her? Of course he would have, wouldn't he? Did she want him to? God, no! And yet she shuddered to think that he should *not* remember.

Abigail rolled to her other side. How could Penelope sleep in this heat? Although they'd left the window open, not so much as a slight breeze stirred the stifling air, successfully ruining Abigail's attempts to slumber. Combined with the distress of her embarrassment that afternoon, she could endure it not one second longer.

She needed fresh air. Perhaps the grass beneath her feet.

With only a few shafts of moonlight for illumination, she climbed out of the small bed and rifled around, locating the gown she'd worn earlier that evening. Once dressed, she slipped out the door and down the corridor. Surely, she could find her way outside through the french doors off the drawing room. She did not wish to attempt opening the large main door, and she did not know her way around well enough to find the servants' entrance.

On bare feet, with her hair tied in one long braid down her back, she opened the drawing room door and tiptoed over to one of the glass-paned doors which exited to a terrace. She turned the knob, but it did not budge. Moving to another door, she tried it with no success either.

"Oh, blast!" she whispered.

****

Ah, so she had found him. Not quite as imaginative as the busted bodice, but he gave her points for tenacity. The uncle apparently had not been exaggerating. For here she was, in the library, so very late, with such a thin excuse as wishing to go outdoors. She had even cleverly managed to stage herself so that the moonlight streamed in behind her, revealing more than a silhouette of what he now admitted to himself was a delectable and voluptuous figure. She was wearing the dress she'd worn to dinner earlier, but without stays or chemise. It was quite transparent when the unfiltered moonlight shone behind her, and the effect was causing a tightening in his groin. He wondered, vaguely, if she had attempted to find him in his bedchamber first. Marco, his valet, would have been tucked away on his trundle off the dressing room and most likely would not have heard her knocking. Perhaps Alex ought to have gone to bed after all. That would have saved them both a bit of effort.

He had known he would not be able to sleep, though. Discussing Hyacinth and the children with Miss Wright earlier had stirred up too many disturbing memories. He'd decided to avail himself of Ravensdale's fine scotch—quite a bit of it, in fact.

"Such language," he said, laughing softly. "And from such a pretty mouth."

Abigail froze. She was not alone. Spinning about,

her eyes searched the shadowy room. She had entered the library several moments ago. Why had the person not brought his presence to her attention then? An inkling of fear ghosted down her spine.

"Who is there?" she asked, attempting to sound unafraid.

And then she saw a movement from one of the large chairs by the fireplace. "Hopefully not your worst nightmare."

She knew that voice. Bored sounding and arrogant, yes, it was the duke.

"They are locked at the top. You'll never reach them." And then, seeming to guess at her confusion, a hand gestured toward the outside terrace. "The doors."

"Oh," was all she said. And then feeling the need to fill in the silence, "The heat upstairs is unbearable. I could not sleep."

The duke rose to his feet and moved quietly across the room. Did he seem just a tad off balance? The lines of his face were all she could make out, cast in shadows by the moonlight. He was holding a glass in one of his hands and his hair was disheveled, as though he'd run his hand through it several times. Even knowing it was he, and that she was quite safe, her heart skipped a beat. He was a man, after all.

"So you thought it would be wise to explore your host's estate in the middle of the night all alone?" His tone suggested an insult. "I'm beginning to think you are not a very smart woman, Miss Wright."

Oh, he really was annoyingly arrogant. And then she shivered. He did have a point. Why had she not considered her safety before making a mad dash to be outside? And after seeing that nasty excuse for a gentleman earlier this evening no less? At the time, all that had mattered was to find some relief from the heat. "I was hot."

She watched as a sly, not a smile really, rather a smirk, passed across the duke's features. A ray of moonlight fell on his face, revealing raised eyebrows and glowing silver eyes. He now stood uncomfortably close to her, holding a brandy snifter.

"And looking for a bit of relief, eh? Perhaps you'd like some company?" He reached up and unlatched the lock at the top of the door. As he raised his arm, his body skimmed Abigail's. She inhaled and a strange energy pulsed through her. He was all male, and he was very close. The sensations caused by his nearness befuddled her. She'd spent little time in the presence of gentlemen. Even less in the presence of worldly dukes.

And then, just as smoothly, he lowered his arm, pushed the lever, and swung the door open. Not moving away, he took a slow sip of his drink and watched her over the rim of his glass. His silver eyes were again caught by the moonlight. They were hooded but focused.

On her.

The air was only slightly cooler in the library than it had been upstairs. That is until the duke pushed open the door.

A refreshing breeze beckoned her outside. But although the cool air tempted her, Abigail was beginning to believe coming downstairs had not been one of her better ideas. It was bad enough she'd run into the duke. What if Farley were wandering about outside? She'd most definitely not used good judgment.

A rush of cool air swirled her gown around her

legs.

If the duke were to stroll outside with her for a few harmless minutes, she would be safe from Farley. The duke *seemed* like an honorable gentleman, after all. And he was awaiting her response. Would she appreciate his company?

"Thank you, Your Grace. That is kind of you." The minute she spoke, an altogether different apprehension settled on her. The duke was not wearing his cravat or waistcoat. The top half of his shirt had come unbuttoned, and a smattering of dark curling hair showed on his exposed chest. Tiny black hairs covered the line of his jaw, and his eyes gleamed amongst the shadows on his face. He'd rolled his shirtsleeves up to his elbows and removed his stockings and shoes. The sight of his bare feet moved her.

"You must be feeling the heat this evening as well," she said nervously.

He merely raised one eyebrow and then indicated with a slight jerk of his chin that she step outside.

The stones on the patio cooled the bottom of her own bare feet. After the duke closed the door behind them, he turned back toward her and offered his arm. She took it hesitantly and they proceeded to stroll toward the front lawn. His proximity sent a shiver racing through her.

"You could not sleep?" she asked. Silence unnerved her.

He did not answer. A shaft of moonlight caught his face again. His eyes appeared more silver than they had in the daylight and his chiseled features set and hard. Even walking casually, he carried a tension. Did he never sleep?

"Penelope had no difficulty falling asleep whatsoever." Realizing he might not remember who Penelope was, she forged onward. "Penelope is my cousin on my father's side. As long as I've known her, and that has been a very long time, she has never suffered from insomnia. What a blessing that must be!" In his continued silence, she babbled nervously. "To lay one's head on the pillow, take a few deep relaxing breaths, and voilà! Be asleep. I can hardly image anything lovelier."

"Has this inability to sleep been with you since the scandal of your come-out?" He spoke the words in that lazy, uncaring voice. Abigail swallowed hard.

Had he known all along? Had he remembered it himself? Her ruin had been public, but she had not thought it would be a matter of consequence to such a high and exalted person as the duke.

"No," she said, remembering. "It began shortly after."

"It took some time then," he pressed, "to realize you would live a different life than you supposed? To succumb to your true nature?"

At the thought of the drastic changes in her life when she returned from London, she chuckled, feeling no amusement whatsoever. "I suppose you could say that, Your Grace."

"But a sleepless night can hold a great deal of pleasure, would you not agree?" His voice sounded gravelly. "For a single woman...and an unattached male."

She inhaled sharply. Surely he was not implying...Surely not! "I often find something productive to do when sleep eludes me, Your Grace. It is amazing what one can accomplish under the light of just one candle." She often did some sewing; she'd embroidered many a stitch sitting up alone at night.

"It is infinitely more pleasurable when one can see what one is doing," the duke agreed. Instead of enjoying the coolness of being outdoors, Abigail was unexpectedly quite, *quite* aware of the heat emanating from the man walking beside her. She tried to focus on the cool grass beneath her feet, and the gentle breeze stirring her dress, but her thoughts defied her and instead directed themselves upon the hardness of the arm beneath her hand and a spicy, male scent that invited her to lean closer.

They continued their casual stroll across the lawn while Abigail gathered her thoughts enough to direct the conversation toward another subject. "I disagree completely with the mark that the ton has chosen to put upon you."

"The Duke of Ice?" His laughter rang false.

"Yes," she responded firmly, warming to her subject. "I think it is childish and cruel, but most of all, untrue. I have come to believe that society is made up of a group of people who collectively possess the maturity of an adolescent girl. Such nonsense, declaring that merely because a person chooses to be reticent he lacks emotions. Everybody has emotions—worries, sadness, wants…needs."

"I will admit, I do have those." This time, a husky tone sounded in his voice.

"Yes. You may be assured that I do not believe a word of it. You have shown me honor, and…and compassion…and kindness. I am going to remind myself, the next time I listen to a piece of gossip, of how untrue hearsay can be. I think that, in fact, Your Grace, you are a kind person indeed."

"Being kind has never been something I have aspired to, Miss Wright." His tone stirred something inside of her. She trembled and lost her train of thought once again. They had reached the edge of the lawn near a path that led around the lake and the duke came to a halt.

When he turned to face her, she moved backward until her back pressed against the solid trunk of a tree.

They should go back. She should edge away and march across the lawn on her own.

But she did not. Instead, she stood as though mesmerized, caught in the intensity of his silver gaze.

He stepped forward and put one hand on the tree, inches from her face. He continued to hold his drink in his other hand. "Now being *friendly* is something else entirely." He then tipped his head down and pressed his open mouth against her neck.

He touched her with nothing but his lips and tongue. So very different than the last time. And yet, the horror of the situation she'd allowed herself to fall into, once again, paralyzed her. She could not cry out for help. She could not scream.

There *was* something different, though.

As he trailed his lips along the line of her nape, he left a tingling awareness as thrilling as it was disturbing. It was almost even enjoyable.

Until his hand moved down and grasped her breast. This was not different. This was the same! And the smell of whiskey suddenly overwhelmed her as well.

"Stop! Please stop!" was all she managed. She struggled for air as the world closed in on her. It could not happen again. Oh, it could not.

She was too far gone to realize that the duke had removed his hand from her breast and his lips from her neck. He had, in fact, stepped back to watch her through narrowed eyes.

And then she fainted.

Alex's reflexes were just barely quick enough to keep Miss Wright from falling to the ground. This was a first for him. One moment he was caught up in the lazy sexual haze of desire for this lush little package of femininity, and the next he was holding that same little package in a manner different from what he had imagined. And after he'd caught her, he wasn't quite sure what to do with her.

And damn, when he'd prevented her from landing on the grass, he'd failed to do the same for his drink. The earth, rather than his gut, absorbed the last sips of Ravensdale's fine scotch.

Hell.

He couldn't leave her out here on the lawn, alone.

Damn his eyes, but she'd fainted dead away. The moonlight shining on her face revealed the delicate and translucent skin around her eyes and on her cheeks. Her lips were slightly parted and dark lashes fanned downward, hiding her exceedingly expressive eyes.

He supposed he ought to take her back into the house.

Sliding one arm under her knees and the other around her shoulders, he lifted her easily. When he stumbled, though, he realized he'd perhaps absorbed plenty of Ravensdale's scotch after all. Perhaps he didn't really need the few drops he'd lost due to her faint.

Perhaps.

The lawn tilted to one side, and just when he'd righted himself, it tilted the other way. He had no idea how long it took to reach the library doors, but it seemed far longer than it ought.

Once inside, he waited for his eyes to adjust. The room appeared much darker than it had when he'd been sitting quietly, minding his own business, just a short while ago. He nearly knocked over a lamp, and then a vase, before dropping Miss Wright into an inelegant heap on the leather couch.

Again, what to do with her. He ran a hand through his hair and considered his options.

He could leave her here alone.

No. He immediately dismissed this notion. The worst case scenario would be that somebody would find her and take advantage; the best case would have her discovered upon awakening and open to censure and scorn. She'd be mired in yet another scandal.

Kneeling on the floor beside her, he gently patted her cheek. "Miss Wright? Miss Wright?" She was breathing softly but did not awaken. Had she, too, been imbibing? He leaned forward to see if he could smell anything on her breath.

Hovering close to her mouth, he inhaled softly through his nostrils.

She smelled slightly of mint and another unidentifiable fragrance that was clean and feminine. One of his hands rested on the couch near her ear and the other near her waist. Unable to stop himself, he leaned forward and pressed his lips against hers.

Most unfortunately, Abigail had always been a fainter. Upon those distressing situations which were either frightening or extremely overwhelming, she became short of breath, experienced that sensation of standing at the end of a long and dark tunnel, and then fainted dead away. This disagreeable tendency annoyed herself more than anyone else. It annoyed her because, whenever she had seen other women faint, they did it so prettily and would be revived after only a few moments. Abigail was quite certain that her faints were never graceful, nor were they feminine. Her dear cousin, in Penelope-like honesty, had adamantly confirmed this for her. Furthermore, when Abigail fainted, it took several minutes for her to be revived. A frightening notion in and of itself. She did not like thinking of her person—her human body—lying defenseless and vulnerable.

When she revived, on this particular occasion, the first thing she saw was a slightly recognizable but utterly handsome face. Far too close for comfort, in fact. And far too handsome. But familiar. Oh, Lord, it was the duke!

Abigail scrambled quickly to sit up and pushed the duke away from her. "Your Grace, I am so sorry. What must you think of me?" She gradually realized that she was in the library at Raven's Park and it must be very late at night. There were no candles lit, and she and the duke were quite alone.

And then she remembered why she had fainted, and she pushed even harder at the duke. "What are you doing?" she demanded accusingly. Her push caused him to fall back away from her. He caught himself with the arm of the sofa and simply stared at her, kneeling on the floor.

For just a moment, his face looked like that of a

small boy who'd gotten caught with his hand in the cookie jar. Only for a moment though.

Relaxing on his haunches, he quickly transformed back into the marble-faced, arrogant, and emotionless duke once again. "My apologies for startling you, Miss Wright." His voice sounded level and controlled. "I was only making certain that you were breathing…which you apparently are, might I add."

Abigail swung her feet off the couch and felt slightly less at a disadvantage, except that her feet didn't quite reach the floor. "How did I get back in here?" she asked suspiciously.

The duke studied the carpet. "I'm afraid that I perhaps frightened you. My advances, it seems, were not as welcome as I had led myself to believe."

And then he met her eyes again. His own were bloodshot, but he appeared lucid and stoic. "After you fainted, I carried you inside. You have been unconscious for several minutes now." And then, "Will you accept my apology, Miss Wright?"

Abigail smoothed her dress. She was nervous that he had perhaps not been honorable while she had been unconscious. But upon finding her gown intact, and squirming with no unusual sensations, surmised that he must have behaved himself. She lifted her chin and met his gaze.

"You thought I would welcome…You thought that I would…" She couldn't continue. Looking away, she did her best to bring her emotions under control. Her reputation obviously would be with her forever. She wiped at one eye quickly, not wanting him to see how upset she was.

A handkerchief was pressed into her other hand.

"Please accept my apologies." His voice didn't sound quite as cold and clipped. "You must allow me to escort you back to your room now. It would not do for you to be seen."

Abigail nodded but did not meet his eyes. "Yes," she managed.

Looking at the pathetic little thing, the duke couldn't help feeling like a heel. And a fool. And a cad. The combination of those three descriptors drew from him an abundance of self-loathing. For he had been careless and reckless. He would have liked to have blamed the drink, or Riverton, the fact that he'd gone too long without sex, or the fact that he'd been imagining the chit's breasts all afternoon, but he wasn't one to make excuses for himself. He'd simply acted foolishly. And his actions had frightened Miss Wright into a dead-away faint.

Walking to the door into the corridor, he peeked out to ascertain they would not be observed. She rose from the couch and followed him. He offered her his arm, and she took hold of it uncertainly. Not another word was spoken as he walked with her all the way to the third floor, for God's sake, and she slipped inside her chamber.

Knowing for certain that he would be departing at first light, Alex returned to his room and awoke his valet. Excuse or no, he would return to Brooke's Abbey post haste.

Chapter 4

Brooke's Abbey

The duke had hoped that when he returned to his estate he'd be able to put the entire debacle of Miss Abigail Wright firmly out of his mind. He wasn't upset by the lady, herself, per se. His own actions concerned him.

He'd overimbibed while a guest in the Earl of Ravensdale's home and then virtually accosted an innocent young woman. His actions had been out of character and unforgivable. Without the demands of his estate and his horses, he'd dwell on this self-loathing and disgust to no end. He needed to wear himself out physically and mentally, and he could only do so at Brooke's Abbey. Then, perhaps, he would find a bit of peace and quiet, late at night.

And so he returned to Brooke's Abbey.

But even then his thoughts haunted him.

Words she'd spoken that horrible night had penetrated his mind and then continued to plague him. *I disagree completely with the mark that the ton has chosen to label you with...such nonsense: declaring that merely because a person chooses to be reticent he lacks emotions. Everybody has emotions; worries, sadness, wants...needs...And it is unkind as well.* She had trusted him. She had chosen to ignore his reputation and think the best of him.

You have shown me honor, and...and compassion...and kindness. I think that, in fact, Your Grace, you are a kind person indeed.

She had thought him to be honorable and kind. But what bothered him most was her statement she had made about gossip. *I must remind myself, the next time I listen to a piece of gossip, of how untrue hearsay can be.*

She had been innocently telling him all of this while he had acted on malicious gossip he'd heard about her. And her actions had proven it to be completely untrue. She had not been a woman of easy virtue. No, in fact, she had acted more like a frightened virgin. She'd fainted, for God's sake! How else could one interpret such a response?

Miss Abigail Wright invoked a plaguing guilt in him. And the foreign sensation of humility.

This woman of whom he would normally take no notice whatsoever had managed to wedge herself into his conscience, and it irritated him. The cumulative effect of these emotions, added to his normal feelings of inadequacy since the accident, further fueled his discontent. He was a worthless excuse of a man, and yet, he was also a bloody damn duke. Even he could almost laugh at the combination of fortune and tragedy in his life.

But he'd accepted his lot in life. His blessings, his fate...his duty.

The best way he knew to handle the warring conflict within himself was to fulfill responsibilities ingrained into him for as long as he could remember.

He must be diligent as a landlord, he must find honorable ways to keep all of his estates prosperous, and he must provide the dukedom with a strong, intelligent, and healthy heir. The first two came naturally for him. The last, he admitted to himself, meant he was going to have to take measures next spring. As much as he had wished to avoid it, he must find another wife. A mistress would not suffice, for a bastard did not become an heir. He would present himself upon the marriage mart next spring.

Just a few days after his return and making such a life-altering decision, his Aunt Cecily, who normally spent the off seasons on the Continent or at various house parties, returned to spend the remainder of the summer at her home, which she made in the dower house at Brooke's Abbey. And since she was to be at home, she had requested Margaret, Alex's only sibling, to spend a fortnight at Brooke's Abbey as well. Of course, Margaret would bring the children.

Not an unusual occurrence. With her home less than a day's ride away, she often visited while her husband, the Earl of Clive, traveled to oversee some of his distant estates. And she always determined that she and the children had a duty to "cheer uncle up," as she put it.

"Margaret and I can visit with some of the tenants while she is here. Ever since the accident you've neglected them." His Aunt Cecily chastised him over dinner the evening before Margaret's arrival. "Not to worry, dear," she told him, placing one gnarled but manicured and be-ringed hand atop Alex's own. "That's why you have Margaret and me. Hopefully, you'll participate in the season next year?"

Alex nodded, noncommittally, despite his decision. Once he expressed his plans to find a wife, he was afraid he would not be given a moment's rest until the deed was done. His female relatives would pursue brides for him in a relentless manner. He'd not escape the matchmaking until some unlucky woman managed to drag him to the altar.

Not that he resented her...interference.

Aunt Cecily meant well. Not maternal by any means, she'd watched out for Alex's wellbeing, nonetheless, after his mother's passing. Like Brooke's Abbey, she remained a touchstone for him. Not many things had been a constant in his life, but he always had Aunt Cecily, Margaret, and his homes.

The next morning, Margaret, along with her twin two-year-old sons, *two* nannies, a maid, and several outriders entered the long drive that led to the ducal manor. His sister's husband, the Earl of Clive, was inspecting his northernmost estates, and in his stead, he'd sent a veritable army of liveried outriders along to protect his family. Margaret and the earl's marriage was a love match. The two had married three weeks before Hyacinth and the children drowned. Their wedding anniversary would forever be a bittersweet one amongst them all.

Margaret and the children waved gaily as the coaches pulled to a stop. Now a mother, her face looked even lovelier than she had as a debutante. She looked mellower, maternal—happy.

Assisting Aunt Cecily down the marble front steps, Alex couldn't help but think the older woman leaned more heavily upon him than usual. She was definitely getting on in age. The two waited patiently as the footman pulled out the step, opened the carriage door, and assisted Margaret, the nannies, and the children out.

"Monfort, you look as cheerful as ever." Margaret's words sounded sarcastic, but her smile carried sisterly affection. After embracing their aunt, she took both of his hands in hers and squeezed them warmly.

"You are lucky I am at home," he told her, "I have only recently returned from a blasted house party. Had I been inclined to stay for the duration, I would not have been here to greet you." In the past, he had spent the summers almost exclusively at Brooke's Abbey. Neither Margaret nor Cecily would have considered the possibility that he would be away.

"A house party? Alex?" she said with raised brows. "Whoever was persuasive enough to engage *you* as a guest?" Despite having given birth to twin boys and embracing motherhood fully, Margaret would always be the only daughter of a duke. As a countess, she remained as regal as ever, with her dark hair elegantly styled and her gown of the latest fashion.

One of the nannies stepped forward with a small boy on each hand while the other nanny gathered baby paraphernalia from inside of the carriage. Bending down to be on level with her children, Margaret addressed her two boys lovingly. "Come give Uncle Alex a kiss, boys." She picked up one, and Alex effortlessly lifted the other. They both had blondish hair, like their father. One was named Michael and the other Christopher, but Alex could not tell the two apart.

"And who have we here?" he asked, looking into the small boy's wary eyes. He saw them often but had not spent much time in their company. He must still seem like a stranger to them. As he considered this, he realized he'd never before held one of them without being forced to do so.

Miss Abigail Wright would have chastised him for this. What was it she had accused him of doing? *Your Grace, you appear to have chosen to ignore the pleasures that are present in the here and now.* She had accused him of dwelling in the tragedies of the past, impertinent wench.

Had she been correct in her accusation? Had he avoided his sister's children, thinking it would lessen his own pain? He bore a lancing pang inside and was not certain if it was guilt or sadness.

A small hand reached up and touched the corner of his mouth. "Kwistophew, I am Kwistophew," a hesitant voice answered his question.

"And I am Michow," the boy in Margaret's arms said with more conviction.

The child in his arms spoke up again. "And you are Uncle."

Alex turned surprised eyes toward Margaret. "They are talking now, Margaret?"

His words caused Margaret to tilt back her head and laugh. "Oh, Alex," she said finally, "They have been talking for nearly a year now." Her eyes danced with mischief. "Let us go inside and get out of this sun. It has been a rather warm summer, don't you think?"

Alex glanced over at the boy in Margaret's arms. "Would you like to come inside, young man? I imagine your nannies are ready to get out of the sun as well. Tea and biscuits will be served in the nursery shortly, I'm sure, or better yet, iced lemonade." Alex set young Christopher down, and a nanny quickly claimed her charge. He then offered his arm to both his aunt and his sister and led them through the large foyer and upstairs to a drawing room.

"Whose house party was this, Alex?" Margaret persisted as they entered the comfortable sitting area.

"The Earl of Ravensdale. I had thought it prudent to consider the irrigation system he's set up. Some of my own estates require considerable modernization, and I wished to look over what the earl has accomplished." Margaret relinquished his arm and allowed herself to recline on the loveseat away from the window while Alex continued talking. "It was time well spent."

But Margaret waved away his opinions of the irrigation system. Her eyes twinkled. "Were any young ladies present at this house party?"

The image of Miss Abigail Wright came to mind immediately, which was ridiculous. "Lord Ravensdale spent considerable energy foisting his daughter, Lady Natalie, in my direction." Alex grimaced. "Don't start with me, Mags. I'm not interested right now."

And again, one of Miss Wright's annoying comments came to mind. *Will you wait until you are a doddering old fool and then take a wife a quarter of your age and impose an old man's body on her?*

Margaret, thankfully, was not in a pestering mood. "Lady Natalie only recently ended her engagement to the Duke of Cortland. It's no wonder her papa is trying to secure her a husband again. Poor girl, such a scandal!"

Aunt Cecily stayed up on the most current gossip. "The Duke of Cortland has already replaced her. He married just a few days following the broken engagement. It is said to be quite the love match, which causes one to wonder exactly how much of the blame really ought to fall upon Ravensdale's daughter."

Alex thought back to when Margaret had married. "It is a relief, I must say, to marry off one's dependents." Margaret had been willful and stubborn, turning down numerous proposals before accepting Clive. She'd participated in five seasons before finally marrying. "Lady Natalie cannot be nearly as difficult as was a certain duke's sister."

Margaret refused to take the bait. "Not a smattering of it matters if the marriage is an unhappy one—as you well know. If the girl wasn't in love with Cortland, then bravo for her, I say." She looked curiously at Alex. "Was she interested in you?"

At that, Alex could not help chuckling as he remembered Lady Natalie virtually shoving Miss Wright into his boat. "Not at all. In fact, I think the notion of marriage to me repelled her."

"Hmpff," Margaret said.

His sister obviously thought any woman who would not be interested in him must be daft indeed. Alex considered the opposite to be true. He was not sociable and completely unwilling to play society's courting games. Why would any chit worth her weight be interested? Oh, yes, but of course, the duke thing.

"Nobody else then? Was she the only marriageable girl at the party?"

That was when another unworthy thought drifted through Alex's mind...*Beddable, if not marriageable. Miss Wright certainly presented a beddable option.*

He was going to have to find himself a new mistress...soon. He'd gone far too long without sex.

Whyever else would he be having lustful thoughts about such a spinsterish, barely genteel lady?

"Not a one," he answered Margaret's question firmly. And in a well-needed change of subject, he asked after Lord Clive. Being enamored completely with her husband, Margaret was more than capable of expounding upon this topic enough to fill in the rest of tea time.

****

The day after the duke had departed from the Ravensdale's house party, Abigail was awakened by Penelope with the news that the Rivertons and most of the other guests would be departing early as well. She was surprisingly relieved to make her escape. The guests had not been as agreeable as she'd thought they had been on the first day of her visit. Perhaps word of her scandal from years before had spread or perhaps it was merely her imagination. But the atmosphere had become somewhat tense, and a few of the guests turned their backs on her on more than one occasion.

But the reason for their departure erased all of Abigail's personal concerns. Apparently, a dreadful scandal was in the making when it was discovered that Lord Hawthorne had absconded during the night with Lady Natalie, compromising her completely. Following several anxious hours, a missive arrived assuring the earl and countess of her safety, but most of the party atmosphere had been eclipsed by Lady Natalie's future troubles.

And so the next day, the Baron and Baroness of Riverton thanked the earl and countess formally and departed from Raven's Park as did most of the other guests. The withdrawal resembled something of a mass exodus.

Although the countess took the time to wish each guest safe travels, the pinched lines around her mouth exposed her worry. She most certainly was still deeply troubled for her daughter. Abigail wished she knew the woman better; she would have liked to have given her a reassuring embrace. The leave-taking already felt awkward, though, because nobody looked *her* in the eyes.

Expecting that she and Penelope would either return to Raebourne together or perhaps travel to the Rivertons' country estate, Abigail was surprised to learn that her aunt would be joining them in order to deliver Abigail, alone, back to Raebourne. Penelope would not be spending the summer with her after all. Her uncle, she discovered, would travel alone back to his estate without his wife.

"But it will be no trouble, Aunt. Mother is most likely completely healed of her injury now. She wasn't really an invalid at all when we left. And Penelope and I can be quite independent. We are not children, you know."

"Penelope will return with me to Helmsley Manor." Her aunt gave no further excuse or reason. Her terse reply brooked no arguments. All plans for the two young ladies' holiday together were cancelled with no explanation.

Furthermore, her aunt's attitude had turned distant and aloof. But for what reason? Abigail wondered and Penelope seemed just as confused.

Although Abigail had experienced discomfort at the imposition of their pending visit during their journey to Raven's Park, she knew an even greater foreboding as they traversed the miles home in an unnatural silence.

Penelope sent her a few apologetic glances, shrugging as if to say she had no idea what was the matter either. Neither of the women were children, but both were dependents, which did not allow for them to question their elders' plans. As they drove, her stomach dropped lower and lower as she gradually comprehended something to be terribly, dreadfully wrong. Could it have something to do with her unfortunate encounter with the duke on that first day of the party? Had he told her uncle? He'd promised he would not reveal her gaffe to anybody. And she had believed him!

By the time they rolled onto Raebourne, Abigail had worried her bottom lip as well as nibbled several fingernails half away.

The carriage surged to a halt at the door of her parents' home, and they all climbed out in somber silence. In response to Abigail's mother's confusion, the baroness frowningly took Mrs. Wright aside to speak privately.

While Abigail's trunks were unloaded, Abigail waited in the parlor with her father and Penelope. They sat somberly, listening to the clock tick between stilted conversation as though awaiting a verdict. What was being said across the foyer? Abigail shuddered upon imagining what the duke had told her uncle. She'd convinced herself by now of his betrayal.

Finally, the baroness appeared in the doorway. Alone. "Come now, Penelope." Her aunt's voice brooked no argument. "We must get back on the road so as to arrive home before nightfall."

Her father merely downed a tumbler of his usual vice and eyed her suspiciously. Penelope met Abigail's eyes and grimaced.

What had Abigail done to deserve this?

Abigail rose quickly and embraced her cousin. "I will write you. Surely whatever this is about will pass soon," she whispered in Penelope's ear as she pulled her close to wish her farewell.

Penelope pulled back and shook her head with a grimace, leaning in again she said, "I fear that there were more scandals brewed this week than just that of Lady Natalie's. Perhaps we are being protected?"

But Abigail knew that was not the case. Her aunt's attitude had changed abruptly toward her.

And her mother, who had finally rejoined them, watched her now with pinched lips and red eyes.

With a strong sense of foreboding growing in Abigail as each minute passed, the Wrights followed their guests outside and then waved while the baron's elaborately crested carriage drove off her parent's small land holding. As soon as it disappeared around a bend, her mother broke into tears.

"Why would you do this to us again, Abigail?" Her voice caught on a sob. "Have you no consideration for your father and me? For your own reputation?"

But she'd done nothing really! "What, Mother? What have I supposedly done now?" The duke *must* have shared her shame. Or even worse, someone had witnessed her while she was on the boat with the duke. *Oh, dear God, no, please, God, no!*

"You were seen," her mother said, seemingly confirming Abigail's suspicions, "in a compromising situation with one of the gentlemen who attended the house party."

No, please God, no!

"He was seen leaving your room in the middle of the night. You were also seen embracing him, in your *nightclothes*, outside, *alone*, in the *middle of the night!*" And then her mother gasped and pressed her face into her husband's shirt front. Her sobs somehow increased in volume in spite of the fact that they were now muffled.

Abigail's father stared at her over his wife's head with disappointment in his eyes.

Abigail, rather foolishly, knew only relief that nobody else had seen her bosoms exposed. This minor reprieve was irrational because she knew all too well how damaging gossip could be. This cannot be happening. Not again!

"But Father, I only went outside because it was so hot on the third floor. I stumbled upon the duke in the library, and he offered his escort out of concern for my safety! I did nothing wrong! He was never in my room. For Pete's sake, Penelope was in there! What were we to have done with Penelope inside?" Abigail was astonished that such an innocent act had been so terribly and scandalously misconstrued. "A duke, of all things! Really? And I was *not* in my nightdress!"

Her father shook his head wearily. "With your history, Daughter, you ought to know it is better to endure the heat of a thousand fires rather than put yourself in another compromising situation. It is unlikely anyone will allow you the benefit of the doubt. I'm not certain I am inclined to give it myself." He pushed his wife away from him and admonished her. "Whatever were you thinking? Sending her to a house party?"

With Mr. Wright's words of criticism hanging in the air, her mother turned and dashed out of the room and up the stairs to her room with quickness, if not grace, wailing loudly all the way. Surprisingly, her ankle had miraculously healed over the past four days. Yes, it had only been four days.

Enough time to ruin Abigail's hopes for the future, this time, beyond all repair.

Abigail stood, still as a statue, and looked out the window onto the drive where her aunt and Penelope had just disappeared. She needed a plan. But what? What could she do? She was used to the powerless conditions of her life. She'd long ago spent her efforts mastering her emotions instead.

But the more she dwelled on her parents' words, the harder it became to breathe. If she was as ruined as they said, Abigail could never be a companion to any respectable lady. She could not be a dressmaker or governess. She was not fit for any employment that could be considered respectable. And there would come a time when employment would most definitely be necessary.

This could not be happening! A dreadful mistake had been made!

Abigail forced herself to meet her father's gaze with a confident smile. "It cannot be as bad as all that, Papa," she asserted, too brightly. "There will be another scandal involving someone else soon enough, and this will be forgotten again, I promise. Please, do not worry about me. I am most forgettable, you realize. It cannot be as bad as the other, surely…All will be well. Of course it will!" Placing her hand over her heart, she boldly went on, "I feel it right here."

Her father grunted, turned on his heel, and marched away. Was all hope truly lost this time? It could not be.

Abigail chuckled ruthlessly to herself. She absentmindedly remembered a biblical verse that was appropriate to her life…Was it in the book of James? Something to the effect of "you do not know what your life will be like tomorrow. You are just a vapor that appears for a little while and then vanishes away…" Like her coming out in London, like her plans for the summer, like the house party…like her life.

The Duke of Monfort had brought nothing but trouble to her. He'd so adamantly told her she ought to be planning for her future. Ha! Plans got her nowhere. She had planned on thanking him the morning after he'd escorted her safely up to her room, and lo and behold, he had already departed. He would never even hear about the repercussions his attentions were heaping upon her.

He most likely was riding his horses and drinking his brandy, happily enjoying himself on his large ducal estate with not a single thought for poor Miss Abigail Wright. Poor Miss Wright and her gigantic bosoms, that is. No, he'd most likely banished her from his thoughts completely. And she, well she, was supposedly ruined forever.

Again.

****

Having Margaret as a guest was really not a bad thing, after all. Her presence, and that of the children, broke up the monotony of his days. Certainly, he kept busy. He normally spent a great deal of time with his secretary, Harris, and his steward. There were always decisions to be made, reports to read, and papers to sign, but Margaret and the children forced him to step away from the dukedom occasionally. The three of them, Aunt Cecily, Margaret, and Alex, took dinner together, formally in the evenings. Each day, they informed him of the visits they had made that day and any interesting gossip they'd stumbled upon. The information was surprisingly...well...informative. Tidbits and news he would never hear otherwise, as the duke. News the women shared only with each other and presumably, their spouses: who was courting whom, who had purchased what, and which scandals were in the making. Some of it explained certain issues Alex had run across with his steward. This evening proved no different. Alex sipped from his goblet of wine and watched his sister as she fussed at her asparagus. From the gleam in her eyes, she had come across something meaty today.

"You were at Raven's Park last week, Monfort? It was their house party from which you departed early, was it not?" She raised a petite bite to her mouth and allowed it to hover there.

Alex merely raised one eyebrow.

"Well, of course, that was where you were. You did not tell me the Earl of Hawthorne was in attendance."

Alex picked up his own fork and knife and cut a tender slice of beef from the steak on his plate. "I did not inform you of all who were in attendance. Was I to have done so, Margaret? Was it my duty to inform you of the guest list at Lord and Lady Ravensdale's party?" He purposefully allowed his voice to sound lazy and uninterested. Something about teasing his younger sister never lost its appeal.

"Did you speak with him? Did he seem as nefarious as his father was?" Margaret asked, not disguising her interest in the least. "For, apparently, he kidnapped Lady Natalie!"

Well. Alex looked up. Interesting. Except, remembering the exuberance with which the young woman had literally pushed Miss Wright into his boat so she herself could partner the nefarious new earl, he doubted that "kidnapping" was an accurate label for what likely occurred.

Perhaps more of an elopement? He doubted Lady Natalie Spencer had much to worry over. She had proven quite adept at handling matters to suit herself.

In a flash, his mind triggered the image of Miss Abigail Wright in the moment before she'd fainted in his arms. A woman, considered to be of easy virtue, who had been so shocked by his touch that she'd literally swooned.

The thought of malicious gossip hurting Ravensdale's daughter struck him suddenly as not so humorous at all. "Mags, I would have that such damaging hearsay stop at my own dinner table." He picked up his napkin and swiped it irritably across his mouth. "Lord Hawthorne is not the sort of man who would undertake a kidnapping, and if some such calamity has occurred to that family, I would suggest the family is more in need of our sympathy than our judgment." He sent an icy and ducal glare in his sister's direction.

Margaret merely stared back at him uncomprehendingly. "You are saying it must be untrue, then? So Sir Bentley and his wife then are now liars?"

Alex pushed his shoulders back and continued glaring at his sister, but his aunt interrupted his thoughts before he could respond.

"They were themselves in attendance at the party after all, Monfort. I've never known Lady Bentley to make up untruths, and I have known her for nearly half a century!" Aunt Cecily sat back as a footman removed her dish quietly. The other footman immediately replaced her plate with a parfait dish featuring one of Margaret's longtime favorite desserts, Rhubarb Fool. It consisted of elderberry cordial and rhubarb swirled over sweet cream. Alex had requested cook prepare it specially for his sister.

As another footman placed a dish in front of Margaret, Alex took satisfaction in seeing her stubbornness melt. "Oh, Alex, how sweet of you." She smiled his way.

He exhaled. If anybody ever dared to drag his own sister's name through the mud, he would have met them on a field of honor. And he would not delope. If the men in Miss Wright's family had shown even an iota of honor, most likely she would not find herself with such an insecure future. Damned unfortunate for the woman.

Margaret glanced at their aunt. "Perhaps that other juicy morsel, then, is not true either—the one about that foolish girl running about at night. Except that she most certainly must be ruined. Whether there is any truth in it or not."

Aunt Cecily dipped her spoon into the dessert. "Oh, most definitely. Especially with her past. I doubt society will forgive her twice."

Alex froze where he sat. No, no, no—it cannot be.

"Did you come out with her, dear? Or did all of

that happen later?" Aunt Cecily dipped her spoon into the cream a bit deeper this time. Her second bite was a little less polite.

"She came out the year after me, Aunt. The year Alex married."

Now he stifled an urge to loosen his cravat. What the devil were they talking about?

Both ladies sighed.

And then reached for another taste of their desserts. Alex's dessert remained in front of him untouched. And then, with barely a sigh, Margaret shook her head. "Poor Miss Wright."

"Poor who?" Alex nearly croaked before clearing his throat and then speaking again. "Did you say *Miss Wright*?" He sincerely hoped the poor girl had not found further trouble for herself following his departure. It was very possible; in fact, it was quite likely. Her uncle had been spouting off to other men in attendance, no doubt.

"Yes, Miss Abigail Wright," Margaret answered with a sharp glance. "Did you meet *her* as well while you were there?"

He supposed he ought to investigate this situation. What trouble had the chit gotten herself into after his departure? "I did," he admitted. "And she is another unfortunate victim of hearsay and gossip. Pray, tell, what are the scandalmongers saying about the poor lady now?"

Raising her brows at Alex's inquiry, Margaret relinquished her spoon and began fidgeting with her napkin. "She was seen consorting intimately with a gentleman out of doors and in the library alone, in the middle of the night. That same gentlemen was also seen leaving her room later."

The ramifications of his sister's words hit Alex with the impact of any physical blow. "Who was the gentleman?"

"His name went unmentioned. Just that he was one of the guests." And then, mimicking the ducal glare Alex had sent her way earlier, Margaret eyed him back with icy arrogance. "It was not you, was it?"

As much as he would have liked to, he would not dissemble to his sister. Instead, Alex nodded in his aunt's direction. "I will take my port alone this evening, Aunt. If you would be so kind as to excuse yourselves, I will join the two of you later in the drawing room."

Both ladies eyed him carefully but excused themselves nonetheless. He was the duke, after all. Damn it!

Meddling women needed to learn their place. He bristled.

But for now, the information he'd just heard required his attention. Was it possible that some busybody guest had spread such malicious gossip? Of course, it would not harm the Duke of Monfort in any way. He was so far above the chit that common opinion would consider it her own fault for offering herself up to him.

But she had not.

She was innocent in every way.

It had been idiotic of her to leave the safety of her bedchamber and gallivant about the house alone. If it had not been himself sitting in the earl's library, it could just as likely have been some other gentleman— one perhaps less scrupulous than himself.

He winced at the thought. He'd not been entirely

scrupulous.

He took a slow sip of his port, leaned his head back and closed his eyes. *Oh hell.*

****

Later that evening, Margaret could keep her peace no longer. "How could you, Alex?" she asked after he had eventually joined the two ladies in the drawing room. "Does the story hold any truth?" She clamped her lips shut then, awaiting his answer.

Alex did not feel the need to explain himself to his younger sister, but he did, however, wish to afford some protection to the lady in question. "The lady did nothing to deserve such malicious gossip. I merely escorted Miss Wright outside for a few moments and then back to her room. She had come downstairs in order to escape the heat on the third floor."

Margaret sat, apparently deep in thought, for a few minutes after he spoke. "This is not Miss Wright's first scandal," she said. "She drew society's scorn that same year you and Hyacinth married."

"How so?" Alex asked. Could it be true? He had difficulty imagining the frumpy young woman he had met deliberately participating in immoral behavior. Of course, the resulting consequences could have changed her attitude considerably. Perhaps she had been fast and easy when she'd first come out. Perhaps being shunned changed her outlook on life. But he could not believe such an explanation. Most likely she had made a few foolish but innocent blunders, as she had by walking outside with him, alone.

Which caused him to consider her in a different light entirely. She had looked quite, quite wistful when she'd spoken of children. She'd also adamantly stated she would never marry.

"It was rather surprising to me," Margaret continued. "The lady had been such a timid wallflower for most of the season. I cannot imagine her seducing anybody. Except…"

"Yes?" Alex urged her to continue.

"She, well…" Blushing a bit, Margaret looked down at the embroidery in her hands. "She was quite well…endowed, if you can imagine." Looking up, she caught her own mistake. "Well, of course you don't need to imagine anything. You met her. Did you think her to be fast? Did you see her as something of a seductress?"

Alex shook his head. "Of course not." He considered the possibility that she had purposely exposed herself to him while out on the lake and then dismissed it immediately. She had truly been mortified. Unless she was something of an incredible actress, nobody could have feigned such abject mortification. Could one?

She had not acted in any manner that could be considered fast. She had in fact, seemed quite naïve. This struck him as especially unusual now that he considered her reputation. She lived her life as something of a foolish optimist. She'd been imprudent to have wandered about at night while attending a house party. This led him to believe she'd rusticated in the country for most of her adult life.

Remembering her faint after he'd kissed her, he knew her not to be fast. And easy?

No, she'd not been easy. She'd been annoyingly difficult at times. Definitely not easy.

"Of course not," he repeated as Margaret looked up

from her embroidery circle with a questioning look in her eyes.

"Well, that's terrible, then—the gossip—I mean," Aunt Cecily added. "She is most certainly ruined, now. Amazing she was not already."

Alex ground his teeth. He ought not to even care about all this. *Damn his eyes.* He should have departed the estate as soon as he'd completed the tour of the irrigation system. People at house parties had nothing better to do than embellish upon indiscretions and flap their jaws merely for the sake of their amusement. "A shame," he muttered, looking into his glass as he swirled the amber liquid about. He didn't even like the woman! He'd conversed with her only for the sake of duty! *Damn his eyes again. And damn Riverton for his insinuating comments!*

Margaret narrowed her eyes. "Is she a woman of independent means?" she asked.

Alex stared into his cognac. An excellent year. Just a hint of sweetness, and then spice, before it smoothly warmed his insides. He took another sip, swirled it in his mouth, and then swallowed appreciatively. "She is not," he answered his sister's question succinctly.

"Oh, Alex, that is most unfortunate!"

Alex continued studying his drink. "What would you have me do, Margaret? Marry the chit?" He allowed derision to seep into his words. She was a nobody. She was practically common. An abhorrent thought to even consider! Duchesses were poised, elegant, beautiful women, raised in noble families, trained to step into their role from birth. And Miss Wright was...well, she was none of that. She was clumsy, reckless, and crushingly naïve. Even if she did have large soulful eyes and bodacious…well, even if she was prettier upon acquaintance, she was most definitely not beautiful.

"Of course not." His aunt spoke quickly. "I mean, she is far too below your notice for that to even be a consideration."

"But you must do something for her," Margaret interrupted. "I think you might perhaps settle some sort of a pension upon her. That way, if she cannot find any employment, of which she most likely will not, she will at least have a means to live by."

Alex considered this. Even now, were her acquaintances shunning her? Might her parents disown her? Had they already? If he were to put her up in a cottage somewhere, would she find herself living a lonely and solitary life? He would have to set her up in a village where she was unknown. Allow her to put the actions of her past far behind her.

Or.

Or…he could set her up in London. She could be his mistress.

The thought was frightfully tantalizing.

As a young woman of gentle birth, most certainly, she would never consider such an option. But now…would she consider it? His mind had no trouble remembering the lushness of her body. His hands remembered the feel of her bottom, and his eyes remembered the glory of her breasts. And her lips…

Except for her mouth. She'd had quite a mouth on her, and he could not imagine her keeping it shut long enough for him to ever find his enjoyment with her.

An absurdly stupid idea. The woman had fainted, for God's sake.

"What do you think, Alex? Will you set her up with a pension?"

He had to backtrack to what his sister was talking about. His body had somehow latched onto his second idea and distracted him.

Oh, yes, a pension. "I will have think about it," was all he said.

"Because you must do something, Monfort. Even though your actions were completely innocent, and I believe they were. For you are not the sort of man who would ruin a young lady and then fail to take responsibility for her. Nonetheless, she must be taken care of. She mustn't have to worry for her financial security over something you were involved in." Margaret dropped her attention to her embroidery circle once again, as though the situation had been settled to her satisfaction.

Alex downed the remainder of his cognac, awaited the pleasant warmth to spread through him, and then stood up abruptly. "Have I not just told you I will think about it?" He spoke more sharply than he had intended. And then he pivoted on his heel and strode from the room. She would forgive his rudeness.

She was his sister, after all.

Chapter 5

With each passing day, Abigail grew to believe more and more that her parents had been correct in their judgment of her situation. News traveled throughout the tiny village quickly, and it didn't take long before she was forced to face the fact that she was, indeed, being shunned again.

Local merchants took money for her purchases but refused to look her in the eye or speak other than to announce the number of shillings she owed. People who had, a mere week ago, taken several moments away from work to chat and laugh with her now kept their lips pressed firmly together and acted as though she were a perfect stranger. The speed at which this sort of news traveled was really quite astounding. Her life, her doings, ought to be of no importance whatsoever, for heaven's sake!

Even the local seamstress refused her offer of free labor that had always before been eagerly pounced upon. Abigail was skilled with a needle and thread, and could accomplish twice the work the older lady could do in the same amount of time, but the woman now refused to allow her to even cross the threshold of her humble shop.

Things were not looking good.

Penelope had written her a brief note, stating that

her parents forbade her to keep any contact with Abigail as she was quite obviously a bad influence. *Ha,* Penelope had written, *if anyone is a bad influence we know it is me.* But, she then added, Abigail ought not to write back as her father would in all likelihood confiscate any such letter and then know to curtail Penelope's own letter writing as a punishment.

Not good at all.

After a few weeks of such malicious and petty treatment, Abigail's ever-present smile strained. And on this day, while walking alone in the meadows, she allowed it to slip completely. For it was becoming more and more tiring to force the corners of her mouth upward as each lonely day passed. This was disheartening. She did not wish to allow herself to wallow in self-pity.

Because she was not the only person feeling the dislike and disrespect of the people in the community. Her parents received such treatment as well. She knew that if her father could send her away again, he would have done so the first day she arrived home.

Oh, but her mother! Mrs. Edna Wright took the news badly indeed. She refused to come downstairs for dinner. She kept to her chamber and remained in her nightclothes both day and night. She only allowed Betty and one faithful friend to enter. Mrs. Wheeling happily kept Mrs. Wright abreast of the town gossip. Her words never failed to provide affirmation for Mrs. Wright's declarations of humiliation.

She refused to set her eyes on Abigail, *ever again,* she had shouted at Abigail's father.

And so Abigail had eventually begun to feel a certain level of self-pity after all.

She wavered upon whom she wished to heap the blame. At some moments, she directed her anger at the Duke of Monfort. If he had not believed what he'd heard about her than he never would have attempted to kiss her! And yes, he had acted inappropriately outside that night, as she suspected he had indoors as well. She was still not certain whether or not she believed his claim that he'd been checking to see if she were breathing. Ha! His mouth had been inches away from hers. His lips had been hovering over hers in that moment when she'd regained consciousness. Oh yes, once she'd analyzed her memory of that evening his actions had become clearer.

But it was difficult to blame him *completely.*

She *had* exposed her bosoms to him earlier that day. What if he thought she'd done it on purpose? The thought appalled her. No woman in her right mind would ever do such a thing! And she had made the choice to venture outside her chamber alone. She'd willingly strolled with him through the grounds in the moonlight. Any man might misconstrue her actions as those of a strumpet.

Just as he had.

But mostly, he had simply been kind. How could she blame him for showing kindness?

Other days, she blamed her mother. If she had not forced her and Penelope to attend the house party none of this would have happened. Abigail and Penelope would have bided away the rest of the summer doing perfectly harmless activities at Raebourne and in the relative safety of Biddeford Corners.

Depending upon Abigail's mood, blame could be shifted at will. Sometimes, after she'd gone through a litany of conspiracies, Abigail simply blamed herself and then tried to hope for the best. What that might be, however, she could not comprehend.

Caught up in her castigations, Abigail marched back to the house and stepped inside. Entering the parlor, she dragged her hand along a row of books and then pulled one out. Solutions to her predicament evaded her. She'd find nothing in a book except perhaps a few hours of escape.

"Abigail!" Her mother's voice jolted her back to the present.

In her mob cap and billowing night dress, Mrs. Wright stood in the doorway red-faced, fluttering, and nearly hysterical. "There is a carriage, a grand, grand carriage approaching down the lane. Betty!" she shouted for her maid. "I must be dressed immediately! Whoever can it be? Abigail, girl, go to your room. I don't want our guest to discover you are here. You mustn't expose them to your scandal."

Abigail sighed and complied reluctantly. Perhaps it was one of her aunt and uncle's friends? Accepting her new lowly status, she tucked the book under her arm and marched up the stairs to hide away in her bedchamber. She would escape in the book—pretend she'd not become a pariah.

A feat easier said than done.

The more she tried to read, the less she comprehended. For she couldn't help but wish things could turn out differently. In her imagination, hope refused to let go. Oh, how she wished…oh, she wished a number of things.

She flipped the pages back and set her mind to reading them again.

"You're wanted in the drawing room, miss." Betty had thrown her door wide open without knocking. "Best make yourself presentable."

****

Alex had decided he would take Margaret's advice and settle a pension upon Miss Wright. But he did not wish to do so through his man of business. He wished to ascertain for himself that such a course of action would resolve the situation. He wished to see for himself that Miss Wright no longer need dread her future. He must also disabuse Miss Wright's parents of the notion that she had been in any way promiscuous while attending the house party. He did not think Miss Wright would suffer her parents' disapproval gladly. Perhaps after this visit, his conscience would cease needling him.

After a bit of investigation into the whereabouts of Miss Abigail Wright's home, he set out in his carriage toward the virtually unheard of village of Biddeford Corners. Her father owned a small property on the outskirts called Raebourne. Thankfully, he needn't travel more than a day. Rumbling down the clean and tidy road, he noted it as a pretty little place, the same as numerous other villages in relative proximity to Bristol and Bath.

He shifted uneasily on the cushioned bench. Unease jostled in his gut with each passing mile, and by the time his coachman pulled up in front of the modest but well-cared-for dwelling, a part of him wished he had left this business up to Harris. Harris would have had no reason to feel anything more than that of an employee doing his duty while making the arrangements for his employer.

Harris hadn't attempted to swive an innocent girl.

Without waiting for the footman to alight and set down the steps, Alex opened the door and jumped to the ground. He confidently stepped up to the door and rapped on the knocker three times with not so much as a glance at his surroundings. He knocked only because it was what one did. They were well aware of his arrival. When one lived in the country, one knew when a visitor was no less than a mile away.

After several insufferable moments, some sort of housekeeper opened the door. Of course, the Wrights would lack the means to retain a butler. They were—what did Miss Wright call it? Barely considered gentry.

"Might I have a word with Mr. Wright?" Alex spoke with no question in his voice whatsoever.

"Yes, sir, who may I tell him is calling, sir?"

Alex produced his card. "Alex Cross, Duke of Monfort," he said in a droll voice. This next part was always a bit annoying.

Bow, curtsey, and then more curtseying. As she backed away, the housekeeper's eyes widened in something resembling both awe and terror. "Of course, Your Grace, right this way, Your Grace." Ah, he would not be kept waiting in the entryway after all. She led him into a small room with worn but comfortable-looking furniture. "I will fetch the master at once for you, sir, Your Grace."

She curtseyed out of the room, leaving Alex to examine the contents of it at his leisure. A few embroidery hoops, a small pianoforte, and a wall filled with what appeared to be well-read books. No sign of dust anywhere. The duke stood with his arms behind his back, facing the door when an elderly-looking man entered slowly. An older woman who most likely was Mrs. Wright could be seen peering around him from behind. Mr. Wright shooed her away with his hand and closed the door behind him.

"So, Mrs. Hartley had the right of it then, good sir. Are you in fact the Duke of Monfort?"

Alex tilted his head in acquiescence. "I am. Are you the father of Miss Abigail Wright?" The man's complexion was both jaundiced and ruddy and the whites of his eyes more than a little yellowed. He stooped a bit.

With these words, the man visibly shuddered. He actually shuddered! "I am at that. Perhaps we ought to have a seat, if you would please, Your Grace?"

Alex lowered himself onto a wooden chair and found himself feeling somewhat...good God, were these nerves? No, definitely not. In fact, he experienced only anger on behalf of the man's daughter. Where had this insanity come from? "It would seem," he said softly, "Miss Wright has landed herself in something of a sticky situation. And I," he added firmly, "seem to be the cause of it."

With these words, the older man flushed. He obviously had not known the identity of the blackguard who had caused his daughter ruin. Mr. Wright stood up and began shaking his head ruefully. He then walked over to the sideboard and poured himself a tumbler of some amber spirits. "These things happen, Your Grace," he said. Did the man not care that his own daughter had no prospects for her future? Lifting the bottle questioningly, he shrugged after Alex declined with a shake of his head.

"She is, of course," Alex continued as though her

father hadn't uttered a word, "completely innocent of any wrongdoing."

The man's eyes looked everywhere but at the duke. "Well, if you say so, Your Grace." He threw back the contents of the drink in one swallow.

The man's attitude both disgusted and infuriated Alex. He couldn't even remember what the chit looked like, and yet suddenly, he was in the position of defending her from her own father?

"You say this because of her indiscretion in London, years ago? Has she not paid already? Does she not now benefit from the support of her own family?"

The older man had the audacity, then, to shrug. "We, me and the missus, never thought she would allow such a thing to happen. Abby has brought more than her fair share of shame upon this family already. How forgiving is a father to be?"

Her father was nearly as bad as the uncle had been. Shameful that the poor lady did not have better men to protect her reputation. If anybody had ever spoken so cavalierly of Margaret, they'd have placed their life in immediate peril.

Apparently, Miss Abigail Wright was in need of a protector.

"May I have a word with her?" He paused. "Sir."

Her father did not demand to know what for, nor did he ask the duke's intentions. "Certainly," he said matter-of-factly, rising from his seat. He disappeared for a few moments, ostensibly to have his daughter summoned.

Alex rose to his feet again and paced over to the window. As he did so, he considered his options. He was looking forward to dealing with this situation and leaving it far behind him. Perhaps it had been best that he came himself. He could be certain he had put matters to right this way. No regrets and certainly no guilt. The young lady would most certainly be more than placated once she knew her future was secure. He would instruct Harris to locate a small cottage in another village for her, perhaps give her a few from which to choose. He would provide for a few servants and perhaps a carriage. Yes, Miss Wright was a lucky woman indeed.

Alex did not have to wait long before Miss Wright timidly looked into the room and then stepped inside. She appeared smaller than he remembered. Dressed in a flowing dull gray dress she stood over a foot shorter than him. She'd pulled her hair back ruthlessly, which ought to have made her appear even more the spinster, but instead somehow drew attention to the delicacy of her skin. Eyes cast downward, she dropped into a curtsey.

"Your Grace, welcome to Raebourne," she said. "Please, won't you sit down?" She indicated the chair that he had previously vacated. She did not meet his eyes. He waited for her to sit before doing so himself. Regretfully, he realized he hadn't stood when she had entered the library that night at Raven's Park.

He'd been an ass.

"Miss Wright." He cleared his throat. "I hope you have been well?"

Finally she looked up. The smile she gave him was strained and brittle and her eyes, haunted. "I have been…yes, I have been well. I admit I am quite surprised that you have come to Raebourne for a visit. Were you traveling in the area, Your Grace? Oh, my, you have been on the road for some time. Let me order tea for you." Without awaiting his response, she reached over to pull the bell pull.

She did not seem nearly as vibrant as she had while at Raven's Park. Had he beheld her as vibrant to him then? The thought struck him as odd. But when he remembered the spunk she had shown after her embarrassing situation on the lake, and then again when he'd talked with her in the library, he thought that, yes, she had been filled with an optimistic light. But now...now, she appeared to be on the verge of shattering, not physically, but emotionally. Her smile was forced, and she was hesitant to look him directly in the eyes.

The same servant who had opened the door to him entered the room, and Miss Wright requested some tea and sandwiches. The woman hesitated a moment, curtseyed in his direction, and then removed herself as quickly as she'd arrived.

"Miss Wright," he began, "I have come because I owe you an apology."

Finally, he had her attention. She stared at him with those big brown eyes, shaking her head. "No, no, Your Grace. You owe me nothing. You were simply being a gentleman. You were merely concerned with my safety and well-being. I was foolish." She stopped and swallowed. "I ought not to have left my room alone. I am the one at fault."

Her hand shook ever so slightly as she lifted it to brush a stray hair away from her eyes. Her dress hung loose upon her frame. She was a tiny little thing really.

"Nonetheless, it was I who was observed leaving your bedchamber. And it was *my* actions that night that have given rise to unseemly gossip. You and I both know that *you* have nothing to be ashamed of. I wish to put matters to rights somehow."

Dropping her shoulders, she averted her face from him, unable to stifle the sound of a choking sob. "I am sorry, Your Grace," she said, wiping a tear from her eyes with the handkerchief she clutched inside her fist. "I suppose it is just that things have been rather...difficult lately. I don't know what has come over me." Unable to stop a flow of tears that had begun, she added, "I never cry."

Yes, a cheerful cottage of her own would set matters to right. She had obviously been living under the strain of her parents' disapproval for longer than just the past few weeks. He supposed they threw her previous indiscretions in her face at every turn. She would find a great deal of relief to be away from them. Perhaps he could send her to Scotland, or Wales. Somewhere far enough away that her reputation would not follow her. She could take on a different name. Yes, a new life completely. He allowed his gaze to drift around the room. She could keep herself busy decorating her new home. He would give her an additional sum for such things.

She looked back up at him with a sincere, but somewhat watery smile. "I had forgotten how difficult it could be when all the people I believed to be my friends turned away from me. Shopkeepers who have always welcomed me with a smile barely acknowledge me now. The local seamstress, who has always been happy to let me sit and work with her, will not allow me to enter her shop. And that had been one of the great joys in my life, sewing, creating new designs, adding beauty to a frock with ribbon and lace."

Perhaps he ought to offer her the position of his mistress after all. He could take her to London and set her up there. Amongst certain circles, she would be received quite well. Being mistress to the Duke of Monfort was something of an honor in itself. He could dress her in the finest fashion had to offer. She could have a lady's maid to do her hair and keep her company. He could take her about town and she could visit places she would otherwise never see. Being his mistress would be quite a step up for her, he imagined.

It would benefit his own needs as well.

"Families I had visited with charity baskets, even, will not open their doors to me." Brushing away her tears with an irritated hand, she continued, "I don't know why I am telling you all of this. It is just that once again, everyone in the world thinks the very worst of me, and now, here you are, telling me that you *know* I have not been a lady of easy virtue."

"But of course," was all he could think to say. There was nothing more tedious to a man than watching a woman cry.

"Over the past several years, I have filled my time by singing in the choir and assisting the vicar's wife in her duties. And now, I find myself banished from church! From church, can you imagine?" And then, as though she had used up all of her energy in the last few minutes, she fell silent. She dabbed at her eyes a few times and shook her head sadly. "I am so sorry, Your Grace, for making such a ninny of myself. I do not want for you to feel badly for…for what you did, nor for having escorted me to my chamber at Raven's Park. I am truly sorry that you went to such trouble to come all of this way. It is I who have been the cause of this situation. I am sorrier than I can possibly say. Somehow, I cannot seem to avoid scandal. It is I who must beg your forgiveness."

With those words, the room, again, fell silent. The ticking of the large clock perched on the mantel above the fireplace echoed off the walls. The sound was somewhat hypnotizing.

"Miss Wright, will you marry me?"

The words bounced off those same walls and shattered all of his plans.

He was not certain who was more surprised by them, Miss Wright or himself. In fact, he had an urge to look around the room to make certain that someone else had not, in truth, uttered them.

Miss Wright did, in fact, peer anxiously around the room.

He, Alex Cross, the Duke of Monfort, had proposed. No one but himself had asked the blasted question.

There was no way he could set her up in some lonely cottage in the middle of nowhere. Miss Wright was a social bird of a woman and would pine away in loneliness. Furthermore, he realized, he could not set her up as his mistress. She was apparently something of a God-fearing woman. Even if she did accept such an offer, he was certain guilt would eat away at her.

In that moment, in truth, he could fathom only one solution to the problem of Miss Abigail Wright. He would realize the new problems this offer created sometime later. After he'd had a drink or two.

"Miss Wright, you are in a difficult, nay, more of an impossible situation. Your parents and friends have turned their backs upon you. You have no opportunities or possibilities of employment, and you have no means to support yourself independently. My solution, of course, is the best possible course of action. I feel certain, if you consider the matter seriously, you will agree with me."

"But—" She hesitated only a moment. "But...You are a duke!"

"Yes."

Abigail could hardly believe she had heard him correctly. He sat there, in his fine ducal attire, with those piercing silver eyes, as calmly as though he had just told her that the sun was shining.

"And I..."

"Yes, Miss Wright, you have told me before. You are barely gentry." His voice sounded almost bored.

Abigail pushed a tendril of hair back that had escaped her bun and tried to wrap her brain around his proposal. Could he actually be serious? "Are you serious?" she asked.

"Miss Wright, this is not something I would joke about." His lips clamped, as though he were holding something back. She studied him for a moment. The only aspect of his person that was not quite impeccable was the growth of beard that shadowed his face. It was late in the day and tiny whiskers peppered his chin and above his lip. His jaw was straight and firm, his cheekbones high. He was lean and yet gave no indication of any form of weakness.

And then Abigail forced herself to consider his offer. It came as something of a miracle and a nightmare all rolled into one. Living with her parents had become more and more intolerable. Their sharing in the ramifications of her disgrace had seemingly diminished any affection they still felt for her.

She did not think her aunt and uncle would help her either. They would separate themselves even more so than her parents. Even Penelope had been unable to alter their convictions.

Abigail had exactly four pounds to her name.

She had no hopes for employment.

She had no one to turn to.

She covered her face with both hands and closed her eyes, lest she begin to cry again. Contemplating her situation did nothing to stem her previously uncontrollable tears. Oh, God. What had her life come to?

Was he, in fact, her miracle?

"Your Grace." She kept her hands over her eyes, lest she jump upon the man and wrap her arms about him. "I must give you leave to rescind your kind offer and forget you ever met me. I cannot hold you to such generosity. Soon enough, upon further reflection, you will thank your lucky stars that you left Biddeford Corners a free and single man." She continued to hold her hands in front of her eyes but peeked through slightly.

He had not moved.

"For you see, Your Grace, the longer you sit there, the greater the likelihood that I will accept your offer…

"You are not moving, Your Grace."

He reclined and shuffled to cross one leg over the other.

"Your Grace," Abigail persisted, "I would not be a good duchess. People would always remember me from my come-out. Your family will not be pleased at all. I am not beautiful. I have no connections. I have nothing to offer you. I am going to count to three, very slowly. You must take your leave while you have the chance, Your Grace, for if you are still here by the time I have finished counting, I warn you that I shall accept your proposal and you will leave here an engaged man. I only have so much self-discipline, you see, and part of me sees you as quite the answer to all of my problems.

"I am warning you…

"One…

"Two…

"Two and a half…" Oh, lord, he still had not moved.

Abigail dropped her hands. "Three," she said.

He was watching her with something that looked like it might be amusement. He lifted one ducal eyebrow. Before either of them could say anything, Betty entered, carrying a tray with both tea and a plate of sandwiches upon it. She set it down carefully on the table beside Abigail.

"Thank you, Betty," Abigail somehow managed. Both she and the duke sat quietly until Betty once again had disappeared. "How do you take your tea, Your Grace? Sugar? Milk?"

"Neither, thank you." He sounded bored again. His eyes were slightly hooded as he watched her stand up and pour. With hands that Abigail did her best to keep from shaking, she poured the hot liquid and handed it to him carefully. She then selected a few small sandwiches, placed them on a plate, and presented them to the duke as well. He set his tea down on the table beside him and accepted the small plate from her.

"Now that that is settled, I suppose we ought to consider how best to go about it."

"It, Your Grace?"

He had taken a bite and was chewing it thoughtfully. He did not answer until he had finished. "The wedding." A perplexed frown marred his smooth forehead. "I imagine I could procure a special license. I am uncertain as to the rest of it. I have several distant relatives who will wish to be in attendance. I am aware that you have some family as well. Would it be best to marry quickly and quietly or ought we to include family and friends?"

"I-I have no idea, Your Grace. What do you prefer?" Taking a sip of her tea, she glanced surreptitiously up to gauge his expression. What she saw could only be described as veiled disgust.

"It is not a matter of what I prefer, Miss Wright, rather what will be the best for handling and eliminating the gossip. My preference, as I am sure you might guess, would be to get the damn thing over with as quickly as possible."

Well.

Would he be even more resentful of her than her parents were? Was she jumping from the frying pan into the fire? She suddenly questioned her belief in miracles.

But if she married, she could have a child, perhaps more than one. And even though she knew they would never fill the hole in her heart from before, she thought they could bring her some contentment, some happiness after all.

"Would it make, well—us—appear to look guilty? Or does being a duke erase that kind of nastiness? Will my apparent indiscretions be forgiven if I am a duchess?"

The duke pondered her question with his gaze fixed on some inanimate object across the room. "I imagine so, eventually." Then he looked around the room before arriving at some sort of decision. When he stood up, Abigail took his lead and rose as well. Perhaps he'd come to his senses and changed his mind.

"I will consult my sister. If necessary, I will obtain the special license." Turning to leave, he stopped suddenly and turned back to face her. Taking her hand in his, he raised it to his lips. Was he mocking her? "You will hear from me again in no less than a week. Until then, Miss Wright." Her hand tingled where he had placed his lips for that slight fraction of a second. Abigail dropped to a curtsey, but did not drop her eyes.

"Goodbye, then," she said.

As he left, she wondered if she would ever see him again. Or perhaps she would merely wake up and discover this all to have been a dream.

****

Alex ran a shaking hand through his hair as the carriage turned out of the drive. What the hell had he just done? What was it about that woman that caused him to veer so completely away from his original plans? It cannot have been lust. He was thirty-eight, for God's sake. He could control his baser needs and had been doing so for years now.

Was he acting out of pity? It cannot have been. Good Lord, marriage? He could hardly believe he had offered for her. And then, unwittingly, he found himself smiling as he remembered her counting to three and urging him to flee.

He ought to have taken her up on her countdown and dashed out to the coach before she reached the count of two. But he knew why he had not.

She'd been refreshingly honest with him. She had not turned coy and pretended to not want to marry him, in fact, she had admitted to him that his offer tempted her. What had she said? Oh, yes. *I only have so much self-discipline, you see, and part of me sees you as quite the answer to all of my problems.*

Something about her brought out his protective instincts. Neither her father nor her uncle had provided her any protection whatsoever.

He, himself, had treated her disrespectfully.

Despite these salient facts, she had attempted, quite valiantly, to remain cheerful.

God save him from a cheerful woman.

Perhaps, scratch that—no perhaps about it. Her tears affected him. They'd not been feigned. In fact, he believed his visit might have actually drawn them from her. It was as though she'd discovered a great relief with him. And it was his opinion that she had not allowed herself any tears until that moment.

Alex shifted restlessly. He ought to have ridden his own mount for this journey. Rapping loudly on the roof, he demanded the attention of his driver. He would ride up front. Far too agitated to remain inside at that moment, he'd enjoy the fresh air. Allow it to clear his thoughts…And then…well…Margaret and Cecily were both still in residence, and he could discuss this with them. Yes, that would be best. And next time he faced an unwanted complication, he would bloody well send Harris.

****

"You what?" Margaret's eyes flew open when Alex casually mentioned that he had resolved the situation of Miss Abigail Wright by betrothing himself to her. Along with Aunt Cecily, they were seated in the most oft-used drawing room at Brooke's Abbey taking tea and enjoying some small pastries.

Alex shot Margaret the look he reserved for occasions when he was unwilling to discuss a matter. "It is settled. I only wanted your input regarding the details of the wedding itself. You have been more active than I amongst the ton. Which would provide the best outcome, do you think? A hasty marriage by special license, or must I make an occasion of it?" He crossed his legs and took a sip of the hot tea Margaret had poured. "In the past, I haven't paid much attention to such trivialities, so I thought it would be best to consult you and Aunt."

Aunt Cecily had narrowed her eyes. She would not be as manageable as his sister. "Good God, Monfort!" She spoke in a tight voice. "If the chit is with child, you merely have to set her up somewhere. You needn't marry her. You haven't told anyone yet, have you? You most certainly will not go through with this unsuitable arrangement." She set her teacup down and wiped her hands on the linen napkin draped over her lap. "You must extricate yourself from this promise as quickly as possible. Even if we must pay her family off."

"I have offered for her, and she has accepted. I will not go back on my word. I am surprised you think that I would." He set his tea aside as well. "I did not come to the two of you for your approval. For with it, or without it, you will accept the woman I marry as my duchess, and you will not speak another word against her. I came to you for assistance in planning the wedding."

Margaret continued to look at him as though he had

grown two horns. It took her a few moments to address his wishes. Alex knew she would not contest him. "Oh, Alex," she wailed, "I am at a complete loss. What happened? However did she manage to draw a proposal from you?" She ventured into uninvited territory in spite of his icy demeanor.

Alex uncrossed his legs and leaned forward. He clenched his jaws tight to keep from blistering his little sister with a scathing set down. "It is done," was all he said.

Margaret sprung to her feet and began pacing. Alex did not rise for his sister as he normally would have with any other gentlewoman—except for when he was in his cups, apparently. Visibly agitated, she was no longer looking at him; rather she stared at the ornamental carpet as she paced back and forth. Finally, after covering the length of the room about a dozen times, she returned to her seat. "I am not sure if a special license is necessary. I need to know more about this…this…Miss Wright before giving you any advice." She paused a moment and finally met his gaze again. "Is she at all refined?"

He pondered her question. When he first had set eyes upon her, he would have said, definitely not. And later, she had been clutching her shawl about her in a death grip (although not tight enough) and wearing a dress which had been a few sizes too small. When he had met her that evening for dinner, however, she had looked perfectly respectable in some dress that she had said she'd sewn herself. Although not glamorous, she had interacted with the other guests with a warm and sweet countenance unique to her. Everybody had presented some level of ennui, but not Miss Wright.

She had embraced the evening as though it would be her last.

As it very nearly had become.

But was she refined?

"With a bit of polish, she might be considered refined," Alex finally answered. "She isn't pretty in a general sense, but she is not the antidote I considered her to be at first glance."

"I think"—Margaret's lips pursed as she formulated a plan—"we ought to take her to London. She will need clothing and various instruction, no doubt. We can do all of this discreetly, at Cross House. Of course, I will have to bring the children, but Aunt and I will act as chaperones." Concern wrinkled her forehead.

He supposed their task might be greater than he'd imagined.

Alex rose to leave his sister to the planning. Best to keep the woman busy. He never understood the workings of woman's brains, anyhow.

Most times, he preferred his horses.

Chapter 6

Abigail sat stunned, in her father's drawing room for several moments after the duke's carriage pulled away. She only roused from her stupor when her mother came bursting in.

Waving her hands around in an irritating manner, Mrs. Wright fluttered with curiosity. "What did he want? What have you done now, Abigail?"

Mr. Wright meandered in behind his wife. "He wanted to apologize to her, I told you. It's the way those nabobs are. Full of himself, that duke is," he added before tipping the carafe on the sideboard and pouring a liberal amount into the glass he'd been carrying.

"Is that all he came for, then, Abigail?" Her mother sat on the loveseat, straight backed. "Fancy that! A duke coming to Raebourne to apologize to my daughter!" Leaning forward, she demanded details. "Well, speak up, girl, is that why he came?"

Abigail paused before answering. If she told her parents the truth, most assuredly they would not believe her. She barely believed it herself.

What if they believed her, and then the duke failed to return? What if he had been out of his head when he'd proposed, and once away from her realized the horrid mistake he'd made?

The situation would be nightmarish if she were to tell her parents she was betrothed and it turned out to be a cruel joke. It wasn't every day that a girl from Biddeford Corner betrothed herself to a duke. Her parents would shout the news from the rooftops.

Was it possible for her to be even more of a scandal than she already was? Perhaps it was.

"He apologized nicely," she answered carefully.

But what if he *did* take this betrothal seriously and then returned in one week expecting her to have made plans to move away from her family and become a duchess? At this thought, she nearly burst out laughing.

It must be a joke!

"He told me he felt sorry such a scandal occurred when he knew I had done nothing to deserve it," Abigail added, her spirit fighting through the lethargy she'd been feeling for the past few weeks.

Mrs. Wright slouched into the back of the settee and frowned. "Hmph," she said. "That doesn't help the reputation of this family! That is all? That is what he came all the way to Raebourne for?"

She would not mention the betrothal. Better for her parents to be pleasantly surprised in the unlikely event the duke returned in one week than for them to be disappointed in her again.

"That is all, Mother," she murmured. Still, a part of her unnaturally giddy. Once alone, she was going to embrace the delight of the fairytale proposal. She'd carried the burden of scandal for nearly a decade now, and the duke had said, as a duchess, she would be free of it. Even in her wildest imaginings, she had never conjured up the miracle he had offered her today. She must enjoy the feeling while she could.

She would ignore the complications of her decision later. Specifically the daunting thought that she had no idea how to be a duchess.

Surely a duchess would have to walk differently. She'd talk differently. Abigail stifled a wince at the thought that duchesses likely did everything differently. And then she stifled a giggle.

Her parents watched her closely. "What are you smiling about, girl?" her father said. "Do you think it is amusing that you have dragged my good name in the mud once again?"

"Oh, no, Papa," she answered quickly, tightening her lips. She should know better than to show any emotion other than remorse while in their company, as of late. "I appreciated somebody finally acknowledging my innocence. That is all..."

"Well, it does us no good." Mrs. Wright shrugged, standing and clutching her handkerchief tightly. "No good at all! I don't understand how you could have acted so foolish...so vulgar..."

And the remonstrations would begin again...

"It was your fault for sending her," Mr. Wright said. "We'll not make that mistake again, not that such an opportunity will present itself, that is."

Abigail stared down into her lap, deflated. As long as she could remember, her parents had browbeaten each other to some degree or another. But more recently, the arguments had worsened.

And it was likely all her own fault.

As expected, Mrs. Wright left the room, wailing and whining for Betty to help her to her bedchamber. And, also as expected, Mr. Wright reached for the decanter of spirits sitting open on the sideboard.

They had managed to emerge from her first scandal with a semblance of dignity, but would they survive this latest scandal? Abigail sat motionless, aware that her father had thrown back one drink and already poured another. Oh, God, but she hoped the duke had not been mocking her. For all of their sakes, she needed to escape.

****

It had been four days since the duke had come through Biddeford Corners and thrown down the gauntlet of his unlikely proposal. Abigail, fully aware that he had told her he would contact her in one week, grew more nervous with each passing day. What if he did not return?

What if he did?

Desperate to escape the tension for the afternoon, Abigail slipped outside, ran, and then, once breathless, slowed to a stroll along the rutted drive, in mind to head into Biddeford Corners. She didn't care if people chose to be rude to her today, she needed away from Raebourne, if only for a few hours. And as she put distance between herself and her parents, the fist around her heart gradually let up.

So much so that she skipped, and then twirled. She wanted to feel like herself again, not this shell of disappointment she'd become.

Hearing an approaching rider, Abigail looked up. Ah, something of interest might happen today after all. Still on her father's land, Abigail hailed the imposing man to stop.

Dressed in full livery, the rider was obviously a nobleman's servant. He pulled his horse to a halt several feet from Abigail and stared at her down his nose. "Do you work at Raebourne, girl?" he asked, gesturing toward the cottage in the distance.

Realizing he mistook her for a housemaid, Abigail smoothed the apron she wore over one of older dresses and laughed. "No, sir, but I am the daughter of the house. How may I help you?"

Waves of doubt rolled off the messenger. "And your name, madam?"

Abigail sighed and then forced a smile. "I am Miss Abigail Wright. Again, how may I help you?" The Duke of Monfort must have sent him. Likely he carried the dreaded missive she had been expecting, signifying his regrets. She glanced over her shoulder, hoping neither of her parents had heard his approach. How would she explain a liveried servant upon their property?

Abigail braced herself for the news. Surely, this was his way of crying off.

As the realization of his mistake dawned on the servant, he threw back his shoulders and then jumped down from his mount. He pulled something out of his satchel and then bowed formally. "I have a missive from the Duke of Monfort. I am to await your response before returning to Brooke's Abbey." Although contrite, the man's features remained formal and aloof.

Abigail reached out and took the envelope from the servant's gloved hands. Ought she to read it quickly so she could then send the man away? Her breaths quickened as her heart began to race. She didn't want the servant to witness her disappointment. The contents were far too important to her to allow a stranger to look on as she read it.

"Return to the village and await my answer in the

tavern." She spoke with as much authority as she could muster. The man showed no surprise at her request. He easily remounted his horse, nodded curtly, and headed back from the way he had come.

He must be crying off. The duke had come to his senses. She reminded herself that she had no business becoming a duchess, preparing herself to read what would surely be a note filled with regrets and apologies.

A short laugh caught in her throat. From the few conversations she had with the duke, Abigail knew there would be no regrets. No apologies. He'd simply state his change of mind. He'd likely not even acknowledge he'd made a mistake.

Abigail stuffed the letter into her apron with shaking hands and studied her surroundings. Noticing a fallen log a few feet off the road, she walked over to it and sat down. Her racing heart echoed in her ears. *Breathe*, she told herself. *In, out, in, out.*

The envelope was made of a fine parchment and sealed with red wax. She rubbed her thumb along the edge of the ducal imprint in the wax before slipping it under the flap and breaking it.

Slowly removing the missive, she inhaled deeply and then opened it.

Dear Miss Wright,

After some discussion with my sister and aunt, who are both more knowledgeable regarding these types of situations, I've decided upon a small wedding ceremony in London. Rather than rush things along with a special license, the banns will be read at St. George's in Hanover Square. The wedding date is set for three weeks from this coming Saturday.

My sister has brought it to my attention that you

will be in need of a new wardrobe and perhaps some instruction in many of the various social duties that will be required of you. A carriage shall be sent to collect you and your mother in six days' time, to transport you both to Cross House in London. My sister and her family shall be in residence when you arrive.

Please advise the courier if you have had any change in heart regarding this matter and will not be needing the carriage. At this point, all can be called off easily. No invitations have been sent.

Monfort

Abigail had no idea how long she had sat there before realizing a crick had begun to settle into her neck.

He had not cried off.

He had every intention of going through with it. He'd even spoken with his family.

Like a giant wave crashing over her, the reality of what she had agreed to hit her with an overwhelming force.

His sister, of course, had seen the faults in his plan right away. She'd obviously then pointed out to him that his chosen bride was countrified and would be unable to interact in society without substantial training.

By accepting his proposal, Abigail might very well be leaving one difficult situation only to put herself into an even more difficult one.

She rubbed her thumb along the edge of the missive and realized that until this moment, she had not truly taken the proposal seriously. For had she done so, she would have appreciated that life as a duchess came with a number of responsibilities and expectations of which she knew nothing. Was she capable of undertaking such a task? She would be going from being a person of perpetual inconsequence to a lady of high rank.

Would he expect her to capably present herself as a true duchess? Had he mentioned the training intentionally to dissuade her? *If you have had a change of heart*, he'd said.

Was he experiencing a change of heart? Was he hoping she would cry off so he would not have to? It was considered to be the height of dishonor for a gentleman to end a betrothal agreement. But was this a true betrothal? He'd not asked her father's permission yet. But he had spoken of it to his own family...

Oh, how she wished she could speak with Penelope about all of this.

At this thought, an idea dawned upon her. *Could* she speak with Penelope about all of this? Perhaps, with this new apparent connection with the duke, Abigail was not as helpless as she had always been before.

As a duchess, instead of being answerable to *every single person around her*, she would only be answerable to the duke himself. *Hmmm*...

If she asked the duke to request Penelope's company for her on the journey to London, would he comply? Her aunt and uncle most definitely would not deny a request made by the Duke of Monfort, would they?

Of course not!

And if she made this match, for once in her life, she could make her parents proud of her. She would no longer be the trial that she had always been to them.

She was being given a one in a million opportunity. She had no choice. She could not have a change of heart.

Jumping up from the log, she turned back toward the house with purposeful strides. She had a letter to write.

****

After writing the note she had in mind and delivering it to the servant who awaited her at the tavern, Abigail resolved to relay the news to her parents. Since her mother remained in her bedchamber, Abigail marched upstairs first.

Standing outside the closed door, she knocked lightly. "Mama, may I come in?"

A commotion sounded inside, and then her mother's feeble voice. "Enter."

Abigail turned the knob and slipped inside. Betty was smoothing the counterpane on the bed, and her mother sat up, propped up against several pillows.

"May I speak with you alone, Mother?" Abigail's voice wavered, but she glanced pointedly at the maid.

Heaving with a dramatic sigh, her mother dropped her head back and closed her eyes. "You aren't going to vex me again today, are you, Abigail? I cannot abide any more unfortunate news. Mrs. Henry visited earlier. She told me the vicar is considering allowing you to return to church. He said he must wait and see if your behavior is what it should be through the end of the year. They will not allow you to return to the choir, of course, as that is a position of privilege." And then sliding her gaze toward the maid, "Betty, will you please fetch me some of my tonic? My megrims are returning again."

As the maid scurried out, Abigail wondered just what exactly her mother's megrims consisted of.

Surely, her health would improve by stepping outside into the sunshine more often. "Mother, I think you will be happy with the news I have for you."

Her mother eyed her suspiciously.

Abigail continued, "I am betrothed to be married to the Duke of Monfort! He is having the banns read in London over the next month. I am to be taken to London so his sister can help to prepare me for the task…" She wasn't sure what else to say. It truly did sound fanciful when she spoke the words out loud.

"You lie, child. For what purpose, I know not, but your wicked nature takes you too far in this joke."

"It is not a joke, Mama. Look here." She held the letter out. Her mother frowned and narrowed her eyes even more. Abigail dropped the missive on to the bed near her mother's hand. "Read it. It is from the duke himself."

Her mother grabbed at the letter and read it hastily. Upon reaching the end, her eyes returned to the top and reread it again, more slowly this time. Abigail waited patiently, the only sound in the room that of the clock ticking.

"Have you shown this to your father?" her mother finally asked, a look consisting of both horror and elation somehow contorting her features.

"I haven't yet. Will you come with me, Mother, to London?"

At that moment, Betty returned.

"Oh, Betty, I must have my tonic. I am overset by my daughter. I don't know what to believe."

The maid instantly grasped the fan off the bedside table and began waving it in front of her mother.

"Abigail, fetch your father, at once. I will have his

opinion on this before saying another word. Oh, Betty, please, pour me a tonic. My heart is beating too quickly."

Backing out the door, Abigail was relieved to be given an excuse to leave her mother alone with the maid. Where was her father? She searched throughout the house to no avail. Surely he had not gone into the tavern himself. She would have seen him when she'd taken the message to the duke's courier. When she stepped out the side door from the kitchen, a commotion drew her to the stable block that sat behind the house.

"Father?" she called out tentatively. "Father?"

After a moment, she heard more commotion, as though something had fallen over. Running around to the stable door, she entered just in time to watch as her father began straightening some tools that had been knocked over. His balance was not sure, however, and the tools went crashing down again. He held a flask in one hand.

"Oh, Father," she sighed. "What are you doing out here? Why have you not stayed inside the house? It's dangerous for you to be out here when you're in your cups like this." She rushed inside and began picking up the rakes and shovels lying at his feet. After righting the mess he'd made, she took hold of his arm and began leading him inside.

"Thought I would fix the gate over by that old oak, Abby, my girl. Been meaning to take care of that." He leaned heavily on her, and his breath reeked of spirits. Abigail's heart was breaking. She'd done this to them! Her father hadn't been so inclined to overimbibe since the terrible scandal following her come-out. And her mother was a wreck as well! Her stupidity was causing everything to fall apart.

"Come inside, Father. I'll get Quinn to go check on the gate later." She wasn't sure what gate he was talking about. Holding tightly around his waist, Abigail painstakingly led her father back into the house and onto the couch in his study. He passed out as soon as she lifted his feet off the ground. "Oh, Papa…"

Her parents would have to discuss her upcoming nuptials tomorrow. Out the window, despite her trials, the sun set as always in brilliant fashion. Her life might come to a standstill or rush incomprehensibly forward, but the world's natural rhythms continued inexorably on.

She could only hope she was past finding herself in scandalous situations. The people in her world, obviously, could not handle another.

Chapter 7

Six days later, Abigail's world had turned upside down. When she had finally convinced her parents the plans were not a cruel hoax, the discussion turned to composing a ridiculously long guest list and London travel arrangements. Her mother could not possibly be ready to travel with such little notice. They also sent word to her Aunt Edith and Uncle Hector. Presumably they would wish to attend their niece's wedding to a duke. They would open up their house in Mayfair, and the Wrights would then stay there. Both her parents were more than pleased to hear of Abigail's plans to travel with Penelope ahead of them. She hoped the duke had been amenable to her request for Penelope to be collected, otherwise she would have to concoct some other scheme for she hadn't anyone else to chaperone her on the journey.

Unable to sleep, Abigail rose at sunrise and had two small valises sitting ready at the door early the morning that the carriage was to arrive. Abigail would leave behind most of her wardrobe, understanding that most of what she owned would not be suitable for a duchess.

Oh, she hoped Penelope was coming! Along with the excitement of leaving Biddeford Corners, Abigail was an absolute bundle of nerves. This was the most impulsive, wild, challenging experience she had ever taken on.

Well, almost.

She was to be married after all!

To a man she hardly knew. Good heavens! She could not even picture his face in her mind. She remembered his gray eyes and that he was tall and lean with dark hair, but she could not remember what his features looked like all put together. He was a stranger!

His missive had been short and to the point. He made it quite obvious that he had no tender feelings for her at all. As she did not for him either. This was a sort of, well, a business arrangement. It still astonished her that he had taken such drastic measures to assuage his guilt over the scandal that had occurred at Raven's Park. Surely he could have found another way?

Lying with her eyes open last night, staring at the shadows on the ceiling, she had come up with a number of solutions to deal with the scandal that weren't nearly as drastic. Why had he chosen marriage?

He presented himself as such a cold man most of the time. She did not think she had seen him smile even once. And he was to be her husband!

Did he intend her to fulfill *all* of the duties that were expected of a wife? Of course he would; he was a man, wasn't he? And he would need another heir, presumably.

And, of course, if she wanted children...

Abigail was simply going to have to find a way to cope with his attentions. Perhaps it would not be so bad. Hopefully it would not be as painful as the first time had been—or as demoralizing. The other time she had experienced the act, the man in question had nearly shattered her soul. She had endured. With the duke, at least he would be her husband. It would be done in a soft bed. There would be no ripping or tearing of her dress or anything else.

She *would* find a way to cope with the marital act and hopefully conceive quickly. At this thought, her heart jumped in wonder. A child that she could keep. She would perform all of her duties and embrace this new life she was being offered. She held tight to this tiny seed of optimism.

****

Morning dragged on, forcing Abigail to wait for what felt like hours before the well-sprung, crested carriage turned onto the driveway at Raebourne and approached the house just before noon. Dressed in a formal black uniform, the driver and the two outriders wore the same livery the courier had worn earlier that week. A few horse lengths behind, Abigail recognized her aunt and uncle's travelling carriage, already laden with several large trunks. Her heart leapt as she realized Penelope must have been given permission to come! When the carriage came to a halt, one of the outriders jumped off and pulled down the step. He wasn't given a chance to assist the passenger, however, as Penelope jumped out on her own and with a squeal threw herself into Abigail's arms.

"I cannot believe it! You cannot imagine how you have shocked me! And my parents, oh, Lord, do they have some humble pie to eat."

Abigail, keeping one arm around her cousin's waist, led them both into the house where Abigail's parents were waiting.

Never shy, never one to hold back, Penelope

stepped forward and gave them each a kiss on the cheek. "Aunt Edna, Uncle Bernard!" She embraced them exuberantly. "Can you believe your daughter is going to be a duchess?" She then turned toward Abigail and curtseyed deeply. "Your Grace"—she mimicked a haughty tone—"shall you wear the ruby tiara or the diamonds today?" Both girls giggled and then sobered up as one of the outriders approached.

"Miss Wright"—he addressed Abigail—"the duke's orders are to continue on from here today so we can arrive in London before noon tomorrow. If you would show me to your belongings, we can load them and be on our way again."

Abigail pointed to the two suitcases by the door and shrugged. "That is all I am taking with me." She spoke apologetically. She did not want to dawdle longer than necessary either.

Turning toward Penelope, whose maid had appeared behind her, Abigail clasped her hands together. "Rosie, it's good to see you again." Rosie had come to work for the Rivertons just before Penelope's come out, so she and Abigail were somewhat familiar. "I'm quite ready to depart as soon as you've both freshened up."

"Thank you, Miss Wright." Rosie dropped into a half-hearted curtsey before discreetly disappearing with Penelope. This left Abigail standing alone with both her parents in the foyer.

Her father was thankfully sober this morning, but nervous and agitated instead. His gaze landed on Abigail, and he smiled a bit sheepishly. "Well, my girl, let's hope this isn't all a cruel hoax."

Oh, the horror if it was!

But she refused to allow her mind to drift in that direction. The duke was intimidating and aloof, but he was not cruel. She was certain she would have recognized cruelty in him if it had been present.

She reassured her father with a tremulous smile. "It is not. You mustn't worry. Would Uncle have allowed Penelope to come if he thought anything underhanded about it?" And then suddenly realizing that she was leaving her home with her papa behind, forever this time, she threw herself into his arms and buried her face in his shirt. "Remember I told you that everything would turn out all right? Don't worry about me, Papa," she whispered. She inhaled the familiar scent of the man she'd depended upon for everything her entire life and relaxed as his arms wrapped tightly around her. He wasn't perfect, but he was her father. He'd done his best.

He cleared his throat and set her away from him. "Your mother and I will arrive in London in two weeks," he said, some warning creeping into his voice. "For God's sake, girl, stay out of trouble this time." He was shaking his head, looking at the floor.

And then her mother was there, holding a handkerchief to her mouth. "Please, Abigail, please, do not do anything untoward. Do not anger the duke by getting caught up in another scandal." Seeing Penelope return to the foyer, her mother turned toward her niece. "Dear, dear Penelope, please do what you can to keep Abigail from trouble. She has managed to ruin herself twice already. If she does anything scandalous at this point, we're certain the duke will cry off. And that would be more devastating than everything else put together."

Abigail disagreed but refrained from saying so. She wished they would show more faith in her. Oh, well, perhaps someday…

Taking one last glance around the foyer, Abigail again reflected that this place was no longer her home. She had lived here her entire life, and her parents, despite all the troubles they'd been through, had been the center of it. She hugged them each again, quickly, not allowing herself to cry, and the three ladies exited the house and climbed into the duke's luxurious carriage.

Penelope and her maid took the forward-facing seat leaving Abigail facing backwards. She hoped she would not get sick.

All smiles, Penelope leaned forward, her eyes sparkling in excitement. "Well," she said, "Now, you must tell me everything. I have simply been dying to know how this all came about! It must have been the duke, then, who compromised you, was it not?"

Really, there were times when Penelope knew not a smidgen of propriety! Although she had known Penelope's maid for a long time, she couldn't be certain the woman would refrain from gossip. It was most likely a servant who had begun the gossip that had set tongues to wagging at Raven's Park in the first place.

Abigail raised her eyebrows and shifted her eyes toward Rosie. When Penelope stared back uncomprehendingly, Abigail shook her head. "The banns are already being read. His Grace has arranged for the wedding to be at St. George's."

"Yes, I am aware of this. The duke included the details in the missive we were sent. What I would like to know is the how, and the why!"

Abigail merely shook her head again and then turned her head to look out of the window. It was bad enough the entire world discussed her misdeeds and judged her, but it was even more hurtful to hear her dearest friend discuss her personal matters with such little regard. She had often overheard her mother discussing what ought to have been private with her own maid as well, usually about Abigail, and that had always bothered her. But now, Penelope, of all people was doing it. Glancing toward her cousin, she could see that Penelope had finally realized what she had done.

Fully confident, Penelope reached up and pounded on the roof, signaling for the driver to stop. Once the carriage was at a complete stop, Penelope turned to her maid. "Rosie, I wish to have some time alone with my cousin. Will you ride behind in the baggage coach?"

Grimacing, Rosie gathered her reticule and shawl and climbed out after the footman lowered the step. After ascertaining that the maid had boarded the other carriage, the door was closed and they were once again on their way.

Leaving her reticule on the rear-facing seat, Abigail gingerly maneuvered herself onto the seat the maid had vacated. She didn't turn toward Penelope, however. Instead she leaned back and closed her eyes. She already experienced the beginnings of driving sickness from facing backward. Perhaps that explained why she'd been so testy.

"Oh, Abby, I'd forgotten you do not do well facing backward. I ought to have told Rosie to take the rear-facing seat. Or I could have!"

Penelope's voice overflowed with contrition. Abigail had not meant to make her cousin feel badly. It was just that always between them existed the knowledge of their different stations in life. Of the fact that Abigail was a spinster due to her circumstances, but Penelope was by choice.

Of course Penelope had never intentionally set out to diminish Abigail's sense of belonging in any way. Likely, Abigail was too sensitive. She reached over and squeezed her cousin's hand. "It has been a difficult month."

They rode silently for a few minutes, nothing but the sounds of the carriage wheels churning up the miles on the way to London. Eventually, Penelope squeezed her hand back. "I am so sorry, Abby. I have just been hoping the wedding was the culmination of a great romance between you and Monfort. I'd imagined all sorts of intriguing scenarios of how your warmth and love had miraculously warmed the heart of one of London's coldest aristocrats—of how you came along to save the Duke of Ice from his loneliness and misery. And of how he had developed a grand passion for you, how he saw what a wonderful person you are and would save you from a life of drudgery and treat you like a queen."

Abigail didn't know if she should laugh or cry at such an outlandish scenario. "Nothing romantic about it at all," she said, remembering the duke's visit. "He is a good man, though." How much ought she to tell Penelope? "He only acted out of guilt. The room you and I were given was so warm that first night at Raven's Park, I stupidly ventured outside to cool off. In hindsight, I realize how utterly foolish that was. I met up with the duke in the library and he…well, he and I were seen together." As Abigail spoke, she again considered some of the details of that night. She remembered that the duke had kissed her. It had even been slightly pleasant for the first few moments, but she had become frightened. What had frightened her? She didn't remember. But she'd fainted.

Had the duke done more than just kiss her? He had carried her back to the library and when she revived he had been leaning over her closely.

He had said he was checking to be certain she was breathing. Why had he attempted to kiss her?

He must have been foxed! That was why. And he must have known of her reputation from long ago. He must have assumed she would welcome his advances. When she had been frightened, he experienced regret.

Had his proposal been made out of honor or had he asked out of guilt? For a duke most certainly would not have been expected to marry somebody as low socially as she. Even had he gotten her with child, that would not have been the case.

Surely a combination of guilt and honor had provoked his proposal.

Wonderful.

****

After staying overnight at an inn, in what was most likely the best suite available, the duke's driver made quick time the next day and they arrived on the outskirts of London only a few hours after setting out. London in the late summer was not quite the same as it was during the spring, when Abigail had last been there. Today, hot, humid air hung about the city with a heavy stench. No wonder the upper crust abandoned the city during the warmer months. Penelope assured her it would get better once they got closer to Mayfair, but watching out the window, Abigail knew more than a few misgivings about her decision to leave Biddeford Corners. She had forgotten how crowded the city was. She wasn't sure she would have had the courage to go through with everything if Penelope had not come along with her. While covering mile after mile, Abigail eventually had told Penelope most of what transpired between her and the duke at the house party. She did *not* tell her about the incident on the boat.

Penelope, in turn, told her everything she knew about the Monfort family and Brooke's Abbey. Apparently the duke had one younger sister, Lady Clive now, wife of the Earl of Clive. Her name was Margaret Knightly, and she had two-year-old twin boys. Twins!

The duke had one remaining aunt on his mother's side and several distant cousins on his father's side. Penelope said she had met some of them, and although they were all quite high in the instep, they seemed to be pleasant enough. Abigail wondered how many of them would be invited to the wedding. On her own side, her parents had sent a list to the duke's man of business that consisted of every relative Abigail had ever heard of, and some whom she hadn't known existed. It was all rather daunting.

She inhaled deeply as they turned down a street that bordered Hyde Park. The air was fresher and slightly cooler. Here, the sights were becoming somewhat familiar. When she'd had her come-out, she and her mother had stayed at her aunt and uncle's townhouse, which was on Curzon Street. She'd taken numerous walks around Hyde Park before that horrible last night and enjoyed those excursions thoroughly. She loved the statues, the ornate bridges, and the pretty walkways that were kept so neatly trimmed. She was surprised to realize she had a few good memories from before, after all.

With a slight lurch, the carriage drew to a halt in front of one of the larger mansions set neatly across the street from the park. The coach bounced a little as the driver and outriders jumped off. Before she knew it, several servants descended upon the coach, opening doors and pulling down the steps. Others unstrapped and removed trunks from the baggage carriage behind them. Her opportunity to turn around and run home was over!

Penelope climbed out first. Abigail nervously collected her reticule, straightened her bonnet, and took a deep breath just as a gloved hand reached in for her.

It belonged to the duke.

Chapter 8

Alex hadn't consciously decided to be at home when his betrothed arrived, but as luck would have it, one of his finer traveling coaches was just arriving as he strolled along the sidewalk, returning from one of his clubs that morning. When Penelope Crone stepped down from the carriage, he was taken back for a moment to the day, just over one month ago, when the two women arrived at Raven's Park.

Knowing his duty, without thought, he stepped forward and leaned into the carriage to assist his betrothed. Concerned brown eyes flew open wide when she realized who was to help her alight. He was surprised to feel anything other than annoyance as he grasped her hand and assisted her onto the pavement.

Miss Wright appeared fragile and delicate, and he could not remember having this opinion of her at any of their prior meetings. Perhaps she had not been eating. Perhaps the elegance of these surroundings diminished her. She'd spent almost all of her adult life in the country amongst cottages and simple structures.

London was a towering collection of mansions, buildings, and general greatness. His own dwelling certainly no exception.

Sensing her feelings of inadequacy, rather than release her hand, he placed it along his arm. "Welcome to Cross Hall, Miss Wright, Miss Crone. I trust your journey has not been taxing?" Beside him, a tremble rolled through her.

But no one else would have known it, for she turned toward him with a cheerful smile and sparkling eyes. "The carriage is a dream," she said. "I did not think it possible to travel in such luxury." She dropped her eyes shyly before looking back to her cousin. "Would you not agree, Penelope?"

Miss Crone smiled pleasantly but with less cheer. "It was quite comfortable, Your Grace," she said and then curtsied slightly in his direction. She was suspicious of him; he could tell at a glance. It was about time Miss Wright had an ally. Other than himself, that is.

This thought brought him up short for a moment. When had he become her protector? He supposed the die had been cast when he'd attempted to kiss her. He supposed the exact moment didn't really matter. She would be his responsibility from now on.

And then he escorted them both inside where his sister awaited them in the front salon. He presented the ladies to one another and then sat down while Margaret rang for tea. Margaret and Miss Crone had a prior acquaintance and exchanged pleasantries for a few moments. Both of the new arrivals sat together on a brocaded velvet couch while he and Margaret sat across from them in elegant, wing backed chairs. He could tell that his sister was reserving judgment on his fiancée.

Shifting slightly, she eventually directed her full attention to Miss Wright. "You hail from a village near Bath?" she asked, directing the conversation smoothly.

Alex crossed one leg over the other and relaxed

into his chair.

"A small village called Biddeford Corners," his betrothed answered a bit breathlessly. "It has been ages since I was in London." She then bit her bottom lip as though she had said something that she ought not to have. Her eyes appeared large in her face. The lashes surrounding them curled back in thick, long waves.

Margaret was not deterred from her inquiry. "That was just after the wars, was it not, Miss Wright?" she asked, all smiles. "I remember you from then. You departed before the season ended."

His betrothed shot him an apprehensive glance and then tilted her chin up. "I did," she said, and then added, "You see, when a debutante is as thoroughly ruined as I was, it is quite impossible to remain."

Alex drew in his breath and did not release it immediately. He was curious to know of this great scandal of hers. It would change nothing, but it might shed more light upon her character. Ought it to be discussed with her in private though?

Margaret spoke with no sympathy. "But you find yourself in a new scandal, and alas, you are returning to London. You are prepared to take on the ton as a duchess, then?"

Alex leaned forward. "Margaret," he cautioned his sister.

Margaret turned toward him at that point. "Well, let's get everything out in the open so we know exactly what we are dealing with. We can be better prepared for problems if we know they might arise."

"My betrothed and her cousin must be tired from the journey. If anyone demands an accounting, it will be myself." He spoke in his ducal tone, the one that even Margaret could not ignore.

"It's all right," a small voice interjected. "I appreciate, Your Grace, that your sister is concerned. I agree with her, in fact." And then she turned her gaze on him alone. "When we discussed undertaking this...er...plan of action, so to speak, you told me I would find relief from scandal, as a duchess. I think it is not as simple as that. I realize we are just entering the Little Season, but there will be some people here, I'm afraid, who might remember me from before. I do not wish for you to be surprised by anything that you hear."

At this point, her cousin reached over and covered one of her hands supportively. This motion reminded him of that evening in Ravensdale's drawing room, when Farley and his gang had barged in.

His betrothed sent Miss Crone a weak smile. "Both the story and the truth are unpleasant, to say the least. But I feel I owe both of you the truth of what transpired nine years ago."

Margaret sat straight and unmoving. Obviously, she had not expected such candidness despite her own willingness to speak frankly. Alex was curious but also concerned. "It is not necessary if you do not wish to speak of it today."

But Miss Wright was shaking her head. "Best to get it over with. And then if you wish to change your mind, we can come up with another plan." She lifted her chin, apparently determined to get this over with.

"Very well," Alex allowed.

Miss Abigail Wright then took a deep breath and began speaking. "I didn't take to the ton as much as my mother had hoped, but there were *some* gentlemen interested in me. I was so very naïve, though, as was my mother. For, in truth, they were not interested in me as a prospective bride, rather in other ways."

She blushed and dropped her gaze to the floor.

"I believed the compliments they paid me. I trusted that their intentions were those of true gentleman and allowed one of them to steer me away from the safety of the ballroom. He'd said a kitten was caught in a rosebush and asked me to assist him in freeing it. I allowed him to walk me far away from the hearing of any other guests or servants, for that matter."

"Oh, Miss Wright…" Margaret nearly groaned. "Of course there was no kitten…"

Looking beyond all of them, toward the windows and blinking a few times, Miss Wright shook her head mournfully. She then pinched her lips before continuing.

"Afterward, he spread his version of what transpired to other 'gentlemen' friends. It is amazing, truly phenomenal, how quickly and viciously scandals spread. Within two days, I was back in Biddeford Corners, having not only disgraced myself but my parents as well. And shortly after that, I was sent down to Cornwall until I could once again appear in my village."

Alex watched her closely. Her recitation failed to fill in a few salient details. He believed he'd require some further explanation eventually.

But was it fair for him to question her now? She had stopped speaking and had looked down at her hands now, still clasped tightly in Miss Crone's.

"You were sent down to Cornwall, Miss Wright?" Margaret had no qualms. "For how long, and why?"

"I was in Cornwall until after Christmas."

Which, if one did the math, allowed for a lady to complete a confinement and deliver a child.

Rage swept through Alex. Not directed at her, but toward the people who ought to have protected her from her foolish decision. He was incensed that neither her uncle nor her father ever brought the bounder to heel. Good God! What had they all been thinking? Unable to sit still, he abruptly stood up.

Walking over to the settee, he held out a hand to Miss Wright. "May I escort you to your chamber?" He didn't want Margaret or anybody else for that matter delving into his betrothed's history any more today. Heaven forbid, but he continued to have this unfamiliar urge to protect her.

Unspeaking, he and Miss Wright climbed the ornate curved staircase, her tiny hand tucked through his elbow. When had he stopped seeing her as a frumpy spinster? Her dress was atrocious and her brown hair pulled back tightly with no semblance of style whatsoever. She did not seem as plump as she had been earlier that month, but she had definitely not lost her lush curves.

She was the antithesis of any woman he had ever bothered to know.

The mental image of some entitled scoundrel taking advantage of the small lady beside him curdled his insides. She would have practically been a child then, susceptible to seduction and flowery words. And then to have found herself with child!

Questions he would not ask suddenly swirled around in his mind.

Had she delivered the child safely? Where was the child now? Had she been in love with the father? Who was the father? Had she been pining for him all these years? Did any of this change the matter of their betrothal? The last question was the only one pertinent to him. Did it change anything where he was concerned? He was a duke. Her former scandal was by far more ruinous than the present one. Both his aunt and Margaret, he was sure, would once again attempt to dissuade him from this unlikely alliance.

They had arrived at the bedchamber he'd ordered prepared for her, and Alex reached forward to open the door.

"I will cry off, if you wish it, Your Grace." Miss Wright did not meet his gaze, staring at her fidgeting hands instead. "I ought to have told you all of this before. I am sorry for putting you to so much trouble on my part."

Without opening the door, Alex wondered why he did not jump at her offer. Instead he studied her intently.

Fragile and sensitive, her skin beckoned his fingers to trace the curve of her cheek. His gaze dripped to her lips, soft and giving.

Had he kissed her at Raven's Park? Suddenly he could not remember if he had actually even kissed her. The motion of her pulse, fluttering just above her collarbone reminded him. Ah, yes, he had kissed her there. He had traced his lips along that delicate slope between her shoulder and her neck. And, yes, he had kissed her lips. But it had only been for a moment. He stepped away from her and brought his wayward thoughts under rein.

"Do *you* wish to cry off?" he surprised himself by asking.

She licked her lips and steadily returned his gaze. "Only if you wish for me to."

At times, she seemed to be a cowering miss but then there were other moments, like now, when she exhibited more than a little spirit. "Miss Wright, my objectives have not altered." But ought they to have? Would her past tarnish the reputation of any children they had together? If Alex were a conservative man, perhaps he should take this opportunity and be grateful to the chit. "I will not allow my life to be ordered by gossip or scandal." At that moment, his intentions were to make his bow and leave her, but she reached out a hand and touched his sleeve.

"But is that not what you are doing? Did you not propose marriage to me so that scandal could be averted?" She spoke tentatively but with a curious look in her eyes.

"Miss Wright," Alex responded, irritated that she was questioning his motives. He would rather not explain himself to her. He was unused to explaining himself to anybody—ever. "I proposed to you because I committed an egregious error in judgment where you are concerned. And my actions were dishonorable. My own sense of honor demands expiation. Marriage is the most effective way to do so."

"Expiation?" she asked, furrowing her brows.

Alex looked away from her and noticed that the carpet in the hallway was looking a bit dull in color. It had not been changed for years. Hyacinth had never shown any interest in managing the décor at any of their estates. Perhaps Miss Wright would have an inclination. "Yes, Miss Wright. Now if that is all, I have some work I must—"

"I have a few other issues I would like to get ironed out." She spoke firmly and then bit her lip again.

Alex glanced up and down the hallway. "Surely, this is not the proper place? Come to my study after you have unpacked and rested. We can discuss whatever you would like at that time." Was she already going to be requesting funds from him? He imagined so. He had not thought she would be so quick to do so.

"It is about our marriage. I know how I shall benefit from it, but how will it benefit you?"

Ah, well.

Moving toward the door, he then pushed it all the way open this time. He walked inside and gestured for her to follow him. Miss Wright did so unquestioningly. A single lady should never allow a gentleman to enter her bedchamber unchaperoned. He would have to tell Margaret that his betrothed needed guidance on such matters. For now, though, her acquiescence was convenient.

Once she entered, Alex closed the door behind him and leaned against it. Best to be crystal clear. He had expectations. Yes, he did.

"How shall I benefit? I shall not be forced to search for a wife on the marriage mart. I shall not be forced at a later date to impose my *old man's body on an innocent debutante.*" Ah, yes, he remembered those words of hers. "I plan to benefit the same as any man who marries. I wish to beget an heir, perhaps more children after. I will perform my ducal duty and shall expect my wife to do so as well. I expect my wife to take her place as duchess and hostess whenever necessary. Although I spend as little time as possible in town, I shall expect my duchess to take her place by my side at the occasional social function. I shall expect her to act with dignity and poise. While in the country, I shall expect her to visit the local gentry and to participate somewhat in the community. And"—he narrowed his eyes at her—"I shall exercise my conjugal rights. I shall expect absolute fidelity. This will not be a white marriage. Are you still inclined to go forward?" A part of him hoped he had frightened her. Another part was merely stating some of what he ought to have been clear about when he'd married the first time. Somehow, he did not believe that Miss Abigail Wright would dissemble with any promises she made regarding her marriage.

She was too pure, which was ironic.

The duke's words swirled around inside her head. He would be so specific so as to leave her with no uncertainty as to his expectations.

It took her a moment to process them.

She was thrilled that he wanted children, for that was part of why she had agreed to marry. She was, however, terrified by the part about having dignity and poise. Could any amount of education make her into a woman who could pass for a duchess? And again her mind was caught on the word *expiation.* She thought she knew the meaning but was surprised he had used it in terms of his reason for marriage.

This man standing before her was the Duke of Ice. That person Penelope described when she'd first pointed him out.

He had impressed upon her a warmth while with his sister, and then protection when he'd offered to escort her to her room. But now he spoke in precise clipped tones. Although he was leaning against the door and ought to have looked at ease, his muscles remained tense. His eyes distant, impersonal.

But he had been kind.

"I will do my best to uphold your wishes, Your Grace," she said demurely. "I, too, want children."

He raised his brows at her last statement. "It is not something you fear?"

Did he mean childbirth or did he mean the procreation process? Heat suffused her face. "I do not fear childbirth." He did understand that she had already experienced it, didn't he? "I did not suffer any complications…before." She blushed even more hotly. When she looked back up at the duke, she saw that his eyes had become slightly hooded. Although he hadn't changed his expression, his eyes were no longer impassive.

The longer he stared at her, the more uncomfortable he made her.

"And the begetting part? Do you not fear it either?" His voice was low. He did not seem to be mocking her.

She turned her entire body away from him. This was all very personal. "I…" she began unsuccessfully. "I…must admit that I do fear it…But I will do my duty by you. I will not be ruled by my fears. You need not worry on that account, Your Grace." And then she felt his body behind her. Close to her. If she were to tilt her head back, it would rest against his chest. Which she found oddly inviting.

The duke placed one hand upon her shoulder and turned her around to face him. "Do you fear me?" he asked, surprising her. The warmth of his hand seeped through the material of her dress. He smelled musky and spicy—expensive—and yet it was subtle. When they'd walked together in the grass—what felt like ages ago—at Raven's Park, he had not acted nearly so ducal. Today he was dressed impeccably—his cravat tied perfectly, his superfine green jacket pressed and crisp, and an exquisite lace at his wrists. He was rather glorious in all of his ducal finery.

And he was eyeing her closely.

"I am not afraid of you, Your Grace," she answered honestly while looking at a golden button on his jacket. "I do not really know you all that well, but I trust you. I could not marry you if I did not. In spite of everything else, I don't consider myself a fool."

"But I frightened you, that night," he reminded her. And then his hand moved from her shoulder to her chin, and he tilted her face back so that she was looking into his eyes. "You were so frightened that you fainted."

The memory caused a tremor to run through her. She did her best to suppress it, but the duke released her and stepped backward anyway. He had felt it.

"I tend to faint sometimes." She grimaced and then she shrugged. "I wasn't afraid the entire time. When you kissed me at first I was fine, it was more…"

"When I groped at you," the duke finished for her. He looked disgusted. With himself? Or with her?

Abigail sighed. "Yes." Was this to be a deal breaker? Was he now going to request that she cry off? Suddenly she did not want this challenge to be taken away from her. She wanted to accomplish this task successfully. "But I was taken by surprise. I did not expect any of it. I will have plenty of time to get used to the idea by the time we are actually wed." She spoke firmly.

A dry chuckle escaped the duke's mouth as he

shook his head. "You think you will be able to refrain from fainting then, upon our wedding night?"

"I will not faint, Your Grace." She spoke with conviction. *She would not.*

Again that wry chuckle. He had the odd ability to do so with no signs of amusement whatsoever. "And how can you be so certain of this?"

Abigail sought to be convincing. "I shall know you better. I will know that I have your protection. It will be done with my consent. I will not be left to cope with any complications alone. In fact, complications shall be the purpose of it. And it will be undertaken in the safety and privacy of a bedchamber. I will have no reason to be afraid."

Alex was stunned by her words. She was fiercely determined to perform this aspect of marriage in spite of having been raped. For she had confirmed that, just now. The bastard who had left her with child had raped her. Could she overcome such an experience?

She had said she trusted him. She had said she enjoyed it when he'd first kissed her. "You are not afraid of me, then?" he asked again, feeling the need to confirm this.

She shook her head side to side. "No." But her voice sounded slightly breathless.

Alex reached forward again and held her chin. Without moving any closer, he bent forward and touched his lips softly to hers.

At first she did not move, remaining passive.

Alex raised his other hand and rubbed his thumb along the seam of her lips. As his mouth hovered tentatively, he coaxed them open with the pad of his thumb.

She was a quick learner. When he angled his head to deepen the kiss, her mouth opened and she pulled at him with a shy sucking motion. A surge of lust rolled through him.

He released her and stepped backward.

"Then we will proceed as planned." He made a quick bow and took his leave hastily. This entire betrothal was becoming far more complicated than he had foreseen. Could one not simply take a wife and have the matter done with?

****

The duke did not attend supper that evening, leaving the ladies alone to partake of the excellent cuisine provided by his staff. Penelope, Margaret, and Abigail were joined, nonetheless, by Lady Cecily Cross, also referred to as Aunt Cecily. A grand old dame, she had a way of looking at Abigail that made her wish she could disappear. Critical and judgmental, she nonetheless had apparently resigned herself to the situation. The proud woman corrected Abigail throughout dinner and even as they walked through to the parlor. Abigail had a great deal to learn but was feeling quite determined.

The duke had been quite clear that they would have a real marriage. She would have a child, possibly more than one. That was her true heart's desire.

And he had kissed her.

It had been unlike any kiss she'd ever experienced up until that point. He'd not touched her body at all except for his hand upon her face and his mouth upon her lips. Without worrying about protecting her body, she had been intensely aware of the feel of his lips and tongue.

He had tasted warm and comforting.

She had enjoyed it.

The mere thought brought a blush up her chest and onto her face.

"What is it, gel?" Aunt Cecily inquired rudely. "You need not dissemble with us about your history. Believe me, we are well aware of all that we must overcome with you. No need to turn up shy. But I must know, is there anything else of which we ought to be aware? Is your mother sane? Does your father drink? Any other skeletons we will need to skirt over the next few weeks?"

Dear God, but Aunt Cecily was forthright. Abigail thought to answer in the negative, but the memory of her father passed out in the mews flashed through her mind rather ominously. And then the thought of her mother remaining in her room for weeks on end took up residence…

"My parents have been rather troubled by my situation. It has put both of them under considerable strain…" She tried to answer honestly.

Aunt Cecily tilted her head back as though to examine the ornate ceiling before once again pinning her gaze on Abigail. "So, your father drinks and your mother is unstable?" It was more of a statement than a question.

Abigail winced and then raised one shoulder apologetically. "Well, I suppose…"

The older lady raised her brows and lifted her quizzing glass.

"A little, yes, to both of your questions. But I am hoping those matters right themselves now that I no longer live under their roof. The entire village has ostracized them, and what with my marriage, hopefully this will no longer be the case. I am quite optimistic, as a matter of fact."

Margaret waved one hand toward her aunt and nodded in agreement. "Of course, such matters will right themselves. What parent would not find satisfaction in their daughter marrying a duke?"

At this point, Penelope carefully set down her utensil and came to Abigail's aid. "Aunt Edna and Uncle Bernard have had hard times but most assuredly looked fit and well when we collected Abigail yesterday. There shall be no trouble from those quarters." Then her brows drew together in a worrisome frown. "What I am concerned about is how Abigail is to deal with the people in London who remember her. For most certainly, the gossips will dust off the scandal and happily air it again."

Margaret waited while her plate was removed before addressing the servants present. "Smithy, Fredrick, would you be so kind as to leave us alone until we remove ourselves to the drawing room?"

"Of course, my lady," one of them answered before they silently disappeared without so much as blinking.

And then Margaret returned her attention to Penelope. "I have a plan. But, ladies, firstly I must instruct all of you—including you, Aunt Cecily"—this was said with a stern look in her aunt's direction—"that it is crucial for private matters to remain private. Especially when it comes to speaking in front of servants. Although Monfort places a great deal of trust in his staff, it only takes one of them to overhear gossip to share it with their counterparts working in other society homes."

Abigail nodded, and Penelope dropped her hands into her lap and looked down. Aunt Cecily shrugged arrogantly and pinched her lips together. After a few moments of silence, in which Margaret apparently accepted their acquiescence, she spoke again. "I have made arrangements for my modiste, Madame Chantel, to attend to us tomorrow in order to begin working on Miss Wright's wardrobe and for my hairdresser to arrive later in the day. The following day, we shall begin comportment, etiquette, and dance lessons. We have just a few weeks to prepare you to be presented, once again, to society, and so we mustn't waste a moment. I presume you have no objections, Miss Wright?" she continued in determined tones all the while looking directly at Abigail.

"Abby." Abigail spoke softly. "As we are going to be sisters, I'd like it if we could speak informally with each other. But no, I have no objections." She sat up straighter and eyed the duke's sister with conviction. She would do this. She must do this. And she must succeed!

****

Alex intentionally did not spend the evening at home. As the ladies discussed his betrothed's preparations over the next few weeks, he sat comfortably ensconced in a deep leather chair holding a snifter of brandy in his hand at White's.

Brandy; her eyes perfectly matched the color of brandy. He swirled the contents in his glass for a few moments before turning back to his reading, irritated with himself. He was holding a book and appeared to be reading, but had failed to comprehend even a single page.

He was feeling unsettled.

This marriage. Not at all similar to his first trip to the altar. He wondered if he ought to be worried.

There could not be any woman more opposite in nature or appearance to Hyacinth than Miss Wright. Whereas Hyacinth had been tall, slender, and golden haired, Miss Wright was petite and voluptuous, with mousy brown hair. And she was soft.

Hyacinth had not been soft at all.

Oh, God, how he'd made a hash of things with Hyacinth when they first married. She'd been the same age as Miss Wright.

At the tender age of seventeen, Miss Wright had been raped by a cad in a garden.

Hyacinth's husband had forced himself upon her.

Alex let the book fall to his lap and closed his eyes. Had it been rape? It had felt like it at the time. She'd consented, yes, at first. She'd been his wife, after all.

She'd been rigid as a board, her hands clenched at her side on the bed when he'd raised her nightgown upward. She'd told him to please just get it over with. She had not wanted him to kiss her or fondle her.

Alex had been a stupid fool. It was his right, he'd thought at the time. Most certainly after the first time, his wife would lose her inhibitions and allow him greater liberties.

When he'd first gone to her, he'd been excited.

Hyacinth was beautiful. Throughout their courtship she'd allowed a few chaste kisses which had merely stoked the fire of his desire for her. He'd wanted to anticipate their wedding night, but she'd been quite firm in her insistence that they wait.

Hyacinth had demanded he extinguish the candles

before approaching her bed.

Alex furrowed his brows as he contemplated now that he'd never seen his wife unclothed, in spite of the near six years they'd lived together as man and wife.

Good God, he'd already seen more of Abigail Wright's flesh than he'd ever seen of Hyacinth's!

Had he raped Hyacinth that night? His blood ran cold at the thought. It might as well have been.

She'd been dry and tight. The only wetness they'd experienced together had been from her blood and his seed.

She'd cried and begged him to stop, but he'd been determined to complete the act.

Which had taken longer than he would have thought. The memory tormented him. He was no better than the man who'd ruined Miss Wright.

Alex lifted one hand and rubbed his eyes. Miss Wright would not fight him, he had no doubt of that— as long as she could remain conscious. The thought ironically lightened his heart briefly. And then he remembered how she'd kissed him this afternoon.

She'd pulled at his mouth with her own.

She'd experienced sexual desire. He was certain of it. And what had she said? She's said she would not be afraid. *I shall know you better*, she'd said. *I will know that I have your protection. It will be done with my consent. I will not be left to cope with any complications alone. In fact, complications shall be the purpose of it. And it will be undertaken in the safety and privacy of a bedchamber. I will have no reason to be afraid.*

She was not a beautiful woman by any means, but he *was* attracted to her.

Although a part of him derided the lackadaisical attitude she'd taken toward her life in the past, tinges of admiration for her courage were beginning to emerge. So strong in some ways, and in others, so soft...

Her lips—her cheek—her entire body. For some reason, her body was inviting and comfortable—to his.

Perhaps he could find pleasure in a marriage. For a while anyway.

But then Alex remembered again how she had fainted dead away when he'd touched her. He was annoyed with himself for giving any credence to what her damned uncle had said.

What in the hell had he been thinking that night? He'd been thinking with his nether regions, that's what. And he'd been foxed. For years now, he'd prided himself upon his control, on his self-imposed discipline. That night he'd let down his restraint for some reason. And now look at the consequences of that!

He would have loved to look upon this betrothal with a semblance of optimism, but he knew better. He knew himself. Yes, he knew himself well enough to know that this would only lead to disappointment later.

He could have a hopeful outlook for his sister, for his tenants, for his horses, hell, even for his country, but when it came to his own ability to achieve some sort of contentment, he knew it was not possible. His emotions had locked themselves inside a permanent prison of lethargy. Like a wounded soldier, returning from war without one of his limbs, his feelings had been amputated. He hadn't been dubbed the Duke of Ice for no good reason, after all.

Some sexual satisfaction and an easing of his guilt was the most he would hope for from this marriage.

And an heir. God help him, he needed an heir.

"Alex, Alex Cross? Surprised to find you in town. Thought you'd gone back to Brooke's Abbey."

Alex pulled himself out of his uncomfortable musings to acknowledge the man standing before him. He'd wondered about this fellow since seeing him at Raven's Park.

"Danbury." Alex set aside his drink and book to rise to his feet. Clasping the hand of the man he'd gone to school with years ago, he wondered that he'd not sought him out at Ravensdale's house party. "No bastards trailing around behind you today?"

Danbury shrugged sheepishly. Alex hadn't looked closely at the man earlier this summer. The brown eyes were familiar, but small wrinkles had formed at the edges, either from too much sun or too much laughter.

Of similar height to himself, Hugh Chesterton portrayed himself as an indolent type. It was well known amongst the ton, that he spent most of his energy chasing trouble and avoiding commitments, often both at the same time.

"Not today," Danbury responded. Laughter threaded Hugh's voice, but a glint of steel cooled his eyes. Hugh had inherited at a young age, the burden of his family and title falling upon him before he'd been ready. Whereas Alex hadn't seen a choice but to take up his duties, the viscount had rebelled.

Which described the viscount's behavior mildly.

Alex motioned to a nearby waiter to bring a bottle of his favorite scotch before indicating for his long-time acquaintance to take the chair beside his.

Running a hand through his chestnut hair, Danbury sat down, crossed his legs on a nearby ottoman and leaned back. Expelling a deep breath, he met Alex's eyes and shook his head. "Last time we kept company, you were grousing over having to miss out on the war. I haven't seen much of you in London." Glancing at the ducal ring on Alex's hand, the viscount frowned. "My condolences for the loss of your father."

Alex clenched his jaw. Going to war had not been an option for him. His father had been visibly ailing at the time. Alex had loved his father.

A great deal had transpired to change himself and his circumstances. Alex had no wish to rehash any of those years.

"Your mother is still quite active in society. I'm surprised you haven't settled upon one of her matches yet." Alex took a casual sip of the spicy liquid and directed the conversation away from himself.

Hugh raised his brows and grimaced. "Oh, hell, Monfort, escaping her debutantes is an old habit by now." Looking into the amber liquid, he chuckled derisively. "I've spent a good deal of time travelling. I imagine I'll have to settle eventually. Must be going soft…"

Without thinking, Alex surprised himself by speaking. "I'm to be married again in a fortnight."

Danbury's head snapped up. He did not gush with effusive congratulations. "Thought you'd hold out longer than that."

Alex sighed but nodded. "Yes, well."

Danbury stared into his glass again. "So much has occurred in the last decade. Life truly has not been the great adventure we imagined as boys, has it?"

"It has not," Alex agreed. He appreciated the sentiment. But that was enough of such maudlin talk.

Besides, he was interested in some of the political maneuvering Danbury had been involved in. "Tell me about this amendment you and Cortland passed last spring."

Danbury leaned forward and rested his forearms upon his knees. "I'm more interested in your horses…"

Chapter 9

Abigail's first full day at Cross House proved considerably distressing. And embarrassing. She was scrubbed, measured, pinned, squeezed, and snipped. By the time she lay down for bed, she was exhausted and overwhelmed. She had not seen the duke since he'd left her room the afternoon they'd arrived in London. She was certain he would not recognize her the next time they met.

And after a string of similarly rigorous days, Abigail's misgivings continued to grow. With her wedding day fast approaching, she was beginning to feel as though she would be pledging herself, body, heart, and soul, to a stranger.

And she would be giving this stranger the right to have intimate access to her body. As he pleased. He knew nothing of her mind, nothing of her thoughts and dreams. And she knew nothing of him.

And this, quite simply, would not do.

On the fourth day after her arrival, Abigail awoke at dawn. She had formulated a plan.

Her body heartily resisted venturing out at such an ungodly hour, but catching the duke before he went out was more important than a few hours of sleep. Alas, it was imperative to the success of her marriage. So despite her sleepiness and the nerves knotted in her stomach, Abigail dressed in her brand new riding habit and rushed downstairs to await the duke in the morning room.

She'd discovered from her lady's maid, Harriette, who had been appointed to assist her, that her betrothed went riding early every morning. Apparently, he was quite interested in horses in general. Margaret had told her that Brooke's Abbey was home to one of the most successful breeding stables in all of England, and Abigail intended to utilize this information to the fullest.

She wished to befriend her future husband.

She'd also discovered that his given name was Alex—Alex Cross. She hoped he would invite her to use it.

So once awake, full of nervous energy, she skipped down the stairs and whirled around the doorway into the room she expected to still be empty.

It was not.

Alex was glad he'd set his coffee back down upon the table; the appearance of Miss Wright was *that* startling to him.

In more ways than one.

Firstly, people did not normally go rushing around Cross Hall at any time of day, let alone at sun up. But Miss Wright was not to be counted on to do that which was expected, that which was dignified. No, she practically flew into the room before catching the doorframe to stop herself upon seeing him seated.

Secondly, she did not look like the Miss Wright who had formed in his mind. He'd intentionally kept his memory of the spinster who'd stepped out of the carriage at Raven's Park, with her hair pulled back tightly and her dress a frumpy brown color. When he thought of her thusly, he could push back the memory of her assets prominently displayed in the rowboat. He could ignore the desire she'd ignited in him with a simple kiss.

She looked different this morning. Something was different with her hair. Margaret's doing, he supposed. Wisps of it framed her face. It looked softer. *Good God, that word again!*

A few golden strands sparkled as the weak sunlight fell upon her. Her eyes, of course, were large and nearly as startled as his own, he supposed. And her lips formed a small *O*, as she let out a feminine-sounding gasp.

And thirdly, she was wearing a riding habit.

Alex paused only a moment before he realized that he was still sitting. Yes, this was his own home, and yes, she was an unwelcome morning intruder, but she was a lady and he was a gentleman.

He stood and made a slight bow.

Miss Wright released the door frame she had been grasping and made a graceful low curtsey. "Your Grace," she said. Her voice sounded breathless.

"Miss Wright," Alex returned, before stepping over to another seat and pulling it out for her. "I did not expect company this morning." It was not necessary to ask one of the footmen to fetch his betrothed a cup and setting. The man had crossed to the sideboard immediately upon seeing the additional diner.

Miss Wright graciously accepted the seat he offered and smoothed down the fabric of her habit. It was quite fetching, really, a soft apricot color that did wonders for her complexion. "I hope you are not disappointed, Your Grace, to be interrupted." She looked up at him from under her lashes. "But I have not seen you since my arrival and was beginning to wonder if you were, indeed, a figment of my imagination."

Her words startled him nearly as much as her appearance had a few seconds ago. She was an interesting mixture of both timidity and an unusual forthrightness that he was not accustomed to from subordinates. He set his gaze upon her and allowed his jaw to clench. He did not wish to have his actions rebuked. "I have business to attend to, Miss Wright. And I did not wish to interfere with my sister's plans."

Miss Wright merely chuckled before smiling at the footman who was pouring her a cup of coffee. "Thank you," she said to the servant, surprising Alex again. And then, turning back to Alex, she continued, "Oh, I do not think a charging army could interfere with your sister's plans for me."

Alex sipped his coffee and continued watching this creature who was injecting herself into his morning routine. "You are dressed for riding." His statement demanded an explanation.

Miss Wright swallowed hard and then looked up, more directly at him this time. "I was hoping you would teach me to ride."

Resisting the urge to roll his eyes heavenward, Alex stared at her expectant face. He had plans to meet up with Danbury shortly.

"I will make arrangements for you to have lessons when we've returned to Brooke's Abbey." Did she think she could demand his attentions at a moment's notice? "I have commitments for this morning already."

"Oh," she said, suddenly seeming to lose her nerve. "I thought we could come to know each other better. I was hoping we could spend some time together. I would have asked you about this sooner, but you have not been at home." Her hand shook as she reached for her coffee. "It is just that I told you I was not afraid of you. And I am not, really! But I am nervous about being a wife. And I was hoping…I was hoping…that if I knew you better, then well…Things could be different this time…"

She took a hesitant sip of her coffee, holding the cup with both hands. She *was* nervous. She *was* afraid.

Alex sighed. He really did not want a repeat of his first wedding night. Perhaps her words contained some merit.

But this morning, he would be meeting Danbury.

"I cannot take you out this morning," he found himself saying. "I will need to find you a suitable mount—to your size as well as your inexperience. I have several at Brooke's Abbey, but I only keep a few here in town. We can begin lessons tomorrow. Would that be acceptable to you, Miss Wright?"

One might have believed he'd handed her the keys to Buckingham Palace.

"Oh, yes!" she practically gushed, her relief so great. "That would be wonderful."

"Very well," Alex said, while rising to his feet. "I will adjust my schedule accordingly." But before he could reach the door, her voice stopped him.

"Will you address me by my name?" she said. "May I address you by yours?"

She was impertinent! But she was also his fiancée. "Abigail?" he questioned.

"Yes. And may I call you Alex?" Her eyes were so innocent, so naïve as to the intimacy of her request.

Even Margaret rarely spoke to him by his given name. He was Monfort. He was His Grace.

"Monfort," he said firmly.

Miss Wright, oh hell, *Abigail,* scowled at his word and his tone of voice. But he would remain firm on this. Best to begin how he wished to carry on.

"Monfort? As in the Duke of? Am I to address my husband by *his title* then?"

Alex clenched his hands at his side. She had raised her chin to look at him more directly which in turn effectively stretched the material of her bodice. Her damn bodice! What the hell was wrong with him? "Yes," was all he said before turning on his heels and leaving her alone. Danbury would already be waiting, and Alex was never late for anything. *Never!*

****

The next morning, Abigail made certain to arrive in the morning room before the duke. She wished to give herself plenty of time to consume her coffee and at least a bit of toast. She was not nervous of horses. She was not even nervous of riding. It was the sidesaddle that frightened her. She'd known of a woman who had been killed while riding thusly—when her mount had fallen, the woman had been unable to extricate herself from the saddle and gotten herself crushed. All for the sake of propriety.

But ladies never rode astride. They rode sidesaddle.

Before Abigail had grown into a young woman, her mother had unthinkingly allowed her considerable free rein at Raebourne. Her father kept a few old plow horses and had fortuitously come into the ownership of a smaller pony. With some assistance from a few neighborly children, Abigail learned to ride the pony astride, with no saddle at all.

When her mother became alerted to such unladylike activities, her father sold the pony and that had been the end of that. She'd not been allowed to ride since then.

But her memories of those long ago days were happy ones. She'd enjoyed both the affinity with the animal as well as the exhilaration of the ride. That had been a long time ago.

Margaret had informed her that she would be expected to know how to ride. And in society, a lady only ever mounted a horse sidesaddle—silly and dangerous as it might be.

She pushed away her fears as the duke entered the room.

Glancing at her almost dismissively, he seated himself several chairs away and allowed the footman to pour him some coffee. Abigail's heartbeat accelerated in his presence.

"Were you able to find a suitable mount?" She broke the silence intentionally. The duke ignored her question for a moment before pushing his coffee away and looking over at her.

"I said I would, did I not?"

Abigail could not help but smile. "So we can go ahead with the lesson then?"

Monfort sighed. "Yes, Miss—Abigail. I am prepared to give you your first lesson." With a glance at her empty plate, he raised one eyebrow. "You are ready now? Shall we get this business over with then?"

Abigail chuckled. She was beginning to learn how he'd gotten his nickname, the Duke of Ice. He hadn't been so shuttered the first time they'd met. Something about London brought it out in him. Or perhaps it was merely being in his own home, surrounded by all of these ducal servants. She was going to have to do something about this. "Where shall we go?"

Rising to his feet, he tossed his napkin onto his chair, crossed the length of the room, and turned to offer her his arm. "Today we will not go anywhere. There is a small riding paddock in back, and we shall see how you manage there."

"I've ridden before," she said, all too aware of his person as she placed her hand on the wool of his jacket. Inhaling deeply, she then caught her breath. Even under these ordinary circumstances, his maleness filled her senses. He carried a masculine scent that was clean and spicy. His arm was warm and firm. He loomed above her so that she had to look up to meet his eyes. "Just not recently—and never sidesaddle."

His silver gaze flicked over her casually. Suddenly, the memory of his brief kiss four days ago wedged itself into her thoughts. Had this man really touched his lips to hers? Even this near his demeanor was distant— quite untouchable.

"I'll assess your skills today." He walked purposefully toward the back of the house, where the mews were located. "And decide if and when you're ready to leave the grounds after that."

Abigail's legs, considerably shorter than the duke's, struggled to keep abreast of him. But she didn't want to call his attention to this. She knew she was already disrupting his normal activities—forcing him to change his gait for her would only irritate him further.

As they exited the back doors, the morning air felt crisp and cool. They descended the service steps and followed the stone path together in silence. Except it wasn't silent really. Birds chirped nearby, a dog barked, and some muffled voices drifted across the lawn from within the stables. Abigail was gradually losing her apprehension and feeling anticipation instead, for the exercise. "Margaret tells me you breed horses at Brooke's Abbey. Do you do this because you like horses, or to generate funds?"

"Must the two be mutually exclusive?" He did not look at her but grimaced. Monfort pulled her around a corner, revealing two gated paddocks, one of which was already alive with activity with workers exercising a tall, fine-looking stallion. The other paddock, although not empty, was much calmer, holding a small white and brown mare already fitted with a lady's sidesaddle. A mounting block awaited her near the gate.

The duke led her toward the paddock, dropping her hand when he reached the fence. His entire demeanor changed as he neared the animal. He didn't use the gate, but effortlessly climbed the rails of the fence and stepped inside with the horse. Reaching into his pocket, he pulled out a carrot and beckoned the animal with it.

"This is Lady Page." He glanced back toward Abigail and actually grinned!

The horse approached this very different duke and trustingly took the carrot out of his hand. Appearing more relaxed than Abigail imagined possible, Monfort reached up and rubbed the horse's forelock. Stunned for a moment, Abigail simply watched this man she'd known to be aloof and stern as he crooned and petted the horse.

She'd seen that look before.

After she'd thrown herself to the floor of the boat.

He *had* been gentle. He had been quite *tender*, really.

"Lady Page, meet Miss Abigail Wright. I know you'll be on your best behavior today, my lady, and we'll see what kind of a horsewoman Miss Wright is." He was talking to the horse!

At his words, Abigail approached the mounting block, but with his sudden change of mood, found herself feeling hesitant and shy—as though she were imposing herself on a friendship that had been in existence for years. Standing atop the block, she bit her bottom lip while Monfort walked the horse over to her.

"I'm not sure how to do this," she said, her fear returning again as she studied the strange-looking saddle.

The duke's smile fled as he looked over and up at her. But his face remained relaxed. He was not glaring at her in irritation as he'd done earlier that morning.

Releasing the horse, he climbed the fence again and stepped up onto the mounting block with her. The horse was placed so that Abigail would mount from its left side. There were two pommels. She'd only ever seen such saddles with one pommel.

The horse stood unmoving as Monfort explained the mechanics of the saddle to her. "This is a brand new design from a fellow I met a few months ago. Didn't think I'd have need of one until yesterday. Now this pommel"—he pointed at the taller, more centered one—"is for your right leg. You place your right thigh above it and let your foot fall along the horse's shoulder. This other pommel is for your left. You'll find it gives you greater support as you improve. You'll be able to gallop more securely." He was guiding her shoulders so that she leaned over the horse and then he placed his hands upon her waist. Abigail turned her back toward the horse to mount, but Monfort twisted her around.

"You are riding sidesaddle, but I want you to keep your spine in line with that of the horse—just as if you were to ride astride. You must remain as centered as possible, both for your safety as well as the horse's."

Abigail lifted her leg, hooked it into the top pommel, and allowed her weight to settle onto the horse. As she tried to pull her left leg over the other pommel, it would not move, as her habit had gotten twisted beneath her. Panic swept through her when she tugged her leg at the material of the habit and could not free herself.

"Monfort, Monfort, I'm stuck," she cried softly, trying to not sound as flustered as she felt.

Alex identified the problem immediately. Crouching down, he knew it was important to keep Abigail from feeling panicked. The horse would sense her tension, and that would not be good for either of them. Soothingly, he placed one of his hands upon her thigh and the other along the horse's neck, grasping the bridle. "Not to worry, Abigail. I'll not let you come to any harm." Through the fabric of her skirt, his palm met with firm, warm thigh. He patted her and rubbed it, the same as he did to the horse. He needed to lift her leg to pull the material out from beneath her.

He admired her attempt to remain calm even as she wound her arm around his shoulders and grasped him tightly. This close, above the regular familiar scent of the stables, the fragrance of her soap, the allure of her perfume teased his sense. As she let out a few tiny gasps, her breath carried hints of coffee and mint.

Alex swallowed some unknown emotion and, forcing himself to address the task at hand, slid his hand downward to tug at the fabric.

It refused to budge.

In one swift movement, he released the bridle, slid his hand under her skirt, up her leg, and then pulled hard at the fabric with his other hand.

Voila! She was free.

Except that his right hand remained under her skirt, on the bare skin of her leg.

His palm lay upon the silk of her stocking, but his fingers were able to stroke the fragile and delicate skin of her thigh. The tiny gasps of her breaths quickened at his touch.

Unconsciously, he grasped the bridle again with his other hand as his gaze traveled up to meet her eyes. She returned his stare almost questioningly. It was as though she was intrigued, somewhat aroused, but also…confused? The hand on his shoulder slid down to his elbow, but she did not push him away. Her other hand grasped the pommel tightly.

"You aren't going to faint on me again, are you?" he asked softly, remembering the last time he attempted to touch her intimately. He allowed his hand to slide higher, massaging her skin lightly. His thumb drifted over her inner thigh, finding skin that was even more delicate, like the wings of a butterfly.

"I ought to." She surprised him then. Her voice a little huskier than normal, not quite a whisper. "I'm doubtful Lady Page approves." And then as though sheer exhaustion had set into her, she tilted her head forward and leaned into him. The warmth of her forehead pressed into his shoulder. She was so trusting of him. "I won't faint, Monfort, but—that—what you are doing—is not calming at all."

Her words had a strange effect upon him. Was this fondness? Protectiveness? She was not fighting him off. She wasn't pushing him away.

"If another man ever attempts to touch you, to take liberties with you, you will scream and bite and scratch. Do you understand, Abigail?" He pushed her away to meet her eyes clearly. "Do you understand?"

She paused and then nodded. "But not you?"

"If you do not want my touch, then all you must do is say so. And if I do not remove my touch quickly enough, then I want for you to scream and bite and scratch."

Abigail's eyes narrowed slightly, and then she nodded again. "I don't."

"You do not want my touch?" Alex went to pull away, but she stopped him with her next words.

"I don't *not want* your touch..." Her delicate complexion suddenly flushed.

A surge of satisfaction rolled though him at her confession. She was looking down at the horse's mane, one hand plucking at the long hairs. *Oh hell*, she was almost perfect. Perhaps he ought to have made her his mistress after all.

Alex allowed himself just a few more strokes of skin, skin he had the sudden desire to press his lips against, and then withdrew his hand slowly. An unusual urge to take her in his arms swept through him—an unusual urge to hold her. Simply hold her so that she would feel safe. Leaning back, he handed her the reins and deftly secured her left leg in the lower pommel and her foot in the stirrup.

This was to be a riding lesson, for God's sake.

Returning to the ground, he stepped away from the horse and then turned back toward the horse and rider. "Sit up straight and tall, remember, stay centered—yes, just as if you were riding astride. The horse needs to feel your balance as well as you do."

Abigail drew upon every ounce of willpower she possessed to pay attention to and follow Monfort's instructions. The skin where his hand had stroked her still tingled—no, it burned.

He'd not asked if he could touch her, but he had been adamant that she could stop him if she wished.

She hadn't.

And then she'd admitted as much to him. What must he think of her?

She'd wanted his hand to slide higher. Good God, she'd wanted him to touch her *there!*

And now she could hardly breathe.

She took a deep breath and patted Lady Page on the neck. She needed to focus on her lessons, on her balance, the horse's gait…Monfort's voice. "Stop a minute, Abigail. Whoa, Lady Page."

As the horse halted, Monfort walked toward her and Lady Page purposefully. When he reached them, he grasped the saddle and made a few adjustments before making certain all was secure and then barked out more instructions. She was not afraid of the animal, nor was she afraid of him. In fact, she found herself quite at ease. Monfort ordered her to walk around the paddock, stop, start, turn left, turn right, and go around several more times before calling an end to the lesson. She could become an accomplished equestrienne if she chose to do so. A thrill of excitement shot through her.

This was fun!

****

In no time, their riding lessons became the highlight of Abigail's days, for her future sister-in-law was relentless in her plans to shape Abigail into the perfect future duchess for her brother.

Abigail was trying her best.

It was just that her best was proving to be not quite good enough.

With so many different dances to learn, at times her feet tied themselves into knots. Often the French dancing instructor who'd been hired would stop in frustration and roll his eyes heavenward. "*Mon dieu*," he cried out often when Abigail stepped to her left instead of right. He was even louder when she tread upon his toes.

Margaret had also arranged for Abigail to undergo pianoforte lessons alternated with vocal training. Abigail had known for years that she was not musical, but her voice coach insisted such training was necessary for any lady of the ton—even if the resulting performances were less than inspiring.

In addition, there were lessons using watercolors on paper and paint on satin. These were at least enjoyable in that Abigail often found humor in her handiwork. The art master did not.

But above and beyond all of these, Abigail suffered her daily lessons in deportment, Debrett's, and etiquette. Margaret and Aunt Cecily, of course, led these teachings themselves. Instructions involved memorization, physical endurance, and something Abigail had never even considered for herself: detached ennui.

Margaret insisted that Abigail's comportment, the look in her eyes, and tone of her voice should demand the respect she'd require to succeed as a duchess. The vocal training, the dancing, the arts—these vocations were embarked upon to instill in Abigail a pride in herself. She must master them to achieve the confidence required to stand in a room under close scrutiny and know that she was better than all those around her.

This last statement extracted a stifled giggle from Abigail, causing Margaret to glare at her disapprovingly.

For in truth, the more lessons Abigail endured, the less worthy she considered herself. Even when she *did* manage to produce acceptable results, she felt like a fraud. The incessant criticism from her teachers was in fact, eroding what little confidence she'd brought with her into this betrothal. As each lesson progressed, her sense of failure grew.

Except in the mornings when Monfort took her riding.

Ironic, really, as she endured more barking and correction from him than anyone else.

But when he praised her…Ah. The sincerity of his praise straightened her spine and lifted her chin. It sent a glow of warmth travelling from the top of her head to the tip of her toes.

Because she *was* improving keenly under his tutelage. And as she progressed, she found opportunities each day to know her future husband better.

Chapter 10

Alex kept his mount in check as he followed Abigail and Lady Page along the path that led to Rotten Row. It was early yet, and the park was empty of any society—the way he liked it. He had told Abigail she could gallop this morning. She had a natural affinity with her horse and was fast on the way to becoming a skilled horsewoman.

Her right hand held the whip loosely along the horse's right side, and she appeared to have complete control as she effortlessly guided the horse onto the path. Her spine was straight and centered, and she held the reins just high enough to exert control over the well-behaved mare.

Alex was quite pleased with himself.

Alex had also managed to avoid lusting after his betrothed this past week.

Almost completely.

This sprite of a woman, whom he'd once considered a frumpy spinster, was spending a great deal of time with his sister and the benefits were beginning to become apparent. The clothing, the bearing, her language and manners. Yes, perhaps this hadn't been such a ghastly mistake as he'd first feared.

He urged his mount forward and came abreast of Abigail as they stepped onto the Row.

They both halted, and Abigail looked over at him expectantly.

"She's nice and warmed up," Alex said. "We're going to trot first, then urge into a canter, and we'll gallop after that. When you can see the Serpentine, we're going to slow again to a trot and turn around."

Abigail narrowed her eyes in concentration, serious and determined. She nodded and did exactly as he'd instructed. After they'd made the same pass twice, they slowed back to a walk, and Alex turned to lead them back toward Cross House.

"Can we not take a different path?" Abigail had the effrontery to bring her horse to a halt and call out to him. "I'm having fun and...I'd like to enjoy the park for a while before returning to the house."

This brought him up short. She did not wish to return to Cross House yet? She'd visibly winced at the mention of it. He studied her and for the first time noticed the dark circles under her eyes.

"Can we not simply walk...and talk?" Upon speaking these words, she looked lonely, and then...defeated. A posture she'd not had while on horseback the entire time he'd been training her.

"Sit up straight, Abigail." He spoke automatically. But then her eyes filled with tears. She'd not been reduced to them since the day he'd proposed. What in the devil had he said now?

Turning her head away, she wiped her arm across her eyes. Lady Page stood patiently, seeming to understand that her rider needed a moment.

An unbidden memory intruded. Alex didn't know why, but suddenly his mind's eye conjured up the moments when he had rowed her on the lake at Raven's

Park—before she'd exposed herself—when she'd found such pleasure in the fish swimming near her hand. In those few minutes, she'd been chatting and smiling without reserve. Since she'd come to London, he had not seen her thus even once. Was she unhappy? Was *he* making her unhappy?

Not that he considered it his duty to provide her constant pleasure, but he truly did not wish to cause another woman such misery as he'd caused Hyacinth.

Without considering his intentions, he dismounted, handed off his horse to the groom who'd followed them, and approached her with careful steps, as though afraid she might spook.

When he reached her, taking the horse by the bridle, he placed one hand upon her foot. "Abigail? You are unwell?" She shook her head, still looking away from him. "Come now, you are unhappy?"

She turned watery eyes to look down at him. Her throat worked, but no sound emerged.

Reaching for her waist, Alex decided it was best she dismount for now. "Come here, Abigail. Let's walk by the water."

She trustingly put her hands upon his shoulders, leaned down, lifted her legs out of the pommel, and allowed him to take her weight as she slid off the horse. Once she landed, she stepped away from him and looked as though she were attempting to shake off her melancholy. "I'm just tired, I suppose...and..." But then she clamped her lips shut and refused to meet his gaze.

"And?" Alex persisted.

A brittle smile. "I am trying so very hard, Monfort, but I am afraid...afraid I will do something wrong—at the prewedding ball, or when I'm out and about. I am afraid somebody who remembers me is going to say something to me about before...and although Margaret has been working with me so I can glare and frown at such a person, I am afraid I will become afraid and then I will...faint. I do that when I am very frightened of something. And if I faint, I will dishonor you and your family and all that you have done for me..." Her voice trailed off, and Abigail looked away from him.

Alex had to pinch his lips together to keep from grinning at her statement. She would not appreciate him finding humor in her fears. They really were not funny, but..."You are afraid of being afraid?"

"I know it sounds silly, but you have seen what happened when I was frightened once before." She was serious. *Very* serious and *very* concerned. She swiped her arm at her eyes once again.

Alex took a few steps closer to her, allowing the groom to take control of the mare. Grasping her elbow, he led her away from the servant. As they walked, he formulated a plan. Several moments passed until they reached the edge of the water.

"Abigail, you are a courageous woman. How can you not realize that?"

She sniffed and then gave him a watery smile. "You have to say that. You are my betrothed."

But he was shaking his head. "I don't have to say anything. I am a duke." But he spoke gently to her.

"I am only here because you have decided to take pity upon me."

Again, he was compelled to deny her words. "Do you know why I proposed to you, Abigail? Not because I pitied you, but because I took *advantage* of you. I was an ass. I listened to the gossip and assumed the worst about you. And that night at Raven's Park, when you came downstairs, I'd had too much to drink. *I dishonored you.*" And then he turned to stare across the water. Why was he telling her this? "The only honorable thing I could do was to offer you the protection of my name."

Abigail watched him closely. Those large eyes of hers seemed to peer beyond what he was saying… Did she see his guilt? Did she see the contempt he held for himself?

"It takes a courageous woman to take on the Duke of Ice." He spoke the words derisively. "You have nothing to fear from the ton."

"I wish I believed that." She sighed.

So lacking in confidence. Alex abhorred this in most people.

Up in the sky, a colorful object floated lazily over the park.

Until the past few weeks, his betrothed's entire world had been a backward village; he couldn't recall the name. And those people had judged her and found her wanting. Her own parents had done the same. Nobody had done anything to bolster the poor girl. As he considered her predicament, the color in the sky again caught his eye and an idea struck him.

She had been brave after her dress had torn on the lake. She'd turned and faced him, in fact. She'd even made conversation with him afterwards. She was not a timid spinster. She simply needed to discover this fact for herself. Lowering his gaze, he took in her countenance once again.

"We shall have to address that then, now won't

we?" As he considered his notion further, it began to take root in his mind firmly. And *by God,* his own heart even jumped at the prospect.

****

Monfort instructed Abigail to leave off her riding habit the next morning. They would be doing something other than riding, he said, but he would not reveal what. He'd changed their plans after she'd told him of the doubts she had in herself. She was to trust him. He was her betrothed and surely would not plan anything that would be too daunting, would he? Abigail did not like surprises, but she had liked the light shining in Monfort's eyes when he bid her good day. She welcomed the temporary crack in his demeanor. He hadn't quite smiled, but she had seen a gleam in him that hadn't been there before.

Recognizing warmth in him that she'd suspected before gave her a renewed hope. And this hope energized her to tackle the daunting lessons Margaret ran her through again that afternoon. Even Aunt Cecily noted that she was showing improvement. Her dancing was less stilted, her memorization more accurate, and her deportment more refined. Numerous new dresses arrived that afternoon, and even the fittings and alterations couldn't suppress her optimism.

Less encouraging, Penelope's parents had arrived in London and her cousin was departing the duke's residence for her parents' townhouse, not quite a mile away. Abigail would remain alone with, not exactly strangers, but not quite friends. Penelope was family, and although Margaret had begun to exhibit signs of friendship, her company wasn't the same as having one's best friend there to support her.

And so with a sense of impending doom, Abigail awaited the arrival of the Rivertons' carriage in Abigail's richly appointed suite with Penelope. Her cousin, never one to sit quietly, opened the wardrobes and sighed wistfully over a few of the new gowns that had just been delivered.

"Could you ever have imagined such a fine wardrobe as this, Abby? Even I envy you some of these."

Abigail ignored the gowns. "I wish you didn't have to leave. Who is going to encourage me as you have?" It had already been a trying day, and she was not looking forward to residing at Cross House alone.

"Oh, posh, Abby. Stop feeling sorry for yourself. You are doing wonderfully. You certainly don't need *me* here to hold your hand. You are going to make a wonderful duchess. I have no doubt of this whatsoever. And besides I cannot abide another day of these lessons, and since I am *not* going to marry a duke, I have something else I wish to look into. I intend to purchase myself one of those Lady Accelerators."

What?

"Not one of those two-wheeled machines! Oh, Penelope, you'll kill yourself!"

"Of course I will," she said mischievously. "Can you imagine the wonder of it? Moving along at such a quick rate without a horse pulling me. The device will be completely under my own control. I have been reading articles about it and can hardly wait to learn how to balance and steer the contraption. Just you wait, you'll be wanting one too after you've seen me."

Abigail shook her head and laughed. She could only imagine the gossip if she ever took to the streets of

London on one of those two-wheeled contraptions. She would most likely crash right into a building with it—or a carriage—or the river! But Penelope would manage just fine. She always did. If only Abigail could be as certain of her own success at this duchess thing.

"Well, Penny, do be careful. Don't break any limbs before my wedding." As the words left her mouth, she shivered to think that she'd be married in less than two weeks. And before the wedding came her reentry into society. Up until now, Margaret and Aunt Cecily had kept her hidden away at Cross Hall. They were determined to use as much time preparing her as possible. She'd be introduced at her prewedding ball.

And with the summer's end, much of society was returning to London for the Little Season. The ball planned for the eve of her wedding promised to be a squeeze. Of course, anybody who was going to be in town wouldn't dare miss the remarriage of the Duke of Ice! And to a scandalous spinster, no less!

"I'll see you soon enough. It's not as though I'm returning to the country." Penelope smiled encouragingly as a knock sounded at the door. When beckoned to enter, a footman informed the women that the baron and baroness awaited them in the yellow salon. Abigail's heart dropped. She already missed Penelope's presence.

Abigail stepped into the salon and was nearly bowled over when her Aunt Edith rushed forward. The same aunt who'd only weeks ago declared her utterly ruined and forbidden her from even corresponding with Penelope. Abigail endured the awkward embrace with a forced smile.

"My dearest niece! You are looking wonderful

indeed! Town life suits you!"

Her uncle, only slightly less enthusiastic, glanced around and behind her, as though waiting for somebody else to enter. "His Grace is not at home? I was quite looking forward to meeting with him this evening as well."

Penelope kissed the baron on his cheek. "Hello, Father. I assume you had an uneventful journey?" Noticing the attire both her parents wore, travel clothes—a bit wrinkled—she raised both of her brows. "You have come directly to Cross House?"

Aunt Edith waved her hand dismissively, "Oh, pish, Penelope! But of course, we were quite anxious to see our daughter and niece! Your father finished his business at home, and we set to the road as soon as we could." Turning to Abigail, she continued effusively, "I am so very sorry, my dear, that I could not travel with you and Penny last week! It was just that there has been so much to do to prepare for the wedding."

Abigail furrowed her brows. What had her aunt and uncle found necessary to do for her wedding?

At the confused look on her face, Aunt Edith laughed and continued. "Oh, darling, there have been so many letters to write! All of our family must be invited to witness your nuptials! A duke? A duke! Splendid, my dear! However did you manage such a coup?"

At these unfortunate words, an awkward silence fell in the room. Abigail glanced in the direction of Penelope's horrified gaze.

Monfort himself stood, quite unmoving, stoically observing her aunt. Abigail's breath caught at the coldness in his eyes.

As immaculately turned out as ever, Monfort

appeared arrogant and unapproachable. He wore a maroon jacket over a waistcoat finely trimmed out in gold embroidery. His breeches had obviously been tailored to fit him perfectly, and the gold buckles on his shoes gleamed nearly to a sparkle. He wore no pomade in his hair but had tied it back, emphasizing his hawkish appearance.

And his eyes flashed the color of ice.

Abigail's uncle stepped forward first and made an awkward bow. "Your Grace, it is indeed a pleasure to make your acquaintance again."

Monfort merely inclined his head. Aunt Edith made several rapid curtseys before placing one arm around Abigail and squeezing her in an unfamiliar affectionate manner. "We stopped over at Raebourne before setting for London. Abigail's parents shall be embarking on their own journey here within the next few days as well."

"I am aware of this, as it will be one of my carriages in which they shall travel." The duke's words were clipped. He was not angry; that would imply some sort of passion. Abigail suppressed the urge to shiver at his tone.

Her aunt effused obliviously. "We are in agreement that upon the arrival of my dear brother and his wife, little Abigail must remove herself to Oak Manor. But it is like a second home to her! And then, after the wedding, like a baby bird in flight, we shall release her into your esteemed protection once again, Your Grace. For it is only proper that a lady be with her family before her wedding."

The duke turned his eyes toward Abigail, his jaw tight. "If that is your wish, my dear?"

My dear? *My dear*? He'd never addressed her with any sort of endearment before.

Abigail struggled to locate her voice. "I…er…yes, I suppose that would be best." And then she could not help but to smile at her betrothed. My dear, indeed! "Aunt and uncle's house, here in town, is not far. It won't be troublesome to visit during the daytime to continue all of my lessons. Do you think that Margaret…er…Lady Clive will have any objections to this?"

Aunt Edith looked confused and looked to the duke for an explanation.

But the duke did not explain anything to anybody. "She will not," was all he said. Then making a slight bow in Abigail's direction, he turned on his heels and left the room. Ah, yes, here was the true Duke of Ice. He could be quite adept at freezing people out when he so chose. He could also be warm…

But had her aunt really deserved it? What had the duke overheard her saying? Something to the effect of Abigail having made an advantageous match? Yes. Well. She had at that. Although not due to any effort on her own part to do any such thing.

"I will have a special guest room made up for you at Oak Manor."

Remembering the small attic room her aunt had provided to her for her come-out, Abigail could not help but grimace at Penelope.

Her aunt continued, oblivious to the secret exchange between the two girls. "Countless relatives shall be arriving in London over the next few days. For the wedding, of course! All in your honor! Dozens of Hector's relations shall be descending upon town, as will all of my own sisters and brothers and cousins and their parents. This is so exciting, Abigail."

Abigail turned her attention toward her aunt once again. The words *my dear* echoing in her brain.

"Mother." Penelope interrupted her mother's recitation of relatives of whom Abigail had never heard. "The carriage is waiting for us. My bags have been loaded, and I'd like to settle in at Oak Manor sometime today." Rolling her eyes heavenward she added, "As must Papa."

Uncle Hector was in fact fidgeting to leave. Apparently, he wasn't keen on staying around with only women for company.

Abigail embraced Penelope one last time and suffered through another from her aunt, before bidding them goodbye, with promises to call upon them tomorrow—if she could find time, that was. The only problem with having a cousin such as Penelope was that in order to see her, she had to endure her parents.

And then as her own parents came to mind, she decided Penelope must think likewise.

Her own parents.

They would be arriving in London shortly as well.

Would they be an even greater embarrassment? Her mother often spoke loudly and without much thought to what would be flying out of her mouth. And her father...well, he was fine as long as he did not dip too deeply into any available spirits.

Abigail worried her bottom lip with her teeth and climbed her way back upstairs. She had just a quarter of an hour before deportment lessons commenced, and she did not wish to waste it with worry. What good would worrying about her parents do anyhow? She could no more control their actions than she could hold back the tide.

****

Alex disliked the Rivertons, specifically the baron.

The last time that man had deigned to speak with him, he'd all but called his niece a whore. And yet, after the wedding, he'd be a relation.

And then there were Abigail's own parents to consider. He'd not met her mother, but he'd not been overly impressed by the man who deigned to call himself her father either.

Most of all, he was unimpressed with the manner in which they'd handled the attack on Abigail when she'd been just a girl. Either Abigail's father or her uncle ought to have called the cad out. It wouldn't have taken much to put a period to his existence, or to merely force him to leave the country. Why had nobody done this for Abigail?

Monfort had been developing a theory as to who the perpetrator was. His suspicions had begun to develop when he recalled the horror on Abigail's face in Ravensdale's drawing room nearly two months ago.

At the sight of the three bounders, Alex remembered, Abigail had gone white. Would any of them have been present during the season in which Abigail had been ruined? Ruined, hell, she'd been raped!

Damien Farley had never been known as an honorable gentleman.

Alex was grateful, in an odd turn of thought, however, that nobody had forced the bounder to marry her. The criminal—the bastard—the sorry excuse of a man would have made her life miserable.

But.

But she would have been able to keep her child.

Alex experienced that far too familiar stab at the memory of losing his own children. What had it been like for Abigail? And then his own words came back to haunt him as well. *You do not wish to have any little boys to chase after? No little girls' hair to braid?*

He'd been goading her. Taunting her for her inability to obtain herself a husband.

And she'd already lost a child. He wondered if it had been a boy or a girl.

****

Although Monfort had promised a surprise the next morning and Abigail generally didn't appreciate surprises, she was not nervous.

She trusted Monfort.

He would not do anything that would hurt her. She didn't understand why she believed this, but she did, nonetheless. She found him thoroughly dependable.

Yes, he could be cold and arrogant and dismissive; he was a duke, after all. But when her dress had ripped and she'd been alone with him on that damn boat…he'd been kind.

And he'd told nobody about it.

Taking a bite of toast as she awaited him early, she surmised how that fact alone caused her to trust Monfort a great deal. He'd never mentioned it again.

Even when he'd touched her on that morning. She nearly shivered at the memory of his hand caressing her leg. She couldn't forget it. He'd taken liberties, but he'd left her in control.

She swallowed hard, flustered even contemplating the memory.

It was as though, by his touch alone, he could relax all of her muscles and turn her bones to liquid. And as odd as the situation had been, she'd wanted him to continue touching her. To move his hand just a few more inches and—

"Good morning, Abigail." His voice pulled her into the present as he entered the room and took his seat. He wore no cravat this morning, and his coat appeared softened and worn—like an old favorite. Watching those capable, long-fingered hands take hold of the coffee pot, Abigail squirmed. Only moments before she'd been remembering the sensations those hands had created in her most personal…Those hands had touched her intimately.

"Good morning," she returned, attempting to focus on the day's planned excursion. "Are you going to tell me where we are going yet?"

"I am not." He narrowed his eyes at her, and just when she thought he was going to rebuke her for asking, she realized he was teasing her! This was the duke being playful! One side of his mouth pulled up slightly. The footman placed a dish before him, and he dug into it heartily.

Abigail's heart lightened to watch him do such an ordinary thing as eat. He was a duke, but he was also a person. In the time Abigail barely dented the morsels of egg, bacon, and fruit on her plate, the duke had eaten most everything set before him. Rather than stand or leave, he placed his cup solemnly upon the table and absentmindedly smoothed down the linen.

He dismissed the servants who'd been attending them and then met her eyes.

"Abigail." He lacked his normal resolve as he

searched for his next words. "I do not wish to make you uncomfortable in any way. In fact, I'm sure you would prefer never to have this conversation. But as your fiancée there is something I must do." He watched her carefully, as though waiting for her to make an objection. But she could not speak. Her heart lodged in her throat. What was he leading up to? Did he wish to cry off? Roaring filled her ears, but she forced herself to listen.

At her silence, he continued. "It is my duty to mete out justice upon your attacker. I will only say a name, and all you need do is say either yes or no. I must be certain, you see, before taking any action."

Oh no! No, no, no. She did not want him to do anything! It would bring it all up again. She pushed her plate away from her and went to stand up, but the heavy chair behind her would not move. Seeing her difficulty, Monfort himself rose and pulled it out for her. Not wishing to have to look at him, Abigail paced over to the window. He would think her a coward again, for not allowing him to defend her honor. He would accuse her of putting her head in the sand. But it was for the best. Surely he must understand this? She gazed unseeing at the spectacular greenery of the nearby park. The sun had not quite risen yet, but an orange glow lit the sky.

She could not allow him to pursue this course of action. "Please, Alex, Monfort, Your Grace. Do not. I beg of you. It will only make matters worse." She was shaking her head. "Can we not simply allow the matter to rest?"

He watched her closely but only considered her request for a moment. "I cannot. I will not, Abigail. Something ought to have been done years ago, and I cannot allow such a deplorable situation to remain unresolved." He pressed his lips together into a straight line. "It will not be done in a way that will expose you to ridicule. When I demand satisfaction from him, it will not be done publicly. You have my word. This situation will be righted, Abigail. As it ought to have been long ago."

Abigail covered her face with her hands. She did not want to think about this. She did not want to speak of it to anybody, let alone Monfort.

"Was it one of the men at Raven's Park?" His voice sounded gentle, and yet it also carried an edge of steel.

She dropped her hands. "How?" How did he know? Were people still speaking of it?

Monfort returned to his seat. "At Raven's Park. You looked as if you'd seen a ghost when Danbury and the others entered the room. I know that at least one of them has been a pestilence upon society for years." He spoke matter-of-factly, as though they were discussing the weather.

Feeling quite foolish, Abigail returned to her own seat and drew her plate forward in attempt to appear unaffected. Her hands shook, though, as she spread jam on her toast, which surely must be cold by now. She did not want to reawaken all of this. She wished to look to the future. Leave the past in the past. "Please, let it be."

Monfort's eyes bore into her as though he could read her thoughts. And then, apparently willing to table it for now, he reached for his coffee and took a slow sip. Abigail hoped it was the end of the matter, but his easy capitulation gave her reason to suspect otherwise.

They sat silent for several moments after that,

Monfort perusing the newspaper that had been placed beside him, and Abigail lost in thought. Abigail was surprised at how contented she felt in his presence, even after such an uncomfortable discourse.

Desperate to change the topic of conversation, Abigail happily recalled a question she'd been wanting to ask him. "Have you made any plans for what we shall do following our wedding ceremony? I was not certain if you would wish to remain in London or return right away to Brooke's Abbey."

Glancing up from his newspaper, Monfort grimaced. "I would rather not stay in town for the season. Were you wanting to participate in the Little Season?"

"Oh, heavens, no!" Abigail nearly flinched at the thought. "I am most at home in the country. At Raebourne, I had a garden to tend. It is too late to plant anything this year, of course, but I was hoping you would allot me a small plot that I could begin preparing for the winter months. I also would like to meet some of your tenants, other landowners, and villagers who abide nearby. That is, if you do not have any objections?"

He merely waved a hand in the air. "You will be free to do all of that at your leisure. I was rather thinking of a wedding trip. I have an estate—actually it's a castle—near the sea, just west of Cornwall, which I haven't checked in on yet this year. If you are amenable, we could spend a few weeks there and return to Brooke's Abbey before the cold sets in for the winter."

Cornwall? Abigail's heart dropped. It would be fine. No one would remember her from before. It had been ages, and she had been kept quite—quite—

isolated. She forced her lips to smile before he suspected her misgivings. A wedding trip would be good for them. It might allow them to come to know each other better as husband and wife. She did not want him to change his plans. "That sounds delightful." She did enjoy the sea. It would be nice to be away from London again. The city was not one of her favorite places.

"Very well, then. We will travel south the day after our nuptials."

At which point, she would be his wife in truth.

She nodded in response, and Monfort returned his attention to the newspaper in front of him. Abigail picked up her knife and toyed with her food for a few minutes before giving up on it completely. She was intrigued by his consideration of her wishes and yet his utter confidence that she would fall in line with his plans.

When she pushed her plate away from her for the second time, Monfort glanced up and lifted one questioning brow. "If you are finished, we should leave now. Our outing requires that we have the cool of the morning air."

He was being mysterious. And that gleam had appeared behind his gaze once again.

The slight hint of enthusiasm rubbed off on her immediately. "Let me fetch my bonnet." She grinned. "And I'll meet you in the foyer. Are we walking or taking the carriage?"

"I will drive us in my curricle."

As Abigail stood, her anticipation grew. Was he going to take her to a stable to see some horses? Were they going to a race somewhere? He'd thought of this activity when she'd been talking about her fears. What was he up to?

She thought again, for all of two seconds, that she ought to be frightened. But no. She trusted him. Since he'd come to Raebourne and proposed, he'd acted in her best interest on every occasion.

Monfort easily assisted her into the gleaming yellow curricle. He showed her where to grasp and then, placing his hands upon her waist virtually hoisted her onto the platform. The seat was so high perched, she wondered if perhaps the ride itself was the surprise. But Monfort made no indication that such was the case.

In no time at all, he sauntered around and climbed on unassisted. And then, looking very comfortable and self-assured, took the reins and urged the cattle forward. Although she sat several feet above the ground, she knew herself to be safe with him. He would never knowingly put her in any danger.

After a few blocks, she wondered if he was taking her for a drive in the park. Were they going to go onto the water? Was he going to take her rowing?

That must be it. He was going to take her rowing since the last experience she'd had...well...things had gone so awry. He was going to prove she could have a perfectly lovely outing on a rowboat.

But then, as he turned into the park and down a path, Abigail's breath caught in her throat. For awaiting them in an open stretch of lawn hovered a large colorful balloon attached to a basket that was meant to carry passengers into the sky. The fully inflated scarlet balloon reached higher than the trees off in the distance. It contrasted brightly against the greens of the grass and trees and the blue of the sky. Surely he did not intend for them to ride in such a conveyance? And yet...the duke was looking over at her with questioning eyes.

And he was smiling.

Chapter 11

Monfort pulled the curricle to a halt and handed the reins to one of the grooms before jumping off and coming around to assist Abigail. Although Abigail's misgivings at the thought of being carried away in a basket were enormous, this almost boyish excitement in him kept her from protesting.

With a little impatience, he placed her hand upon his arm and dragged her over to introduce her to the pilot. Both men were discussing details and weather conditions, but Abigail failed to hear much of what was being said.

When she could finally speak, she was not eloquent at all. "Surely not…? Monfort, you don't intend for us to…?"

But he was grinning and even laughing a bit as he took her hand. "I won't force you, Abigail," he said, momentarily serious. "But I believe that if you have the courage to fly above the rooftops of London, then surely you will feel better about looking its inhabitants in their eyes. What do you say, Abigail? Shall we fly today?"

He looked so earnest, and so proud of himself, but what *could* she say? "Of course!" Hugging herself with her arms, she shivered. "What do we need to do?" This time she addressed the pilot.

"Not much for you to do, m'lady," the pilot answered cheerfully, "but climb into the basket."

Before she could say anything else, Monfort's strong arms swooped her up and over the sidewalls of the basket. It was not reassuring at all to feel the squishy basket material beneath her feet as she stood directly under the balloon. And then with no hesitation whatsoever, Monfort hoisted himself over and stood beside her.

"It is safe, isn't it?" Abigail asked, feeling in need of more reassurance.

Monfort laughed. "These have been around for nearly half a century now, Abigail. The heat from the burner causes the balloon to rise. Only the balloon isn't called a balloon; it's referred to as the envelope. Hydrogen balloons are all the rage right now, but I prefer the simplicity of this design. The heated air in the envelope causes the balloon to take flight." The duke was telling her the ins and outs as well as the history of balloons, even that the first passengers to ever ride in one were a goat, a pig, and a rooster. And before Abigail could act on her misgivings, the ground receded and she was looking down upon the tops of the trees.

"Monfort! We're flying!" The unexpected exhilaration sweeping through her could not be contained. It was as though she were dreaming. As she clutched the side of the basket, looking downward, the duke's arms wrapped around her from behind. He rested his chin atop her head.

Not thinking for even a moment, Abigail brought one of her hands off the basket and covered the duke's arm with hers. She liked the feel of him behind her. She liked the security of being held by somebody who was good.

The rhythm of his breath flowed through her as his body pressed flush against her own.

It *was* a rather small basket, and he *was* most likely only standing so close to her so the pilot had space to maneuver his torchy thingy.

Pleasure coursed through her veins, and in that moment, her emotions lifted higher, even than the balloon.

The duke removed one of his hands and pointed. "Look there, Abigail, and you can see Cross Hall. And just beyond it is Grosvenor Square." His breath caressed the skin just beside her ear. The sensation warmed her. Never had she experienced such…tingling intimacy.

They went higher and higher and higher, straight up into the sky. With no wind to move them, they hovered directly over Hyde Park. Abigail could make out the spot where they'd taken off from, and a tiny little dot for the curricle they'd ridden over on…just barely. They were so very high up in the sky.

She was jolted from her reverie when something the pilot was saying led the duke to step away, rocking her sensation of safety. Suddenly feeling quite alone, standing in a basket in the sky, she grasped the edge of the wicker wall with all her might.

"So you still wish to go ahead with it, Your Grace?" The pilot lifted up a vest with straps from the floor.

And the duke was nodding eagerly as he took hold of it and slipped his arms through the openings. "The conditions are perfect," Monfort said as he tied the canvas vest snugly. "Mightn't be so lucky next time."

The pilot was assisting him now, tightening the straps and tugging at the buckles. Abigail then noticed that ropes attached to the vest were strung up to the side of the balloon. A horrible foreboding struck her. She'd heard of such daredevil acts. She'd heard of such careless individuals who wished to test the boundaries of new inventions.

"You aren't thinking of—? You cannot possibly! Monfort! Alex, what in God's name are you thinking?" Her outburst caught both Monfort and the pilot's attention.

The pilot rolled his eyes and moved to the opposite corner of the basket. Monfort stared over at her with some concern. Being careful of the ropes around him, he stepped closer and grasped her elbows. "It's known as parachuting. I've been of a mind to try it since I saw it at a festival a few years ago. It's quite safe, Abigail."

"Don't you 'it's quite safe, Abigail' me! I know when something is dangerous, and I know that jumping out of a balloon is one of them. Excuse me, an envelope!" Seeing the determined look upon his face, Abigail fought the tears threatening to overflow. "But if you want to kill yourself, don't mind me! I'll just sit up here and watch you throw yourself to your death. I'll explain to your sister, your aunt—to your nephews— that their uncle just 'wanted to try it,' and that it was all really quite safe, not at all dangerous, as they scrape your body off the grass." She was nearly sobbing as she spoke. Why would he do such a thing? Did he not really care if he were to live or to die? Life was precious! *He* was so very precious! How could he even *think* of doing something like this?

And then she was in his arms, and he was shushing

her softly.

"Hush now, Abigail," Alex said, shaking his head at the pilot. He would not do the jump today. Good God, the woman was becoming hysterical. She trembled in his arms. He pulled her closer and rubbed the back of her neck with one hand. Her skin delicate and soft, with a few wisps of dampened hair clinging to it.

"I couldn't bear it if you died," she mumbled into his shirt. "I simply couldn't bear it."

He knew he would not die. Well, he was relatively certain he would not die. He'd merely been attracted to the thrill of it. How magnificent to fall from such a height with only the silk of a parachute to slow his descent.

But this woman. This woman in his arms was terrified for him. And discovering this, somehow melted his insides just a little bit. "I won't die, Abigail," he promised. "I won't jump."

Silly promise, really. He of all people ought to know that such a promise was a joke.

What had Hyacinth said when she'd threatened to go out on the ice that day? *You worry far too much, Monfort. Don't be such a spoilsport!* And then she'd died. And she'd taken the children with her.

"I won't jump, Abby," he repeated, something of a lump forming in his throat. And then he turned her around so that she was looking away from him. He stepped away and began removing the jumping vest. The pilot assisted him in silence until it was once again stashed in a corner of the basket. He was a little bit annoyed with himself for allowing Abigail's fear to stop him from doing what he'd wanted to do, but he was even more annoyed with himself for planning to try the jump with her in the balloon in the first place.

There *were* a tremendous amount of people who depended upon him. In the event of his death, no apparent heir stood by, ready to take up his responsibilities. He'd acted on impulse while setting the flight up, just yesterday.

Abigail, herself, was dependent upon him—for virtually everything now. And they were not yet married. If he were to be killed, she probably assumed she'd be right back in that terrible predicament she'd been in before he'd proposed.

Was that why she'd been so terrified?

"I've changed my will to provide for you in the case of my death," he said, warmth draining out of him.

He preferred this cold feeling.

Emotions were like a disease.

Abigail looked at him over her shoulder.

She'd composed herself somewhat, but her eyes were still pink and a little swollen. She furrowed her brows as though confused. "I…didn't even think of that."

Was she lying? Her hands shook visibly as she brushed a wayward piece of hair back from her face. She released her hold on the basket and turned around to face him fully, both of her arms now wrapped in front of her abdomen. The expression on her face hardened as she realized his insinuation.

"Well, if that's the case, go ahead and jump, by all means. Don't mind me. If I've nothing to lose, then give it a try, Your Grace."

Ah, well, Miss Abigail Wright was angry.

He'd not seen her angry before. Weepy, frightened,

charmed, and yes, even sexually aroused, but he'd not seen the woman angry before. Angry and proud.

She gestured toward the corner of the basket where he'd tossed the jumping vest with a nod of her head and then turned her back to him. The pilot raised his brows at Alex in question, but Alex merely shook his head.

Abigail Wright was more woman than he'd realized.

He stepped up beside her putting his hands along the edge of the basket. He could almost physically feel the tension emanating from her. "My apologies."

Abigail raised one hand to wipe at her eyes. "You don't need to apologize. I understand how you might think that." She spoke into the empty air. Now it was she who sounded emotionless.

"I didn't do it to scare you," he said. "I simply wanted to do it."

She slid her eyes toward him without turning her head. "I beg you, don't do it in my presence then, Monfort."

It was Alex's turn to look off into the distance. "I didn't think of how you might react. I suppose I thought you'd think it something of a lark." Just as Hyacinth had when she'd gone out onto the ice without his approval.

A small hand landed atop his. He turned his head just in time to see her swallow hard.

"I'll be taking her back down now, Yer Grace." The pilot was tinkering with the burner. "If you're ready, that is."

Alex nodded his assent and then turned back to watch the skyline of London rise before them. It was unusually clear today, the warmth of the weather precluding the necessity for most homes to build fires. And it was still early.

When he'd proposed to Abigail, he'd not considered having any feelings for her. Feelings were never a good idea. Best to keep things cool—to keep his distance.

Was that possible, though, to have a satisfying sexual relationship with one's wife? Even Elise had become emotional when he'd called things off. And before that she'd become possessive.

Hyacinth had never been possessive. She'd been thrilled when he'd finally directed his attentions elsewhere.

But his relationship with her could hardly have been deemed to have been satisfying sexually. He could count the times they'd been together on less than two hands. And there had not been much satisfaction for either of them. Hell, truth be told, there'd not been any satisfaction in it at all.

He glanced over at Miss Wright.

Miss Abigail Wright.

He liked to think of her thus. He was safer that way. Safer to think of this marriage in terms of saving Miss Wright, rather than taking Abigail to be his wife.

And yet something about her affected him. Looking at her evoked a *physical urge* to take her in his arms. She had been brave this morning. Not only in going along for the flight, but she'd stood up to him. Good God, she'd not only stood up to him, but she'd ordered him not to take the parachute jump. *Ordered him!*

And she'd succeeded.

Oh hell.

If Abigail could handle him so easily, she had nothing to fear from the ton.

****

Penelope was true to her word, and just two days after removing to her parents' house, she made a visit to Cross Hall.

On her Lady Accelerator, no less.

Her eyes were bright and her cheeks flushed with exertion. "Oh, Abigail," she said as they walked the contraption around to the back of the house together. "You must give it a go. The trick is to continue to move your feet as though walking while keeping your head up. If you run, you can lift your feet and glide."

They arrived in an open area, and Penelope handed the contraption over to Abigail. Abigail's first thoughts were that the large thin wheels looked impossible to balance upon and the seat incredibly uncomfortable. In spite of her misgivings, she stepped over the middle bar and straddled the apparatus with one foot on each side of it. Her dress made it impossible to see her feet. "How on earth, Penelope?"

Penelope took hold of the front handles and urged Abigail to scoot onto the seat. With a tremendous amount of faith in her cousin, Abigail slid upward and back. Once sitting, she began to walk the contraption.

Penelope's strength alone prevented her from careening onto her side. "This is impossible!" Abigail declared as Penelope moved around to her side and ordered her to move her feet faster. But Abigail did as she was told and found herself moving ahead of her friend. She went all of about ten feet before toppling over, banging her hip and arm rather painfully into the ground.

She endured a few more attempts until she was able to traverse about twenty or so feet. And it *was* something of a thrill, terrifying and painful though it might be. By the end of the lesson, more than a few scrapes and bruises adorned Abigail and she'd torn her dress. But she'd experienced something singular. Empowerment.

Propelling the Accelerator, or hobbyhorse as some called it, required physical exertion of the rider. It was not at all the same as riding atop a horse. After setting it aside, the ladies found a bench under a shady tree and both sighed. They were worn out and tired, but Abigail wanted to enjoy her cousin's company longer.

"Monfort took me up in a balloon yesterday, if you can imagine." She went on to tell Penelope the entire story of how Monfort had thought to jump out of it and how she herself had experienced something of an apoplexy at the thought of him doing such a dangerous thing. "It's as though he thought nothing of what the people who cared about him would do if he were to be hurt...or worse...as most likely would have been the case had the parachute contraption failed him."

Penelope was looking down at her hands but glanced over at Abigail when she spoke. "Do you? Care for him, that is?"

Without having to think, Abigail nodded. "I do. That's the problem. And he had the nerve to accuse me of only being concerned for my own security."

"Were you?" Penelope asked. "If I were in your predicament, I cannot honestly say that isn't the first thing that would come into my mind." Penelope knew all too well what Abigail would be forced to face if this marriage were to fall through. And if the duke were dead, it would most definitely fall through.

"The crazy thing is," Abigail almost whispered, "all I could imagine, as he stood there attached to that silly contraption, ready to jump to his death, was waking up the next morning to a world without him. He is so full of energy, vitality, I feel as though I absorb some of it each morning when we go riding. It's silly, really, in that most of the time he is critiquing me or telling me to sit up straight, but there are moments, Penelope, when I feel we are growing somewhat close. And I…"

"You what, Abby?"

"I love those moments." It was a difficult admission to make. Frightening in that, even as his wife, she could easily be set aside from him any time after they married. A peer could do such a thing with an inconvenient wife. In fact, it was quite unexceptional.

Penelope didn't respond right away. "So he did not jump after all, then?"

Abigail shook her head. "Thank God, no. We had a bit of a row, and then the pilot brought us back down to the ground. And then Monfort cancelled our riding lesson this morning. Sent me a note explaining that he had some other commitments to attend to."

She'd been very disappointed. Was he going to cancel them indefinitely? Was he so very angry at her outburst? She'd thought they were growing closer, but…He'd wanted to make that ridiculous jump and she'd made such a fuss about it…

"Perhaps you can continue with them after the wedding. From what I hear, he's mad about the sport," Penelope interjected.

"I hope so." Abigail rested her chin upon her hand

as she slumped forward.

And then Penelope rose to her feet. "I'd best head back, or Mother will have an excuse to journey here herself in search of me." She lifted the Accelerator, brushed off some dirt, and climbed onto it confidently.

"Do be careful, Penelope," Abigail urged. "And tell Aunt and Uncle hello for me."

At Penelope's departure, Abigail's spirits deflated considerably. She would need to clean up and prepare for more dancing lessons. Margaret had said it was important that she have absolute confidence in her dancing abilities. She and the duke would be leading off the first set at their prewedding ball, and all eyes would be watching. Margaret told her she mustn't have any doubts in her abilities whatsoever. So they had lengthened the allotted time practicing in the ballroom.

Forcing a determined smile onto her face, Abigail braced herself for the rest of the day. Oh dash it all, who was she kidding—the rest of her life!

Chapter 12

"Abigail, child! Stop your fussing and don your fichu!" Her mother was in top form. Her parents had been in London only three days but had managed to thoroughly disrupt the routine she'd finally gotten accustomed to at Cross Hall.

Their first demand had been for Abigail to remove herself to Aunt and Uncle's house. As excited as they'd been for her to spend the first weeks at a duke's residence, they were adamant now that the last few days before her marriage must be spent under the protection of her own family.

As hectic as the days before their arrival had been, the sheer boredom of time spent with her mother and aunt was nearly enough to drive Abigail batty. They'd insisted she stay indoors with them, coddled. The only time she'd left the townhouse had been for her daily dancing instructions at Cross Hall where she'd seen Margaret only briefly, and her betrothed, not at all.

The extent of her mother's hovering and lack of contact with Monfort elevated her nerves to a level she'd not yet experienced.

Monfort had told her she was more than welcome to go riding with a groom, but that he was too busy to continue instructing her himself. He told her this when she'd made the assumption the lessons would resume a few days after the balloon ride and been so bold as to appear early in the morning to take coffee with him.

He was icing her out again.

And tonight was their prewedding ball.

Margaret had sent a missive for Abigail and her parents to arrive early, as they would be expected to participate in the reception line. But glancing at her mother, Abigail was terrified that all of the lessons she'd taken to shape her own behavior in society would be of no use if her mother could not behave herself.

Her mother's tongue ruled her brain all too often.

She wished she'd considered this earlier, and perhaps even confided in Margaret. She'd been embarrassed though.

And her father was no better. She'd forgotten how he became more morose than usual when forced to spend time in Uncle Hector's company. As long as she could remember, her uncle's titled personage had always had a demoralizing effect on her father. He tended to drink even more than usual and sit in corners, dismissing conversation or activities while looking somewhat dejected. However was he going to behave when faced with an entire ballroom of nobles?

She hoped he had not already dipped into her uncle's liquor this evening.

"I cannot say I approve of today's fashions, Abigail."

Her mother plucked at the gown sent over just this afternoon, the modistes having finally completed their last-minute alterations. It truly was a gorgeous creation. Far too gorgeous for the likes of Abigail.

Fashioned from fine ivory-colored gossamer material, with a tight bodice and wispy sleeves, the waist was high and the skirt draped elegantly, barely brushing the floor. An intricately woven golden lace fell over the underskirt.

The maid, whom Margaret had insisted accompany Abigail to the baron's residence, had styled Abigail's hair elegantly atop her head in a number of braids, all entwined with a golden ribbon that matched the lace on her dress.

The effect surprised even Abigail. Her mother, however, announced the bodice to be too tight and too low. She'd insisted the maid locate a matching fichu in order to cover the cleavage pushed up by Abigail's stays.

Margaret had assured Abigail that the dress was perfectly appropriate.

Just as she tucked in the covering garment, a knock sounded on the door. It was one of her uncle's servants. He carried a package for Abigail, specially delivered from the Duke of Monfort's home.

Abigail's mother snatched the package up and began tearing away at the paper.

"Mother," Abigail protested. "It is from my betrothed. Please give it to me."

Turning away from Abigail's outstretched hands, her mother ignored her and stripped away the last remnants of paper. Abigail could barely make out a long black velvet box as her mother opened it hungrily.

"Mother—" Abigail reached, but her mother turned away further.

"Anything a man deigns to send to an unmarried woman ought to be approved by her mother first." And then dropping onto a nearby chair, Edna Wright set the box aside and opened the missive within.

Her brows furrowed as she read it. "The man is daft, Abigail! Whatever can he mean by this?"

"Let me see it, Mother."

Her mother read through it a few more times before carelessly shoving it in Abigail's direction.

Abigail, it read. *Never forget you are a woman who can fly over rooftops. This stone matched the color of the sky from on high. I am proud of you. —M.*

Abigail shrugged off the fichu and asked her maid to help her with the necklace. It consisted of a delicate gold chain and an oval sapphire pendant. It *did* remind her of their sky. She suppressed a shiver when her maid attached the clasp at the back of her neck. He was not made of ice. *He was not!*

****

The duke's butler escorted Abigail and her parents into the same drawing room where she'd met with Monfort's family upon the first day of her arrival. Monfort stood, and Margaret and Aunt Cecily nodded but remained seated as they entered.

As Monfort's eyes fell upon her, Abigail dipped into the slow, graceful curtsey Margaret had forced her to practice multiple times. She was oblivious to the bobbing curtsey her mother performed beside her and the shallow bow her father made. For Monfort's eyes captured her.

Taking her hand, he raised it to his lips and brushed his mouth across her knuckles. He did not speak, but Aunt Cecily's voice carried across the room.

"You look elegant this evening, Abigail." She spoke in that haughty tone of voice.

Monfort's voice was low. "Very pretty, Abigail." His eyes dipped to her mouth, and then to the stone that rested above her cleavage.

Abigail reached for the stone, unthinking, and spoke breathlessly. "It is, isn't it? Thank you, Monfort. The necklace was a thoughtful gift. I've never owned anything quite so beautiful."

"It'll be the first of many such treasures, I hope, Abigail." Her mother glanced meaningfully at the duke.

Alex was more than a little taken aback by Abigail's appearance.

Tonight, she looked…breathtaking. The gold of her dress was not quite as vibrant as the golden highlights in her hair, and her bodice exposed creamy, smooth skin. He appreciated how the whimsical curls artfully arranged to fall around her neck emphasized the fragility of her person. She looked soft and delicate.

And surprisingly, she puzzled him. How was it that she could be so vulnerable, cowering even, at some times, and yet so courageous at others?

Tonight she was somehow…both.

Her mother, on the other hand, was a blight. She'd been introduced to him, of course, when she'd come to Cross Hall to collect Abigail, but he'd not taken much mind of the women then. Tonight, however, he noticed a derision in the way the woman glanced at Abigail.

Her father eagerly accepted the drink one of the footmen offered him and looked on as his wife grasped Abigail's wrist tightly and pulled her over to the settee. "Be careful, Abigail!" she carped. "You're going to wrinkle your gown. Sit up straight. What must Lady Margaret and Lady Cecily think of you, slouching like that?"

Abigail hadn't been slouching, she'd been shrinking. She summoned a bright smile and addressed his sister.

"Margaret, Lady Cecily, thank you again for all of the time and effort you have both put forth in assisting me the past few weeks. I hope it has not been in vain. I'll do my best to ensure it was not."

Margaret, after catching Alex's eye briefly and sending him some sort of silent message, smiled graciously at Abigail. "It has been our pleasure, Abigail. You have been an excellent prodigy."

Edna Wright nearly snorted but somehow just managed to stifle it when she caught Alex glaring at her.

"The guests will begin arriving shortly." Margaret continued. "I wanted all of you to be here early, of course, as you are to be a part of the receiving line." And then she turned her haughtiest stare toward Mrs. Wright. "There will be a long line of guests, and I must direct you to speak only briefly with each of them." She paused and waited for agreement from Mrs. Wright before continuing. "Keep your greeting simple. Many of the guests are titled. You will make your curtsey, say that you are pleased they could attend, and wish them a delightful evening. Do not address any questions they might have about Abigail or her past. If they deign to comment, merely smile, turn away, and address the next guest."

"Well, I would never!" Mrs. Wright gasped. Obviously, she wanted to be outraged at Margaret's instructions but knew herself to be quite outranked— and outclassed.

Margaret smiled at Abigail again. "Abigail, you do look beautiful tonight. I have every faith in you."

Thank you, Margaret. Alex caught his sister's eye

again and gave an almost imperceptible nod.

And then the sound of carriages outside signified the arrival of early guests. Most likely a line would have already formed near the entrance. It had been years since he'd known anxiety over a social occasion, but for Abigail's sake he experienced a twinge of unease. He strode toward Abigail and offered her his arm. "Shall we face the dragons, then?"

She nodded demurely and stood, placing her tiny hand on his arm. Alex reached over and covered it with his own. They both wore gloves, but he could feel the tension in her. He patted her hand reassuringly, and she raised her lashes to look at him in surprise. And then she chuckled softly.

"What is it?" he wondered what amusing thought had run through her mind.

"Just that…" She gently nudged him. "I don't think even the fiercest of dragons would dare breathe fire upon the Duke of Ice."

Alex shook his head. She'd referred to his nickname as though it was a joke between just the two of them. As though she knew the truth of it: he was only a man.

****

Margaret had not exaggerated in saying that many of the guests were titled. If one did not hold a title themselves, then they were either sister, brother, or heir to one. Not half an hour into the welcoming ritual and Abigail's brain was already overwhelmed with new names and faces.

It was pleasantly surprising to see some familiar faces in that several of the guests who'd been at Raven's Park for the summer house party had been invited. The Ravensdales were present, of course, and Abigail delighted to see that Lady Natalie was well recovered from her harrowing experience earlier in the summer and her fiancé, the Earl of Hawthorne, attended with her.

There were a few other dukes: the Duke and Duchess of Cortland, a newlywed couple; the Duke of Waters; and the Duke of McDuff. For a brief moment, a sense of panic threatened when she was introduced to the Marquess of Lockley and Viscount Danbury. These were the fellows who'd shown up at Raven's Park along with Damien Farley. But Mr. Farley was not with them. Thank heavens! Abigail had not given any names to Margaret or Monfort. What if they'd actually invited him?

Upon making her curtseys to the two well-dressed gentlemen, she glanced at Monfort. He seemed well acquainted with the viscount, even shaking his hand heartily. The exchange had the effect of reassuring her.

Perhaps it was merely Monfort's steady presence.

He stood close and quite often took hold of her hand to impart some of his own strength. He'd glanced at her curiously just then, but the moment passed quickly as they were obliged to welcome an elderly couple who were next in line. What had Monfort said their names were? Good Lord, she was never going to remember them all!

The reception queue drew out for all of fifty minutes but could have very well been hours. She experienced relief when Monfort finally drew her away. It would not be necessary for them to greet the stragglers.

Her reprieve, however, dissipated when she

realized it was now time for them to enter the ballroom.

Abigail had danced in the ballroom several times, of course. She'd spent literally hours of time in the grand room practicing. But tonight brightly lit chandeliers, adorned with hundreds of candles, along with profusions of flowers throughout transformed it into a magical setting. An orchestra played softly at the dais toward the far end of the hall, and the terrace doors were thrown open so guests could enjoy the fountains and moonlight outside.

Clasping the duke's arm, Abigail knew the time had come to leave his side and face these people on her own. This was the moment she'd been dreading. She must release him so that he could mingle alone. Removing her hand from the safety of his escort, she curtseyed with practiced ease.

"The dancing is not to commence for an hour still." His eyes glimmered. "I shall return then."

"I look forward to that."

And then he was gone, and Abigail's mother appeared at her side. *Oh, where was Margaret? Where was Penelope?*

"Abigail, I wish you had left on the fichu. The neckline on that dress is borderline vulgar. Did you see the headdress on the Duchess of Waters? One would think the quality would show a bit more taste." Edna Wright had dressed somewhat austerely for the evening. She'd attempted to persuade Abigail to dress similarly. Thank heavens, Margaret had insisted on sending over the new gown. One did not usurp Margaret's authority on such matters.

Her mother pulled Abigail toward a wall lined with cushioned chairs and settees. "I need to sit down,

Abigail. All of that standing has caused my gout to flare up."

Abigail looked around helplessly for Margaret again. She was supposed to mingle now. It would not be good for her to be seen sitting with her mother, with old maids and chaperones. She was one of the guests of honor! But her mother's grip clamped onto her like a vise, and she could not very well have a tug of war right there, could she?

And then, as though the universe heard her, Lady Natalie Spencer appeared.

"Miss Wright! What a delightful turn of events for you! I cannot believe you are actually going to wed the duke. And I must tell you that I am going to take all of the credit for this marriage." Addressing Abigail's mother, she smiled brightly. "It was I who brought the two of them together, you must know." The girl's eyes sparkled, but something brittle lurked behind her charm and beauty.

Abigail could not help relaxing upon Lady Natalie's refreshing openness, though. She freed her hand from her mother's grasp and curtseyed before the esteemed earl's daughter. "And you are to marry Lord Hawthorne. Whoever would have guessed that two weddings would be the result of your mother's house party? When is your wedding? Have you and Lord Hawthorne set a date yet?" And then, just before she turned to introduce her mother to Lady Natalie, the older woman spoke up.

"My lady, how positively delightful to meet you. And yes, what a coincidence it was, was it not, that both of you girls quite nearly ruined yourselves at that same house party. Lucky for both of you the gentlemen turned out to be honorable. Unlike the first time, with Abigail."

Lady Natalie's eyes flew open wide at such a faux pas on Mrs. Wright's part. Abigail steered her mother toward her original destination. "Please, Mama, go sit down. Your gout, remember?"

But her mama chose to ignore her gout for now.

"When are you to be wed, my lady?" her mother queried the lovely young woman, uncaring that she'd not only insulted her own daughter, but the daughter of an earl. "I do not believe we've seen an invitation as of yet, have we, Abby dear?"

But Lady Natalie did not take offense. Abigail had been right in thinking, when she'd first met the girl, that she was not only a lovely person, but a *nice* person. "Oh, I'm quite certain my aunt and mother sent an invitation around to the baron's town residence. You and Mr. Wright are most certainly included." Turning back to Abigail she answered, "Lord Hawthorne and I are to be wed two weeks from tomorrow." But her brow furrowed. She did not resemble a carefree bride-to-be.

Somewhat satisfied with Lady Natalie's response, Abigail's mother excused herself to make herself comfortable on one of the loveseats which lined the wall. Left alone, Abigail leaned toward Lady Natalie conspiratorially. "I can hardly wait for it to be over. I have never been so terrified in my entire life!"

Lady Natalie laughed warmly. "I, too, am terrified. It seems there are a thousand things to go wrong! I love making the decisions, but then I second-guess myself. So many people are invited! Too many!" And then the uneasy expression crossed her lovely features. Despite having met only briefly, the two girls shared an unexpected bond. "I'm ever so anxious he'll change his mind."

Her words lit new anxiety in Abigail. What if *her betrothed* changed *his* mind?

He would not. He could seem cold and emotionless at times, but he would not change his mind.

How could Lady Natalie fear such a thing? Perhaps because she herself had jilted the Duke of Cortland last spring.

But Abigail had seen the way Lord Hawthorne watched Lady Natalie. "He will not, Lady Natalie. Anyone with eyes in their head can see that he adores you. You must know you have nothing to fear."

Lady Natalie smiled and then winced. "I hope you are right, Abigail."

The girls chattered on about other wedding concerns for several moments before various gentlemen approached to add their names to both of their dance cards. Yes, both of them. Abigail was shocked, but Lady Natalie took it with equanimity.

And then her duke approached. He strode across the room just as he should—proud, flawlessly attired, and utterly confident—arrogant even. Which was only proper.

The moment to lead off the dancing had arrived. It was to be just the two of them. All the other guests would be looking on, watching, waiting for her to take a wrong step. Her heart raced, and her breaths grew shallow. Where had all the air gone? Ringing threatened to fill her ears as he positioned one hand at her waist. The quartet, which had been playing softly, fell silent as the entire orchestra poised to begin playing.

She watched his mouth move as though from a great distance but for the life of her could not hear a word he said.

And then he leaned in and whispered, "Rest easy, my dear. You've no need to worry." When she still didn't move, he leaned in again. "Won't you trust me?" And with a twinkle in his eyes, he added, "I'm a fabulous dancer."

He'd used that endearment again: my dear. And he'd boasted of his dancing skills. With a short laugh, she exhaled.

Smiling tremulously, she placed her free hand on his shoulder. He grasped her other hand in his—not too tightly but with just enough confidence to convey some of his courage to her. "Of course." *I have since the day we met.*

Margaret had insisted the dance be a waltz. "Much more fashionable than a reel," she'd maintained. "The two of you are not ducklings just out of the nest. It will be most appropriate for a couple of your age."

The orchestra sprang to life, and Monfort took control. And he had been right, he really was a fabulous dancer. Abigail hardly had to think as he took long steps, guiding and twirling her around the shiny parquet floor. Before she knew it, other couples joined them.

The terrifying moment had passed, and it hadn't been all that terrifying at all.

"I didn't faint." Abigail blurted the words before thinking.

Monfort chuckled and swept them around a few of the other couples. His hand lay firmly upon her waist, making it impossible for her miss a step. Her body responded to his direction perfectly. Abigail was not so confident as to think this was because of her own skill. But she was surprised to realize she was enjoying herself. In fact, dancing with her future husband was more enjoyable than practically anything she'd experienced before.

Except for those moments when the balloon had ascended and he'd wrapped his arms around her from behind. In spite of her fear at the unknown, at being far above the ground, she'd felt safe with him. And she'd experienced exhilaration.

Just as she did now.

Perhaps their wedding night would not be something awful to endure. Perhaps it would be something…dare she contemplate the thought? Pleasant? Enjoyable? Even…wonderful?

But then the music stopped. Monfort tilted one side of his mouth up, ever so slightly, before leaning down to her and speaking quietly, "I hope I've lived up to my boast?"

Abigail held his eyes and nodded. "Thank you, Monfort. The dance was lovely."

He escorted her back to where her mother and now, Aunt Edith, were seated. He did not speak to either of them. Rather he confirmed with Abigail that he would partner her again for the supper dance and then pivoted and withdrew.

Ah, if only the ball could have ended then.

Chapter 13

Something was decidedly off.

Foreboding pricked at the back of his neck. Standing unaccompanied for a few moments, observing, Alex noticed a subtle wave of excitement fluttering through the guests. Had one of Abigail's family spoken out of turn? He'd been concerned having had first-hand experience of Baron Riverton's lack of discretion. The ballroom overflowed.

He'd expected a crush, but had Margaret really invited all of these people? Most likely not. It was not all that exceptional for the uninvited to attach themselves to legitimate guests in order to gain entry. He ought to have told his butler to show no leniency tonight.

It was too late, now, however.

Against his own inclination, he casually mingled with various clusters of guests hoping to discover if salacious words about Abigail were being brandied about. But of course, nobody would speak of such a thing to him.

Until he found Hugh Chesterton. Or, rather, until Danbury found him.

"Why, in God's name, would you allow him entry?"

"Who?" Alex demanded.

"Damien Farley," Danbury said in disgust.

Abigail's attacker was in attendance at her prewedding ball? Alex had become more certain than ever that Farley was the one. And as if his own conclusion was not sufficient enough, Danbury confirmed it with his next words.

"It was he who drove Miss Wright from London, I believe. The bastard practically admitted as much to me this spring." He frowned at the look on Alex's face. "I figured you knew. You did know, did you not? That she'd been ruined as a girl?"

Danbury's words were not meant to demean Abigail. Nonetheless, a slow burn of anger rose inside Alex. Abigail had not been ruined, by God, she'd been raped! And the bastard was here, inside his home!

"Where is he?" he ground through clenched teeth.

Danbury glanced about. "He came in about twenty minutes ago, but I haven't seen him since. Oh, wait, he is dancing with Mrs. Gormley. Good God, Monfort, whoever drew up your guest list?"

A cloud of red swarmed Alex's vision. Elise Gormley had not been invited either. And Margaret would not have invited Damien Farley. No wonder the ball was such a crush. More than one uninvited guest had crashed the ball. He would have them both ejected immediately. Damn it, he would do it himself.

His gaze settled on Farley and held steady as he approached the man who'd nearly ruined Abigail Wright's life. He did not stop to think of the consequences of an altercation. He experienced none of the indifference that had taken hold of him over the past few years. He had but one purpose and would not be dissuaded.

Grasping Farley's arm, Alex jerked the vermin away from his own former mistress. He did not take note of the pleased expression on Elise Gormley's face. All of his attention focused upon Farley, obviously already well into his cups.

The man snarled a smirk in Monfort's direction, and then made the mistake of speaking. "What's the matter, Monfort? You cannot be upset that I'm poaching your leftovers. It's only fitting, wouldn't you say, seeing as you are marrying mine?"

In his mind, Alex conjured unwanted images of Farley forcing himself on a much younger and innocent Abigail. Of Farley forcing his mouth on hers. Of Farley's clumsy hands lifting her gown.

His control snapped.

He acted not as a duke, but as a man.

And he was not even aware of his own intentions until his fists began stinging as he meted out a vicious punishment on the younger, heftier fellow. It could have been mere seconds, or perhaps several minutes, before several sets of strong arms pulled him off the blighter's nearly inert body. Blood gushed from Farley's nose and mouth, a few teeth had dislodged and were God knows where, and the man was crying and begging for mercy.

Alex wasn't done, though. He lunged forward a second time, only to find himself again restrained by the men who'd come up behind him. "Let me at him. The bastard deserves to die." A growl tore through him as he broke free to launch another attack upon the bully who'd hurt Abigail so badly years before. In that moment, Alex did not care if he killed the man. In fact, it would likely be the best outcome he could imagine.

This time he set his fists to the man's midsection.

Again, arms from behind pulled him off the villain.

The Duke of Cortland, along with Lords Hawthorne and Danbury, managed to bring a halt to Alex's rage.

"You've made your point, Monfort. If you kill him, there'll be an inquiry. Even *you* cannot murder a man in the middle of a ball without consequences." Hugh's calm reasoning penetrated Alex's haze of anger.

"He'll not be the same after this, Monfort. Allow Cortland and me to take over from here. We'll force him to leave England for good. He deserved every punch you've given him. Let him live with himself and his sins on another continent." Lord Hawthorne's words indicated a thorough understanding of Monfort's motivation. He gripped Alex's shoulder tightly. "I only wish I'd gone at him first."

Elise stepped forward, pushing herself through the men who'd gathered around the spectacle. Her eyes sparkled with a manic sort of excitement. "I didn't know you cared, Monfort. Don't you know I'll always take you back? Farley is nothing to me, darling."

What the hell?

Did she think…?

Had she thought he did this for her?

And then the gathering parted again, and through it he saw Abigail's large eyes fixed upon the woman he'd once enjoyed often and thoroughly. A roar of murmured whispers spread throughout the room as Cortland and Hawthorne dragged Farley away. A few footmen had stepped forward and were mopping the floor with some handy linens.

Without thinking, Alex took the drink Danbury

handed to him. The impact of what he'd just done slowly settling upon him.

At first, Abby was confused. She did not know what to think.

Had she been asked even one day before if she would have liked to see her former attacker punished, she would have said, of course. The thought would have given her tremendous satisfaction.

But seeing Monfort so utterly out of control, his eyes wild and fists pounding relentlessly, gave her pause. This was unlike him. Had he done this *for her*?

For a fraction of a second, a warmth spread through her. He'd admitted to wanting justice for her. He must care somewhat, mustn't he? In order to relinquish his proud and rigid control?

But then she heard that woman speak. *I didn't know you cared, Monfort. Don't you know I'll always take you back? Farley is nothing to me, darling.*

Whispers carried shamelessly across the room.

"Mrs. Elise Gormley, Monfort's mistress…"

"Her protector for over two years…"

Abigail glanced from the sophisticated beauty who'd been dancing with Farley to her betrothed.

Monfort's eyes looked haunted.

What had this been about? Did he love this woman? Had he been keeping a mistress all along? *Oh, Abigail, you stupid, stupid fool!* Of course he had a mistress. A man, a duke such as Monfort, would have his most primitive of needs met regardless of a timid fiancée.

But did he love Mrs. Gormley?

Of course he did! Why else would he fly into such an uncharacteristic rage? Jealousy was an extremely powerful emotion. Mrs. Gormley had been dancing with Damien Farley.

And Monfort had attacked her partner.

The display of violence had nothing to do with Abigail. She'd not told him the name of the man who ruined her.

He'd been fighting for Mrs. Gormley.

Margaret appeared as though from thin air. Without saying a word, she grasped Abigail's elbow and steered her away from the dance floor.

No more dancing tonight.

"I don't know what came over him, Abigail. In all of my life, I've never seen him turn as violent as this." And in a more soothing tone, "Don't worry, dear, all will be just fine. Probably just too much drink and an unfortunate disagreement. Not at all well done of my brother, though. Not at all well done."

Abigail's lessons had not been for naught. She lifted her chin and met Margaret's eyes. "We've spent hundreds of pounds for the food laid out in the dining room. Shall we announce supper early? Or send these people away?"

Margaret blinked and then nodded slowly. "You are right." Signaling a nearby servant over, she whispered instructions into his ear before turning again to Abigail. "They'll announce supper immediately. Perhaps we can salvage what is left of the evening." Looking closely at Abigail, she frowned. "You are certain you are not too overset? I can make excuses for you, you know."

Abigail nodded. "I am fine for now. But I think Monfort has left."

Understanding Abigail's concern, Margaret waved

her husband, the Earl of Clive, over. "Darling, Miss Wright needs an escort into the supper room. Please do the honors for me? Monfort, I believe, will be indisposed for the remainder of the evening."

Giving Margaret a warm look of approval, he nodded and then winged an arm for Abigail to take. "Of course." Winking at Abigail, he smiled charmingly. "Shall we, Miss Wright?"

Abigail endured supper by nodding and smiling, experiencing it all as though she were watching from outside her own body. Nobody dared broach the subject of the duke, her *betrothed's,* attack, nor his absence. That would be bad ton.

But they were all speaking of it.

And speculating.

Eyes averted from her far too easily.

Of course they would all be talking about it. Whoever would have imagined that the *Duke of Ice* would put on such an exhibition? As she went through the motions of making inane conversation in a vain attempt to divert attention from the earlier spectacle, she herself endured a number of conflicting emotions.

Part of her wanted to lash out at him for ruining everything. After all the lessons and training she'd undergone so as to not make a spectacle of herself, how dare he make such a scene over his mistress? At their prewedding ball, no less? He was a bastard! A cad! A phony and a fake!

How dare he propose marriage while having relations with another woman? How dare he speak of honor while in the midst of an affair?

But then other thoughts defended him. He'd never spoken to her of love. He'd never promised fidelity or any other sort of husbandly regard. He'd known she was in a bind. He'd spoken of having been the cause of her scandal.

He'd offered her protection.

Nothing more.

And then her heart cried out.

He'd bought her a horse and given her riding lessons. (Heart).

Only because you demanded them. (Head).

He took you up on a balloon, to help you to conquer your fears. (Heart).

So that you would not embarrass him. (Head)

He kissed you. He wrapped his arms around you. (Heart).

Silence.

And on and on the inner argument continued.

They were to be married tomorrow.

Abigail nodded at some unknown question as she contemplated the status of her would-be wedding.

Was he going to cry off? She'd be ruined forever if he did that. Ought *she* to cry off? She glanced over to where her mother and father chatted amiably with a few friendly guests. She could not return to Biddeford Corners. She could not live as a dependent upon her parents any longer. She would go through with the wedding.

As long as the duke was still willing. She turned her head and smiled at another mindless comment. The evening proved to be the longest of her life.

****

Alex's sister took hold of Abigail's arm and led her away from the remnants of the scene he'd created. He then raised the glass to his lips and downed the liquor

229

handed him in one satisfying swallow.

Elise was standing before him, one gloved hand upon his chest. "Oh, Monfort, that was brilliant! I had no idea your affections persisted, my darling." She glanced around the room before leaning closer still, "Shall we go to my house now? I've missed you so!" She pressed herself against him.

Steeling his eyes, he gently, but firmly, pushed the lady away from his person. "You misunderstand, Mrs. Gormley. You are not the cause of my disagreement with Farley. The man had it coming to him for other reasons entirely. As I am certain you received no invitation, I'd appreciate you making your way home, alone, at this time. Your presence here is an abomination to my future wife. Whyever would you think you might be welcome?"

Her eyes flared just a moment before she purred once again. "Monfort, you needn't be so proud with me. I realize—"

But Alex would not allow her to finish. If Abigail knew Elise was his former mistress...If she suspected...Oh, hell, his fiancée already suffered enough self-doubt. She most certainly mustn't be allowed to think he'd invited his former mistress to their wedding ball.

Especially when he'd made a spectacle of himself *for her*!

"If you do not leave on your own, I shall have you physically removed...by a servant." He flicked her a stern look. "*Now,* Elise. As I told you last spring, we are over. I'm sorry if you have misinterpreted my actions tonight, but my mind has not changed in the least. I have moved on. You must as well." He lifted one arm and gestured for a nearby footman. When the man neared he said, "Niles, escort Mrs. Gormley to her coach."

Without waiting for a response, he spun on one heel. Where was Abigail? She had most likely absented herself from the ball, retreating to her uncle's house. She would be too overset to remain. Margaret, he knew, would salvage what remained of the evening. Most likely, his sister would have Clive announce a premature end to the ball. Or not. At that moment, he didn't really give a damn.

Alex would not stay around to bid the guests farewell.

Exiting through the terrace doors, he headed around back to the mews. Damn his eyes, but he did not regret his actions. Farley more than deserved it. It had taken far too long for anybody to punish the villain for his actions years ago.

No, Alex did not regret it.

He did, however, regret that Elise had been the person dancing with the blackguard in the moments before justice had been served. Society would have a field day with all of it. And, goddamn it, he was to be wed tomorrow.

Stepping into the stables and bending forward, Alex grabbed his knees and took a few deep breaths. A drop of red appeared on the newly swept wooden floor. He raised a hand to his lip, and it came away wet with blood. Farley had managed to land a few blows himself. Alex's left eye throbbed.

This was not what he'd planned for this evening.

"You're going to have a shiner tomorrow, Monfort." Danbury's voice interrupted the litany of swear words currently running through his head. "I've a side of meat for you to put on it."

Alex stood up and accepted the cold piece of beef held out to him.

"One question." Danbury raised his brows. "Did you pummel the bastard because of what he did to your fiancée years ago or was it because of his involvement with Elise Gormley?"

A damned impertinent question. "What the fuck do you think?" he answered gruffly.

"What *I* think is of no matter. The trouble is everybody in that blasted ballroom thinks it's because of Mrs. Gormley, your fiancée included."

Alex touched his eye and winced. More due to Danbury's words than physical pain. *Goddamn it,* this situation had become far too complicated. It should not matter what the hell Miss Wright thought. It should not matter whether he chose to maintain a mistress or not. He was a bloody duke, for God's sake.

"She can believe whatever she likes," he said impatiently. "It's not a bloody love match, for Christ's sake." As soon as he spoke the words, guilt beset him.

Because it *did* matter—what she thought that is.

She trusted him.

And for the love of God, he'd done it for her. He'd done something that ought to have been done ages ago.

"I did it to punish Farley. He more than ruined Miss Wright years ago. He forced himself upon her, and nobody did a damn thing about it." Why was he telling Danbury this? Where had his control gone to?

"So Mrs. Gormley had nothing to do with it." Danbury stated. Handing Alex a handkerchief, he added, "Here, take this, your lip is bleeding all over the place. You'll make a colorful groom come tomorrow morning."

"I ought to call the whole thing off," Alex said wishfully, "take her up to Gretna, and have it be done with there."

Danbury chuckled. "Why don't you?"

But Alex was already shaking his head. "We decided on a proper wedding to put an end to the scandal surrounding her. The only way to face this situation is to go ahead as planned."

"I don't envy you, my friend." Danbury pulled a flask out of his jacket. "The least I can do is celebrate your last night of freedom with you. Shall we head over to one of the clubs?"

Alex considered his options. Return to the blasted ball and face polite society after the spectacle he'd made of himself or retreat upstairs to his chambers for what promised to be a sleepless night. The obvious choice, of course, was to drink himself senseless with Danbury.

"Lead the way, good man, lead the way."

****

Abigail climbed into one of the duke's coaches along with her parents and then leaned back into the plush upholstery. Tonight had been, although not the worst in her life, among the top three. She'd heard the gossip but had done her best to hold her head high. She'd even given the cut direct to a matron who'd had the gall to comment upon Monfort's absence.

Her head pounded, her neck ached, and her slippers pinched her toes something awful.

And her heart was bleeding.

She'd known the duke had no affection for her.

He'd proposed out of his sense of duty and honor. What had he said? How could she forget? *I proposed to you because I had committed an egregious error in judgment where you are concerned. And my actions were dishonorable. My own sense of honor demands expiation. Marriage is the most effective way to do so.*

She nearly choked on the sob rising in her throat. But she could not cry with her mother there. She needed to press forward bravely. She instead looked up at her mother and smiled. Her father had already nodded off, and soft snores hummed from his corner. "Well, I'm certainly glad that's over. Are you as tired as I am, Mother?"

Her mother let out a short huff. "To think Lady Margaret thought that *I* would say something scandalous, or untoward, and then her brother creates such a spectacle. And with his mistress, no less! I don't blame you for putting up with him, Abigail. He is a duke, after all. And you shall not want for anything. Did you realize he has settled an annuity upon your father and myself? We spoke this evening, and we are proud you've managed to net such a lofty gentleman. And as I've said, you shall not want for anything. And really, if he has a mistress, you shall not be forced to perform the deed so often yourself. Give him an heir and a spare, and you will be left alone after that. At least we know you are good at childbirth." She chuckled at her own joke.

Every word her mother spoke twisted a knife in Abigail's gut. For, although she'd known the duke did not love her, she'd wished to make something more of her marriage. She'd wanted affection between the two of them. How was she to endure intimacy knowing he was enamored of another woman? She knew she was already tarnished, but to share him with another…

The act was so *very* intimate. And allowing her person to be violated thusly without trust and intimacy would be unbearable.

But she'd promised him.

"Abigail? Abigail? Are you listening to me?"

Abigail glanced back up at her mother. "I'm sorry, Mama. I am more tired than I'd thought. What did you ask me?"

"I was telling you that I did not intend to give you the talk…the one about what a wife is to do with her husband on their wedding night. You know, because you've already experienced it for yourself. Nothing I can say that you don't already know."

Her mother's words ought to have hurt, ought to have drawn a bout of tears, but the pain of the evening had left her feeling numb. Thankfully, blessedly numb.

She wanted to be alone. Only then would she wrap herself in a blanket and allow herself to feel the pain. But for now she stared out the window and saw only darkness.

"You are quite right at that, Mama," she said dully. "Nothing I don't already know."

Chapter 14

"Hugh—" Hiccup. "Danbury, the sun is on the horizon. It's my wedding day already." Alex peered through gritty eyes just enough to make out the hazy image of his butler. Although the man stood at attention holding the door wide, the rest of the house rocked alarmingly to the left and then to the right quite indiscriminately. Alex blinked until it settled and then grasping the door frame, and then a wall, he entered Cross Hall.

"See, I tol' you we had plenty o' time, Monfort." Danbury's mouth apparently wasn't functioning normally either.

Both men leaned upon each other for support. When Danbury nearly toppled over, Alex steadied them, and when Alex lost *his* balance, Danbury miraculously kept them from falling. They'd spent the entire night traversing from White's to Brooks's and then on to some other, less elevated, establishments, each time emerging deeper into their cups than they'd been before. A few familiar fellows joined them for most of the night, Lords Hawthorne and even Cortland, but Alex could not remember the names of the others.

He grasped the doorframe again to stop it from swaying and then allowed the butler to assist him along the foyer. "Set my good friend up in one of the guest rooms, Montgomery." He formed the words carefully, his mouth not quite responding to his brain's instruction. "One o' the finest fellows of my acquaintance."

The butler and footman dragged him across the foyer until his valet appeared to guide him upstairs.

"Your Grace," Villiars was saying. "You are to be wed in less than four hours. You can only rest for a short while, and then we need to get you cleaned up and over to the church! Lady Clive is mad with worry."

And then Margaret appeared, coiffed and already dressed for such an early hour. "Oh, thank God, you've returned." Her arms flew around him. "I've been so worried. Thank the heavens Abigail is not here to see you thusly. She would be frantic!" And then, pulling away from him, she made a disgusted face. "You reek. I could kill you! And your eye!" She stared at him with a combination of horror and disapproval. "And your lip is swollen! Oh, dear God, we've got to get you cleaned up."

Alex scratched his head, trying to follow his sister's lengthy monologue. "Plenty o' time, Meggie."

Her eyes flew wide open after he'd spoken. "You are out of your mind with drink, Monfort." Turning her head, she shouted directions at the servants. "Coffee, bring plenty of coffee to His Grace's chambers immediately. And Villiars, you have a bath prepared? Yes! Very well. We must get His Grace sobered up and clean. And see what you can do about his face. It's a godawful mess."

"It'll be jus' fine, Meggie." Alex tried again to reassure his sister as he was pulled up the long staircase. "How many stairs are there? I don' member there being this many las' night."

But Margaret ignored him. She threw her hands in the air and merely shouted, "You'll be the death of me yet!"

It took a considerable amount of tugging and dragging, but eventually Alex arrived in his chambers. When he saw his bed, in a surprisingly agile motion he climbed the step and threw himself on top of the coverlet. As his head hit the pillow, Villiars tugged at his boots.

"I can allow you to lie there for one hour, Your Grace. Any longer and her ladyship will have my head."

"Iss fine...fine," Alex muttered into a pillow. He wanted to rest, but the bed suddenly began spinning. This must be the sensation he might have experienced had he jumped from the balloon, before being caught by the parachute.

Except this whirling motion was getting out of hand.

Crawling to the edge of the bed, Alex moaned. Villiars just barely managed to arrive in time with a chamber pot before Alex heaved up what must have been the entire contents of his stomach.

"Probably for the best, Your Grace," Villiars tutted, "getting most of the spirits out of your system. That way the drink should wear off more quickly."

This did not feel like it was for the best. In fact, this was the worst Alex had felt in years. Stupid thing to have done, really, consuming so much scotch—and brandy—and wine—and...he couldn't remember what else. Too much everything, really. Oh yes, gin. There had been some gin. Horrible stuff.

And then his stomach convulsed again.

After a knock on the door, a footman entered with what smelled like a pot of coffee. The aroma was just enough to bring on another bout of retching. "Oh, hell." Alex spoke into the disgusting pot being held in front of him. "Oh, hell."

****

Just a mile away, a small sense of relief ebbed into Abigail when the sun finally made its appearance. She'd slept little. Not at all, really. Tossing and turning with worry, sadness, and yes, anger. She tried desperately to be optimistic about this day, but a stubborn, selfish part inside of her grew louder and louder. It was telling herself that she deserved to be happy. She deserved to *matter*.

And then another, calmer voice interjected to argue that this marriage would give her more than she ever could have hoped for while living at Raebourne with her parents.

Along with her scoundrel of a husband, she would gain a sister! And nephews! While staying at Cross Hall, she'd often found time to steal away to the nursery for a few moments at least once a day to hold and play with little Michael and Christopher. They were adorable!

And she could look forward to having her own children after all.

A sob escaped her upon this thought. Always— always the memory of having her own flesh and blood ripped away from her.

A good deal of the night she'd wept silently. Over the years, she'd perfected the talent of crying without making a sound. By morning, her pillow was quite damp and her eyes red and puffy, but she'd awakened no one.

Abigail turned and hung her bare feet over the side of the bed. Slipping off the edge, which was farther down than she'd remembered, Abigail tiptoed across the cool floor to stare out the window.

The sky was still mostly dark, but a hint of red, orange, and pink glimmered on the horizon. A few stars still twinkled. What was Monfort doing right now? What was he thinking? Did he regret his proposal? Most likely. Mrs. Elise Gormley was a glamorous and beautiful woman. When Margaret pulled Abigail away from Monfort last night, her last sight of him had been of the woman throwing herself into his arms.

Had he gone to her last night?

Abigail forced herself to breathe as that possibility hit her. She held no claim on his person—nor his emotions—and of course he'd never promised her affection.

A quick knock on the door and then Penelope's face peeked in. "You are up? I thought I heard a sound in here." Her face disappeared for a moment. "Fetch the hot chocolate and biscuits, Harriette, will you? Miss Wright is awake now."

Penelope slipped inside, wearing only her nightdress and dressing gown, and pattered over to where Abigail was standing. "Oh, Abby, you've had a dreadful night, haven't you?"

Abigail shook her head. She thought her tears had all but dried up, but apparently a few more would demand escape. "Oh, Penelope," was all she managed before moving into her cousin's arms.

"Hush." Penelope smoothed Abigail's hair and

rubbed her back. "You must remember, Abby, who it was that your duke beat into a pulp last night. From what I understand, he set Mrs. Gormley aside last spring. It may have simply been a coincidence that she was the one dancing with Farley."

Abigail pulled back and blinked several times. "It seems too much to hope for."

Penelope tilted her head to one side. "Perhaps. But would he have beaten Damien Farley so severely for merely dancing with his ex-mistress? Husbands and wives dance with people who are not their spouses all the time. In fact, it is expected. Can you imagine if they only danced with one other? What a dreadful bore it would be! But if Monfort were to somehow have gotten wind that it was Farley who'd ruined you all those years ago, I think it highly likely he would wish to punish him. Monfort seems an honorable fellow. He's marrying you, after all, you ninny!"

Abigail choked as ironic laughter caught in her throat. "That is true," Abigail said, retrieving the handkerchief she'd already used throughout the night and dabbing it at her eyes.

"Your eyes!" Penelope exclaimed, appalled. "We need to soak them in lavender water to calm the redness. What will your groom think?"

Her devoted cousin threw open the drapes and gestured for Abigail to lie on the bed. She then dipped a cloth into the basin on the dresser before hovering at her side. "Close your eyes." She pressed the cool cloth firmly against Abigail's eyelids. "And for God's sake, no more crying."

"How long will it take?" Abigail mumbled, trying to hold still so the cloth wouldn't dislodge.

"Not long; a quarter of an hour ought to do it. It won't remove all the swelling, but it will help. And it will make you feel better." Penelope must have sat down on the chair by her bed as her voice drifted away. "I think you were wonderful last night, by the way. Surprisingly, even your mama managed to avoid saying anything mortifying."

"I thought if I left early, matters would appear even worse. It was bad enough form, wouldn't you think, for Monfort to depart?" She wasn't sure of this. She was not familiar with all that a duke could get away with.

"Oh, pox on him." Abigail could picture Penelope waving her hand through the air. "I think you were brave to have stayed until the guests began leaving. And you looked so lovely last night, Abigail. You are going to make a wonderful duchess. I don't think the duke yet realizes what a gem he has in you." And then Penelope fell silent for a moment. "Or perhaps he has."

Both girls pondered the idea. But only for a moment or two.

"What makes you think that?" Abigail asked timidly into the silence.

Another pause. "He flew into quite the rage when he went after Farley. It was not a cold-blooded sort of punishment. Rather a fit of passion. One does not exhibit such an emotional outburst if one does not care—if one does not have strong feelings. Especially the Duke of Ice."

"He does have feelings, Penelope." Abigail would address this issue. "I would ask you please not to refer to him by that name. It is not flattering. Imagine how he must feel for people to be referring to him with a word that reminds him of his family's death each time he hears it."

"I had not thought of that, Abby," Penelope said contritely. "You know I wouldn't be deliberately cruel. I've not been as considerate as I ought with you lately. I'm sorry if I've hurt your feelings."

"Please don't feel badly. You are my only cousin, and I love you to distraction. But I do hate hearing him called that." Abigail spoke softly. She didn't mean to chastise her cousin, but she'd been thinking about this for a while now.

"I won't speak of it again." Penelope's voice lightened. "I promise. I'll merely refer to him as *your husband.*"

"Thank you," Abigail barely managed before the sound of the door opening alerted her that they were no longer alone. Was it possible Monfort had feelings for her? Again with the wondering. The endless cycle of hopefulness and doubt.

"I've your chocolate, miss," Harriette was saying. "And water heating for your bath." Then apparently noticing the moist cloth on her mistress's face, she addressed Penelope. "I've more lavender oil on the table over there. If my mistress has need."

"Thank you, Harriette. Add some to the bath water, will you?"

Abigail's bones relaxed into the mattress as she listened to the maid and Penelope rummaging around, opening drawers and laying out clothing. Ah…finally, maybe just a wink of sleep.

But only a wink.

Roused not long after drifting off, Abigail began the day for a second time with a long indulgent bath. She sipped on chocolate and coffee, and even managed to eat a few pieces of toast. Unable to attempt anything else to break her fast, Abigail then turned herself over to Harriette, who assisted her into her undergarments and the dress Margaret had chosen for the ceremony.

Abigail had never been one to fuss a great deal with her hair, but found her maid's abilities fascinating as the woman twisted the sides away from Abigail's face, except for a few wispy strands, and then curled two long spiraling locks to hang past her shoulders. She completed the romantic effect by placing a wreath of flowers with dangling ribbons atop Abigail's hair. The headpiece had been made up of blue daisies, hydrangea petals, and baby's breath woven throughout.

The entire effect was stunning.

When Harriette was finished, Abigail opened her jewel box and pulled out the necklace Monfort had given her the day before. Had she really opened it less than twenty-four hours ago? Yesterday, now, seemed a lifetime ago.

She handed it to her maid, and the blue stone settled just above her bodice.

In spite of getting hardly any sleep at all, Abigail looked into the mirror and saw that her eyes were sparkling. She was excited.

She was going to marry the duke, and she was going to do everything within her power to ensure they both found some happiness together. For she knew that, as much as she needed joy in her life, the duke needed it even more.

She touched the cool stone and rubbed it, as though for luck. She only hoped she was the person who could help him.

Penelope peeked her head into the room with a

cheerful smile. "You are ready? Oh, Abigail, you look perfect! Your future sister-in-law has a wonderful sense of style and fashion. That gown looks as though it was made for you!"

But of course. It had been.

It was a different style from the gown she'd worn last evening, with a tight bodice formfitting to the waist where the gathered skirt then flowed freely. The sleeves were large and puffy and an abundance of lace set off the blue. Abigail hugged her cousin carefully and promised she'd be down shortly. Penelope was to travel to the church with her parents, in their own carriage. Margaret was sending a special landau over to transport Abigail and her own parents.

Penelope's abrupt departure provided only a moment of quiet before her mother stepped inside the room. She fussed and plucked at Abigail's gown, but in the end merely stepped back and blinked several times. "You look quite pretty, Abigail. I am so proud of you today." She then kissed Abigail softly on the cheek and left the room.

And then her father entered. "I'm afraid to hug you. I'll ruin your gown." He smiled jovially. Abigail suspected he'd already raided the liquor cabinet but refused to chastise him for it. She wasn't going to allow anything to ruin her surprisingly optimistic mood.

Instead she simply allowed herself to take comfort in her father's rare embrace. "I'll be fine, Papa. Nothing could possibly ruin this day!"

Her father hugged her tightly for several moments before turning away and wiping at his cheeks, more than a little embarrassed. "Now, I don't want you to be a stranger to Raebourne and Biddeford Corners simply because you are a duchess, Abigail. I want you to bring all the grandchildren around as often as possible."

Abigail laughed, daring to imagine herself and the duke visiting her parents' home, with a handful of children. "I promise, Papa." Tears threatened once again. Blasted tears. She was not going to cry anymore today. Her eyes were finally looking normal again. "Off with you, now. You'll make me cry. I'll be down in but a moment."

But her father hugged her one more time. "You've been quite a bit of trouble for us, Abigail, for your mother and me. But I want you to know that we—both of us—love you dearly." He kissed her on the cheek softly and then gave her a watery smile. "Best finish readying yourself. We'll see you at the church."

With those parting words, he kissed her again and then left, closing the door behind him.

Abigail waved her hands in front of her eyes for several moments to keep any new tears from falling. Who would have thought she would ever have been able to make her parents so very happy? After all she'd put them through, years ago and again this summer, she was pleased to make such fabulous amends with them.

All thanks to her duke.

And then her father's parting words echoed in her brain. *We'll see you at the church.*

We'll see you at the church?

Gathering up her pelisse, Abigail rushed toward the door and ran down the stairs, the ancient townhouse sounding surprisingly quiet. In a blaze of incomprehensible panic, she rushed past the butler and threw open the door.

No carriages awaited her.

Turning back to the stodgy man in the foyer, she shook her head, not quite believing this was happening. "Where are all of the carriages? Where has everybody gone?"

The man did not blink or make even the slightest expression as he answered. "Why they've left, miss. They said you were to ride in a separate carriage."

Except that had not been the plan at all.

"There isn't another one coming. Have one of the baron's carriages brought around immediately!" She never shouted at servants, but her voice rose nonetheless. "Anything at all. I'm going to be late for my own wedding."

A dawn of understanding and sympathy appeared on the butler's face. "There aren't any left, miss. Even all of the horses are out already. I suppose I could send a footman in search of a hackney, but there's no promising he'll be able to hail one."

At this, Abigail rushed through to the back of the house to the mews to verify that not even an old nag had been left in the stable. He was right. There were no conveyances left that she could take to the church.

And then, a gleaming piece of metal caught her attention.

But no.

She could not.

Except...it was her only hope.

****

"I cannot eat a bite, Margaret," Alex told his sister, who'd managed to become the bossiest woman alive this morning. "You're lucky I'm upright."

After vomiting earlier for what seemed like an eternity, Alex managed to steal not much more than a wink of sleep before Villiars insisted he arise to bathe. The hot water had felt heavenly, but drinking coffee proved to be the opposite. His stomach protested on and off in varying waves of intensity while his valet shaved and dressed him.

When the time arrived to depart for St. George's, all he wanted was to throw himself back into bed. Damn his eyes, and on his blasted wedding day! A fine bridegroom, for certain!

As much as he wished to blame Danbury for encouraging him, it had been his own decision. The last of an unfortunate string of bad decisions made the previous night.

He should not have attacked Farley publicly. Not that he regretted pummeling the man, but he'd promised Abigail he'd not do anything that might draw public criticism.

He also ought to have gone to Abigail afterward. He ought to have reassured her that he'd not been fighting over his former mistress. Not that he needed to answer to anyone regarding his sexual exploits, but it would have been kind of him to reassure her, nonetheless.

She'd told him once that she believed he was a *kind* man. It was the least he could have done for her.

The remaining poor decisions he'd made had come every time he'd raised a glass or flask to his lips over the course of the night.

And now he was to pay for them all.

"Are we sending a carriage for Abigail and her parents?" he inquired of his sister absentmindedly. She would already have taken control of all these details.

"Already done, Monfort. I've appointed them use

of the ivory landau. The weather is simply gorgeous, and so we've left the top down," she answered over her shoulder as she straightened her husband's cravat. Clive was watching Alex with laughter in his eyes.

"You look like death warmed over, Monfort." He sounded droll and insolent. "I don't think I've ever witnessed a bridegroom as battered and green." And then laughing at his own joke, he winged an arm to his wife. "Shall we lead the way, my lady?"

Alex's brother-in-law was not a bad fellow, but at that precise moment, Alex considered landing him a facer. Clive at least ought to have had the decency to get foxed along with him last night. Not right for the fellow to look so well rested and cheerful.

Danbury appeared at the top of the stairs. Oh, hell, if Alex looked anything like the viscount, then Clive's insults were thoroughly justified. Danbury's appearance only lacked the blackened eye and swollen lip.

"You are all speaking far too loudly," Danbury stated, descending carefully. "There won't be loud music at this affair?" Hugh would be standing up with Alex. Just last night Alex had assigned him the duty.

"It's a wedding, Danbury." Clive's grin persisted. "Magnificent pipe organ, playing a march."

Danbury groaned.

"You have the rings, don't you?" Alex would confirm such an important detail. Especially in light of Danbury's current state.

"Right here, old fellow." Danbury pulled them from a pocket inside his jacket. "Both shackles, safe and sound."

Good to know his friend still possessed a sense of humor. Perhaps Alex himself might feel human again soon as well. "What are we waiting for?" he groused.

Margaret and the earl climbed into a lightweight horse chariot while Alex and Danbury climbed on to their mounts. Alex needed all his concentration to do something he normally wouldn't even have thought about. Stay atop his horse.

The church wasn't far, and a large crowd gathered below the steps. Alex refused to acknowledge any of them. He'd already given in to an exorbitant amount of undukelike behavior over the past twenty-four hours. He dismounted and handed his horse to one of the liveried servants who'd jumped down from Margaret's coach.

Where was his bride? Had Abigail arrived with her parents yet?

He did not see the ivory landau parked anywhere nearby. Of course, the bride would be last to arrive. The twinge of nervousness he experienced at that thought surprised him. Of course, she would arrive. What woman would fail to show up to marry a duke?

A woman who feared the ton. A woman who would perhaps believe her bridegroom had fought over his mistress the night before.

Ignoring these unproductive thoughts, Alex strode confidently up the church steps and into the vestibule. A sacred song reverberated throughout the sanctuary, but he was not so obtuse as to be ignorant of the judgmental whispers rolling through the pews. He gestured Danbury to follow him as he strode down the aisle toward the altar. His fob watch revealed the time to be five minutes before nine. Abigail and her parents would be arriving shortly. Rather than take his official place at the front while awaiting Abigail, he dropped onto the bench in front of Margaret and the earl. Numerous familiar faces of distant relatives and acquaintances who had traveled far and wide for such a momentous occasion as his wedding went completely unnoticed.

"You have the rings?" he whispered to Danbury, again, thinking something surely would go wrong at this point and time. Apparently, the world worked in concerted effort to make his wedding day into a mockery.

"Right here." Danbury chuckled. "Ah, I believe your bride has arrived."

Alex glanced over his shoulder and sure enough, Mr. and Mrs. Wright were settling themselves into the front row on the opposite side of the aisle. Abigail would be waiting in the back.

Alex stood, and Danbury followed him as he took his place beside the bishop. The music ceased and then, in a great crescendo, began again.

Except Abigail was nowhere in sight.

Chapter 15

Abigail wrestled with Penelope's Lady Accelerator, all the while steering it from the stable out into the small road behind the house. If she were to have any chance at all of arriving to her wedding before everybody gave up on her, she must travel at much greater speeds than she could walk, or even run. She suppressed the anxiety rising inside and forced herself to remember that she *had* managed to remain upright for short distances without falling the other day.

Very short distances.

She leaned the two-wheeled vehicle against the side of the carriage house and rushed back into her aunt and uncle's townhouse. Upon locating the butler precisely where she'd left him, she caught at his sleeve breathlessly. What if Margaret or Penelope or anybody realized the mix-up and sent a carriage back for her? What if she were to attempt to ride the Accelerator and they missed her completely? Surely they would realize her parents' thoughtless, incomprehensible, stupid mistake? Surely the duke would not think that she was jilting him? Nobody jilted a duke!

Except Lady Natalie had.

But that was different. She was not Lady Natalie. Under no circumstances whatsoever would she ever jilt Monfort!

"Has a carriage returned for me yet?" she gushed breathlessly, her chest tight.

Perhaps she ought to wait.

The butler shook his head apologetically. "What would you like me to do, miss?" He was far too calm, far too contained. She was missing her own wedding, for heaven's sake!

She had to do s*omething*!

"If a carriage comes for me," she gasped, "tell them I am coming! Tell them I have not cried off! Do you understand?"

The butler nodded somberly. "You are going...on foot?" he asked, his brows furrowing slightly.

"I am going to ride to the church on Penelo—on Miss Crone's Lady Accelerator. I shall be there as quickly as possible. But it is important, do you understand, that you tell them *I am not crying off*!"

"Very well, miss." He nodded somberly again. "If a carriage comes for you, I am to tell them you are riding a contraption to the church and that you are most definitely *not crying off*."

"Yes." Abigail nodded. And then before she could change her mind, she dashed back out to the mews again and pulled out the Accelerator. Grasping the handles, she pulled up her skirts and lifted one leg over the middle bar. Not giving herself time to think, she began shuffling her feet along the ground to propel herself forward. Raising her bum to the seat, she daringly increased her pace.

She was moving!

The Accelerator wobbled slightly, and she put even more effort into propelling herself forward. *Rrrip!*

Her beautiful dress! A large piece of the lace had

caught on the wheel and now trailed along in the dirt behind her.

But she could not worry about it right now. Monfort must think she's crying off!

She forced herself to look up, just in time to avoid running into the side of a neighboring stable. She was on the road, however, and she was moving.

Not as fast as she'd like, but faster than she could walk.

As she emerged onto a cross street, it took her a moment to contemplate which way she needed to drive. To the right.

She moved the handle just a fraction to the right and nearly lost her balance when the contraption began to tilt. She caught herself with her foot and pushed off again.

And it worked! As she stepped, kicking her feet along furiously onward, she ignored the gaping pedestrians who stopped to stare. She needed to focus all of her energy on steering and balancing.

The road to the church was not without obstacles.

Oh, she hoped this wasn't all a colossal mistake. Likely a carriage awaited her at her uncle's house by now! She ought to have waited. When she rode through a puddle of water, she wondered if she ought to turn around and return to the house.

But no, she was almost there.

Her legs burned, and perspiration dripped down her face.

This was considerably more exercise than she'd experienced since she'd been a child. But she rode determinedly onward. She was not going to jilt her duke!

****

She was going to jilt him.

Alex was stunned. The music played on for a full minute before the organist, realizing something was amiss, fell silent. And then in a valiant attempt to bring forth the nonexistent bride, the organist pounded out the bridal anthem one more hopeful time.

Still, no Abigail.

Alex looked down into the row where Margaret sat and raised his eyebrows at her questioningly, as if she might have an answer for him. But Margaret only frowned and then turned to stare curiously across the aisle at Abigail's parents. Abigail's father shrugged and mouthed something in Alex's direction. Alex jumped down from the altar, ran over, and grasped the man who was to become his father-in-law, by the arm. "Where is she?" he asked through gritted teeth, his pounding head and rolling stomach all but forgotten. Was she truly jilting him?

The breath that rolled off Mr. Wright brought forth the nausea Alex had temporarily forgotten. But the words he spoke caused Alex to stand up straight. "What do you mean she was coming right behind you? She was to come *with* you, you blathering idiot!" He did not stop to think that he was publicly insulting his bride's father. The organ had gone silent, and Alex's voice echoed throughout the large cathedral.

They'd left her behind. They'd forgotten to bring the bride!

Disgusted, Alex rejoined the bishop and then addressed the congregation in a surprisingly ducal tone. "Please, ladies and gentlemen, wait but a moment. There is to be a wedding here today but after a slight delay. If you will all be patient, I shall return momentarily." And then, catching himself, he added, "*With my bride.*"

He strode swiftly down the center aisle and stepped out the heavy doors he'd entered just moments before. He could not dwell upon the spectacle this wedding was fast becoming. He would locate his mount and fetch Abigail on horseback. Quite romantic and heroic, really, he thought ironically. He'd never viewed himself as being a romantic and most certainly hadn't planned on being heroic today. Perhaps Abigail would appreciate the gesture.

As he reached to wave one of his waiting servants over to fetch his horse, an unexpected, loud, and frightfully familiar voice carried along the street.

"Give way! Move, please, I cannot stop! Please move!" a woman's voice cried out in panic. The crowd that had gathered around the cathedral to witness the comings and goings of all the nobles at an aristocratic wedding magically began to shift and part.

He did not want to look but knew he must. Just as he turned to see if the unseemly vision approaching was his bride, a flying, swirling mass of blue skirts, flowers, brown hair, and hard, solid metal and wood careened into him.

He barely had a moment to wrap his arms around Abigail before they both went tumbling to the ground. Relief that he'd protected her from the fall barely registered before all of his breath sucked out of him at the same time his head slammed into the paving.

His poor head.

His poor aching head.

"Monfort!"

Was he underwater? Asleep? Dreaming?

"Are you alive? Talk to me, Monfort! Alex? Alex! Oh, God help me, I've killed you! Monfort?"

She was talking. He knew she was talking, He wasn't certain what she was saying and for the life of him couldn't answer.

And then soft lips pressed against his. Honeyed kisses feathered about his mouth and eyes as he was gradually able to capture some air into his lungs once again. He should stop her, he knew, but honestly, her lips on his skin truly made the nicest feeling he'd had all day.

She smelled of lavender and mint and woman. And her lips were supple and tender. He opened his eyes and willed her to look at him.

"Abigail." He managed to speak. "Abigail, don't we have somewhere to be?"

When she heard him, she pulled back, allowing a sob to escape. "Oh, Monfort, I did not want you to believe I was jilting you. And then when I saw you, I couldn't make the Accelerator stop. I know it was foolish to ride, but there was no other way! There were no coaches or horses or hackneys! And now my dress is ruined and my hair is a mess. But I didn't want you to think I was jilting you."

Alex forced his aching body to sit forward, setting her slightly to the side of him. "I knew you weren't jilting me." His mouth twisted ironically. So much for his heroic gesture. "I was coming to get you. I was going to save you!"

Danbury and Penelope appeared at the top of the church steps. "What are you two waiting for? An entire congregation is waiting," Danbury reminded them.

"My Accelerator!" Penelope stared in horror at the sight of her new contraption twisted and broken, one wheel still rolling several feet down the road.

The footman intending to fetch Monfort's mount was already gathering the remaining pieces together. Danbury groused at Penelope. "Really, Miss Crone? Is that your greatest concern at this moment?"

Requiring all of his strength and all of his resolve, Alex managed nonetheless to rise to his feet. His head pounded and his joints ached, but he had no choice but to enter the church. "Milton will take care of it." He acknowledged Penelope's concerns. He did appreciate Abigail's cousin. "Take it to Cross Hall, Milton," he ordered, "and have it put to rights."

He then winged his arm for Abigail. Her hair was in thorough disarray, and her dress was torn and splattered with mud. But she was here. And she was smiling tremulously. "I believe we have an appointment with the bishop."

Chapter 16

"Abigail, your gown!" Penelope lamented. "And your hair."

Abigail glanced down at her torn and muddied skirt. As she did so, several locks of hair fell forward. The beautiful twist Harriette had created earlier had come completely undone. All that remained was the wreath of flowers and a tangled mass of her hair flowing freely.

She suspected a few drops of mud might have splattered on her face as well.

Danbury laughed heartily. "She's a perfect match for you, Monfort."

A perfect match?

How? What? Abigail forgot about her dress and hair and glanced toward her bridegroom.

Who was, quite possibly, in worse condition than she.

His left eye was blackened, streaks of purple reaching toward the bridge of his nose and temple, and his bottom lip was scabbed and swollen as well. Behind the colorful patchwork of bruises, his skin looked...yellowish? Was that green? Regardless, he wore a pallor, unusual for his normal impeccable self.

And then she glanced at his beautiful embroidered ivory coat, now scuffed and torn, thanks to her.

He winced as he reached up and ran a hand through his hair. When he rubbed along his arm, a streak of crimson smeared across the cuff.

"Monfort, you are bleeding!" Worried now, she inspected him from all angles and noted a small but dark and glistening spot on the back of his head.

But he was pulling away from her. "I'm fine, Abigail." His eyes looked so very tired, but his voice sounded as determined as ever.

"Danbury and I will enter first. When the music begins, follow Miss Crone down the aisle. Do not worry about your dress, Abigail. You are going to become a duchess this morning. Remember that. Nothing else matters." He paused and looked into her eyes intently. "A duchess, Abigail. Do not forget that."

Then, leaving her alone with Penelope and limping slightly, he and the viscount reentered the church. Abigail blinked.

A duchess.

In a torn dress, muddied.

Her wedding day…

A burst of giggles erupted from Penelope. Abigail wanted to hush her cousin, chastise her for laughing at this predicament, had it not been for the absolute absurdity of her situation. Abigail held back her own gurgling laughter, fearful that if she lost control, she herself might go into hysterics.

A most ludicrous situation indeed! Even she could not have imagined this.

Scandal was not to be hers alone now. She and her duke would share it.

The memory of his face, bruised, battered, and pale, did something odd to her heart. A duke, but really, just a man.

Deep sounds of the organ escaping from the front of the church brought Penelope up short. Both sober now, they stared at one another and then crept toward the opening of the large, intimidating cathedral. Upon entering the vestibule, Penelope smoothed her own gown and then met Abigail's gaze with a tight smile.

And then, ignoring the expectant eyes watching them, she gave Abigail a long and tight hug. "You are the most amazing person I know, Abby. Always remember that. Monfort is the luckiest man alive!" And then, wiping her eyes, she turned, lifted her chin and began walking slowly down the long carpeted aisle as though nothing untoward had occurred.

Abigail, feeling more than a little emotional, watched as her cousin took long, even steps toward the alter.

Where Monfort and Danbury stood waiting.

Her groom was almost even more handsome disheveled and bruised. It showed his humanness. She hoped those who saw him now might understand that he was not made of ice. He possessed feelings. He bruised. He bled. And he bore the scars of having lost two small children and a wife in a tragic accident.

But he did not wear his emotions on his sleeve for all to gape at. He merely exercised a great deal of discipline over himself. Even now he stood tall and proud. Ever the duke.

His expression might have looked grim, but his eyes gave her courage. *You are becoming a duchess*, he'd said, *remember that. Nothing else matters.*

She brushed at her skirts, futilely, pushed a lock of hair behind her ear, and marched toward her future. She did not look to the left or the right, at the censuring stares she knew she'd see. She ignored the whispers, swallowed hard, and continued moving. Where was her father? Was not her father supposed to escort her on this long, torturous walk?

Oh, yes, he'd forgotten her.

She swallowed another lump, which again formed in her throat. She could not imagine how nice it would have been to have leaned upon her father at this time. She focused her gaze upon Monfort. She could almost imagine herself floating. Her hands and feet tingled, but she was almost there. *Breathe, Abigail, breathe.* A loud gushing sound roared in her head, and darkness encroached upon her vision.

Monfort stepped forward to meet her, placing her hand upon his sleeve. Although his expression did not soften, she knew an odd sense of comfort when he placed his other hand atop hers and squeezed slightly. Her heartbeat slowed to its normal pace, and air once again filled her lungs.

Later, Abigail would not remember a word the bishop said, she was so focused on the warmth emanating from the man standing beside her. She barely managed to answer in the affirmative when both the duke and the bishop looked to her expectantly. The ceremony took no time at all, and yet it went on forever.

And then the bishop declared the two husband and wife.

Monfort turned and took both of her hands in his. Rigid and tall, he leaned forward. What was it about this man? Why had he chosen to save her? Abigail closed her eyes and tilted her head up slightly. He was going to kiss her. In front of a church full of society's loftiest citizens.

The warmth of his breath reached her in the instant before his lips landed softly upon the corner of her mouth. It lasted no more than three seconds, but the jolt of his touch travelled to the bottom of her toes.

And into her heart.

For the kiss was soft and tender and sweet. She opened her eyes and stared up at him in wonder as he drew back. He was not smiling, but his silver gaze conveyed an unfamiliar warmth.

With shaking hands, she signed the papers set before her, noting Monfort's bold scrawl just above her own smaller flourish.

The loud music echoed in her ears even as she allowed herself to be led out of the church by her husband.

Her husband.

The ceremony had passed in a blur. Had it been a minute? Had it been an hour? Cheers rose to greet them as she and Monfort emerged from the cool of the ancient church. Those same onlookers who'd watched her come barreling down the street on Penelope's Lady Accelerator now gazed at her in awe.

In fact, the enthusiastic crowd barely opened up enough to allow her and Monfort to tunnel through to the landau awaiting them. Amidst a flurry of flower petals raining down, Abigail wondered vaguely if this lovely vehicle were the one meant to have carried her to the church earlier.

It didn't matter now. She'd arrived in time. She had not jilted him.

Monfort, looking even more exhausted than he had

earlier, hurried to help her climb up before flinging himself in and falling onto a seat. "Drive!" he ordered, tilting his head back and closing his eyes.

The carriage rocked slightly as it pulled away.

She'd thought he would stand and toss some coin to the crowd, but he was not moving. Those who'd come hoping for a bit of fortune would be disappointed. As though reading her mind, Monfort reached a hand into his coat and pulled out a small purse. Setting the jingling pouch on the seat beside him, he looked to be asleep. "Will you do the honors?" His eyes remained closed as he murmured.

Her newlywed husband was not well at all. Concerned, Abigail snatched the bag and poured the coins into one of her hands. In a hurry to fuss over Monfort, she hastily stood and threw the coins in one bountiful toss. The crowd cheered some more, a few racing to run along beside them.

"Faster," she said to the driver. She wished them away from curious eyes.

What had he done to himself?

Dropping back into the seat, she dared to reach up and tenderly brush her fingers along his brow. "You are in no condition to attend the breakfast." Margaret had planned a large meal to be served, with only relatives invited, but that was still going to be close to fifty or so people. Both her maid and Monfort's valet would be at Cross House to attend them, but somehow she did not think a change of clothes could revive her husband enough to appear publicly again.

He opened his eyes and slanted them in her direction. "I am thinking a storm is hovering, and it might be best to depart for Rock Point posthaste. If we are quick enough, perhaps we can be gone before the guests arrive at Cross Hall."

Abigail's brows shot up.

Was he suggesting they forgo their wedding breakfast? Oh, that would be marvelous! "If you are expecting an argument from me, then you shall be sorely disappointed, Monfort." She couldn't stop herself from grinning.

Monfort studied her intently before speaking again. His complexion was not only pale, but slightly…green. "Very well. Do not take time to change, but have your maid pack you an overnight bag and then meet me in the mews. I'll instruct Villiars to follow us at a more leisurely pace with your maid and our luggage. I shall leave a message for Margaret, and if we don't dawdle, we can forgo any arguments."

A breeze lifted her hair, and the cool air soothed the skin at her nape. She didn't know whether to laugh or cry. She only knew a great sense of relief.

"I will take but only a moment." And then she could not help adding, "This is brilliant."

Monfort chuckled dryly as the carriage rocked to a halt in front of Cross Hall.

****

Alex was not looking forward to several hours riding inside of his traveling coach. Far better, though, than spending the next couple of hours making inane conversation, eating, drinking, and acting the part of host and bridegroom. It took all of his will to remain upright and conscious.

He paused only a moment to watch Abigail dash up the stairs for her belongings before he turned toward Walkins to relay his orders. "Have the traveling coach readied immediately. Her Grace and I are leaving for Rock Point before the wedding guests arrive. Tell Lady Clive that, as a storm is approaching, I found it necessary to get an early start on our travels."

"Very well, Your Grace," the elderly retainer said before bowing and then removing himself. Alex had every faith that his butler would see to any other necessary details. Alex then located Villiars, gathered a few items for himself, and headed outside to find Abigail already waiting. Several grooms and liveried footmen were buzzing about the carriage house and stables efficiently readying the coach. Not even a flicker of guilt pricked Alex's conscience by adding this additional burden just as they were expecting more than fifty guests to arrive.

And then all was ready. He lifted a basket of what he assumed to be light fare for their journey onto the floor of the plush carriage and then climbed in behind Abigail—his wife now. The reality of his wedding had not yet truly set in.

The activity and need for haste had temporarily given him a brief spurt of energy, but once he sat down, his body immediately made known to him every slight it had received over the past twelve hours. He hoped Abigail did not expect him to make pleasant conversation as they traveled.

With a jolt, they were off.

"We've done it, Monfort!" Abigail was peeking out the window, holding the curtain back. "And barely in time. All of the guests are just now arriving." She was smiling and her eyes shone bright. *She'd* obviously had a good night's rest. And she'd ridden to the wedding on that blasted Accelerator no less! He could not help but remember the moment when he'd realized it was *his bride* storming through the crowds on the metal contraption. Someday, he hoped the oddities of their wedding would be forgotten by all. But it most likely would not. Ah well, it was over.

Once the driver gained a bit of speed, Alex reached for a handy pillow, placed it on the bench beside him and turned sideways to try to get comfortable. Abigail sat on the bench across from him. She was facing backward, her brows furrowed.

"What is it?" he asked, sounding gruffer than he'd intended. She shifted her gaze away from him. "Did you forget something? We cannot return. If it's important, your maid will have it with her when the luggage coach arrives behind us."

Abigail hesitated just a moment. "Oh, no, it is just that...I don't do well traveling with my back facing front. But it is of no matter. I shall be all right."

He would not do well in the rear-facing seat either.

"Come here, then," he said, shifting to the side.

"But you wish to lie down."

"Abigail," he said sternly.

After a rustling of skirts, she crossed the empty space and then primly sat beside him, hands demurely folded in her lap. Hands, he noted, that bore scratches and scrapes from her earlier fall. She sat ramrod straight leaving several inches between the two of them.

At a momentary loss, Alex examined the pillow for a moment before tossing it onto the floor as useless.

Unable to overcome his exhaustion, he gave into the gravity pulling at his weary bones and lay down again along the bench, this time using Abigail's lap as a cushion. With one foot on the upholstery and the other bracing himself upon the floor, he waited for her to squirm and push him off of her.

He waited in vain.

Instead, cool and tender fingers begin combing through his hair, around his eyes and across the bridge of his nose.

His heart raced. For some unknown reason, he wasn't one for this sort of... affection. He'd give in to it for only a moment. He'd move across to the other bench...and yet he sunk deeper into her at the same time.

"Monfort?" she asked quietly. It seemed he'd never be allowed a moment's peace.

And yet he didn't mind so much. He mumbled something in order to effect a response while her hands worked magic on his aching head.

"Why did you fight Damien Farley?" she queried him in a timid voice. Her hands continuing to soothe and comfort and the sweet, clean smell of woman filled his senses.

He'd feign sleep if his conscience would allow it. "Why do you think?" he mumbled the question and turned onto his side, burying his face into the cotton of her dress. He wondered if she believed, like the rest of the ton likely now did, that he would attack a man for dancing with his ex-mistress at his own betrothal ball.

"Was it because...you figured out that he...was the person...and you..." She shifted restlessly beneath him. "Or was it because he was dancing with Mrs. Gormley?"

He wrapped one arm around her waist, so as to secure his position comfortably. At the same time, he was annoyed that she did not simply know the answer.

He'd told her before that the man deserved to be punished. Instead, she had listened to the gossips.

"After you disappeared last night, most of the guests were whispering that she was your mistress and you wanted her back. I did not wish to believe it. She is very beautiful, though, and although you told me you would expect fidelity from me, you never said anything about not keeping a mistress, yourself. And she *is* very beautiful…"

Wait, she had stayed at the ball? "You did not leave the ball early?" He'd been certain she would have left. He attempted to sit up, but she exhibited a surprising amount of strength and ensured that he remain prone.

Or perhaps he was just that exhausted.

"I did not." He could feel her shaking her head. "I stayed with Margaret for the supper and then waited until most of them departed before leaving with my parents. It was not easy. People were saying the most dreadful things—not to my face, mind you—but I overheard many of them."

With closed eyes, Alex absorbed her words, surprised by her courage yet again. Her fingers continued threading through his hair, mesmerizing him.

But she required an answer.

She deserved one.

Pulling back from his comfortable position, he met her gaze in order to ascertain her response to what he needed to say. "I attacked Farley for no other reason than justice demanded it. It ought to have been addressed years ago. From what I understand, Cortland and Hawthorne put him on a packet today. He knows that if he returns to London anytime soon, a greater punishment awaits."

Her eyes studied his before she released a soft sigh and settled comfortably again. This time her hand rested along his jaw.

All was quiet, finally, but for the sounds of the coach and horses as the driver steered them out of the city. For a moment, the desire to take hold of her hand tempted him.

And then she spoke in barely a whisper. "Thank you, Alex."

****

Monfort had been sleeping for nearly an hour when the rain began. At first it was a light sprinkle, but it did not take long before the storm had worked itself into a deluge. In falling into a deep sleep, he gave Abigail a rare glimpse of this man she'd married. She could stare to her heart's delight at the tiny wrinkles forming around his eyes. She could examine, in detail, the prickly whiskers already reappearing on his jaw and throat

Awake he vibrated with intensity, likely ingrained into him from an early age.

In sleep he was merely a man.

She enjoyed the feel of his hair as it slid through her fingers, wincing only when she discovered the crusted blood from when he'd hit his head on the pavement.

Her poor, poor duke.

So very stubborn, so very determined. She traced the barely noticeable wrinkles beginning to etch themselves into his forehead and smoothed the straight lines of his brows. She enjoyed the very weight of him resting on the tops of her thighs.

And eventually she relaxed as well, content to offer him this small comfort.

At the first clap of thunder, Abigail started, but Monfort remained nearly comatose. It wasn't until the coach nearly slid off the road that he roused and sprang into a sitting position.

Alert to the conditions, Monfort opened the window to the driver's box and ordered the man to stop at the nearest inn. When he returned to the seat, he sat up straight, tense and alert. Oddly enough, Abigail was not afraid of the storm.

In spite of having slept for a short while, his eyes were bloodshot, his skin retained that sickly pallor, and his bruises contrasted even more vividly against his skin. Every now and then he'd blink slowly, almost as though even the slight movement itself was painful. When he turned to stare out the window, Abigail noticed again the crusted blood in his hair from when he'd knocked his head on the pavement after she'd crashed into him.

"Did you sleep at all last night?" she asked.

He grimaced but then glanced at her with that arrogant expression of his. "It is no matter, Abigail."

Ah, so he had not. Just then, the carriage slowed and turned off the road. Thank heavens! They were lucky to find themselves so close to an inn. A flash of lightning, followed by another loud clap of thunder, seemed to shake the earth.

And then the realization of what was to come hit her.

They would take a room.

The sky was dark.

Her wedding night loomed close indeed.

Chapter 17

Due to the torrential downpour in the area, the inn was filling quickly. Even being a duke, Monfort was lucky to get them a room with a large clean bed. One room. One bed.

Since no private dining rooms could be made available, a tray with some stew and bread was delivered upstairs. Monfort excused himself in order to ensure the drivers and outriders found their quarters without hassle. Needing to be of some use, Abigail ordered a hot bath filled and set up for her husband behind a privacy screen. He'd require it. She herself was covered in splattered mud from her short trek from the carriage to the inn but dared not strip down and bathe while Monfort could reenter at any moment. Instead, she cleaned up with a washcloth and then changed into her night rail and dressing gown. She had packed only one spare dress to wear, and she would be needing that tomorrow. It was not likely that the baggage coach would find them here, at their unscheduled stop. A bolt of lightning lit the room, shortly followed by a shock of booming thunder, and Abigail shivered.

She glanced at the bed longingly but didn't want to be in it when he returned.

It was their wedding night, and *he had attacked*

Farley for what he had done to her.

She was a wife now.

She was caught somewhere between abject fear and hopeful anticipation.

Another clap of thunder shook the inn just as Monfort tapped on the door and entered. He'd been gone nearly an hour and was soaked through to the skin. If it was possible, he appeared even paler than he had before.

"I've a hot bath prepared for you," she said. He regarded her as though she spoke a foreign language so she gestured toward the far side of the room. "Behind the privacy screen."

Monfort nodded before limping slowly to the area set away from the bed. Mud covered his left side from hip to boots. The poor man must have slipped and fallen. Abigail restrained herself from assisting him and hoped he wouldn't keel over before he could bathe. The poor maids would not appreciate the mess he was making. Maybe Abigail could find a broom somewhere?

But not right now. She wondered that poor Monfort was able to move at all. Somehow marrying her had turned him into a mere shadow of his normal ducal self.

Studying her sock-covered toes, Abigail wondered. What did a lady do while awaiting her newly married husband to prepare for bed? She glanced toward the privacy screen curiously.

A tall man, Monfort's head and the top of his shoulders were visible above the divider. With nothing else to do, she unapologetically observed him as he bent his head forward and attempted to unbutton his shirt. His brow furrowed, and his hands ineffectually fumbled at his neck cloth. "Bloody, blasted thing." He cursed as though alone.

And then he reappeared from behind the screen—still fully dressed. He scowled as he gestured to his jacket helplessly. "I can't get this damn thing off."

It was tightly fitted. And wet.

He was stuck, poor thing.

In the face of his physical discomfort, Abigail shed her concerns about their wedding night, padded across the room, and went right to work tugging at his jacket. As the sleeves peeled away from him, her bare hands brushed his. They were damp and freezing cold.

She'd lacked any boldness, up to that point, tentatively taking the liberty of touching Monfort. But in that moment she wrapped her hands around his and rubbed them vigorously to lend him some warmth.

He likely was cursing his decision to have his valet follow them at a distance.

Hesitating but a moment, Abigail knew only a desire to comfort him. She released his hands and reached up to untie his cravat.

He still did not move.

He'd given her protection. He'd given her his name. He'd finally punished *that man*. Monfort was chilled. He was practically asleep on his feet.

Deciding she had no alternative but to assist him further, Abigail unfastened the buttons at the top of his shirt. As the material fell away from his neck and chest, she found herself looking not at the button she was working on, but at the taut, pale skin she'd revealed. And at the short, dark, and slightly curling hairs. As a duke, he was a symbol of responsibility and tradition, but his naked skin reminded her of his humanity.

Sensing a rare vulnerability in him, she resisted a mad urge to lean forward and press her lips against his neck.

What would he think if she gave in to such a fanciful thought?

Like a small boy, he lifted his arms and allowed her to tug his shirt free of his breeches and then over his head. But he was not a small boy. He was very much a man.

Unaware of her disquieting thoughts, Monfort's eyes remained closed. A few times, he swayed slightly so that Abigail had to steady him.

His arms were sinewy, smooth, and shadowed where pale skin stretched over corded muscles and short hairs began, again, just below his elbows. She was fascinated by the elegance of his capable hands. He ought not to be so fit and strong. He was a duke.

But he rode nearly every day. He loved his horses, she reminded herself.

And then her gaze drifted back to his torso.

Abigail's breath caught at the sight of his full upper half—unclothed.

With eyes open, he didn't move but watched her now as she examined him. Her heart quickened, but not in fear. He stood frozen, as though he were an artifact, to study, to admire. He did nothing but stare back at her with hooded eyes, his lips slightly parted.

Abigail pointed to a nearby wooden chair. "Sit down," she ordered him. "I'll remove your boots." She did not know how she had such temerity. She imagined she'd been cast under a spell.

He obeyed without question. Perhaps this spell had been cast upon both of them.

With a confidence unusual for her, Abigail knelt

before him. Curling her fingers under the leather of his boot with one hand, she placed the other along his heel. The warmth of his calves brushed against her knuckles as she pulled at the fashionable boot. Monfort reached down to secure himself on the chair when she tugged with vigor.

As the boot gave way with considerable difficulty, Abigail allowed her hand to slide down the length of his stockinged calf. She was even so bold as to allow her fingers to linger slowly.

Chastising herself, she forced herself to dawdle less as she removed his other boot and stockings.

Assisting him in this way pleased her. Up until this point, their connection had been all about what he could do for her. Him saving her reputation. Him giving funds to her parents. She'd not like to think that he pitied her.

"Stand up," she commanded softly. And then, licking her lips, she added, "Please."

Monfort stood.

Abigail pushed to her feet, walked around to the back of him, and reached her arms around his waist for she could not be so bold under the scrutiny of his gaze. She'd often assisted her mother's housekeeper in the washing and pressing of her father's clothing. She knew how the placard of a man's breeches fastened.

With nimble fingers, she dipped her thumbs under Monfort's waistband and unfastened the buttons easily. They slid off the duke with a little tugging, and then he stepped out of them without protest.

Staring at his back, she took a deep breath. She'd touched his naked skin as she'd peeled his trousers downward. Like his arms, black hairs grew along his slim calves and muscular thighs. She'd caught more than a glimpse of pale, masculine buttocks. Her face flushed hot with embarrassment. She could not look him in the eyes now...

"Climb into the bath before it cools." How was it that her voice came out sounding so controlled?

Suddenly overwhelmed by the intimacy of what she'd done, Abigail needed to retreat. "There are linens here when you are done." She was tempted to glance back once more but was already shocked by her assertiveness. So she slipped out from behind the screen and sat upon the bed. Her mind whirled. Whatever had come over her?

Being practical, she reasoned with herself. The duke needed assistance, and she was the only person available. Her assistance had been nothing.

Really, it was nothing.

He likely had been barely aware of her. Her undressing him was probably no different for him than when Villiars performed the task.

The rain continued falling outside, but a fire in the hearth warmed the room. She placed the screen in front of it and climbed into the bed. Maybe if she were asleep when he finished his bath, he would forget all about her.

****

Alex had not thought he had the energy to think of anything but sleep, but after Abigail's innocent ministrations, he found himself not thinking of sleep at all. No, his thoughts gravitated toward exploring hands tugging at his clothing, rubbing warmth into his skin.

He finished bathing and climbed out of the tub. Amazingly, he was aroused.

How was it that this—he could no longer refer to

her as a spinster—*woman* had excited him as no woman had since his younger days? When she'd first begun undressing him, he'd thought to stop her but then changed his mind. Her actions had been daring, indeed. He'd no wish to shake her confidence. He was far too aware that the only time she'd been intimate with a man, it had been against her will. Perhaps if he remained passive, she would be comfortable with him. And so he had continued, unmoving, while she'd removed his clothing.

She'd been tentative in her touch at first, really. But her gaze…

She'd eyed him with sensual boldness.

And watching her watch him, watching her devour him with those eyes, had been one of the most seductive experiences of his life.

Baffling, really.

He'd restrained himself from pulling her to him. She was his wife. This was their wedding night.

Wrapping the linen around his waist, he stepped out from behind the screen.

Abigail had climbed under the counterpane and lay still—far too still to be sleeping. His head throbbed and his muscles ached. Without warning, an overwhelming weariness assaulted him.

And with it, all sexual arousal fled. If he were too tired to make love to his new wife properly, she would likely end up hating him as Hyacinth had. No, he would not consummate their marriage tonight.

He stepped around to the opposite side of the bed, dropped the towel, and climbed under the large quilt.

He fell asleep almost immediately.

Abigail hadn't thought she would be able to sleep.

She'd heard Monfort climb under the counterpane and into the bed and then...nothing. Not much time passed at all before she heard deep steady breathing coming from her newlywed groom. She ought to be relieved, but her traitorous body experienced disappointment. Removing his clothing—touching his person—had left her feeling edgy and...frustrated. Monfort had not touched her once. He'd watched her, and she'd thought he'd been affected somehow, but he'd gone from his bath to the opposite side of the bed without saying a word.

She remembered when he'd touched her leg before her first riding lesson. She'd thought he was attracted to her. Could she have misread his attentions? Had she deluded herself into believing he was forming an attachment to her?

She let out an exasperated sigh.

Monfort slept on.

To think he did not wish to bed her was disheartening...which made no sense at all. She'd dreaded it, hadn't she? And of course, he'd proposed to her for honorable purposes only. But she had thought things had changed between them...

Here she lay, seven-and-twenty, alone on her wedding bed, untouched by her husband. Turning to her side, she wrapped her arms around her stomach. She would be content. She was safe. Her parents were well taken care of. She closed her eyes and willed sleep to come quickly. It probably would not.

She was wrong.

****

The bed was soft and giving.

And warm.

And tendrils of hair tickled him indulgently, just below his chin.

Alex pondered the insane events of the previous thirty-six hours as he lay abed listening to the rain fall gently against the window. The woman he'd taken for his wife was tucked in beside him, her breaths warm against the skin of his chest.

His head no longer pounded, and the aches he'd experienced the previous day had abated. He never slept past dawn, but today no urgency compelled him to move from where he was. The wind blew steadily, rattling the windowpanes, and he knew they would not be leaving by coach anytime soon.

Abigail squirmed and made a little mewling sound. Opening his eyes, Alex studied this new wife of his as she slept.

She had one hand tucked under her face and the other had drifted down over his abdomen, dangerously close to the one part of himself that was suddenly very much awake.

He'd not had the chance to examine her so closely before. Usually she appeared so animated, a person became caught up in her words—or reeled from her emotions. No one would have ever held her close like this, to watch her—unguarded and defenseless. Alex sent his gaze roving over her long dark lashes, the line of her jaw, the fullness of her lips.

Several strands of her hair had escaped the long braid she'd tied before going to bed, framing her delicate features softly.

That word again. It dangled in his thoughts each time he thought of her: soft.

Without thought, he drew a line with his finger

down the curve of her cheek.

Her eyes fluttered open, searched for focus, and then held his own.

Awakening in the morning with his new bride pressed against him, Alex now found himself quite prepared to consummate this marriage. He hoped she would not turn squeamish. Would she?

Not moving his eyes away from hers, his hand drifted downward to her neck, her collar bone and onto her breast, which remained demurely covered by white cotton. Her own gaze fixed upon his, trusting him as he cupped the plump flesh gently. Ah, yes, perfect. Glorious. He stifled the urge to lift her gown then and there and press his mouth to such fullness.

Opting instead for a tentative squeeze, he watched as her lips parted with a catch in her breath.

He leaned forward and caught her lips with his own.

Ah, even in the morning, she tasted sweet and clean. "Abigail," he whispered. He kept his eyes opened. She had closed hers, but he wanted her to not be afraid. "Open your eyes."

After a moment, she obeyed and looked at him. He was pleased to see no fear, only that a sensual haze had come over her. Sweet God in heaven, she did something to him.

"Tell me if you become afraid." He wished to show her that sex was not violent. He wanted to show her that they could both find satisfaction with each other. He was going to have to take things slowly.

And then he trailed his lips along her jaw, allowing them to follow the path his hand had taken just seconds before. He drew lazy circles with his tongue and was pleased when she reached up and clasped his head to her.

Damn, but he was hard.

With sure fingers, he gathered the material of her nightdress and pulled it upward. Together, they both yet lay beneath the large quilted counterpane. She could keep her modesty.

For now.

Pulling back, he interpreted her stillness for acquiescence and used both hands to pull the gown up and over her head. She lay close to him now, no barriers between them. The softness of her legs and the roundness of her curves touched and then pressed against him.

Her eyes closed tightly, she'd pressed her lips into a thin taut line.

"Breathe, Abigail," he whispered and began trailing kisses around her face once again.

She relaxed when his mouth returned to hers and his tongue explored the tender skin behind her lips. He nearly came undone when she joined him in the kiss, nipping and pulling at him. Whether she meant to or not, she arched her body into his.

"Remember, Abigail, I am your husband now," he reminded her, his lips trailing down her throat in search of heaven. "You have my protection. You are safe."

Both of her hands gripped his head, her chest rising and falling rapidly.

"I know, Monfort, I know," she answered.

And then his mouth opened over her breast. His tongue circled her pert nipple and flicked it before he latched on greedily. Had he been waiting all summer for this moment? Had he wanted her since he'd first seen her looking so vulnerable in the boat that day?

Or had the wanting come afterward? When she'd turned and faced him boldly? Or even later when she'd warned him to retract his proposal?

He wasn't sure when it had happened, but at last he could admit to himself that he wanted this woman in a most carnal way. His arousal, so acute that it was nearly painful. It was an exciting, promising sort of pain, though.

He ran his hands down to grasp Abigail from behind. Ah, soft, and full of promise. Her sweet body so very full of promise.

Touching her, kissing her, tasting her nearly brought him to completion prematurely.

****

So many sensations rolled through Abigail, all of her restraint was required to keep from crying out. These were not bad sensations, though. They were good, though they were unfamiliar.

And, oh, but exquisite.

Monfort was tugging at her, molding her to his hands and mouth, making her his. His actions would have been terrifying if she were not also experiencing this hunger to bring him inside of herself. She'd had such yearnings before, when alone, but had not dared acknowledge them.

But now Monfort was bringing them all to the surface. This was the Duke of Monfort touching her, *her husband*. He was the man she had married.

When his hands clasped around the softness of her thighs, she gave in to the most natural urge to part her knees and allow him complete access.

His hand found her first, and he slid it around those

places she'd forbidden herself to ever linger. Then his finger slid inside of her, moving rhythmically, creating even more wanton sensations.

How could this be? Such intimacies ought to be mortifying!

And then he climbed atop her, and he replaced his hand with something harder, larger, altogether more demanding, pushing against her.

Her eyes flew open wide.

She remembered this from before. The pain. The intrusion. The humiliation. She raised her hands to his shoulders and pushed. "Monfort, stop! Wait! Please!"

He stilled instantly. But he was breathing heavily and dipped his forehead so that it pressing heavily against hers. "Alex," he said.

He was Alex.

He was not a dark, menacing, and laughing acquaintance. He was not drunk with spirits. She was not in a public place. She was a wife.

He was Alex.

She opened her legs wider and pushed upward toward him.

He came into her large and hard, but as she took him inside of her body, she experienced a rightness she'd never known before. She let out a sigh of satisfaction and he pushed deeper, farther, to her innermost core. He must surely be touching her womb.

"Alex," she breathed.

And then he was moving. Slow at first, but with a gradual increase in pace and intensity. Abigail held onto him as though her life depended upon it. She clasped her legs tightly around him, and her hands gripped his upper arms. She moved with him. She reached forward with her mouth and clasped it upon his shoulder, her neck straining.

He consumed her as she consumed him. And she sensed even more coming. More sensation, more exhilaration. A sharp, infinite crash of…something…took hold of her body. Alex held himself above her as he thrust himself deep and hard into her one last time. He pushed higher though, and higher, and then a rush of warmth inside. An agonized look took hold of his face before he buried it in her neck. His breath, damp and hot. Both of them were perspiring and gasping.

He was not a small man, and all of his weight rested upon her.

But she welcomed it. When he went to roll away, she tightened her legs around him. "Not yet," she whispered.

He stilled and allowed his weight to press her into the mattress once again.

And then, before she could utter another word, he'd rolled her over so that she was atop him.

They both slept.

Chapter 18

Abigail woke with her cheek pressed against her husband's chest and the unexpected sensations of intimacy nearly engulfed her. It startled her that not only was she so close physically to a man, but that that man was the Duke of Monfort.

Alex.

At some time while they'd slept, their conjoined bodies had separated, but the way she lay atop him, she absorbed his every breath. The rhythmic beating beneath her ear terrified her in that it was the sound of this man's heart. That fluttering was all that kept him alive. Just a tiny little sound—his life, so vulnerable. If it were to stop, he would cease to live.

She pushed the thought away. He was very much alive—very naked—and very much trapped beneath her.

How on earth had he managed to sleep?

She tilted her chin upward and studied the beard appearing darkly upon his jaw and chin. Even shadowed, the strong lines of his face were apparent. Her eyes drifted upward to the angular lines of his nose and cheeks.

In sleep, his lips relaxed. And long black lashes fanned out upon the skin beneath his eyes. They even stood out against the dark bruises which had developed quite magnificently over the past twenty-four hours.

His hair was ruffled and springing out in several different directions. She had to still her hand to keep from reaching up to touch it.

But should she? He was her husband, after all. Would he awaken cold and distant?

As she argued with herself about what would and would not be acceptable the morning after—well, when one awakened after…two hands reached around and clutched at her bottom.

"You are thinking very loudly, Abigail," Monfort murmured. Ah, so he was not sleeping after all. Abigail tensed at the sensations his hands created.

She was further distracted by the feel of him between her legs. That *particular part* of him had grown and hardened in a matter of seconds. Abigail herself experienced a heat rising inside, a sensation surely considered inappropriate for a lady. And her a duchess no less! She certainly didn't *feel* like a duchess. She'd known she was a scandal, but was she wanton as well? She buried her face against his chest.

Monfort's hands continued to caress her bare skin. "Will you sit up?" he asked. "I want to look at you."

What? Oh, good Lord no! Although the sun was not shining outside, daylight lit the room nonetheless. Why would he wish to *look* at her? It would be too humiliating. But he was pushing at her shoulders, and she found her body obeying his hands. "Please? Abigail?"

Abigail opened her eyes and watched his face as she allowed him to maneuver her upward. His eyes were slightly hooded, and his lips parted as he inhaled deeply. His gaze move from her face to her breasts and abdomen. Self-consciously, she wrapped an arm around her stomach. It was soft and had silvery little lines near her navel. This had never bothered her before, but with his intense gaze, she ducked her face in shame.

Alex gently pushed her hand away and replaced it with his own. His fingers traced one of the silvery lines and his thumb reached downward, touching and rubbing her intimately. He then adjusted himself at her opening and pushed up and into her warmth. Obliging his knowing hands, Abigail could not move her gaze from his face as she watched the desire on his.

His thumb made little swirling motions, intensifying her own want. She no longer experienced any embarrassment; only intent upon *him*.

His hard length prodded exquisitely inside of her. On pure instinct, Abigail reached behind herself and grasped onto his solid, hair-roughened thighs. As she did so, she arched her back and rubbed herself against her husband. Monfort grasped her hips, and they began moving together once again.

Alex thought that perhaps he'd died and gone to heaven. For his little spinster of a wife was, rather, something of a sexual goddess.

And not only because of her lush, warm, welcoming body. No, it was the way she responded to his touch. Her head was thrown back, and her bosoms heaved as he pushed himself deeper and deeper into her wet hot warmth. She moved against him eagerly, creating a friction that was nearly his undoing. Her eyes were closed, and she was breathing heavily—as was he.

He'd admitted to himself that he'd desired her body, but he'd never expected…this.

This was, indeed, a pleasant means of

entertainment for a rainy day.

And then she gasped and moaned softly. Alex slowed his own movement and watched as satisfaction washed over her. Just as he thought to begin moving again, Abigail slumped, bent her head forward, and mumbled. "I am so sorry. Please forgive me. I don't know why…" Was she *crying*?

Ignoring his own need, he pushed her hair out of her face and looked on in astonishment when he noticed that tears were indeed present.

"But whatever for?" he asked softly. Had he scared her? He traced his thumb up the side of her face and smoothed the moisture away. She was perhaps more complicated than he'd imagined. He could not help himself. He moved his thumb to trace the line of her ripe, soft bottom lip. Abigail opened her eyes and looked at him mournfully.

"This is not seemly of me at all! I am not supposed to be…this way!" And then she closed her eyes and dropped her face again.

Alex nearly chuckled but realized this was clearly a serious matter to her. She would have no idea that the last thing he'd wanted from his wife in bed was decorum. He'd already had that, and it did not make for a pleasant marriage. With Abigail, he'd hoped for a bit of mutual enjoyment at best. He was beginning to realize even greater possibilities—for a while, anyhow.

"But I am pleased that *you are*…this way," his voice rasped. Emotion caught in his throat. Abigail stared back up at him skeptically, and so he added, "It is what I would have in a wife."

"It was not like this before…that other time. This is different."

Alex nodded. "I am glad."

"You do not find it...distasteful?" She required further reassurance.

Alex flexed his muscles and pushed himself up into her more deeply. "Does it feel as though I find it distasteful?" And then he watched as a delightful blush crept up her breasts, her neck, and into her face. She was sitting astride him, gloriously naked, and she was *blushing*! Grasping her behind the neck, Alex pulled her face forward and placed his lips on hers. "Sweet is what you are," he murmured into her mouth.

And suddenly he not only felt aroused, but extraordinarily tender. Silken strands wound themselves around his heart. He was not certain that he liked it.

He pushed the images of her soulful brown eyes out of his mind's eye and instead focused on the pure physical pleasure he was feeling. Hot, wet, tight. It was a rainy day, and there was not much else he could do.

Deep, soft, moist.

There were no pressing responsibilities to attend to. No clubs to visit, no letters to dictate.

Sweet puffs of breath, tender lips tasting his skin, soft, feminine, little mewling sounds.

No secretaries and no valets.

Tentative hands exploring him boldly. A tiny blue vein, nearly invisible beneath the almost translucent skin of her breast. He nipped gently with his teeth. He pulled her ruched nipple into his mouth and sucked at her deeply.

What harm was there in spending the day pleasuring his new wife? It did not need to become more than what it was.

This was, by God, no love match.

He was fulfilling a duty of honor.

He was protecting a woman who had experienced a great lack of it so far throughout her lifetime.

And she was nibbling at his ear.

****

Several hours later, Abigail and Alex had only moved from their bed to retrieve a tray delivered by one of the inn servants. They'd eaten, made love, and slept randomly, lazily, without any desire to do anything differently. Lying beside her husband now, with her cheek resting upon his smooth, strong arm, Abigail raised a finger to trace the color around his eye.

"Did Farley know why you attacked him? He did not think it was over Mrs. Gormley, did he? Because that would just seem wrong…"

Alex chuckled, slid his eyes toward her, and then grinned wickedly. "Feeling a little bloodthirsty all of a sudden, are we, Your Grace?"

His grin was too beautiful to ignore. She slid her finger down and touched the corner of his mouth. She answered him truthfully. "I told him to stop, over and over again. I told him to stop, but he wouldn't. But when you touch me, you say I can tell you to stop at any time, even though you are my husband." The words escaped her with a sense of wonder.

Alex shifted into a more comfortable position and then tilted his head back to stare at the ceiling. He raised one hand and grasped her fingers to keep them from moving. Almost subconsciously, he placed a kiss upon one of her knuckles. "I have no wish to make love to an unwilling woman."

Abigail remembered Farley's eyes gleaming at her resistance. The wild look that had come into his eyes as she'd squirmed and pushed at him. "You are different from him."

Alex released her hand then and drew his forearm up to cover his eyes. He seemed almost irritated by her words. "Men are not so complicated, Abigail. Neither are we all that different from each other."

What was he trying to say? "But if I told you to stop, you would stop. Farley did not. This is a significant difference."

He fell silent for a moment. "There are ways for a woman to tell a man to stop that do not involve any words at all. And a man ought to listen to her. He ought to heed the messages her body sends."

Abigail wasn't certain what he was talking about. So she simply cuddled closer to him and let her hand rest upon his chest. She turned her head and placed a kiss upon the skin she rested upon. "What messages?"

Still talking to the ceiling, Alex answered her, "Rigidity. Tightness…dryness."

After the past several hours, Abigail had somewhat of an understanding as to what he was referring. But who? Lady Hyacinth?

"She did not tell you to stop?" It must have been the deceased duchess.

At her question, he let out a short bark of laughter. But it was not laughter, really. It was more of a self-deprecating gurgle. "She told me to hurry. She told me to get it over with."

Abigail contemplated his words. "And so you did what she said…even though she really did not want it?" What a horrible situation! "Was this on your wedding night?" The room had grown dark with shadows. She wondered if they ought to light a candle soon. But for now the darkness wove a comforting intimacy around the two of them. And Alex was talking with her, about himself no less!

His eyes were closed, but he emanated tension. "And a few other times." His voice sounded cold. "How does that make me any different from Farley? It does not." He went to pull away from her and out of the bed, but Abigail used her weight to push him back into the pillow. He could have moved if he'd tried harder, but he allowed her to hold him down. He did not meet her eyes, however.

"You did not enjoy it? Without her participation and satisfaction, you did not find a particular thrill?"

"God, no, Abigail!" He stared at her in horror.

"So why did you do it?" she asked him, remaining calm. He squirmed for a moment, but Abigail was almost lying completely on top of him now. Finally, he lay back in defeat.

In a resigned voice, he answered her. "I was excited to bed her. It was our wedding night. We were supposed to have relations. She was *a lady,* she said. I'd never bedded a virgin before. I thought I was doing my duty. I hoped it would be better the next time, and then the next time after that. But it never was. And then she hated me for it."

She'd never expected to be given such insight into his previous marriage. Lady Hyacinth was nearly as guilty as Damien Farley when it came to violating another person's body. "She made you do it even though she didn't want to. And when she didn't want to, it made you not want to. So you did it even though you didn't want to."

Alex chuckled. "You're insane." But he didn't say

anything after that. Abigail did, however, feel a brief kiss on top of her head.

Imagining what she must have looked like riding Penelope's contraption to the church in her wedding finery, Abigail chuckled. "Well, that's nothing I haven't heard before."

And then his hands were sliding down her sides and his mouth was forging a path all its own. "Alex!" she said in some surprise. What on earth was he doing? Except—oh my!

Neither of them did much talking for a while after that...

****

By the following morning, the rain had abated, and the driver declared it safe to travel. The going would be muddy, but Alex agreed that if they took it slowly, there was no immediate danger in resuming their journey.

His more pressing need was to reestablish separation between himself and his new duchess. For if he were to allow himself to spend another day making lo—no, *having relations* with her, he would find himself spouting poetry, for God's sake.

Yes, he definitely needed boundaries to fall back into place between the two of them. For God's sake, between bouts of sex, he'd talked of his childhood with her. He'd talked about Hyacinth. Good Lord, what was the matter with him?

He'd also delved into her own past.

She'd been an only child. Perhaps if she'd had a brother, her life might have turned out differently.

But after she'd left London that first time, she had not wallowed in self-pity. She'd made friends, developed a skill, and embraced any goodness she could find in life.

Whereas after the tragedies of his life, he had…what? He had barely gone through the motions of living since Marigold's and Elijah's deaths, focusing only upon his horses and his estates. He'd ignored how his abandonment of hope affected his aunt and sister. Was he such a cynical self-indulgent bastard as all that?

Alex dismissed these thoughts as he climbed into the carriage behind Abigail. On this day, he chose to sit across from her with his back facing front. He would not spend the day cuddling and fondling her like some lovesick fool.

Her questioning gaze irritated him. He'd yet to speak to her today except when he'd informed her they would be leaving after breakfast. He'd not touched her. He'd not looked her in the eyes. And she had not pushed him for further affection nor an explanation.

Yet.

As they pulled away from the inn, she sat with her lips slightly parted and fixed her gaze outside the window.

Alex resisted the urge to cross to sit beside her and take up where they'd left off just before dawn. The air was damp and cool. She pulled her shawl around her delicate shoulders and leaned against the side of the vehicle.

Her lips looked soft and swollen. Her neck was red, rubbed nearly raw by his beard, no doubt. Alex reached up and touched the two days' growth on his face. No razor, no starched cravat, and no valet, damn it. No wonder he was so overly engulfed in feelings of affection and sexual desire. He'd become most uncivilized.

He glanced outside to see what was so fascinating as to hold her attention. Children. Running wildly about in a field by a nearby farmhouse. Abigail reached up a hand and touched the window pane.

"Do you wonder about your child ever?" he asked despite his resolve.

Abigail turned and looked at him in surprise. She didn't answer right away. It had been an impertinent question to ask. He would have been angry if she'd asked him the same of his own children.

"I used to think it would have been easier had they simply died." She spoke after a full minute of silence. "Because of the not knowing. Not knowing if they were well—or cared for—or loved. Are they sick? Are they lonely?" She paused and returned her attention to outside the window. "Had they simply died at birth, I would not listen for them now. Every single day. But neither, then, would I have any hope. Hope that they are happy, hope that they bring joy to somebody else's life. Hope that they will love and be loved. Had they not lived, there would be no hope." She looked back at him and shrugged.

Wait a moment.

"They?" More than one?

Abigail dropped her lashes to study her gloved hands. "Twins—a boy and a girl."

You do not wish to have any little boys to chase after? No little girls' hair to braid? His arrogant words taunted him again.

"They will be all of nine years old on Boxing Day." Of course, she thought of them. "I gave birth to them the day after Christmas." They were but a few months older than Marigold would have been. But two of them?

"They were born safely?" Why should he care? They were another man's children. Farley's bastards, no less.

But they were not Farley's.

They were Abigail's.

Abigail nodded, pinching her lips together into a straight line. Her knuckles had turned white as she gripped her reticule tightly. "I experienced pains all throughout Christmas Eve and Christmas. They were early, but the midwife assured me it was normal for twins. She had guessed that there were two babies. She could feel them from the outside, she'd said." Abigail stared outside again, seemingly lost in her memories. "They were tiny, the girl first and then the boy. Two perfect miniature humans came out of my body."

She'd stunned Alex with her words. She ought not to speak so openly with him, and yet he found himself craving such details. Hyacinth had banned him from the birthing room. She'd insisted he stay away.

"But they were healthy." More a statement than a question.

"I was assured that they were." She swallowed hard. "The baby girl was set beside me as I gave birth to my son—the boy. But after he was born, both were taken out of the room." She blinked rapidly several times and then flashed him a watery smile. "They didn't allow me to hold them. They said it would be easier that way. It would make it easier to forget them."

Alex could not return her optimistic expression. Instead, he turned his head to watch the passing scenery. Despite being modern and well sprung, the carriage jostled as it hit puddles of mud and newly formed ruts in the road. It was not slipping, however. And the road was rather flat and straight.

"My property is but a few miles from Cornwall," he said, staring out the window. "If you would like, perhaps"—he turned to watch her expression—"I can make some inquiries as to the well-being of your children." He could do nothing for Elijah and Marigold, but Abigail's children were alive. *They were alive.* He was uncertain as to how she might feel about his offer.

She closed her eyes and leaned her head back against the seat. "What if they are unhappy?" she surprised him by asking. "What if they are not loved and cared for and healthy?"

"*What if they are*? Would it not calm your fears to discover that they are loved, and cared for and healthy?" he asked back. "You do not need to answer now."

"But what if they are not? How could I live with myself if I were to discover them living in want…in need?"

Alex looked at her as though taking a vow. "Then I will set things right," he answered firmly.

Abigail searched his eyes and then nodded. "Yes, then. Yes, please."

To say that Abigail was shocked by Monfort's offer would be the height of understatement. Since those empty days so long ago when she'd returned from Cornwall, her mother had been adamant that she never speak of the experience. The only person she'd ever shared any of it with until now had been Penelope.

And now Monfort was offering to find her babies and look into their well-being?

Already, today, an awkwardness overcame her.

After the shared confidences of yesterday, the heady lovemaking, early this morning even, Abigail had been disappointed to awaken alone. Monfort had dressed, apparently, and sent breakfast up for her to eat.

Alone.

Every inch of her body remembered his touch from the day before, but when he'd arrived back at their room, Monfort's face revealed only passive consideration. And when they'd climbed into the carriage, he'd chosen not to sit beside her. As though he no longer desired her touch.

She did not think she'd done anything wrong. No, she considered to herself, it was perhaps Monfort who was regretting his actions of yesterday.

He'd been Alex yesterday.

The man.

Today he was to be the duke again.

The duke, that is, who was offering to look in on the bastard children she'd given up for adoption nearly nine years ago.

Was he regretting their time together yesterday? Did he think it made him appear weak to her? Was it because she was so very common? Did he regret that he had such a strumpet for a wife? Yes, he'd told her then that he liked her that way, while she was in his bed— good God—while he'd been in her body! But today, as the Duke of Monfort, did he regret that he'd taken her to be his duchess?

And yet he'd offered to find her children for her.

Which wrought an entirely different set of emotions sweeping through her. And more questions. Suddenly, quite uncertain of herself, she pulled her feet up onto the bench and wrapped her arms around her knees. A chill had settled over the carriage today, and not simply because of the rain.

Chapter 19

Monfort's estate, Rock Point, was aptly named. Located in Southern Cornwall, it perched upon high rocky cliffs overlooking the sea. When they turned onto the road that carved its way up to the ancient castle, the sun was setting and the clouds had moved away.

Monfort had been exceedingly polite and proper as the miles passed. It was as though he intentionally needed to create distance between them again. Abigail had followed his lead and not pressed him for any affection. But her body had been awakened, and a part of her wondered if he would come to her this night. And if he did, who would he be? Would he come to her as Monfort or Alex?

Not that it mattered, in truth. Both parts of him were honorable. Both parts of him were genuine.

Yes, she would receive him tonight. She would even anticipate it.

She watched out the window quietly, the estate truly a glorious sight to behold. The water in the distance stretched forever a crystalline blue and the hills a verdant green she'd not remembered from when she had traveled south before. As the carriage turned and climbed, Abigail began to feel as though she were in something of a dream. She had a new life. She was married. She would be expected to act like a duchess.

Abigail glanced away from the ocean to peer out the other window as the carriage rocked to a halt. They had come to a stop below a towering structure that was to be her home for the next several weeks. It was more than a little intimidating. It was a castle, for heaven's sake. One of the gigantic wooden arched doors swung open and several black- and white-clad servants stepped out in an orderly fashion. Abigail was relieved to see her maid and Monfort's valet among them. The rest were quite unfamiliar.

Margaret had warned her about this. She had told her she would be expected to greet and approve the servants upon arriving at any of Monfort's estates. She was not fearful of this, but instead rather hopeful to make some friendly new acquaintances. They were servants, of course, but first and foremost they were people.

She smiled for the first time that day as each of them was presented to her. Margaret had instructed her to be restrained. Aunt Cecily advised her to tilt her head back and look down upon them in spite of her own lack of height. But Abigail could not do this.

No, she found herself clasping their hands and thanking them each for such a kind welcome. Most of the servants warmed to her quickly, except of course the butler and a few rather starchy footmen. The housekeeper and cook were smiling and bobbing by the time Abigail and Monfort entered the castle itself.

She'd been left cold by Monfort's demeanor all day, reminding her of the name he'd achieved with the ton, even though she hated it.

And then her maid turned to lead her off to her suite, admonishing Abigail over the state of her hair and dress. The duke excused himself to abandon her for some other unknown part of the ancient castle, but Abigail stopped him with her voice.

"Monfort," Abigail called out. Noting the servants around them, she leveled her voice slightly. "Your Grace?"

He turned back to look at her and raised one eyebrow. In spite of having traveled all day, he appeared perfectly elegant. How was it that he could look so fresh and pristine when her own gown must appear as though she'd slept in it, which she might as well have.

"Thank you."

He'd given her something she'd never expected.

"For…everything," she added.

He dropped his eyebrow and searched her eyes but said not one word.

Nothing.

Abigail curtsied quickly and left him standing there in his own thoughts. Yes, he had "saved" her. And yes, he had made her a duchess. She did appreciate all that he'd done. To thank him had only been polite. But his distance today hurt.

More than she wished to admit.

And a "you're welcome" would not have been remiss. He was a damned duke, after all. Where were his manners?

****

Alex retired to the study, which he'd always associated with his father. He'd only visited twice since taking over the dukedom himself. But it was tidy. He'd sent word ahead of their pending arrival, and he presumed the castle had been prepared just as he'd ordered.

A fire burned in the hearth. As he entered the room, the heavy drapes were pulled closed by a nearby footman and another man lit several candles about the room. When Alex took his seat behind the large mahogany desk, the servants discreetly disappeared, leaving him alone with his thoughts.

Alone, after being in Abigail's presence for nearly two entire days, he did not feel the relief he'd expected.

No, he felt...bereft—which bothered him. It bothered him that her mere existence was somehow changing his life, no, not only his life but his *thoughts*. He'd not bargained for *this*—for *feelings*. He'd entered into this marriage for rational purposes. He'd believed so, anyhow. He needed to marry and beget an heir. He wanted her physically and was in need of a sexual partner. And lastly, he'd harmed her reputation at Ravensdale's house party.

But something else had entered into it all.

Abigail herself.

Something of her character, her behavior and attitude, affected him emotionally. It was as though she passed judgment upon him with every optimistic thought she voiced. But she did not really. She consisted of something that he wasn't really used to...goodness...openness...At first, he'd presumed that these traits made her weak and simple, but now he wondered.

Perhaps they didn't make her weak so much as they made her vulnerable. That was it. And being with her, being close to her, made him feel vulnerable as well.

Vulnerability, in any form whatsoever, was

something he must squash. Wanting her made him weak. Wanting her was a weakness.

She had thanked him. For what, he wondered. For losing himself in her body? For taking that which he'd craved since they'd met? For treating her like a polite stranger today after the previous day's intimacies?

Alex ran his hand through his hair and sighed heavily. Even now his body came to life at the thought of being with her. Being in her body—no, he would not allow himself to ponder their encounters. Emotions were unsettling. He hated feeling unsettled. All day long, he'd forced himself to harden against Abigail's allure. It was exhausting. At moments, he even questioned his reasoning for doing so.

Perhaps she'd thanked him for offering to find her children. Yes, that was quite likely the reason.

He located a sheet of foolscap and went to open his inkwell before realizing he was going to require more information from her. What was the name of the midwife? Where had she stayed? He knew the date of the children's birth, but quite likely that would not be enough.

He set the pen down and placed the lid back onto the glass container of ink.

He would speak with her over dinner. The servants would have prepared an elaborate affair for the two of them this evening. He would need to endure Abigail's company for longer today, after all.

He rose from the desk and went in search of his valet.

****

Abigail's maid insisted the evening's meal would require her to dress formally. The servants had been frantically preparing for it for weeks, they'd told her. And now, having met Abigail, they most certainly would be anxious to please the new duchess.

And so for this evening's formal meal, she wore another of her new gowns. This one a delicate peach silk, simple yet sophisticated and flattering to her figure. Abigail nervously fingered the short string of pearls she'd donned for the evening. She'd not worn them often but had owned them most of her life. They'd been left to her by her grandmother.

The only other jewelry she owned was her wedding ring and the sapphire pendant Monfort had gifted her. The sapphire was far too glamorous to wear for an evening at home.

If only she and her maid could locate her slippers! They'd been dyed the exact shade of the dress and had inexplicably gone missing. As her maid returned to search for them in the dressing room, Abigail dropped to her hands and knees and crawled around peering under the furniture. Catching sight of them under a table, she ducked her head down farther and was just barely able to reach them. "They're right here, Harriette! I've found them—" She turned her head to alert her maid, but in doing so instead found herself staring into her husband's astonished gaze.

Monfort had entered the room and was watching her with something of a dumbfounded expression. Well, of course, she had her bum in the air and her dress pulled up past her knees. Not duchess-like at all.

"I knew I'd brought them out with the dress, Abby. It's no wonder I think I'm losing my mind." Her maid had not seen Monfort either. Abigail gestured toward the door, and Harriette's expression turned into one of abject submissiveness. "I mean, Your Grace, I'll fetch your shawl for you now. This castle is chilly in the evenings."

Abigail pulled herself to a sitting position as her maid disappeared and grimaced up at Monfort. "I lost my slippers."

Monfort appeared somewhat hesitant. Which was quite unusual for him. Normally he inhabited a room as though he owned it, as though it had been built for him. Which, in some cases anyway, it quite possibly may have been.

"Abby?" he spoke her name with raised brows. "Your maid addresses you as *Abby*?" At the same time, he walked toward her and held out a hand to assist her from the floor.

Abigail stared at his gloved hand and then grimaced. The material was perfectly white. Not giving her a chance to wipe her hands from crawling on the floor, he grasped hold and pulled her up to stand.

"I *like* my maid. She is a devoted companion to me. Why would I not allow her to address me by my name?" She was still a little irritated by his chilly demeanor from earlier today.

Monfort released her hand and examined the dust she'd left on his glove. In spite of his natural arrogance, she again had the impression that he was not altogether comfortable entering her chamber.

"I'm not quite ready to go down." Abigail reached for a linen and wiped her hands and then bent forward and brushed at her skirt to smooth it.

"Of course, my apologies, madam." He looked as though he were going to back out of the room. "I would not have—"

In spite of the haughty tone in his voice, he could not hide an emotion that had appeared in his eyes.

He looked…rejected? Surely not?

And then something dawned on her. But of course! He had not been welcome into his wife's room when he'd been married to Lady Hyacinth. Abigail gritted her teeth at this thought.

"Monfort," she interrupted him. His head snapped up. He again looked arrogant and proud. "I'll be just a moment. Do you like this dress? Margaret chose it for me. Harriette tells me dinner will be formal this evening. She said the servants have been planning this dinner for days now. Since they first heard we would be coming here, in fact." Abigail intentionally set to babbling, thinking Monfort needed it in that moment. "And I'm starving! It seems as though we ate our luncheon ages ago. Oh, thank you, Harriette," she said as she took the shawl and sat down for her maid to tie her slippers. "Nearly ready now."

She looked up from her feet as Harriette went to work and smiled at her husband. "Are you as hungry as I am?"

He'd relaxed slightly, and she thought she recognized a ghost of a smile. "I do." And then he looked about the room curiously. He was uncomfortable, but not as much as he'd been at first. "And yes, I suppose that I am."

"You do?" Abigail furrowed her brows.

And then he was looking at her again. "I like your dress."

Abigail swallowed hard but didn't say anything. He liked her dress. But even more than that he actually—really and truly—listened to what she said.

With her slippers tied securely, Abigail took Monfort's arm and they exited the room together.

****

Alex was pleased that the servants hadn't positioned Abigail at the far end of the table as was often done on formal occasions. Instead, she sat to his right. Numerous candles glowed and a profusion of flowers decorated the long dining hall.

He almost chuckled out loud as he recalled the sight that had greeted him when he'd entered her chamber. Rounded derriere pushed into the air, clothed in thin, nearly transparent material. And then her face peeking around with a shocked expression at his appearance.

To be fair, *he had knocked.*

Hyacinth had demanded he always knock before entering her domain. And on many occasions, she'd refused him entry.

Abigail could not be any more different than his first wife.

Always so cheerful, so forthcoming, so accepting of what life handed her. She never complained or whined, constantly searching for silver linings. The mere fact that she'd had to look for so many ought to have diminished her outlook.

"Did you know, Monfort, that your cook speaks Cornish? I was unaware that the people of Cornwall had their own language. When she first greeted me, I thought she might be Welsh, but she assured me that she was most definitely not." Her eyes sparkled as she chattered on about certain servants who'd made an impression on her when they'd arrived.

Alex nodded, soothed by her endless stream of

words. She would be an adequate duchess, he imagined. Already the servants had taken a liking to her. He, himself, had not given much notice to any of them. "My mother spoke Cornish." It was a surprising memory. He'd not thought of her in years. But he held onto a few vivid memories. She'd died after giving birth to Margaret. Alex had not yet been ten years old. "This castle was a part of her dowry."

"Did you come here much as a child?"

"We did." Like an ocean wave, a plethora of memories crashed into his thoughts. "Mother liked to swim. I have fond remembrances of the beach here during the summer. We must have traveled down every year." Alex found himself lightened by the recollection. After his mother had passed, his father had not ever been the same. The visits to the beach had ceased completely.

Abigail tilted her head. "So you must be a good swimmer, then. Will you swim while we are here?"

He'd not thought about it. He'd been inclined to inspect the stables, perhaps seek out what horseflesh was available in the area. He'd also been considering the search for her children.

"Perhaps." The idea was intriguing. "Are you a swimmer, Abigail?"

She laughed. "Less so than a horsewoman. I've waded into the stream that runs through Biddeford Corners, up to my knees. But the ocean is a different beast, I'm sure. Perhaps I'll be so daring as to let the surf curl around my toes while we are here."

The thought of her being pulled away by the strong tide stole his breath. "If you wish to do so, I'd have you not go down alone. I can go with you. If I'm not available, you will take a footman." He ought not to promise her his company. "From what I remember, the path down to the beach is steep. And the tide can be strong. I've no wish to lose another wife so quickly." Good God, had he actually spoken such words?

Abigail's eyes were wide. "Of course not, Monfort. That's a horrible thought." And then, uncharacteristically, Abigail was apparently at a loss for words as she stared down at her plate solemnly.

Why had he said such a thing? "I'm sorry, Abigail. That was uncalled for."

But she shook her head in denial. "It is what I experienced when you were going to parachute from the balloon." And then she looked him straight in the eye. "I've no wish to lose *you*, Monfort."

For a moment, he was back at that infernal inn and he was gazing into her eyes as he drove himself into her. His heart quickened at the thought. "Well, then." He cleared his throat and then placed his napkin upon his plate. He did not deign to speak again until the servants left them alone.

"I will make inquiries after the children for you first thing tomorrow, but I've need of more information." He glanced at his fob watch. The candlelight was barely bright enough to illuminate the face. "Do you remember the name of the midwife?"

He glanced in her direction casually. She was gazing at one of the flickering candles as though mesmerized and then took a sip from her glass. "I stayed at the Periwinkle Farm. The midwife was Mrs. Wells. The date of delivery was the twenty-sixth of December in the year 1815." Her lips were shiny from the red wine. A wisp of hair curled seductively along her cheek.

His breath caught. How had he ever thought her to be an antidote? He'd considered her a harmless spinster who did not even have the strength to affect her own life. Now, if he was not careful, she would have his own life in ruins.

Alex nodded and then pushed his chair back to stand, signaling that the meal was over. "It has been too long since I've looked over my steward's books here, so I am going to forgo port this evening." Her eyes were questioning and a little disappointed. "If you will excuse me," he added.

She looked as though she were going to ask him something but instead answered with a nod. "Of course."

Alex left the room without another word.

He needed time alone.

The feelings he'd indulged in with Abigail were somewhat...terrifying. If he continued to allow them reign over his person, there could only be disappointment. How ironic that he was called the Duke of Ice. He'd not been married a week and already Abigail was chipping away at what he'd considered to be his frozen emotions.

And then he chuckled at his own uncharacteristic thoughts. He'd not frozen his emotions in any way, he admonished himself. He simply did not wish to give Abigail the impression that he would be a doting husband. He'd already learned the folly of making such an emotional attachment.

He would not go to her this evening.

****

Abigail had not been married to the duke for even

one full week and yet, he'd already tired of her.

After only one day of relations.

He'd not come to her again. It was as though she'd thoroughly disgusted him with her amorousness at the inn. What on earth had she been thinking? She'd dared to think that she was worthy of more than pity—worthy of notice.

She must have been wrong, fooling herself into believing their lovemaking had meant as much to him as it had to her. Such foolishness! Every night since arriving at Rock Point she'd lain awake, hoping he would come to her. And later, after that, she'd chastised herself for allowing herself such ridiculous hope.

More than anybody, she ought to know that life was not a fantasy.

She'd been fortunate, yes, very fortunate to have married into a position of great security. She ought not to press her luck into wishing for more.

She had shared one wonderful day with her husband. She'd shared more than she ever could have imagined with him in that cozy little room while it had rained outside.

She'd felt beautiful, powerful, and...loved!

And she had thought Monfort had felt love as well. Why did love not matter to him?

He'd shared parts of his soul with her, she'd thought.

Oh, foolish, foolish Abigail! She had been warned about his lack of ability to show emotion, let alone love. She deserved every ounce of heartache she got for thinking otherwise.

In the days since their arrival, Abigail decided to make the most of the independence her husband had given her through his indifference.

She'd met with all of the staff. Every cook, maid, footman, and stable hand. There were forty-eight of them altogether. They were, each and every one of them, human beings and deserved to be given some notice and appreciation for their efforts. At first, they had been hesitant and surprised by her unannounced visits, but as word spread of her endeavor, she was finding herself received quite positively.

Some of them even went so far as to share a few of their opinions and needs with her. She carried a pencil and paper and took diligent notes away from each meeting. The staff in Cornwall was not nearly as loyal as those who worked at Cross Hall had been. They had been mostly ignored for the past decade. She hoped she could do a few small things to rectify their outlooks.

Between these meetings, Abigail explored the grounds of the estate. She could not run about alone, as she had in Biddeford Corners, but the footman assigned to watch out for her kept his distance.

Abigail followed the trails into the hills behind the castle, and she picked her way down the paths that led to the beaches below.

She did not venture into the sea. A foolish part of her was waiting for an opportunity to do so with her husband.

She explored some nearby ruins and toured the well-kept but empty rooms within the castle itself.

She found optimism in her busyness. She'd been a fool to look for optimism from Monfort.

****

After a few days of correspondence with his local man of business, a man who he trusted to act with the utmost of discretion, and Alex easily obtained the location of the people who had taken custody of the two Wright children. The records were supposed to have been closed, but a few sovereigns from his man of business persuaded the midwife to give up the information.

The couple who adopted Abigail's children had presented themselves as the owners of an inn located about fifteen miles west of Cornwall. They had wanted just a boy but, in light of the children being born twins, had taken on both. They had told the midwife the girl could ease the missus's duties and the boy could earn his keep in the stables.

The situation did not sound promising.

After reading the missive, he summoned Abigail. They'd hardly spoken at all over the last few days. She'd taken to marching about the property without him, and Alex had filled much of his time with meetings and a few tenant visits.

He knew he ought to have invited Abigail along with him, at the very least offered to give her a tour of the estate, but considered it best to reestablish detachment.

He'd hurt her with his lack of attentiveness. And as much as he tried to convince himself that she would not have welcomed his nightly visits, he knew his continued absence from her bed hurt her as well.

And all of this damn hurting of Abigail was making him angry with both her and himself. He'd not married her so that she would be unhappy, damn it! He'd been *saving her*, for Christ's sake. He'd not promised moonlight and roses. He'd promised her security and comfort. Why should he feel guilty now for not giving her…?

Love?

Was that what she'd been asking for with her eyes when she'd watched him leave the dining room that first night? Was that what he was afraid of giving to her?

Impossible!

It had been about sex. Their time together had been about sex. That is what she had been offering him, her body—pleasure—sensual entertainment.

A knock at the door interrupted his musings. "Enter," he stated firmly. It would be Abigail. He chastised the part of himself cheered by her impending presence. Nonetheless, when she entered, his eyes devoured her. She stepped in quietly, wearing a yellow gown that was reminiscent of the gown she'd worn for dinner that first night at Raven's Park. It was of similar style but of a heavier material, and of a subtler tone— more golden than sunny.

She stood straight, her hair perfectly made up of artful braids into an intricate coronet.

She looked rather…like a duchess!

What had he expected? The waif he'd rescued from Raebourne earlier that summer? And yet.

She was still Abigail, with a light in her eyes and a soft glow to her cheeks. Surprisingly, she was not smiling at him, which caused a dull ache to take residence in his heart.

But she was still Abigail.

Alex swallowed and then gestured for her to be seated. He would not beat around the bush. "I have located the children. They are not far from here—half a day's drive, if that."

His words brought him her full attention. She jerked her head up and stared at him in a straightforward manner he'd not seen since arriving at Rock Point. "They are well?"

Alex glanced at the letter sitting atop his desk. "I have ascertained the name and location of the people who adopted them. I merely wished to inform you that I would be traveling there tomorrow to investigate their situation further. I did not think it fair to do so without informing you."

Abigail jumped to her feet while he was speaking. "I will go as well." A gleam had appeared in her eyes. The same one he'd seen when she had come careening toward him on that damned Lady Accelerator the morning of their nuptials.

"Perhaps it would be best if you were to wait he—"

But she would not allow him to complete his sentence. She was shaking her head adamantly. "No, Monfort, I will see them for myself. I will not state who I am. I do not wish to disrupt their lives. But I wish to see with my own eyes that they are well. It is the only thing that will suffice for me now." She turned and walked away from him, seemingly as though she were perusing some of his bookshelves, but he knew that was not the case. As she reached up to pull out a book, her hand shook.

"In light of this marriage, and your offer to find them for me, I have come to realize that this is important for me in order to move on. I shall always carry them with me in my heart regardless, but I just need to know..." She spun around and faced him again. "I need to know, Ale—Monfort."

Her eyes were shining, but her voice carried

conviction, or had until she'd nearly called him by his Christian name.

"They are likely servants," Alex told her. He did not wish for her to build a fantasy in her mind as to how the children were living. "It mightn't be the most pleasant of circumstances."

Abigail held his gaze. She was not looking at him meekly. He glimpsed a fire inside he'd not seen before. Was it because of him? Was it because he'd rejected her? Was this how Abigail Wright looked...angry?

"If they are not in a suitable situation, then we shall change that. Is that not what you promised?" By God, she *was* angry with him.

And Abigail Wright, looking proud and angry, was nearly as enticing to him as when she'd tossed back her head and found her pleasure atop him.

He would have her tonight.

"Of course." Her insinuation that he would not keep his word drew some of his own ire. "We shall depart tomorrow after breakfast. This will allow us to return home before dark." And as she twirled about to leave, he stopped her again with his voice. "I will come to you tonight?" It was not a question, and he was irritated with himself for allowing it to sound like one. "You shall receive me."

Abigail stilled. But for the tiniest nod of her head, he would not have thought she'd understood him.

But she'd nodded because she had.

By God, she had.

****

Tonight she was to receive him.

How could she keep herself from falling into this death spiral of hope if she continued to allow him such intimacy with her person? For there was no way to have relations without intimacy.

Except there was.

There was, and it had been absolutely horrible.

Could she hold herself in reserve? She imagined herself, lying passive as Alex—no Monfort—touched her, opened her up. As he explored and tasted and...loved.

It would be impossible to not want him back. She was not at all like his first wife. She *wanted* him!

But he had not indicated that any of it mattered to him. Ever since they'd left the inn, he had been cold, aloof, and arrogant. *But still she would not resist him.*

And as she waited for his arrival to her rooms, her conviction grew stronger. The hour she normally went to bed was long past. She'd been attempting to read but in her nervousness failed to comprehend more than a page or two. Why was she waiting for him? He'd obviously forgotten his request of earlier. Was a wife so easy to forget?

Defeated by the inconsideration of her blasted husband, Abigail set her book aside, shed her dressing gown, put out the few candles she'd left burning, and then climbed onto the vast canopied bed she'd been allotted. She did not realize how cold she'd become until she lie cocooned beneath the heavy coverlet. Turning to her side, she pulled her knees up to her chest and burrowed for warmth. Next time, she would simply tell him no. That way she would avoid the torture of being disappointed by him.

Why must he be this way?

One tear escaped before Abigail surprisingly fell asleep. Her last thought of the night was of the children she would see tomorrow.

****

He'd come after all.

She awoke to the feel of his lean warmth behind her. He had wrapped one arm around her waist and was kissing the skin behind her ear. "Abigail," he whispered, "forgive me?"

And then his lips were moving around her face, across her eyes, down her cheeks. "I'm sorry I have come so late. The stable master was injured, and I needed to wait while the doctor attended him." His mouth traveled along her jaw, her neck.

And then his lips found her mouth.

Abigail parted them and arched into him. She *could never* resist him. His tongue explored behind her teeth, inside the tender skin of her cheek. Abigail opened wider for him.

"God help me," he mumbled inside her mouth.

Abigail's hands grasped the back of his head. She wanted him closer, tighter. Their teeth made a clashing sound as they both fought for something deeper.

With a rumbling growl, Alex swept her nightgown up and over her head. He'd already shed all of his clothing. He smelled of soap and sandalwood. He must have bathed before coming to her.

They found each other again quickly. There was no playing, no teasing. Instead there was pushing, pulling, and deep, oh so deep, thrusting. In burying himself inside of her, he not only reached for her womb, but her inner essence.

"Alex," she cried out several times. It was all she could coherently manage, so engulfed she was by the sensations of him. "Alex!"

****

Alex very nearly had not gone to Abigail that night. After the accident in the stables, he'd almost convinced himself the hour had grown too late.

He was also somewhat wary. He'd ordered Hyacinth to receive him and look at what that had achieved. Now, he'd ordered Abigail. What if he went to her and she resisted him? He would not demand her acquiescence. He was not so stupid any longer. He'd been an insensitive, rutting cub with Hyacinth. He was no longer that man.

He'd been granted Abigail's trust. He would not do anything to cause her to feel unsafe ever again. Perhaps he would simply go to her and apologize.

He would apologize for hurting her feelings the first night they'd arrived. He would apologize for ignoring her for the past four days. And then, perhaps...If she received him...

He ordered a quick bath and donned a dressing gown before sending Villiars away.

When he entered her room, all was dark. She lay beneath the coverlet, still and breathing deeply. She was asleep.

He should leave. He could speak to her tomorrow. But even as those thoughts drifted through his mind, he found himself climbing under the coverlet and wrapping one arm around her. She smelled clean and delicate. He inhaled as his lips found the pulse at her nape.

She was his.

She would not refuse him. She was not Hyacinth.

Alex whispered his apologies into her neck as he sensed her awaken. He had intended to be gentle and coaxing tonight, but her enthusiasm for his touch ignited a passion inside him he'd long suppressed. It was physical. It was emotional. It was almost even spiritual.

And she chanted his name, as though in prayer. No time elapsed at all before he buried himself in her sweet, wet warmth, her legs spread wide, her hands clutching at him. It was not enough.

He drove into her hard and deep, her returning thrusts surprisingly strong. They merged into one being. And when her body shuddered and began clenching around him, he drove into her one last time, deeply, powerfully, and released his seed. As he pulsed in completion, he pushed into her even harder before relaxing and rolling onto the bed. She curled onto her side and placed one hand upon his chest.

"Are you afraid for tomorrow?" he asked into the darkness.

Her breath tickled his shoulder when she sighed deeply. "I am terrified, and yet nothing on earth could keep me from coming along."

Alex pulled her closer to him, his arm trapped beneath her neck. "I will tell you everything. You do not need to be there. If their situation is remiss, I will make arrangements to right it."

That soft sigh again. "I know…" She trailed off. "But I have a yearning"—she brought one hand up to her heart—"inside, to see them with my own eyes. I have to go, Alex. I cannot let this opportunity pass me by."

Again, he gave her a gentle squeeze.

But she was not finished speaking. "If you could see your children once again, nothing would stop you.

You must think of them often. I know you must...It would be impossible not to."

At her words, a familiar coldness crept into his limbs—through his head, his legs, and into the area where surely his heart must be.

"Is that why you are assisting me in this matter, Alex?" she persisted.

Alex removed his arm from around her and sat up abruptly, causing her hand to fall away from his chest. A roaring filled his ears. He closed his eyes and envisioned little Marigold trapped under the ice, enshrouded in eternal darkness. And Elijah, not old enough to swim, his lungs filled with ice cold water, frightened and unable to draw in air.

He remembered the efforts of himself and his servants. He'd tied a rope around himself and gone into the water in search of them.

But the temperature had dropped quickly that day. The servants had pulled him out, wrapped him in blankets, and dragged him inside as the lake froze solid.

"Their bodies could not be retrieved until springtime." The sound of his own voice in the darkness surprised him. "So you see, I was given one more opportunity to see them after all."

Abigail crawled to her knees and wrapped her arms around him. She held him tightly. She infused warmth into him. He would not give in to the urge to reach up and clasp onto her hands with his own—to turn around and bury his neck in her softness.

Instead, he removed her hands. He needed to be away from her. Retrieving his dressing gown from the floor, he shrugged into it quickly.

Her voice reached out to him. "Why do you resist

this?" she pleaded. "What are you afraid of?"

He would not answer her. He *could* not answer her. Instead, he turned and sketched a low bow. "You have my full gratitude for receiving me. Until tomorrow." And with those words, he returned to his own rooms.

Chapter 20

After a sleepless night, Abigail preceded Monfort into the coach that was to take them to see her children.

It was an older coach, without the ducal insignia. Monfort had informed her that he did not wish to draw any undue attention. They were traveling today, not as a duke and a duchess, but as Mr. and Mrs. Cross. They were to make their visit as though Monfort was interested in purchasing a horse. Ironically, the people who'd taken in her children were known for their horse breeding.

Her children.

As much as she wanted to be angry with her husband for his parting words to her the night before, she knew that she'd prodded at something painful. And like a wounded animal, he'd coiled back.

Was he so very broken? She was beginning to think that perhaps the only closeness he ever wanted to share with her was of a physical nature. He tended to close himself off after he talked to her about himself.

Would sex be enough? For each time they came together, Abigail gave him a part of herself. If she were to continue to do so, without him giving back something of himself, she might be left with nothing. Which hardly made any sense at all.

Shaking her head at her own dramatics, she peered

out the window at the passing countryside. The leaves on the trees were beginning to change color, even though it was barely October. Fall was arriving early; perhaps winter would as well.

She wanted to talk with her husband, but he'd shut her out again, completely, by opening a lap desk and pouring all of his concentration into the contents of some paperwork. Occasionally, he would make a note with a pencil.

How could he concentrate on contracts and whatnot when she was less than a few hours away from laying her eyes on her children for the first time in nearly nine years? Just when she thought he cared for her feelings, he put her opinion in doubt. She turned her head away from the window and stared unabashedly at him.

Tiny wrinkles spread out from the corners of his eyes. He squinted slightly as he read. He was going to need spectacles at some point, she imagined. His hair was combed back neatly. It was longer than when she'd first met him. His valet had even tied it into a short queue in back.

She knew the texture of his hair, intimately. A heady sensation, imagining that just last night he'd been inside of her. She'd been able to touch his body wherever she'd wanted. And now, today, she dared not risk reaching out to touch even the length of his jaw.

Sensing her appraisal, Monfort's eyes slid over to her impatiently. "Did you need something, Abigail?" He spoke as though bored with her. This tug of war between them was beginning to aggravate her as well.

"I am nervous—and excited…It's difficult to sit quietly and wait for our arrival. Is there anything else you might be able to tell me about their family? About the people who took them in?"

After placing the lap desk on the floor, Monfort nodded slowly. "I sent word that we would be coming to look at a few of the Cripes' horses. I will speak with Mr. Cripes about the boy while you speak with Mrs. Cripes. Hopefully, you shall be able to glean information about the girl."

"What if they are not forthcoming?"

"If we do not succeed, I will have my man of business use more straightforward means to see to the children's circumstances. Hopefully, this will not be necessary. I've given my solicitor only the most pertinent of information in regards to his inquiries." As though struck with a surprising thought, he raised his brows. "I do hope you haven't discussed any of this with your maid?"

"Of course not!" Did he think she was a fool?

And then he grimaced at her ruefully. "It was my intention to protect you from scandal, Abigail, but it seems I've caused even more to rain down upon you. If society got wind of our visit, and why..." He shook his head. "It will be better if we do this quietly."

His eye still showed some yellow bruising beneath it.

She nodded solemnly. He was correct, of course. "Of course." She echoed her thoughts out loud. And then she voiced a regret she'd known for years. "I do not even know their names."

Monfort averted his eyes from her to stare at the opposite corner of the coach. He looked as though he would say something but was keeping himself from doing so. She wanted to ask him more about the children he'd lost. It was something they shared.

But her children lived, whereas his did not.

He had known them. He had held them and watched them grow.

She had not.

Abigail turned her head back to stare out the window.

****

As they pulled in to the modern-looking inn, which advertised the large stable block in back, Abigail's complexion had turned as pale as a ghost. She hadn't spoken for much of their journey, which was somewhat unnatural for her. He'd learned quickly that his new wife could prattle on about nearly anything. It was strangely endearing.

Today she must be nervous, indeed.

The coach rocked to a stop, and Alex jumped up quickly to push open the door. The driver had alighted as well and stuck his head in before Alex could exit. "It's muddy, Your Gr—ahem—Mr. Cross. Allow me to set down the step."

Glad that he'd worn an older pair of Hessians, Alex stepped onto the ground tentatively. His feet sank nearly four inches. When Abigail peeked out, he reached up his arms for her. "You'll ruin your slippers, my dear. I'll carry you to the door."

Her brows puckered at his words, and then her eyes drifted down to the mud and puddles that surrounded them. "I'm too heavy." She bit her bottom lip.

Sometimes, she was such a practical lady and at others…Alex reached in and tried putting one arm under her arms and the other at her knees, but she bolted backward. "You cannot!"

Damn woman! Did she not want him putting his hands on her? She hadn't been so reluctant last night. The driver, waiting patiently, observed them. He would be wanting to remove the horses to the stables for a rubdown and some water.

Alex reached in, wrapped his arms around Abigail's thighs, and toppled her over his shoulder. Before pulling her out of the coach, he could not resist patting her bum and then giving it a quick squeeze.

She shrieked as he pulled her from the carriage. The driver grinned, and Alex winked at the man.

Had he really done that? Had he really just shared a joke with one of his servants over his wife's inverted form? Oh, hell. He had at that. But today he was not the duke. He was Mr. Cross, and his wife was being silly and difficult.

He grinned as he crossed the muddied yard toward the entrance to the inn.

"Alex? I can walk, you know! Whatever are the Cripes' going to think of us? Alex! Please? Put me down, Alex!" She did not stop imploring him until he lowered her to stand upon the wooden platform just outside of the inn.

And then he laughed at the look on her face when she swung around to face him. "I cannot believe you just did that!" Red faced, she glared daggers, but he knew she wasn't really angry. Embarrassed, but not angry.

Alex stomped his feet a few times to remove some of the mud and then, upon seeing a boot scraper, went about removing most of the debris. "Hush, Abigail," he ordered her. Then winging her an arm, he raised his brows. "Are you ready?" They were both serious now.

She took a deep breath and then nodded.

"Very well then…Mrs. Cross. Let us see about some horseflesh."

****

A few guests sitting at the wooden tables in the tap room glanced up curiously upon their entrance. Monfort ignored them and approached the long wooden counter. A heavyset woman, who looked to be well into her forties, greeted him cheerfully. "Ah, Mr. Cross? I am Agnes Cripes. Mr. Cripes, my husband, told me to expect you. You are welcome to head out back toward the stable. You'll find him out there along with our stable master."

Monfort sent Abigail an encouraging nod and then, thanking Mrs. Cripes, took his leave.

Abigail wanted to rush through the doorway behind the counter. Was her little girl back there? "Hello, Mrs. Cripes," she spoke firmly, while extending her hand. "I am Abigail—er—Cross. What a lovely inn you have! Do you perhaps have any tea? How long have you lived here? Your stables must be successful for your horses to have captured my husband's attention." She knew she was jabbering. She was so very excited—and nervous—and terrified. The anticipation of seeing one of her children was likely going to kill her.

"Oh, for certain, that I do." With a glance at the men seated in the taproom, Mrs. Cripes reached for Abigail's arm. "Come back here with me and I'll make you a spot of tea. Your husband likes his horses, does he? That's a fine carriage you come in."

Abigail nodded and eagerly allowed the woman to take her into the back. A small girl of about five was stirring a pot, whilst a lad of about fourteen brought in some firewood. There were no others in the kitchen. "Are these your children?" Abigail asked cheerfully. Smiling at the little girl, she added, "What a pretty little thing you are."

"Mary, fetch the lady a cup for tea," Mrs. Cripes ordered the girl. And then, "Johnny, I told you not to bring mud into my kitchen. You get your dirty boots outside and then come back in here with a broom to clear this out." Turning to face Abigail again, she scrunched up her nose as though a smell offended her. "The children are from the workhouse. Labor comes cheap, but I need to take the time to train 'em up right." The woman rambled on about her heavy workload and the trouble she had finding good help. Mrs. Cripes' hands were callused. When she spoke, Abigail wondered if the woman's heart was callused as well.

Abigail's own heart nearly stopped beating at the woman's casual dismissal of the children's humanity.

The woman didn't seem malicious, but a tiredness lurked in her eyes. Her hair, although tied back, was dull, and the skin of her jowls sagged. Abigail swallowed the huge lump that had suddenly appeared in her throat. Interrupting the woman's long-winded discourse, Abigail could hold back no longer. "How do they end up in the workhouse? Are they orphans?"

Mrs. Cripes was taking the cup from young Mary's hand and pouring hot water over the tea into it. "That and their own parents don' want 'em. Figure at least here with me and Mr. Cripes, they can learn how to make a living and whatnot. Mary and Johnny ain't the first ones I've taken in and probably won't be the last. Sit down here, Mrs. Cross. Would you care for some biscuits as well?"

Abigail could barely comprehend Mrs. Cripes' words as she dropped into the seat held out for her. Oh God—Oh God—Oh God. "You've had many children then? Are they apprenticed out? Do they find other work then?"

"Some of 'em run away, mind you," she said, frowning. "Thankless little buggers, at that." And then, handing Abigail the cup of steaming hot liquid, she added, "And some of 'em just die."

Chapter 21

Alex wasted no time returning to the main building of the inn as soon as he heard about the scarlet fever epidemic that had swept through this tiny hamlet last year. He didn't want for her to hear about it alone. Trying to get to her through the mud eerily reminded him of that day the ice give way at Brooke's Abbey. He needed to move faster, but distance and terrain would not allow him.

The news would devastate her. He never should have suggested this. Why had he done something so foolish without obtaining the facts first? She'd never needed to know. He could not get to her quickly enough walking. He needed to be with her when she heard the truth. Maybe he could prevent her from finding out altogether.

By the time he reached the back entrance where a young boy was carrying wood, his legs burned from traipsing through the mud. Through an open doorway, he watched from a distance as Abigail reached for the cup Mrs. Cripes was handing her.

Something the woman was saying upset Abigail. He knew the instant it happened.

An emptiness entered her eyes, and she no longer paid attention to the hot water in her hands, spilling the contents onto her lap. But she did not jump up. She did not even cry out. She sat unmoving, listening to whatever the lady innkeeper was saying.

She'd poured steaming water on herself. He needed to get it off her.

"Why, just last year a pair of twins I'd finally trained up were taken by the fever. After all the effort and time I'd put into them, 'twas a shame to lose 'em. A boy and a girl. Hard workers, too." The woman's voice carried across the threshold.

Surely Abigail would faint at the woman's careless words. Abigail only nodded, but all color had drained from her face.

"How old were they?" Her voice came out sounding flat, lacking its normal lilt of optimism.

"Oh, I suppose around seven or eight. Took them on as babies but hard to remember exactly when."

Alex stepped into the room and squatted behind Abigail. "We must leave now." He grasped both of her elbows from behind and nearly lifted her from the grimy wooden chair. When she'd risen, he pulled the fabric of her gown away from her skin. "If we're to make it back before dark, sweetheart, we need to get on the road now."

He'd shouted at John, his driver, to ready the coach as he'd made his dash from the stables. He needed to get Abigail out of this place. As he steered her nearly lifeless form through the tap room, he cursed himself again for bringing her here. She didn't deserve this. He ought to have allowed her to continue believing the children were happy, healthy in a loving home. She could have gone on believing the world held more benevolence in it than despair.

Once outside on the front verandah, he scooped her

up to carry her to the waiting coach. She did not resist him this time. She hadn't said a word. He didn't think she'd even blinked. It was as though she were frozen.

Ignoring the tragic irony of his own thoughts, he lifted her into the open door of the coach and then leapt in after her. She sat straight against the aged leather upholstery, staring ahead as the vehicle shuddered to move out of the muddy yard. Alex pulled out a flask and poured some water into a handkerchief. He pressed the cool water against the angry welt which had appeared on her hand.

Abigail turned to look at him, oblivious of the burn. "They are gone," was all she said. "I would have thought I would know. I would have thought that, as their mother"—she pulled her hand away from him and pressed it to her stomach—"I would have felt it, inside. But I had no idea. I imagined them happy, growing into little people. I imagined them cossetted—playing outside, learning how to read. And it was nothing like that, Monfort. I abandoned them to *that woman*. They were raised to be *servants*. As children, even, *they* were servants. I am a horrible person. I abandoned them to that life!"

Alex could not bear to see her so hopeless. He scooped her onto his lap. "Hush, Abigail. Hush. You did not know! You were given no choice. You are not a horrible person, never a horrible person. I am so sorry. This is my fault. I never should have brought you here." He tucked her head beneath his chin and clasped her tightly against him. She did not relax against him, however. She remained rigid, unyielding.

"I could have run away. But I was selfish. I wanted to regain my parents' approval. They told me the scandal would go away if things were kept quiet. It was why Farley was never confronted. I didn't want any more scandal. I didn't want to live as an outcast. But if I'd been willing to face a *stupid scandal,* then my children would still be here. *They would still be alive!* It is because of my selfishness." She turned her head and looked into his eyes.

What Alex saw there frightened him. That glimmer of light was gone. There was no optimistic tilt to the corners of her mouth.

"I am such a stupid fool. I was hoping that seeing them happy and loved would give me some sense of comfort. That it would give me absolution for giving them up."

She pushed his arms away and moved to the other side of the bench. Pressing herself into the corner, she looked down at her hands. One of them was reddened from the hot water, but she continued to ignore it. Her gown was damp, but she gave it no notice either.

"When first we met, you chastised me for not being pragmatic about my future. But, fool that I was, I continued to view the world through rose-colored glasses." She stared at him with a cold light in her eyes. "I did nothing for those two children. Dare I even call them mine? They never were." And then she looked out the window again. "Perhaps if I'd been braver somehow. Taken control somehow…I could have saved them."

And then a tear escaped to roll down her cheek. Alex almost felt relieved to see them begin to pour from her eyes.

"I didn't save them, Alex. I did nothing, and they…died."

The sentiment was hauntingly familiar to him. But he ignored that and slid across the bench seat to her again.

She pushed him away at first but eventually relinquished her threadbare control and leaned into him. "I did nothing, Alex," she cried again as he wrapped his arms around her. Sobs wracked her body as she allowed more tears to fall. They traveled for several miles as Abigail gave into her grief. Just as it had been a relief for him when she'd finally cried, it was equally so when she went quiet. She hiccupped a few times and burrowed into him. "I seem foolish," she mumbled.

"You do not," Alex said firmly, not allowing her to continue such train of thought out loud. "There is nothing worse."

"I never knew them," she said. "Why do I feel so empty inside?"

"Because they have been in your heart all this time, Abigail." As he said these words, he confronted a bit of his own grief. "Just as they shall continue to be." Was the memory of his own children locked inside of his own heart? He allowed his mind to picture Marigold, with her golden ringlets dancing about the hearth singing Christmas carols in her small little voice. And Elijah, watching his sister, clapping his hands together.

He'd purposely not thought of them thus since that last day. It hurt too much. He had been unable to save them. He'd been unable, even, to retrieve them from the cold dark waters until the spring thaw had come. He'd not allowed himself to remember the joy they'd given him. That had struck him as disrespectful. Unloving.

"I never learned their names, even."

Without thinking, Alex spoke. "Marigold and

Elijah."

Abigail stirred and then looked up at him with questioning eyes.

And then he realized what he'd done—what he'd said. How thoughtless of him! "I'm sorry. Mr. Cripes said the children, *your children*, were called Flor and Timothy. He said they succumbed quickly to the fever. Apparently, many children died that year."

"Flor and Timothy," Abigail said the names softly, as though trying them out upon her lips. "Your children were Marigold and Elijah." And then she studied his eyes with an intensity he'd not allowed anybody in a long time. "I think I understand, now, some of what you feel. Dead inside. Not just a loss of life, but a loss of hope. I will not belittle your loss by telling you that at least you knew them as a father. That at least you provided a home for them, a family. For your attachment surely made it worse."

"Abigail, you are not to be faulted for their death." But how many times had he been told this by Margaret? By his aunt? Nothing could undo what had happened that day. Just as Abigail could not change the past, neither could he. But she'd not had any choice in the matter, surely! "Abigail, you are not to blame yourself! You believed they were given to a decent family! Your parents would not have supported you if you'd brought them home with you. You would have been turned out. And you and the children would have lived in want. Perhaps then, none of you would have survived." And then, taking her face between his hands, he held onto her fiercely. "You are not to blame yourself for this, do you understand me?"

More than ever before, Alex understood the

tenuous situation she'd been in when he'd arrived to ask for her. Her parents would never have allowed her to bring two bastards into their home. They were not evil, or monsters, but they were weak in character. They were all too humanly susceptible to the opinions of the folks who lived in the community around them. They would have shunned Abigail and the children. "Do you think it *my* fault that *my children* died?"

Where had those words come from? He'd embraced the fault for their death, all of them, even Hyacinth's for so many days, weeks, months, and now years, that it seemed odd to voice them aloud. "I could have stopped them from venturing outside. Hyacinth was careless sometimes. Even though I warned her to stay clear of the lake, I should have known better. Do you know why I did not go with them? She annoyed me. I was glad for her to be out of my presence so that I could get some work done. I had accounts to balance. I had some contracts to read. I should have gone with them, Abigail. One thoughtless decision of mine cost all three of them their lives."

And then Abigail was touching his face. In wonder, almost. She brought her thumb up to the corner of his eye and drew it away. It was wet. Was he to cry now? When she mourned the loss of her own children? He tried to turn his face away from her, but this time it was her hands that stilled *him*.

"You blame yourself," she finally said.

Alex just gazed into her eyes. Warm, soft, comforting eyes. "I should have gone with them," he said weakly.

Abigail was shaking her head. "I should never have abandoned them." She continued touching his face tenderly. "What a pair we are. Would you believe me if I told you that you never could have known Hyacinth would take the children out onto the lake? I've known my entire life never to trust an iced-over lake before the new year. I'm sure Hyacinth knew that as well. Had you thought, for even a second, that she would walk out onto that ice, would those contracts have mattered? Would you not have left off the accounts to stop her?"

"I would not have allowed it, Abigail, but I didn't think...I had no idea..." He turned his face away from her. "I should have, though...I made so many mistakes with them..."

Both of them sat quietly as the coach rambled along the muddied road. Abigail rested her cheek on Alex's shoulder so that when he spoke, his words vibrated through her.

"If you'd known, Abigail, if you'd suspected that the children were not going to be placed in a loving home, would you have allowed them to be taken away? Even knowing you had no power over any of it, would you have allowed it to happen?"

"I would not have, Alex. I would have fought them tooth and nail. I would have found a way to live, a way to care for them. I would not have allowed it." And then she sighed.

The magnitude of their words would take a lifetime to set in. But something had shifted in both of them. She was no less human than him. She was a woman. She was also a mother.

He was a duke, yes. But he was also first a man; a man who'd once been a father. A man who would *always be* a father.

Perhaps fate had steered them all along. He choked

on the wave of emotions he'd disdained for years now.

He'd loved his children.

He'd even once loved Hyacinth.

They had died, but he had lived.

Where there is life, there is hope, Abigail had said to him. Was there? Hope that was?

"I'm squishing you," Abigail said, squirming in his arms.

He tightened his grasp around her. "Hush," he said softly. "You are not squishing me. You are…" *Saving me*…The words died on his lips. All along he'd been telling himself that he was saving Miss Wright, when in truth it was quite the opposite. Miss Wright had been saving him, a duke!

He nuzzled his chin atop her head. From the moment she'd been shoved by the impetuous Lady Natalie into his rowboat, he'd been awakened somehow by Abigail's spirit. With no prospects in life whatsoever, she'd found joy from a simple boat ride. She'd laughed and smiled all the while he'd sat there pompously judging her. He remembered how her eyes had glowed with pleasure when that damned fish swam by her hand. And then that ridiculous dress had given way, adding fuel to an attraction he'd never thought to admit to himself, let alone anybody else.

He'd wanted her from that moment on. But he'd not only wanted her physically. He'd wanted to live in the halo of her joy.

He'd not needed to propose. He'd claimed that his honor demanded it. He remembered how she'd covered her eyes and counted to three, daring him to stay—daring him to take her on.

And he'd done so, all the while allowing her to

believe he was magnanimously granting her his favor.

"Abigail..." He allowed one hand to play with her hair. "Would you mind very much if we left Cornwall for Brooke's Abbey tomorrow?" They'd planned on spending at least a fortnight at Rock Point, but he knew a pressing desire to go home. To return home and take Abigail with him.

He continued to twirl some stray hairs around his fingers, wondering if she was going to feign sleep.

"I don't mind," she said softly. "It will be home, won't it?"

"It will," he said.

He held her the rest of the way. She cried a few more times and then apologized for it. She needed time to mourn. Apparently, it seemed, so did he.

****

Back at Brookes Abbey, Alex was uncertain how to deal with his grieving duchess. Her sorrow frightened him. It frightened him because he was afraid he was going to lose her when he'd just barely realized how vital she was to him. Not that he was going to lose her, per se, but perhaps that she was going to lose herself.

Since he'd first met her, she'd always had a smile for him. She'd always had encouraging words and a positive attitude. But since that horrible day, she'd become a shadow of herself.

And Alex didn't know how to fix her.

For the first month, she diligently went through the motions of familiarizing herself with her duties as the Duchess of Montfort and as the mistress of Brooke's Abbey. Alex could find no fault.

But she lacked her normal enthusiasm. She spread

her time evenly between the housekeeper and the butler and even some of the lower servants and would then disappear for hours at a time. He'd thought perhaps she was spending time abed, but when he'd looked for her in her chamber, she was never there.

It was as though she were a ghost, appearing and disappearing at will.

Except during the nights.

At night, he both gave and found comfort with her.

On this night, they'd made love slowly, leisurely, and now she lay spent in his arms. Alex tucked her head below his chin and pulled the coverlet over her naked shoulders. Sometimes, she silently cried afterwards. She did not think he noticed, but he had. Thankfully, tonight she was peaceful.

"Will you begin riding again in the mornings?" he asked. He'd been wanting to pique her notice again, in anything, but the time had not been right. It was odd for him, somebody who'd so often disregarded other people's feelings, to now find himself tiptoeing around her melancholy moods.

She tilted her head back to look up at him. "Is Lady Page here?" The question held more interest than he'd heard from her in days.

He laughed softly, somewhat relieved. "She's been here since our nuptials, waiting for you."

"Poor thing, and I've neglected her."

Alex slid his hand up and down her arm. "You've had other…things…on your mind."

Abigail snuggled closer to him. "I'm fine, Alex. I've just been sad. I know you've been worried, but I had to take some time." She sighed deeply as she rested against him.

343

He didn't want to push her. He didn't want to ask, but it frightened him when she disappeared for so long during the day. The air was growing much colder now. Winter storms would be blowing in any day now. "I worry, Abigail, when I cannot find you." It came out sounding like an accusation. He was no good at this sort of thing.

"I talk to them," she said. And when he didn't say anything to that she added, "I go for long walks, and I find myself talking to them. As though they can hear me. Silly, I know. But it helps…"

He'd not expected this. An odd thing to do, and yet it was so…so *very Abigail*. "What do you say to them?" He was curious. He'd not hardly allowed himself to think of Marigold and Elijah, or even of Hyacinth, after the accident. Since those first moments.

"I tell them how sorry I am. I tell them I would do anything if I could make things turn out differently. I tell them they were both the most clever children in all of England. I'm proud of what they accomplished in their short lives. I tell them I will see them someday, likely far off in the future. But that I am glad they have each other for now. I tell them that I love them.

"And I tell them about you. I tell them about how you lost two little children as well. I like to think of them all in heaven, all four of them, playing and laughing together."

At this point, Alex brought one hand up to cover his own eyes. They were stinging and hot. Picturing Marigold and Elijah playing with other children in heaven was ridiculous, and yet…

And yet it was comforting. He gulped and without thinking spoke aloud. "I'm so sorry." Who was he speaking to? To Abigail? Or was he speaking to Marigold, Elijah, and Hyacinth. He'd tried so desperately hard to save them. He had to swallow hard before going back to his original train of thought.

"I won't ask you to have a groom follow you about, but will you tell your maid where you are going?" He didn't like her traipsing about the estate alone, but did not wish to curtail something that brought her a small measure of peace.

She sighed deeply as her hand played with the hair on his chest. "I will."

Abigail heard the remorse in her husband's voice. And she knew…She knew he was speaking to Marigold and Elijah, and likely even Hyacinth. He'd not been a cold man because he didn't care. Rather, he'd made himself appear cold because he'd cared so much. He'd been so wonderfully tender with her, but he still held something of himself back.

And for a while she hadn't cared. No, she'd hardly even noticed.

In those first days she'd spent at Brooke's Abbey, Abigail experienced a lethargy she'd not known before. She'd nearly taken to her bed—not sick, but unable to force herself to face the world. But she could not allow herself to do such a thing. It reminded her of her mother too much. So instead, she'd found solace in nature. Winter loomed, but the sun still shone brightly. On a few of the warmer days, she'd simply lain down in the meadow and fallen asleep.

She was exhausted.

It was as though all the optimism she'd held onto for the past nine years had drained away upon the discovery of Flor and Timothy's deaths. And without

345

her optimism, she did not know how to face the world. The days blurred into weeks. Or had it been a month? She went through the motions of life but could not remember what joy felt like. She would find herself at times, as she had in the past, wondering what her children were doing in that moment. And then she'd remember quickly. They were dead.

So she began talking to them.

Flor and Timothy.

Marigold and Elijah.

Monfort had shared his own loss with her that day. He'd cried, even.

He'd come to her every night since their arrival. At night, under darkness, he found comfort in her and she in him. At first, Abigail thought she ought not to do so. That she ought to refrain from relations just as she'd thought she ought to wear only black. There should be no color in her life.

It gave her some understanding of her husband. His grief. His fear of finding happiness again. And now he had spoken aloud, with her, *to his children*.

"I have to go away before the weather turns." He spoke softly, almost as though he thought she'd fallen asleep.

Abigail didn't want him to leave her, but neither did she want him to feel as though she was so needy she could not live without his presence. "We're halfway through November. Do you have business in London?" She made her voice sound even. Not a tremble or wobble to be heard.

"And a few other estates." He rubbed her arm soothingly. "I don't want to leave you like this…"

Abigail stopped him. "I am fine, Alex. I promise

you I am fine." And then unable to stop herself she asked, "How long do you expect to be away?" She did not want for him to go. She almost even allowed herself to ask him to take her with him.

"Just a few weeks. I'll make haste." And then he kissed her on the head again. He did that a lot. Something she never would have predicted in a million years.

And so she added softly, "I'll miss you." God knew, she already did.

Lying beside her, Alex realized what he must do. For her, for him, for both of them as a married couple.

She was struggling. She'd always, in the past, been able to pull herself out of her doldrums but discovering the death of her children was something she'd not been prepared for. She had lost weight, but even worse she'd lost something else.

She'd lost hope.

And so he was going to take matters into his own hands. He would not allow her to shut down as he had. He'd allow her some time alone for grief, but they were going to face their future together. When she said she spoke to the children he'd gotten an idea...

But first he needed to see if it were even possible. It would be. He would make certain that it was. Relieved to have a plan, he closed his eyes and slept.

Chapter 22

Ten days later, when Alex returned, he didn't tell Abigail what he'd done. He'd arrived home late. She'd already retired for the evening. He'd been surprisingly pleased to find her sleeping in his bed.

He was home. He'd made the journey, completed the arrangements, and overseen the execution of his plan. For now, he was glad to be home.

This morning, he held her. She'd awoken and greeted him warmly. Passion was something they didn't need to work on. It was the loving that needed work.

They would work on that together.

She curled against his side. The fire had burned out sometime during the night leaving the air in the room to cool. Alex pulled the coverlet over her shoulder and nuzzled her forehead. He knew she was awake as her hand was playing with the hairs on his chest. The sun was just beginning to rise. "I have something to show you," he told her, finally. "I'd like to take you there this morning."

She didn't speak right away. "Now?" she finally asked.

"If you don't mind." Now that all was completed, he urgently desired to share it with her.

She sat up in the bed and looked down at him. "Are we going riding?"

For the first time in weeks, he saw something of anticipation on her face. He ought to have insisted she ride sooner. She'd enjoyed their lessons while in London. He'd enjoyed them more than he'd been willing to admit.

"We will ride to our destination. Do you need breakfast before we go?" He realized he was holding her wrist. The cover had fallen away from her, and she was naked from the waist up. Seeing her unclothed never failed to arouse him. He ran his hand up her arm for the sake of simply touching her.

Goose bumps rose on her flesh.

"I don't need any breakfast, but…" Her breathing hitched, and she licked her lips. She was a gift from heaven indeed.

But they could be together later. He needed to get this over with first. Oh, hell, he hoped it had not all been a mistake. "Awaken your maid, my lady, and don one of those delightful new riding habits Margaret chose for you. Wear one of the warmer ones." And with those words, he forced himself to climb out of bed and find his valet.

****

Not half an hour later, atop Lady Page, Abigail followed Alex's lead across the fog-covered fields surrounding the estate. The haze was just beginning to burn off as the sun rose, but the frost of winter hovered in the air.

Abigail had wandered the grounds extensively but had not ventured nearly so far on her own. She was curious and pleased to realize that she actually felt *something*…some life…inside of her today. The listlessness she'd come to expect each morning had faded.

And then she realized their destination. They climbed a hill, and at the top, an iron fence surrounded several gray and black stone monuments protruding from the ground. Only a few trees grew nearby, so the markers stood out starkly against the moss and grass on the ground.

This must be the family plot—Monfort burial ground.

Monfort dismounted when they were still several hundred feet away and then assisted her from Lady Page. He must be taking her to see the plots of his children. Of Marigold and Elijah…and of Hyacinth.

Without speaking, he clasped her hand, and they walked together toward the fenced-in cemetery. When they reached the gate, he released her to swing it open.

And then she knew.

Two fresh burial plots stood out against the grass, off to the left. So fresh that they had obviously been dug and filled in recently. The scent of overturned earth permeated the air.

The two graves were identical in size, and they were very small.

Abigail dropped his hand and approached them tentatively. The grass dampened her hem, wet with dew, but she didn't care.

Placed at the head of the plots was one marker, newly carved, decorated simply with two angels flying near a crescent moon. One angel was a girl and the other a boy. It read *Here lie Flor and Timothy Cross. Beloved children of the Duchess of Monfort. Wanted and loved, cherished forever*.

Abigail blinked back tears for as long as she could.

And then she could hold them back no longer.

So perfect.

Her children were home.

Alex stepped up behind her. And then gestured to the next plots over. "I thought they ought to all be together."

Another marker for two plots, also decorated with angels and the moon. Marigold and Elijah. Abigail raised her fist to her mouth. "Oh, Alex." She could barely speak. Her voice clogged with tears.

Alex's arms wrapped around her tightly as he pulled her body close to his. "It didn't feel right, leaving them in Cornwall. I thought they needed to be here, where you could visit them occasionally and assure your heart that you could never forget. They are children of your body. Although they never knew you, they were loved by you."

A sob shook her, and she turned to bury her face in his chest. "Oh, thank you, thank you, Alex. I never thought…No one has ever…" But she could not complete her words. Alex had dipped his head down and was pressing his mouth against her neck. He held her for minutes, hours, days? They stood together as the sun rose over the hill until a gentle peace settled over them both.

"I haven't been completely honest with you, Abigail." Alex began tentatively.

Abigail dropped her arms and took a half step back. Looking up at him she tilted her head in question. "Oh?"

He reached forward and grasped both of her hands in his and then squeezed them reassuringly. "I realize you believe that when I proposed to you, I only did so because I had to, but that was not the case. Something inside of me—I know it's makes no sense—but something inside of me *wanted* to make you a part of my life… needed to make you a part of my life."

Abigail wanted to smile at him, but he was quite serious. And so she nodded solemnly and allowed him to continue.

"You intrigued me. I was attracted to you. The more I've come to know you, I find myself respecting and admiring you." He dropped one of her hands and lifted his own to wipe it across his forehead. His hand was shaking.

"Until I met you, I didn't realize…I have been so damned judgmental…And of course, making love to you is…well…" He held her eyes then, and there was just a hint of devilment there. "What I'm trying to tell you is that I didn't plan any of this, but I've come to realize that I…I—well, I need you, Abigail. But even more than that." He swallowed hard and stared at her with a gaze filled with warmth.

"I love you."

At which point, Abigail's heart took flight.

Because she'd hoped for this, suspected it even, but not been sure he would ever admit it to himself, let alone her. She herself figured she'd fallen in love with him the moment he'd tossed her that blasted shawl that she'd dropped while she'd been lying on the bottom of the boat.

"When?" she asked. If he said that day on the boat, she would strangle him.

Alex lifted one elegant shoulder and shrugged ruefully. "I don't even know." He touched the side of her cheek. "When I first met you, you planted a seed of love inside of me. Each time I saw you after that, it took root and has grown stronger every day."

"Oh, Alex," she said, placing her hands over his and chuckling softly. "I think I've known all along."

At which words, he took her by the shoulders and leaned her back so that she had to look into his eyes. "You knew?" he repeated incredulously. "*You knew?*"

Abigail allowed one side of her mouth to lift into a rueful smile. She stared lovingly into his dear face as a breeze stirred his hair. "Well, I suspected as much, but you have certainly made it difficult."

"But…how on earth?" He did not appear arrogant to her. He was strong and safe and real. He was loving and honorable and all those things she ever could have dreamed of. He was not made of ice. Oh, no, her duke was made of flesh and blood and feelings and emotions. He did not wear them on the sleeve for all to see, but he would show them *to her*. And now she'd made him smile.

"Well, Alex, you *were* kissing me after I'd fainted, and even *I* know that you needn't have married me just to uphold your honor. You could have asked me to be your mistress. You could have offered me money so that I would disappear. But you did neither of those things. But I didn't know for certain until you made love to me. When we made love, you told me with your eyes. You told me with your hands. You told me with every part of your body. How could you love me so wonderfully if you didn't actually love me?"

"I could not," he said solemnly, pulling her into his arms once again.

She reached up and touched his face. "And is it so very hard? Is it so very hard to love me?"

"It scares the hell out of me, Abigail," he admitted, even as his hands caressed her back. "Even now, I'm terrified that I will make a mistake…that I will lose you…That I will do something stupid and…"

"And?" she urged him.

"That you will come to hate me." He touched the corner of her mouth with his thumb.

"I love you, Alex. I cannot promise that something will not ever happen to me, but you will never lose my love. You will never do anything that could make me hate you."

"You are stronger than I. It's what drew me to you from the first time we met. How could anybody who'd lost so much continue searching for joy? I'm afraid of it, you know."

"Joy?" Such foolishness, her poor, dear duke.

Alex slid his thumb along her lower lip. "I fear it is an explosion that will eventually burn itself out."

"That is why, my love"—Abigail leaned into his mouth—"we must constantly find ways to feed the fire."

"I have wondered if you would want to be left alone by me, but could not help but come to you each night. Do you need more time to grieve them? Would you wish I had left you alone?"

"I've spent a good deal of my life mourning the loss of them. Just as you have mourned. Too long, perhaps, for both of us." She looked away and blinked a few times as new tears threatened to overflow for the second time that day. "But we must celebrate life, in death, I think. There is a verse of the Bible that I've held onto over the past few years. It is part of what has allowed me to hope. Would you like to hear it?"

She knew he was not particularly religious; she herself had questioned some teachings of the church. But there were truths in the Bible that had given her great comfort.

"I would," he said softly.

"It says that there is a time for everything; to everything there is a season. A time to be born and a time to die; a time to kill and a time to heal; a time to weep and a time to laugh; a time to mourn and a time to dance; a time to get and a time to lose; a time to keep and a time to cast away, and a time to love and a time to hate. There is more of it than I remember, but I love those verses. They always gave me hope somehow...that my life was not made up of one long season to weep, or just to mourn. There would be a season to love and to dance as well."

Alex leaned forward and kissed her lips softly. "It is your time to be loved."

"And yours," she said.

And they did.

Epilogue

"We're ready, Papa." Four-year-old Nicholas Cross, the Marquess of Hunter, could barely make out his father's face from behind the scarf, woolen cap, winter coat, and newly knitted mittens that nurse had insisted he wear. He carried two small skates in his arms and was bouncing up and down in excitement. This was to be the first time skating this year, and he'd waited all year for the ice to be frozen solid enough for them to venture onto the lake.

"Where is your mama, Nicky? And Fiona? You didn't leave them alone in the nursery, did you? Your mama might need help."

"No, we're here, Alex. And quite prepared to endure the cold."

Nicolas looked over to where his mama had appeared holding baby Fiona. Mama was almost always smiling, except when Nicolas pranked Nurse Spencer. No, Mama had not been smiling when she'd been told that he'd released all of his frogs into Nurse's room.

Neither had Nurse.

But today she was smiling and looking at Papa.

Papa took baby Fiona from Mama's arms and picked up his and Mama's skates as well. Papa could do things like that. He was even carrying Fiona's skates!

"Nurse will be grateful for the afternoon off,"

Mama was telling Papa before she looked sternly down at Nicholas.

Nicolas grimaced and then grinned. "Can we go outside now, pleeeeze?"

Mama grinned back. "Very well, then." And as good as her word, she led them all outside and marched down the path that would take them to the lake. The sun was shining, but the air was freezing cold! Colder even then it had been on New Year's Day. Nicholas pushed down his scarf and blew air out his mouth. Yep, smoke, just like when Grandfather lit his pipe.

"Look, Papa! I'm making smoke."

Mama and Papa gave each other one of those secret looks before Papa spoke. "It's not smoke, it's water, Nicky," Papa explained. "The moisture from your mouth condenses, and that makes your breath look like a cloud."

"Like fog?" Nicky asked.

"He's getting too smart for us, Alex," Mama said to Papa, laughing. "Now, no more lessons for today. Let's get these skates on before I turn into an ice cube!"

Mama helped Nicholas, Papa helped Fiona, and after about ten thousand hours, they were finally ready to step out onto the ice. For just a minute, Nicholas thought his father looked scared, but that was silly. Papa wasn't afraid of anything.

And then they were skating. After holding Fiona for a little while, Mama handed her to Papa and then twirled and glided around by herself. Mama liked to sing while she did things like this.

Nicholas wasn't as good at skating as Mama, but he was much better than baby Fi.

Papa glided around holding baby Fi and after a

while he held Mama's hand too.

Nicholas was too big to need them to hold his hand when he skated. But sometimes the skates made his feet hurt. "Are we almost done, Papa?" he asked finally.

"I'm cold!" Baby Fiona said while sucking on her thumb through her mitten.

Leaning past the baby, Papa kissed Mama on the nose. "Cook promised hot cider when we were done. Are you ready to go inside, sweetheart?" And then he whispered something in her ear which made her face look even redder.

Nicholas impatiently waited while Mama and Papa helped take off all the skates, and again after about a thousand hours, they were headed back to the house. They stopped outside to make a few snow angels and then rushed into the warmth of home.

Nicholas could hardly wait for tomorrow.

Papa had promised him a snowball war!

A word from the author…

I've been a writer all my life but not completed a manuscript until autumn of 2014. I'd worked in numerous fields, even owned businesses, but nothing panned out for me. My default job was bartending. Having my days free, something finally clicked, and I figured out that I could write books.

With my husband and kids cheering me on, I've recently been able to quit tending bar and stay home to write fulltime. The trick now is to find something that makes me get dressed, go outside of my home, and interact with other human beings. Still working on this adjustment, but really, my PJs make a most excellent uniform!

Writing romance novels is a dream come true. I hope my books can provide a fraction of the comfort Mary Balogh's books have brought me.

I love keeping in touch with readers and would be thrilled to hear from you! Join or follow me at any (or all!) of the social media links below!

andersannabelle@gmail.com
https://www.annabelleanders.com
https://www.amazon.com/Annabelle-Anders/e/B073ZLRB3F/ref=dp_byline_cont_ebooks_1
https://www.bookbub.com/profile/annabelle-anders
https://www.facebook.com/groups/AnnabellesReaderGroup/

Read more by Annabelle Anders

Nobody's Lady
(Lord Love a Lady Series, Book 1)
Dukes don't need help, or do they?

Michael Redmond, the Duke of Cortland, needs to be in London—most expeditiously—but a band of highway robbers have thwarted his plans. Purse-pinched, coachless, and mired in mud, he stumbles on Lilly Beauchamp, the woman who betrayed him years ago.

Ladies can't be heroes, or can they?

Michael was her first love, her first lover, but he abandoned her when she needed him most. She'd trusted him, and then he failed to meet with her father as promised. A widowed stepmother now, Lilly loves her country and will do her part for the Good of England—even if that means aiding this hobbled and pathetic duke.

They lost their chance at love, or did they?

A betrothal, a scandal, and a kidnapping stand between them now. Can honor emerge from the ashes of their love?

~*~

A Lady's Prerogative
(Lord Love a Lady Series, Book 2)
It's not fair.

Titled rakes can practically get away with murder, but one tiny little misstep and a debutante is sent away to the country. Which is where Lady Natalie Spencer is stuck after jilting her betrothed.

Frustrated with her banishment, she's finished being a good girl and ready to be a little naughty.

Luckily she has brothers, one of whom has brought home his delightfully gorgeous friend.

After recently inheriting an earldom, Garrett Castleton is determined to turn over a new leaf and shed the roguish lifestyle he adopted years ago. His friend's sister, no matter how enticing, is out of bounds. He has a rundown estate to manage and tenants to save from destitution.

Can love find a compromise between the two, or will their stubbornness get them into even more trouble?

~*~

Lady at Last
(Lord Love a Lady Series, Book 4)
Coming in 2019